The Footsteps on the Stairs

The Troublemaker

Two Novels by

Jean Potts

Introduction by Curtis Evans

STARK HOUSE

Stark House Press • Eureka California

THE FOOTSTEPS ON THE STAIRS / THE TROUBLEMAKER

Published by Stark House Press
1315 H Street
Eureka, CA 95501, USA
griffinskye3@sbcglobal.net
www.starkhousepress.com

ISBN: 978-1-951473-55-6

Book design by Mark Shepard, shepgraphics.com
Proofreading by Bill Kelly
Cover Art by James Heimer

First Stark House Press Edition: January 2022

Jean Potts

By Curtis Evans

Crime writer Jean Catherine Potts had storytelling in her blood, judging from the case of her paternal grandfather, John, who could certainly spin colorful tales, at least when it came to the Potts family lineage. John Potts, who was born in 1803 and passed away in 1886, nearly a quarter-century before his granddaughter Jean was born, used to regale his family with legends of his own paternal grandfather, who was also named John. In his youth the elder John Potts, who was allegedly born in Dublin, Ireland in 1729, ostensibly had been a "schoolmate and fast friend" of no less august a personage than Great Britain's King George III—although the British monarch was in fact eleven years older than the Potts' paterfamilias. As the story goes, Potts, having become a topographical engineer, had been present in North America at the rout of the British expeditionary force commanded by General Braddock at the Battle of the Monongahela (1755), early in the French and Indian War. Fortunately Potts—like George Washington, the future father of a new country—managed to survive the terrible affray at the Monongahela, although "his servants were all slain." Undaunted, Potts settled in Cumberland County in the British colony of Pennsylvania, where, rather prosaically given this eventful history, he operated a grist mill. Whether later in life he kept up with his "fast friend" George is unrecorded.

Potts' imaginative grandson John removed from Pennsylvania to the little railroad boom town of Moulton in Appanoose County, Iowa, where for many years he served as a county surveyor and notary public. John's son William Stitt Potts, born when John was sixty-two years old, served in the Spanish-American War before moving some 350 miles west to the small town of St. Paul, seat of Howard County, Nebraska, and later marrying Lola Law, a Moulton carpenter's daughter whom it appears had previously been briefly wed to widowed railroad laborer Samuel S. Frost. In St. Paul Will was employed as a rural mail carrier and with Lola fathered two daughters, Edith in 1908 and Jean in 1910.

Another member of the Potts clan who evinced a certain literary bent was Will's cousin John Vinton Potts, an earnest Ohio Christian Socialist minister, teacher, poet and publisher, who, according to his 1909 obituary, fervently believed in "the brotherhood of man and the ultimate ideal life here on earth...realizing human weaknesses but trusting to the divine father to bring excellence as a result of effort." Certainly Will and Lola Potts' two daughters, Edith and Jean, from early ages did just what their father's virtuous cousin John envisioned in bringing excellence out of earthly effort. In their endeavors the two young women were greatly influenced by their mother Lola, an early and active member of the P. E. O. sisterhood, an organization which promoted educational opportunities for women (and continues to do so today). Even after Lola expired nine weeks after suffering a sudden paralytic stroke at the age of fifty-seven in 1927, when Jean was still a high school student, her beneficent presence was still felt in her daughters' lives.

Both Edith and Jean played the piano, although it was elder sister Edith who excelled at this particular branch of art. In 1930, Edith, then a music student at Nebraska Wesleyan University in the city of Lincoln, gave a piano recital consisting of Chopin's Piano Sonata #2 and pieces by Brahms, Godowsky, Debussy and Villa-Lobos. Six years later, when she was working as a music teacher at St. Paul College, Edith performed Rachmaninov's Prelude in C-Sharp Minor at a P. E. O. home recital. (Vintage mystery fans may recall that in Ngaio Marsh's 1939 detective novel *Overture to Death* a pianist is shot dead while playing this ominous prelude.) Not long after this event, Edith left St. Paul for New York City to enroll in the Juilliard School.

Jean, on the other hand, pursued a literary course. Her proud father later recalled to a newspaper interviewer that "as soon as she could talk, [Jean] entertained other children with stories which blossomed in her imagination." By the age of nine she had published, in the pages of the *Omaha World Herald*, her first work of fiction, a short story entitled "The Runaway" (presumably not a crime story). After graduating from St. Paul Hugh School, Jean worked briefly as a stenographer before going to work in 1929 as the "cub" reporter and compositor at the *St. Paul Phonograph*. The rest of the tiny work force at the small-town newspaper, which served a community of fewer than 2000 inhabitants, consisted of an editor-publisher, an associate editor and a foreman. Making note of Jean's resignation two years later to enroll at the Colorado Women's College in Denver, the paper noted regretfully: "The junior editor will miss her quite a bit when he has to devote so much of his time to setting stuff for the paper. The senior editor will miss her a great deal too, because he will have a lot more copy to write, news to gather, details to run down and proofs to read." However, Jean, like Kansan Harvey Merrick in Nebraska author Willa Cather's famous short story "The Sculptor's Funeral," had begun a slow climb to bigger and better things than her modest little burg could offer.

After a year at the Colorado Women's College, where she was invited to join the Quill Club, a national collegiate literary society, Jean returned to her home state to enroll at Nebraska Wesleyan University, whence she graduated in 1936. On a visit to Edith in New York City the next year, she fell in love with the great metropolis, like so many others before had done; and she resolved to remain there for the rest of her life. By 1940 Jean and Edith resided together at a six-story Beaux Arts style apartment building in Greenwich Village. Both sisters worked for a publishing company, although Jean soon quit her day job, as she began successfully publishing short fiction in lucrative "slick" magazines like *Woman's Day*, *McCall's* and *Collier's*.

Jean published her first novel, *Someone to Remember*, in 1943, but another decade passed before she penned her Edgar Award winning book *Go, Lovely Rose*, the first of her successful and critically-lauded run of fourteen crime novels, which spanned the two decades between 1954 and 1975. Neither Jean nor Edith ever returned to their native town, their father having departed St. Paul (probably in the late 1930s as well), for St. Cloud, Florida with his second wife, Virginia, although the sisters did stay in touch with cousins back home. Unhappily Will's marriage proved a failure and he and Virginia divorced in 1942, six years before his death at the age of eighty-three. (The newspaper interview in which Will boasted of Jean's writing success was published in 1946 in the *Tampa Tribune*.) In the late 1940s, Edith left New York to work as the secretary for the Berkshire Trout Farm in Sheffield, Massachusetts, located about a dozen miles from the home of prominent midcentury crime writer Hugh Wheeler. Edith held this position until her resignation in 1952, incidentally providing material years later for Jean's 1966 crime novel *The Only Good Secretary*.

Even after she ceased writing novels, Jean continue to publish the occasional short crime story, the last of which evidently was the intriguingly titled "Lady Macbeth Case," published in *Ellery Queen's Mystery Magazine* in November 1990, when the author was eighty years old. During the Nineties Jean unfortunately began suffering from dementia and she passed away in her beloved New York on November 10, 1999, just one week shy of her eighty-ninth birthday. Her remains were returned to Saint Paul, the little town which she had left behind six decades earlier, and interred at Elmwood Cemetery beside those of her mother. As was the case with other superlative mid-century women crime writers, Jean Potts' body of bloodwork had fallen into a criminal state of neglect by the time of her demise, but today I am pleased to report that it is in the rosy bloom of an amply-merited revival.

□ □ □

The ninth of Jean Potts' fourteen crime novels, *The Footsteps on the Stairs* (1966), reflects the author at the height of her considerable powers. This compelling and moving crime novel starts with the story of New York interior designer Enid Baxter, who four years later is still recovering from her breakup with married architect Vic Holm. Unexpectedly encountering Vic again in New York, where they have both relocated from Philadelphia, she finds that their flame for each other still more than flickers, although Vic remains resignedly married to Thelma, on whose account he had earlier broken off his and Enid's affair. The two rekindle their relationship, rather against Enid's will, but to her earnest younger neighbor and friend, Martin Shipley, who is still trying to recover from the trauma of his own stormy relationship with his late wife Jean (which ended in Jean's "accidental" death), Enid's action seems decidedly ill-advised—for certainly love is a many-endangered thing.

When Enid is found stabbed to death in her apartment, Martin, drawn in by Enid's business associate and friend Hazel Nicholson and her daughter Rosemary, becomes a reluctant investigator into Enid's untimely demise, which police evidently have written off as the panic-stricken action of a burglar. Just whose footsteps did a neighbor hear on the stairs on the fatal night? I predict you will find yourself compelled compulsively to read on to discover the answer to this and other vexing questions, all of which are not finally resolved until the final line of this remarkable crime novel.

The Troublemaker, Jean Potts' penultimate crime novel, also explores the perilously wayward courses of love and death. Published in 1972, the novel, which details the consequences of married, middle-aged college professor Quentin Leonard's reluctant romantic fling with a fey, waiflike college student named Lisa (whose body soon ends up broken and battered on a rocky Maine coast), comes complete with references to hippies, tattered jeans, guitars, "phony folk ballads," an avocado and chocolate brown living room (with pimiento accents), the generation gap and the failure to communicate. Indeed, in its very up-to-dateness *The Troublemaker* ironically seems more dated than its predecessor. Yet the author's empathy for people's emotional pain comes as powerfully through as ever, as does her compelling portrait of a sociopathic preteen named Emerson, who with his binoculars and his birdwatching oddly prefigures the criminally nosy character of Stephen Norton in Agatha Christie's own penultimate published detective novel, *Curtain* (1975). During her short life Lisa may have been a troublemaker, however carelessly, but she was not a patch on, to quote from the book's American dust jacket, this "memorable and monstrous small boy."

—September 2021
Germantown, TN

Curtis Evans received a PhD in American history in 1998. He is the author of *Masters of the "Humdrum" Mystery: Cecil John Charles Street, Freeman Wills Crofts, Alfred Walter Stewart and British Detective Fiction, 1920-1961* (2012) and most recently the editor of the Edgar nominated *Murder in the Closet: Essays on Queer Clues in Crime Fiction Before Stonewall* (2017) and, with Douglas G. Greene, the Richard Webb and Hugh Wheeler short crime fiction collection, *The Cases of Lieutenant Timothy Trant* (2019). He blogs on vintage crime fiction at The Passing Tramp.

The Footsteps on the Stairs

Jean Potts

1

Four years after they had said Goodbye Forever in Philadelphia—life being what it is, a mesh of dangling threads—they met again, at a press party in New York. One of the Glasbrix publicity staff, an overwrought girl in a flower-bucket hat, introduced them. Enid Baxter. "She does the most divine interiors, Vic sweetie, simply fabulous." And Victor Holm. "Mark my word, Enid dear, some day we're all going to say we knew him when. He designs the most fabulous houses. Simply divine."

"How do you do," said Vic.

Enid waited until the flower-bucket hat had been washed back into the main stream. "I'm ahead of the crowd. I already knew you when." Her first impulse, to turn and run, passed; she felt remarkably calm, especially after noting the wobble in Vic's hand as he held a light for her cigarette.

"It's been a long time," he said. "Not that you look a day older."

He did. His sandy hair, though it was still thick, was frosted with white. All the way through, no longer just at the temples. His ruddy, blunt-featured face was not the type to wrinkle, but she saw—it hurt her to see—the first subtle blurring, the token of sagging to come. And there was something different about his eyes. They were the same hazy gray, of course; dreamer's eyes, she used to think. Different dreams now, maybe. Or it could well be that the change was in her own eyes more than in Vic's. This amazing calm of hers. She was proud of it. But a little saddened, too: she had been so sure that Vic was the one she would never get over.

"You're looking very well," she said kindly. At least he hadn't gotten fat. He had the stocky, sturdy build of a peasant; it made him seem shorter than he actually was. Enid tilted her head to smile at him. "I'm glad to hear you're going places."

"That's me. Always en route. Never quite getting there."

"Maybe you aim too high."

"Not anymore," he said grimly. "I'm strictly a money-grubber these days. It may not be soul-satisfying, but it's a damn sight more comfortable."

"If you say so. I just dabble myself." She was quoting him; her freedom from financial worries had always enraged him. Even now, she thought, observing the spark of temper in his face. "I don't have the professional attitude."

"I know, I've kept track of you. Especially now that I'm in New York too."

"You are?" She felt the first ominous tremor. His use of the first person singular signified nothing, of course; he was an expert at ignoring Thelma's existence. When it suited his convenience. And anyway, Enid assured herself, his present marital status was a matter of supreme indifference to her. She didn't care where he lived, either; certainly New York was big enough for both of them. "When did that happen?"

"Three or four months ago. Matter of fact, we're practically neighbors."

"Really? It's a small world, as they say."

"Very small. But then you knew as well as I did that wasn't the end, that day in Philadelphia. We were bound to run across each other again sooner or later. Just a question of time."

"I never had any such notion," she lied. "As I recall that day in Philadelphia, you sounded pretty final."

"I sounded final! You were the one. Didn't I beg you not to get on that train to New York? But no. You walked away and left me—I can still see you, switching off in that damn purple suit—and you never looked back, not even so much as a glance."

Naturally not; it would have been fatal. And how typical it was of Vic to insist, now as then, that the breakup was entirely her doing, no responsibility whatever of his. When the truth was that the crucial decision had been his alone. For the choice he had made—Thelma instead of her; that was what it amounted to, whether he admitted it or not—left her with no alternative except to get on the train to New York. Walk away and leave him, as he put it, and never look back.

Only here they were again, face to face. Yes, and he was looking pleased with himself, as if he knew all about the tremor she had imagined she was hiding so successfully. "How's Thelma?" she asked, to even the score.

His face stiffened, and at that moment Thelma's famous laugh rang out. Her trademark: that delightful, delighted laugh, uninhibited as a child's, and because it was the thing about Thelma that had rankled most, Enid was now acutely aware of the change in it. It no longer rang true. The bell was cracked.

"There she is," said Vic. "Over by the window."

Apparently her taste in clothes had improved. (Well. Nowhere to go but up.) She was wearing quite a smart dress, deep blue, good with her eyes, and cleverly cut, good with her tall, willowy figure. Even the hat wasn't too bad, except for the veil. Enid remembered her hair, which she still wore in bangs, as being a duller shade of brown. Had she taken to touching it up? It seemed out of character. So did the clothes, when it came to that. The Thelma of four years ago had been blithely unconcerned about such matters.

She was talking—not to the customary cluster of people who used to gather around her like tacks drawn to a magnet—but to one lone young man, who in spite of his polite smile was clearly on the lookout for an escape route. His eyes darted this way and that, he made nervous, unsuccessful little attempts to edge away from Thelma's hand on his sleeve. A tableau of desperation: his growing restiveness spurred her on to more and more anxious animation. The charming Mrs. Victor Holm, thought Enid, not quite so charming nowadays.

But the spark of wry triumph she might have felt flickered out at once. Vic too was watching his wife, inspecting her with coldly clinical interest, as if she were a specimen under a microscope. "Don't look like that," Enid said sharply.

"Like what? I'm just gauging the saturation level. One more drink and I'll have to get her home."

Thelma a lush? But she used to drink hardly at all. Hadn't needed to, any more than she had needed to bother much about the right clothes or make-up. So why should she turn to drink now? After all, she was the winner. He had chosen her, not Enid.

The restive young man had escaped, in spite of all her efforts. She was left standing by herself, smiling (yes, a little glassily) at everyone and no one.

"Don't let me keep you," said Enid.

"Wait. Let's get out of here. Go some place where we can talk—"

"What about? It's all been said. It's all over. I have a dinner date, anyway. Not to mention your other obligations."

"Trust you to mention them, though. You haven't changed, have you?"

"The point is that I have," she said. "You don't know me anymore. Wouldn't like me if you did."

"Who's talking about liking? That's a nothing of a word to use about us."

All right. Yes. They had either loved each other or hated each other. The heights or the depths. No golden mean. "Makes no difference now," she said, and smiled brilliantly into the distance.

"We'll see about that. Later, then. After this dinner date of yours. I'll ring your bell."

"Thank you for warning me. I won't answer it."

"I'll take a chance," he said. "I walk past your house often, and there's your name under the mailbox, and the bell— Once I actually rang it, but there wasn't any answer."

"Naturally not. I never answer anonymous doorbell rings."

"Very sensible of you. A woman living alone can't be too careful. Assuming, of course, that you are living alone..." He paused, his eyes hardening. He had always been jealous, even in the days when he had no reason to be. On top of that, had dismissed her resentment of Thelma as utter nonsense. He had no claim on her now. Let him stew.

"That's quite a place, the house you're living in" he went on. "Straight out of Chas Addams. Is it as spooky inside as out?"

"Spookier. I love it." Vic would be enchanted with it: she could see him in the middle of her living room, peering at the chandelier that hung like a stalactite from the cavernous ceiling, at the dim, full-length mirror with its ornate gold frame, at the marble fireplace and wide floorboards that creaked underfoot and gleamed like brown satin. She could hear his delighted chuckle when he spotted the hand-painted door knobs. Hastily she pulled the damper on her imagination. He was never going to see any of it, and that was that.

"Do you still have that misbegotten love seat, and the cabbage patch rug?"

She nodded. And the afghan they used to lie under on chilly evenings; the bronze clock that had chimed off the precious fleeting hours. The brandy snifters were long since broken, though, and the lone survivor of their favorite coffee cups was handleless, gathering dust on the top shelf, because she could not bring herself to throw it out. Until now: she would go home tonight and get rid of it. Her years of bondage were over, this final encounter with Vic was a necessary part of the ritual of release. With it behind her, the cycle was complete, she was once more her own woman. And about time, too. When she thought of those first black months when she had carried wherever she went the leaden burden of her heart; of the terrible, rare evenings alone when she had stared at the telephone, battling the urge to pick it up, obsessed with listening—for it to ring, even more tensely (and illogically) for the sound of his footstep on the stairs...

"Enid," he said. "My little blackbird." His hand touched hers, and she pulled away in terror of the remembered current. It was still there, still there; she had not been quick enough. "Just for a little while. An hour. Half an hour. Please, Enid, please."

"Don't. No, no." She got her voice back under control. "Nice to see you, Vic. Good luck." She moved off, waggling her fingers at him, smiling a cocktail-party smile, and resolutely avoiding his eyes.

The cracked bell of Thelma's laugh rang out again, summoning him.

Even so, Enid left before they did. (She had not been lying about the dinner date. It was only with Martin, but it would serve.) As she was going out the door, she caught sight of them, halfway across the room; Vic had a firm grip on Thelma's elbow and seemed to be reasoning with her, in a patient, practiced way. He did not see Enid. But Thelma did.

Her veil was askew; through its cross-hatchings, as through the barbed wire of a concentration camp, she stared out—empty-eyed at first, then, after the click of recognition, sick with fear. She caught her slack lower lip between her teeth, and her hand moved vaguely, in a gesture that was half-defensive, half-pleading.

Enid turned and hurried out. She was trembling with resentment—against herself for pitying Thelma, against Thelma for provoking the pity. What right had she to work on Enid's sympathies? She was the winner, Enid insisted to herself; Vic was hers, all hers, always had been, always would be. Thelma had no excuse for going into such a panic. As if Enid were some kind of a monster or, even worse, a fool who didn't know when she was licked. Well, she did know. And furthermore knew when she was well off: free at last from the spell Vic had cast over her. She was a different person now (imagine feeling sorry for Thelma four years ago!) and so was he (oh yes, it showed in his eyes) and it was no use trying to get back to what they used to be and feel. That old cure-all time had done its work, no matter how determined Vic might be to pretend otherwise. She was realistic enough to face the truth, if he wasn't. The bitterly sad truth; during the cab ride downtown she gave way to a fit of weeping. But this way at least her image of Vic-and-Enid as they had once been would remain intact, unspoiled by the overlay of what they were now. For she knew it would be spoiled. Their heyday was in the past; to try to recapture it now would lead to anticlimax at best, quite possibly to something much more disastrous. She knew it, she knew it.

How did it happen, then, that three hours later she sat on the misbegotten love seat—alone; both she and Martin had been in favor of an early evening—once more obsessed with waiting? Only tonight she waited for a certainty: the doorbell was bound to ring. Vic hadn't changed that much. The question was whether she had changed enough to let it go unanswered. But if so, why was she here at all when she could so easily have dodged the whole issue? That might be precisely the point—to put herself to the test and settle the matter, once and for all. An attractive theory. She grew more and more attached to it.

When the doorbell rang she rose like a sleepwalker and pushed the buzzer. It was beside the door, as the buzzer in her Philadelphia apartment had been, and she stayed there, as she used to do in the old days, listening for the sound of his step on the stairs. She would have known it anywhere: the same quick, heavy thud, with her heart pounding in time. Like Pavlov's dogs. Her hand rose of its own accord and released the bolt, opened the door. They were in each other's arms—more of a collision than an embrace—and for one tremulous moment she could almost believe that nothing was changed and they were back in their lost heyday.

Then she pulled free enough to look up into his eyes.

2

One evening a week later Martin Shipley rang Enid's bell—three rings: their signal—to explain that he had locked himself out of his ground-floor apartment and needed the key he had planted with her against this recurrent emergency.

"Come on up." Her answer over the house phone was prompt and cheerful if a little breathless, he thought as he bounded up the stairs. Maybe she had just gotten home herself.

He was disconcerted and embarrassed to discover, when she opened her door, that she had a guest. She knew how he was about meeting strangers, but instead of simply handing him the key, she insisted on ushering him inside and introducing him to the man who was standing beside the fireplace. A big man, as tall as Martin and much broader, With a ruddy, open face and a shock of sandy-gray hair.

So this was Victor Holm. To Martin the name was more than familiar; in Enid's confidential reminiscences it figured as the major theme on which she played her endless variations of tenderness, grief, anger and longing. (As the name of Joyce figured in Martin's memories.) But somehow he had never attached the name of Victor Holm to a body, a real flesh-and-blood man whom he might some day meet face to face. It was as if a legendary character had suddenly materialized.

"Martin's my neighbor," Enid was explaining gaily. "He has the first-floor apartment. Horticulture brought us together."

It was true enough. Enid had her terrace; Martin the scrap of soil outside his front windows where ivy and a few spindly bushes—leftovers from the previous tenant—struggled to survive. Their friendship had begun with an exchange of nods when, on her way in or out of the house, Enid would see him grubbing there; had progressed to small pleasantries that bloomed, along with Martin's morning glories, into their first real conversation. It was a curiously fast friendship, considering their surface disparities. For Enid kept her loneliness hidden, while Martin's was there for all the world to see; he wore it like a mourning band.

"Horticulture?" Victor Holm bared his teeth in a hostile smile. "How nice."

A jealous type, just as Enid had reported. Poor devil, thought Martin complacently. He had no more designs on Enid than she had on him. Still, the idea of himself as a romantic rival was decidedly pleasant. Feeling very much at ease, quite a man of the world, in fact, he accepted the drink Enid pressed on him, settled down in the easy chair, and lit a cigarette.

She was shamelessly enjoying the situation. He had never seen this side of her, and it intrigued him to watch her playing the female primeval instead of the understanding older sister he was used to. What a charmer she was! Like an ivory and jet figurine come to life—her face sparkling with the vivacity it sometimes lacked, her every gesture full of provocative grace. She was wearing a wide-sleeved robe splashed with colors brilliant as a bird's plumage.

"Martin's with a publishing company, Vic," she said. "He edits textbooks. He just finished one on architecture."

"Bully for him," said Vic, and rattled his ice cubes.

"I'm so sorry you can't stay for another drink, darling. You and Martin would have so much to talk about. Maybe another time. When you and Thelma aren't going to the theater. Do remember me to her, won't you? And have fun."

"You too," said Vic. "Lots of nice neighborly fun." He bared his teeth again on the way out.

When Enid came back from seeing him to the door, Martin said, "What a little bitch you are."

"Only because he asks for it. Can you imagine? He was jealous of you! Not that you're not attractive, of course," she added, and patted his hand. "If you were ten years older he might have a point."

"Thanks." He had no illusions about his own weedy, knobby appearance. Even Joyce had never considered him handsome. If she had loved him at all, it was in spite of his looks. "You're pretty irresistible yourself. For an old lady. How long has Victor the Great been back in your life?"

"He's not. I mean, not really." She shot him a queer, defiant look. "Well. What did you think of him?"

"He surprised me. Though I don't know exactly what I expected. Somebody smoother, I guess. Not such a wholesome farmer type."

"That's what I thought too, when I first met him. If only people's insides matched their outsides! Vic looks so solid, so steady and forthright, when the truth is he's the most confused, the most unstable—" She dropped down on the love seat, weary now, her face drained of the animation that had transfigured it. Martin recognized that withdrawn, mask-like look; he had seen her through more than one fit of what she called The Despondencies. "Even more so than four years ago. It's worse. Much worse. I wish I'd never seen him again!"

"You don't have to go on seeing him," Martin offered, without conviction. "If he upsets you so much, why not just drop him?"

"Because I never do the right thing, that's why not. Or if I do, it's at the wrong moment. It sounds so easy. Just drop him. Don't see him anymore. You don't know Vic. You don't know how he is."

"Of course, if you're still in love with him—"

"Not the way I was. It's all spoiled now. All changed." She stared down at her hands. She was wearing, as always, the ring Vic had given her, a gold band set with squares of jade. A little too heavy for a hand as delicate as Enid's, in Martin's opinion. She had a nervous habit of twisting it round and round. "I feel sorry for him, Martin, and I can't bear it. I can't bear to feel sorry for Vic!"

"Sorry for him? Hell, you were needling him for all you were worth."

"Of course I was. I have to needle him. Because— Oh, what's the use? You'd never understand people like Vic and me. You're too sane."

"Who, me?" It was not the first time she had cast aspersions on his insanity. He suspected her of therapeutic motives, and was all the more nettled. "I'm sicker in the head than you or Vic ever dreamed of being. Just ask Joyce's parents."

"Okay, okay. They think you're crazy. But they didn't convince anybody else."

"Only me," said Martin. "A trifling detail. Hardly worth mentioning."

"Exactly. Because it's not true. If you really thought you were a maniac you'd keep your dark and dreadful past to yourself instead of pouring it out to me. It's not so dark and dreadful, anyway. You've talked yourself into all this guilt business about Joyce just because—"

"Please. Spare me the pep talk. I've heard it before."

"I was going to give you the revised version this time. But all right, I can take a hint." She laughed light-heartedly. When he first knew her these rapid swings in mood had bewildered him; now he was used to them. "Let's have another drink. Would you like to stay for dinner? There's some chicken I'd love to get rid of. I promise not to try to cheer you up."

"Fine. Great." This time the therapeutic motives were his: the more casual Enid was with her invitations the more sincerely she meant them. She disliked admitting that she did not want to be alone. Besides, he had nothing else to do. As usual. His friends had all been his and Joyce's; he had no heart for finding new ones.

Neither of them mentioned Victor Holm until dinner was over and they were having coffee and brandy on the terrace. It was a balmy, starry April evening. The people in the next-door garden were cooking hamburgers, and the smoke wafted up, mingling with the smell of Enid's geraniums. The house backed on an office building, so on weekends and evenings the terrace was pleasantly quiet and secluded.

"The trouble is he's moved here," Enid said abruptly.

Martin did not ask who. He sipped his brandy and waited.

"They've moved here, I should say. He and Thelma. I gather she's turned into pretty much of a lush."

"So that's why you feel sorry for him."

"No, that's not why. After all, turnabout's fair play. Oh yes, that was the thing, you see, he was a problem drinker himself at one time—years ago, before I knew him—and Thelma pulled him through like the loyal, long-suffering, true-blue helpmeet she is. So naturally he couldn't repay all that devotion by deserting her for me. Not to mention the fact that I was his on any terms, and let him know it. Like the fool I was. Why didn't I see it in time? I could have done it, I could have saved him."

"Saved him from what? What are you talking about?"

"He could have been a good architect, Martin, I mean really good. He had originality and flair and this tremendous enthusiasm. He's lost it now, somehow it's all gone, and he doesn't even *care!*" She beat her fists on her knees. "All he wants is money. Security. He's not willing to try anything new anymore, for fear of being called a screwball—that's what he was, in a way, but a brilliant one—and he was almost over the hump, a few more years of developing his own ideas and he would have made it. He's let it all go, settled for this job that's never going to lead anywhere, why, he won't even keep it, once they realize he hasn't got the zing they hired him for!"

"And you think you could have kept him on the upward path. Is that it?"

"I know how it sounds. But all the same... We sparked each other. Call it love, sex, chemistry, whatever. It was there, and it was great. I never *admired* any man the way I did Vic. With all the others, I called the shots. Because I was brainier or stronger or maybe just meaner. But with Vic..."

"Well, all you have to do is say the word. Here he is again, obviously bent on picking up where you and he left off—"

"Wrong again. What he's bent on now is marrying me." She laughed bitterly. "How's that for irony? Four years too late he's all mine. Four years too late. I was dying to marry him then. That's why I came to New York, because I couldn't stand not having him all to myself. And now when I don't want him anymore he's all at once determined to ditch Thelma for me."

"I'm not so sure you don't want him anymore," said Martin cautiously.

"There must be something left or you wouldn't be in such a state."

"Of course there's something left. Bed. And I'm not belittling it. I don't object to having an affair with Vic, picking up where we left off, as you put it. But I won't marry him. I couldn't possibly. I told you, I don't admire him now, I don't even respect him, I feel *sorry* for him! Because he missed the boat and either doesn't know it or won't admit it. He thinks he can go back and do it right this time, but he can't, nobody ever can. Thinks I can wave some kind of a magic wand and give him back what he threw away, but I can't, I can't... Let's have another brandy."

In the darkness her face was only a blur, magnolia-white, with smudges for her eyes, which he knew must be filled with tears, and her mouth, which he knew must be trembling. He could think of nothing to say: she was too proud for comfort, too headstrong for advice. And as always he was too slow-witted; the right words would come to him hours from now, when they could do no good. That was the story of his life.

When she spoke again, it was in a different voice, calm and reflective. "You know, Martin, there's something else. It occurred to me the other night that Vic might be dangerous."

"Dangerous! You mean he threatened you?"

"Of course. But then he's threatened me before. Too often to remember. The battles we used to have! I gave him a beauty of a black eye once. My finest hour."

"Oh well." Martin sank back in relief. "Battles. I thought you meant—"

"I did. I do. I think it's possible Vic might someday kill me."

"What is this, anyway?" His heart beat thickly now, with belated anger. And a sense of betrayal; she had led him on, lured him into trusting her, while all the time she was secretly harboring the same suspicions everyone else had about him. "Your idea of a joke? Or some kind of a trick? You already know all I know about Joyce. What the hell are you trying to do?"

"Oh, stop it. Don't be so touchy. Who's talking about Joyce? You always twist everything around to her. You won't let yourself or anybody else forget it."

"You think it's that easy? Forget it. Shrug it off. It didn't happen to you."

"I know, Martin." She stretched out her hand, and after an instant's hesitation he took it. Such a small hand, but strong and warm, full of life. "Honestly, honestly. No tricks. And no jokes. Anything but."

"Listen, Enid, if you really think this guy is going to kill you—"

"Now, now. I just mentioned the possibility. Very remote. And anyway, it would be my own fault, for needling him into it."

"But my God, you mustn't see him again! I don't care if it's just a possibility. You thought of it. It crossed your mind. That's enough for me. Too much. You simply must not see him again."

She withdrew her hand. "I'm sure you're right," she said politely.

"Promise me. Promise me."

"But I might not keep my word. You wouldn't want to make a liar of me, would you?" She gave a teasing, affectionate laugh. "What's so terrible about dying? It happens to everybody some time, somehow. I'm not all that enchanted with life nowadays, anyway. No, and neither are you, if some of the things you've told me are true."

They were true, all right. "It's quite a different matter," he said stiffly, "going out of your way to get yourself murdered. In the first place—"

"Yes? Yes? I'm all ears."

"I can't believe you're serious! You must be kidding!"

"How can I resist it, with somebody as solemn as you? I declare, Martin, you should have been born an owl. You'd be so lovely stuffed. And then the brandy. I always develop these morbid fancies when I drink brandy. Shall we have another?"

"So you can get morbider and morbider? No, thanks."

"Okay." She yawned. "If you'll go home I'll go to bed."

"And dream about being stabbed, I suppose."

"No, I think strangled. Sweet dreams to you, too. I'll take the tray in, if you'll do the chairs."

"Yes, Ma'am." She was very orderly; the chairs had to be folded and stacked just so, in their special place against the wall. Martin had helped her build the little stile arrangement that led into the living room through the big window. Which he was careful to lock behind him. "Will that be all, Ma'am?"

"Your key. Remember? That's what you came for."

"So it is, so it is." He sometimes played up his absent-mindedness, which by turns irritated and amused her. It was nice, having her fuss over him. A wave of anxious tenderness for her surged through him; he turned at the door. "You really were just kidding me? You're sure now?"

She burst out laughing. "Owl. Always looking for something to brood about, aren't you? Just remember, don't you ever breathe a word of this to anybody, ever, under any circumstances. You do, and so help me, I'll come back and haunt you. That's if I'm dead. If I'm alive— Well, you'll wish I weren't."

"I'll never wish that. That's the whole point. I don't want—"

She was going on as if he had not spoken. "But then I know I can count on you. It's the wonderful thing about you, you never betray a confidence. I can say whatever pops into my head, no matter how wacky it is, and it's safe with you, you'll keep it to yourself. I mean, you always have. You're not going to start letting me down now, are you?"

"Of course I'm not going to let you down."

"Cross your heart? Hope to die?"

He looked down into her face: the round, willful forehead, the jet-brilliant eyes urgently holding his. "You win," he said after a moment. "Cross my heart."

He had promised, she hadn't, he thought as he went slowly down the stairs. He saw now the bargain he should have struck—her word not to see Vic again in exchange for his not to betray tonight's confidences. One more belated brainstorm. He was running true to form.

3

"Morning, Mrs. Nicholson. Hot enough for you?" the doorman said as she hurtled—in a rush, as usual—out of her apartment building.

The cab driver explained, all the way across town, that it wasn't the heat, it was the humidity.

The elevator operator had a variation on the theme: "That thunderstorm last night didn't do a bit of good, did it? Made it worse, if anything."

It was that kind of a midsummer morning.

She opened the office door with its modest gold lettering: "Hazel Nicholson—Interiors" and drew in a grateful breath of air conditioning. Her daughter Rosemary, who was helping out during the summer, glanced up from the *Times* crossword puzzle long enough to say, "Hi, Mom. Tuck your blouse in. You look broiled."

Hazel knew it; she had caught a glimpse of herself in the plate glass window downstairs as she got out of the cab. Red, moist face under wilting gray hair; figure blocky and waistless as a mailbox, solidly based on the clumps of her space shoes. Rosemary herself, of course, looked as fresh and crisp and slim as a stalk of celery.

"Coffee?" she asked. "I got two containers."

"No time." Hazel mopped her neck and dropped her bag, bulging with upholstery samples, on the desk. "The newlyweds will be here any minute, breathing down my—"

"They're not coming," said Rosemary. "They decided to stay out at the beach another day. Too hot to drive into town. They hoped you'd understand." She added virtuously, "I tried to call you at home, but you must have just left."

All that mad rush for nothing. Well, Hazel was used to it. She settled down with the other container of coffee, opened the dog-eared notebook in which she kept track of jobs pending, and prepared to revise her day's schedule. Five minutes of companionable silence, except for Rosemary: "Hero of silent films. Long. Begins with B," and Hazel: "Barthelmess. Don't they teach you anything in college?"

Then the phone rang. "Hazel Nicholson Interiors," Rosemary warbled into it. "One moment, please." She put her hand over the mouthpiece and whispered, "Some guy for you. Sergeant somebody? I didn't catch his name."

Neither did Hazel. His name didn't matter. His message did. She listened, aware of the sweat chilling on her brow, and of Rosemary's eyes fixed on her, round with apprehension.

"Something's happened to Enid," she said when she had hung up. "An accident, he said. A bad accident. They want me to come down there to her apartment."

"I'm coming with you."

"Don't be silly." She stood up heavily and found, to her surprise and embarrassment, that her legs were so wobbly she had to steady herself against the desk. "No need for us both to go. He sounded so— Rosemary, I think it's very bad."

"Let's go," said Rosemary. "What exactly did he *say*, Mom?" she demanded when they were on their way downtown in the cab. "Tell me everything he said."

"Well, he said he understood I was Enid Baxter's—partner? No, business associate, I think that was the way he put it. And of course I am, so I said yes, and a good friend of hers too, from way back. So then he said, 'I'm sorry to inform you that Miss Baxter has met with an accident. We would appreciate it if you would come down to her apartment at once.' It must be the police. The way he said 'we.' And it can't be a car accident or she wouldn't be at home. I know that's where most accidents happen, in the home, but then why in the world haven't they gotten her to a hospital? Why waste time calling me if... You heard me asking what's happened, what kind of an accident, how serious? That's when he said a bad accident, and I would be informed of the details when I got there. And that's all. That's every solitary word I got out of him."

Rosemary's hand tightened on hers, giving comfort, but no doubt seeking it too. When she was in her early teens Rosemary had set Enid apart on a little pedestal of her own. Labeled Sophistication, Hazel supposed, or Glamour; qualities conspicuously lacking in her mother. The gifts Enid gave her were treasured. (And few and far between. She did not know about the pedestal. Children and adolescents bored her.) Enid's most casual comments were seized upon as pearls of wisdom; her mannerisms clumsily, touchingly imitated. That stage was over now, thank God. Rosemary the adolescent had turned into still another stranger: a poised young woman with a brand-new college degree and a mind of her own. But though Enid no longer occupied a pedestal, she still had her special niche, her special charm for Rosemary.

For Hazel too, when it came to that. With her the feeling was partly proprietary pride because she had given Enid her first job, and partly gratitude because four years ago Enid had turned to her again—on quite a different basis this time, with an established reputation, and with a modest legacy from her father's estate which she had eventually invested in Hazel's business. The arrangement was highly satisfactory for both of them: Hazel could afford to expand; Enid could work as a freelance on the jobs that interested her and skip those that didn't. "Business associates." The policeman, or whoever he was, had hit the nail on the head. In spite of the closeness of that association and the fifteen-year span of their friendship, Hazel knew very little about Enid's personal affairs. There had been an impulsive and ill-advised college marriage, already expiring when Enid first came to work for her. There had been a procession of "beaus," shadowy background characters more or less indistinguishable to Hazel. There had been, or so she gathered, an unfortunate love affair in Philadelphia. Enid had never chosen to confide. Hazel had never pried. And just as well, too; she somehow sensed that they would not see eye to eye on such matters.

In an odd way, she thought, Enid was a lonely sort of person. It was the first time such an idea had occurred to her. She decided not to mention it; Rosemary would give her one of those withering looks and say she was out of her mind.

There wasn't time, anyway. "We'd better get out here," she said when they reached the corner of Enid's block and saw all the police cars. The sight of them unnerved her; she had been prepared for only one. Cops swarmed in front of the old four-story brick house, ordering each other around, shooing curious passers-by on their way, now and then admitting somebody with the proper credentials. They let Hazel and Rosemary in eventually. Not, however, before the one word had leapt out at Hazel from a jumble of anonymous voices behind her. The one black word, murder.

She paused at the door and said weakly, "You wait down here for me, Rosemary. Honestly, I'd rather—"

"Don't be silly," said Rosemary. "Tuck your blouse in and come on."

There was a slight commotion as they and their police escort started up the stairs. It was caused by the arrival of the young man who lived on the first floor. (Hazel could not remember his name, though she had met him once at Enid's.) He had a suitcase in each hand. His expression was harried, and his voice was husky with fatigue and strain. "Certainly I live here. You saw my name on the mailbox. This is my apartment, right here. I'm just back from vacation, and I— What's happened? What's going on?"

The reply was mumbled; all Hazel caught of it was Enid's name. When she looked back from the landing she saw the young man propped against the wall—like something broken and discarded, an inside-out umbrella, she thought—his face white under the vacation tan, his eyes blank.

Murder. A black word down there on the street. In Enid's apartment a black reality. They had not taken her away yet; covered by a sheet, she lay beside the terrace window where her maid Carrie had found her when she came to work. The window stood open. Out on the terrace a handful of men milled about among the flower boxes and porch furniture. There were twinkling pools from last night's thunderstorm in the canvas seats of the chairs.

She had been stabbed, according to the gentle-voiced man who took charge of them, stabbed with a knife she used for cutting back bushes. They had found it on the terrace. If Mrs. Nicholson would be kind enough to identify... Hazel nodded dumbly. Nodded again when the sheet was pulled back briefly and she looked down at the small, sprawled body in the gay-flowered cotton dress and sandals. Enid's face had the drained, fragile look of a shell. Her eyes were not quite closed, slitted; her mouth, bright with lipstick, curved a little, so that she seemed to be smiling scornfully at death. Or perhaps at life.

Then the gentle-voiced man steered them into the bedroom, where he sat at the rosewood desk and they perched side by side on the chaise longue. Rosemary was crying fiercely, against her will. With Hazel it was her legs. Wobbling again, even after she sat down. But her voice was all right, steadily, matter-of-factly telling what she knew about Enid Baxter. She knew all the things that didn't matter—what Enid had paid for the chaise longue, for instance, where she had found the rug and the alabaster lamp, who had upholstered the boudoir chair. And none of the things that mattered. Acquaintances? Friends? Enemies? Only a few of the names in Enid's address book were familiar to her. She did not know about any love affair Enid was involved in. Could think of no one who might possibly have a motive for wanting her dead.

"We weren't that kind of friends," she said helplessly. "I mean not intimate in that way. It wasn't all business, of course. We often had lunch together, or a drink after work. Occasionally dinner. We were very fond of each other, but... It doesn't have to be someone she knew, does it? It could have been a burglar."

That was certainly a possibility, the detective agreed. In fact, there were a number of indications that Miss Baxter might have surprised a would-be thief in the act of sneaking in through the terrace window, whereupon the intruder panicked, killed her, and fled without stealing anything. Burglars, particularly amateurs, sometimes did just that.

Apparently Miss Baxter had gone down to the corner delicatessen last night—between ten and ten thirty, according to the owner—to buy coffee and milk for breakfast. The bag of groceries still sat on the kitchen counter where she had put it. For such a short trip, and on such a sultry night, she might very well not bother to close and lock the terrace window. They were checking for signs of such an intruder; unfortunately the thunderstorm that came later in the night had probably washed them away. The terrace was accessible from the roof via a drain pipe, and with no superintendent on the premises—he lived in the house down the street—and a street door that could be opened with a dime, it wouldn't be much of a trick for someone to get into the house and up on the roof. Again unfortunately, the fourth-floor tenants were away on vacation. Like the young man on the first floor; he had been due back last night, but his plane had been delayed by bad weather until this morning. So the only two people in the house had been Miss Baxter and Mrs. Klein, on the floor below her. Mrs. Klein reported hearing someone running down the stairs last night a few minutes after she came back from walking her dog. She couldn't be sure about the time. Ten thirty. Eleven. She hadn't thought to look at the clock. Nothing else out of the way. Just the footsteps. Very fast. Very hard. Bubbles had barked his head off. He was a wonderful watchdog; she never had to worry with him around. She hadn't heard Miss Baxter go out or come back, so the footsteps must have been after her trip to the delicatessen.

To make things even more difficult, there were no neighbors from across the street to observe last night's comings and goings. Almost the entire block opposite Enid's house was taken up by a grade school and a huge new apartment house in process of construction—both of course empty on a Sunday night in July.

Yes, a prowler was certainly a possibility. Though they couldn't rule out the other possibilities yet. Mrs. Nicholson hadn't heard from Miss Baxter or seen her over the week end?

"You mean do I have an alibi?" Hazel asked drily. "No, I didn't hear from Enid or see her over the week end. Last night my sister and I went to the movies to cool off. Got caught in the thunderstorm on our way home. Let's clear Rosemary while we're at it. She spent the week end with friends in Connecticut and came back to town this morning on the train. In case you're interested in names and addresses we can supply them."

"I'd appreciate it," said the detective blandly. "Thank you very much."

Later, when the lawyer called about Enid's will, she realized that checking the Nicholson alibis wasn't such a farfetched idea after all. Enid had been an only child; except for two cousins she had never seen there were no relatives. Her estate was divided between Hazel, who was named executrix of her will, and Rosemary. The amount of money involved was not large; still, people had been known to murder other people for far less. People who had been told the terms of other people's wills, that is. To Hazel and Rosemary the news of their inheritance—the detective could believe it or not—was a shock, a queerly sad jolt of discovery about Enid and the life they had imagined for her, the glittering, crowded social life...

A lonely sort of person. This time Hazel said it out loud. "Don't," croaked Rosemary, and fled to her bedroom.

Hazel herself would have liked a good cry. Instead, she pitched in and made the funeral arrangements.

And after that was over, there were other tasks. Enid's will contained a few specific bequests: her family silver went to the cousins, books and certain pieces of jewelry to friends, her clothes to her maid Carrie. It was left to Hazel to sort out and dispose of the rest—furniture, pictures, dishes, household equipment, all the accumulation of a woman's lifetime. The job, which she tackled with her usual forthright energy, was more time-consuming than she would have thought possible. Each session she spent in that old, high-ceilinged apartment seemed only to open up new pockets of possessions to be looked through and consigned to whatever fate she decided was appropriate.

On the Saturday after Enid's death she arrived bright and early, determined to finish up. Martin Shipley was mousing around in his little scrap of garden. "How about clearing out those books today?" she said briskly. They were his, according to the will, but so far he had put off moving them down to his place. Squeamish about going back to Enid's apartment, Hazel supposed. Well, she hadn't exactly relished the idea, either. But she had done it. "It won't take long, once you get at it. And it will be that much accomplished."

This time, rather to her surprise, he did not stall. "Yes. All right." He straightened up by degrees and wiped his hands along the sides of his faded dungarees. A scrawny, forlorn-looking specimen; once more Hazel wondered how he and Enid had happened to strike up a friendship. Probably a simple matter of propinquity.

But before the morning was over she changed her mind about Martin

Shipley. In the first place, he turned out to be the kind of worker that Hazel's farmer father used to call a hustler. Instead of fading out of the picture, as he had every right to do once he had cleared out the books, he set to and helped her with the kitchen cupboards. She was inclined to dither over decisions. Not Martin. "Throw it out, it's no earthly use." "Give it to Carrie." "The Salvation Army." And that would be that. On to the next shelf.

He had a nice, quiet sense of humor, too. Little jokes sprang up between them. Now and then Hazel had to laugh, just at the sight of him up there on the step-stool: those long arms of his that seemed to angle out in all directions, the stretch of knobby backbone showing between his dungarees and t-shirt, his bony skull with the cowlick sticking up from the crown. There was something engaging about his very lack of grace or good looks. He wasn't all that unattractive, anyway, especially when he smiled; she pointed out to herself his high forehead and steady eyes.

There were one or two sombre moments. In the middle of taking down the drapes he stopped and looked off into space. "I remember helping her put these up. She wasn't tall enough to manage by herself, even with the big ladder... Haven't the police turned up anything? Anything at all?"

"Not as far as I know," said Hazel. "They're still working on it, of course."

But the days had gone by, with no break in the case; the story had receded from glaring tabloid headlines to the back pages; and without realizing it until now, Hazel no longer expected a break. The chances of plucking, from all the swarming city, one anonymous prowler who had panicked and killed and run—too remote, too remote.

"They kept asking me about her friends. You too? Yeah." Martin peered down at her from the stepladder. "They had her address book. I don't know how many times they took me through it, name by name."

"I know. And most of them were just names to me. Didn't mean a thing. Except for the business contacts. You probably knew more about her social life than I did."

"Did you ever meet that friend of hers—what's-his-name?—Victor Holm? He's an architect, I think."

Hazel shook her head. "They asked about him. But his name doesn't ring any bells with me. Why?"

"She used to know him in Philadelphia. He's moved to New York now. I met him up here once—oh, it must have been two or three months ago. In the spring. His name was in her book, so I suppose they talked to him too. I suppose they went right down the list, checking everybody against everybody else."

"Probably." Hazel hadn't thought of it before. It made her feel vaguely uncomfortable. "Well, apparently they didn't find any red-hot suspects. Or if they did they're keeping it awfully quiet."

"That's all they could do if they didn't have any proof," Martin said slowly. "Just bide their time and wait for the murderer to make a slip. The famous, fatal slip they all theoretically make."

"But I thought—I still think it was a prowler." She cleared her throat. "Just one of those senseless things, like being killed by a hit and run driver. As impersonal as that. All the details point to a prowler."

"They could point the other way too, though. If somebody she knew rang her doorbell she might let them in. It could have been like that. Not through the terrace at all." After a moment's silence he reached again for the curtain rod and wrenched it free of its moorings. "Look out below!" The drapes descended majestically, exuding dust. The subject was dropped.

Then there was the business about the ring. Enid had left to Martin, besides her books and anything he might want from the terrace, her jade ring. "I put it aside for you," Hazel told him. "Here. You might as well take it now."

"But that's not the one—" It came blurting out, apparently before he could stop it. He flushed.

"What do you mean it's not the one? I went through all her jewelry, and it's the only jade ring I found. Look for yourself, if you think I'm trying to hold out on you."

"Of course I don't think that!" It was a sign of how far their friendship had already progressed—the way they now glared at each other. "I expected it to be the other one, you know, the one she always wore. It was smaller than this one, and the setting was gold, not silver. Maybe three or four little squares of jade set in a row. She always wore it. Surely you remember it?"

Now that he mentioned it, yes. When Hazel closed her eyes she could see Enid's small, nervous hand, and on it the ring; she had had a habit of twisting it round and round with her thumb. "But where could it be? Honest and true, Martin, the lawyer and I sorted everything out, and this was the only... Unless she was buried with it still on. That's possible, I suppose."

That had to be it, she decided, after they had searched the apartment without success.

"It doesn't matter," Martin said. "This one will do just as well as a keepsake. Something to remember her by. That's all that matters. Not that I'm apt to forget her," he added, and his face was so stricken that Hazel's heart went out to him.

"There. No use brooding."

"She was my best friend," said Martin. "My only friend."

"Oh come on, now. A young fellow like you lonely?" she began. But then their eyes met, and she broke off, inwardly cringing at her own glib heartiness. At that moment he looked like the oldest man in the world, far too old to remember what hope or joy felt like. And lonely, lonely, in a way that was beyond Hazel's ken, except for this brief glimmer. Enid had known, though; she and Martin had been birds of a feather.

And yet when he smiled—as he was smiling now—he changed into the shy, rather unprepossessing, but likable lad she had spent the morning with. Could she have imagined that ancient, tragic mask of a moment ago? "I'm hungry," he said. "How about knocking off and coming down to my place for a sandwich?"

"Fine. The only thing is, Rosemary promised to come down and lend a hand... Well, I can leave her a note, can't I?"

Rosemary arrived as they were finishing their sandwiches and beginning a second round of beers. She and Martin, though they had both attended the funeral services for Enid, had not met formally until now. They eyed each other—Martin with open appreciation, Rosemary with the inscrutable expression she was cultivating this summer. She's so pretty, Hazel thought, with the familiar pang of pride, wistfulness and surprise. She had never been pretty herself; how had she happened to produce a daughter like this? Rosemary's light brown hair, with sun-bleached streaks in it, was hitched up on top today, exposing her neat little ears and the graceful line of her neck. Her nose was pert, her eyelashes extravagant, her dress pink-and-white striped, like a peppermint stick. Martin, poor boy, was obviously and acutely aware of his own sweaty, dust-streaked attire. Not to mention the state of his apartment, which was about what you would expect. Hazel, watching him stumble over his own feet as he cleared a chair for Rosemary, felt suddenly protective.

"Martin's been working like a dog up there all morning," she said. "Wait till you see what we've accomplished. He deserves a medal."

The smile Rosemary dispensed was abstracted. Either this was part of the inscrutable business or her thoughts really were otherwise engaged. Hazel had no idea which. Until a few minutes later, when Rosemary broke off in the middle of something else to exclaim, "Martin Shipley! I knew the name was familiar but I couldn't think where... Now I remember. Of course. I knew Bill Dunning at college, he used to date my roommate, and it was his sister—" Her face suddenly turned fiery red. "Forgive me. I'm so sorry. I shouldn't have mentioned it."

"Why not?" Into the well of silence Martin dropped the two words, small and hard as pebbles. He kept his eyes lowered. His whole body seemed to have locked and gone rigid. "Your roommate. His sister. And my wife. All very cozy."

"Your wife?" said Hazel. "I didn't know you were married!"

At that he did look up; his eyes were stony, his mouth set in a wolfish sort of smile. "Hard to believe, isn't it? I was married. I had a wife. Unfortunately, she died."

"I'm so sorry," Rosemary said again, helplessly, and he turned the wolfish smile on her. With one accord, she and Hazel stood up; Martin unlocked himself and rose, obviously as eager as they to end this uncomfortable little scene. There was no mention of his earlier offer to help with the final chores in Enid's apartment, nothing left of the comradeship that had sprung up between him and Hazel. The few perfunctory words of thanks she mumbled embarrassed them both; they did not even shake hands. But when she looked back, halfway up the first flight of stairs, he was still standing there in the doorway, watching them, with such a hungry expression on his face. Like a stray dog, she thought, and she might have turned back if he had not stepped inside just then and slammed the door.

"What was all that about?" she demanded when she caught up with Rosemary outside Enid's door.

"Joyce Dunning. He was married to Joyce Dunning! And to think I blurted it out like that, why, I could have sunk through the floor! You must have read about it in the papers, Mom, her family carried on like crazy."

"When she married Martin, you mean?"

"Of course not when she married him. When she was killed in that accident. Surely I must have told you— No, maybe not. It was three years ago, the summer you were out in California, and I suppose by the time I saw you again the whole thing had simmered down. I got in on it on account of Penny, she was mad for Bill Dunning at that point, so naturally she was all agog..." They were in Enid's living room now; facing each other—Hazel open-mouthed, Rosemary aware of the effect she was producing. "They suspected foul play, you see. Her family. They tried to get him arrested for murder."

"Martin? They accused Martin of murdering his wife?"

"Well, he could have pushed her," said Rosemary calmly. "He was with her at this quarry when it happened. This old abandoned quarry. He and Joyce were visiting her folks in the country, Massachusetts, I think, and they'd just had a fight. So she went tearing out of the house, and he followed her, and somehow or other she slipped and fell. Broke her neck. Her father screamed his head off to the police, and I don't know whether they decided Martin was telling the truth, or whether they just figured they'd never be able to prove he wasn't. Anyway, they didn't arrest him."

"I should think not," said Hazel, in a voice so much louder and more emphatic than she had intended that it startled her. "I can't imagine anybody looking or acting less like a murderer than that boy. Can you?"

Rosemary's answer was slow in coming. She inspected her pale pink fingernails. "No. But then— Well, who knows what a murderer's supposed to look like? I certainly don't. I've never met one personally. As far as I know."

Suddenly Hazel shivered.

4

So much for the Nicholsons, Martin thought as he slammed the door on them. He grinned to himself, imagining the lurid tale Rosemary was no doubt already pouring out, to the accompaniment of shocked gasps from her mother. And he seemed like such a nice boy, she would repeat at intervals. Past tense. Seemed. The word itself held overtones of fraudulence. Now that she knew what lay behind his false front, she would remember one or two odd moments. Not so much what he said, she would explain, as the way he said it. He couldn't, of course, have had anything to do with what had happened to Enid; but all the same it was strange, first the business about his wife, and now this.

Yes. Very strange. Almost too much of a coincidence. Oh, he could hear them, he could see the frightened flutter of Rosemary's eyelashes, the glaze of dismay settling on Hazel's plain, forthright face.

And they didn't know the half of it. Victor Holm was just a name to them. Enid had spared them her confidences; she had extracted no promise from them. He could almost hate her for the shrewd instinct that had guided her straight to him: the one person she could trust to keep that promise. Once again he toyed with the notion of breaking it. He saw himself marching into the police station, upright citizen that he was, belatedly volunteering the information he had hitherto withheld, explaining in manly ringing tones that on second thought he had decided to put public duty before his personal code of honor. Justice must be served. Yea, yea. Murder must be avenged.

But they must already have checked on Vic, along with everyone else whose name was listed in Enid's address book. Checked and cleared him. Or perhaps not cleared him; they might still be watching and waiting, quietly probing for weak spots in his story. They certainly didn't have to depend on Martin to tell them about the affair between Enid and Vic four years ago; it had been pretty generally known in Philadelphia. As far as its resumption was concerned—well, they didn't need Martin there, either. That was their business, to put two and two together and come up with at least four, more likely five. Vic himself might very well have admitted it. Why not, if he had a good enough alibi for the Sunday night of her death? And if it was all that good, Martin's little tattled tidbits weren't going to break it. There was no guarantee the police would believe him, anyway. Just his word for it, the word of a fellow with a mighty peculiar history of his own...

That, of course, was the crux of the matter, the one angle that made him incapable of breaking his promise to Enid. Because he knew what it was to be accused without proof, he could not point his finger at Vic, at least not at this stage, with nothing more substantial to go on than the memory of Enid's morbid fancies, brandy-induced. Her voice came back to him: "I just mentioned the possibility. Very remote. And anyway, it would be my own fault, for needling him into it."

Definitely not at this stage. But not ever? Never? Supposing he were to come across some solid evidence of Vic's guilt, would he take it to the police? Or would he find some further excuse for not speaking out? With his talent for rationalization, he wouldn't have much trouble. After all, it meant not only breaking his word to Enid, it meant aligning himself on the side of a group he had come to regard, thanks to Joyce's family, as his natural enemies. The sight of a cop could still make him flinch.

Curiosity spread in him like an itch. In addition to his own unpredictable reactions, there was the swarm of questions about Vic: his thoughts and feelings, whatever they might be; how much of them he could hide or not hide; what part of the truth he had dared to tell the police, what part his wife.

He sat down. Absent-mindedly he sipped the remains of Hazel's beer. (They had stood not upon the order of their going.) Yes. He was itching to see Vic. He had a right to investigate the matter on a strictly private basis and settle it in his own mind. That would not be betraying Enid's trust in him. Time enough later to decide about the police.

But he couldn't just barge in and start asking questions as if he were a cop. Victor Holm was no man to stand for any such nonsense. In fact, Martin wondered if he was a match for Vic, whatever tactics he might adopt. A very cagey customer. Still, he had nothing to lose by trying.

Surely he could invent some pretext, some plausible reason for calling Vic...

His eye fell on the pile of books from Enid's apartment, which he had dumped on the floor. A helter-skelter assortment: current novels, Shakespeare, books on gardening, interior decorating, furniture, architecture. Architecture. He plucked one at random; Vic's name sprang at him from the flyleaf.

Five minutes later he was speaking his piece to Vic over the telephone. "Martin Shipley. You may not remember me, but we met once some time ago at Enid—"

"Yes, of course. I've been meaning to call you. I don't know any of Enid's other friends here in New York, and I'd like to talk to you. How about coming over? We're only a couple of blocks away, you know."

"Yes, I know." Thrown off his stride, Martin floundered on. "What I called about, Enid's books, I found several of yours among them, and I thought you might want—"

"What? Sorry, I can't hear you."

Martin went through it again, this time slowly and distinctly. Vic disposed of it in short order. "No, I don't want them back. Thanks anyway. I'd forgotten she had them. If you're not busy this afternoon, drop in for a drink. Any time that suits you. You've got the address?"

Just like that it was settled. He had geared himself for talking to Vic alone. The unknown quantity of Vic's wife both alarmed and intrigued him. But somehow the whole business had been taken out of his hands: a trial sample of Vic's one-upmanship. Where Martin had made his mistake—he decided while he showered and changed his clothes—was in laying out too rigid a plan for himself ahead of time, with no allowance for unforeseeable contingencies. From now on he would play it by ear. He could hardly do anything else, with the performance taking place on Vic's home grounds, very likely with his wife as audience. Thelma. His only source of information on the subject of Thelma was Enid, the barbed comments she had now and then let fly. He knew better than to take them as gospel truth.

Was Thelma supposed to act as a deterrent to Martin? Was that why Vic had avoided a tête-à-tête, because he was counting on her, just the fact of her presence, to keep the conversation within the limits of safety and decorum? The nerve of him! For all he knew, Martin might be loaded with bombshells, with no scruples about dropping them, never mind who might be around. It was galling, to be dismissed as no more of a menace than that.

He was a little startled when he reached the address on Third Avenue: instead of a regular apartment house, it was an old four-story building, jammed in between taller, newer neighbors. The first two floors were occupied by a surgical appliance store and its stock room; the Holms had the top half of the place to themselves. A narrow staircase led to their apartment, which no doubt had great possibilities, as yet unrealized. The big living room into which Vic ushered him—still with that brisk cordiality, quite a change from their previous encounter—had an unsettled look, as if all the furniture were just as the moving men had left it. But Martin's impression of the room and its decor was fleeting; it was the people in it that riveted his attention. There were two women, instead of the one he had been prepared for. Two women, and he didn't know which was Thelma, and he had never been easy about meeting strangers. He felt himself breaking into a nervous sweat.

It turned out that Thelma was the tall one with the bangs. "Lulu and I are about to leave for a matinee. Do forgive us, won't you. And I'm sorry we're still in such a shambles. It's going to be beautiful. We hope." She crossed the room with her hand thrust out: like a child running to meet him, Martin thought, a friendly child who took it for granted she was going to like and be liked. There was a quality of headlong warmth about her that made her seem vulnerable. Dangerously so, from Martin's point of view; she might very well have acted as a deterrent. Thank God for the matinee. She was nothing at all like Enid. (Well, why should he have expected her to be?) None of Enid's miniature delicacy, none of her chic, none of her sleek darkness. All the same, a real rival—as Enid had been the first to recognize. When Thelma smiled, the imperfections of her face, with its overlarge mouth and slightly crooked teeth, were somehow transformed into assets. Really, it was quite a magical smile; you smiled back, whether you meant to or not.

Lulu was an expensive-looking item, polished and tinted and brushed to a high gloss. She had a husky voice, a compact figure, and a coolly appraising, humorous eye. Nothing vulnerable about her. Her last name was McGrath. Mrs. McGrath. A friend of the Holms from Philadelphia. She too had known Enid—well, not really known her, but they had met now and then at parties. Poor girl, what a shocking thing. Dreadful.

"I think Vic said you were a neighbor of Enid's?" said Thelma. "In the same house?"

"Yes. I have the ground-floor apartment." Martin hardened his heart and went on. "We saw quite a bit of each other. That's where I met Mr. Holm, in fact, one evening in Enid's apartment." A small bombshell, perhaps? She was no longer looking at him.

"Remember, Thelma?" said Vic. "It wasn't long after we ran into Enid at that press party. She asked me then if I'd take a look at a job she was working on and tell her what I thought."

Loyally, obediently, Thelma's head bobbed up and down. "So I suppose you had a session with the police too, Mr. Shipley. The same as we did."

"We certainly did," Lulu said. "I was here that week end, too—I sneak off to New York whenever Vic and Thelma will put up with me—and I was just leaving to catch the train back home Monday morning, when here came the cops. What a business! They phoned Vic at the office and got him back here, to double-check Thelma and me, I suppose. Not that they weren't perfectly nice about everything. And after all, that's their job, asking questions. How else are they going to come up with the right answer?"

"They haven't come up with any kind of an answer so far," Martin pointed out. "Maybe they haven't asked the right questions."

"I can't think of any they missed." Thelma laughed tremulously. "Personally I felt as if I'd been put through the wringer and hung out to dry. Not just once, either. They've been back a couple of times, just to see if we remembered anything else. And they've given Lulu the same treatment. We've all three been grilled to a turn, individually and collectively...Vic dear, fix Mr. Shipley a drink. He can have some of my ginger ale if he's on the wagon, poor soul." She made a funny face at Martin. "You're not, are you? Nobody is but me. We've got to run. So sorry. Do come again."

"See you later. Behave yourselves now." Vic kissed her, and over her shoulder exchanged a meaningful glance with Lulu. "Don't worry, I'm in good hands," said Thelma rather irritably. Something of a lush, Enid had reported. Could be. And Lulu's role was to keep her in line? Could be, Martin repeated to himself, and sat down on the couch while Vic got busy at the bar with gin and tonic.

It really was quite a living room. Except for the kitchen alcove, it took up the whole floor. The walls were of whitewashed brick, spectacularly bare and high. At one end an open stairway curved upward, presumably to the bedrooms. There was a handsome Oriental rug on the floor, but no pictures or books. Even Martin, who had little interest in such matters, realized that it lacked the finishing touches.

He had decided on a blunt approach. He would wait till Vic mixed the drinks and sat down. Then he would come out with it: You wanted to talk to me about Enid?

But again Vic beat him to the draw. "What's your theory about Enid?" he asked as he handed Martin his glass.

"My theory?"

"Sure, your theory. Who's in a better position to have one? Knowing her as well as you did. Living in the same house."

"Okay, but I wasn't there the night it happened." Why should he sound so defensive, damn it? And don't think Vic wasn't enjoying it: barely able to keep from smirking. "I wasn't even in town. I was on vacation."

"That's right. I remember now, the police mentioned the house was practically empty. Nobody there but one other woman tenant. And

Enid. And of course whoever did it. When did you get back from your vacation?" A nice sociable question. Vic tacked it on as if it were an afterthought.

"Didn't the police tell you that, too? Monday morning. I was due back Sunday night, but the plane was held up on account of weather. So you know as much as I do about what went on. At least you were here in town. Or so I gather."

"Oh yes. I was here all right. We went to the beach in the afternoon, Thelma and Lulu and I, and I folded up early, right after dinner. Sun affects me that way." Vic sat down and crossed his legs, triumphantly at ease. Well, it was an alibi of sorts. The police must have bought it. No reason why they shouldn't. Even if Martin had chosen to talk, it might not have made any difference. He could see Vic—open-faced, obviously a man of substance with nothing to hide—looking the police in the eye as he answered their questions in his deep, assured voice. Yes. Trust Vic to strike the right note. And Thelma to back him up. "All right. Leaving Sunday night out of it," he was going on now to Martin, "I thought you might have a line on what led up to it. I mean, in case the police are wrong and it wasn't a prowler. I was counting on you to know about her friends here in New York. Or her enemies. Anyway, the people she was seeing."

"I know she was seeing you," said Martin. "Whether your wife knows it or not."

He had the satisfaction of seeing Vic's face turn red. "I had that coming, I guess. Don't bother telling me what you think of me. I agree. I'm sorry about Thelma. I always was. A hell of a lot of good that does. Being sorry. I don't expect you to understand. If you'd ever been married—"

"As it happens, I have been. Didn't Enid tell you?" (But of course she hadn't. His confidences had been safe with her. As hers were with him.)

"She told me nothing about you," said Vic bitterly. "For all I know you were in love with her too."

Martin sipped his drink contentedly. It was pleasant to have the upper hand, for a change. "I don't think you had any real competition. Judging from the way she talked to me. She used to go out with other men now and then, but not after you turned up."

"So she talked about me, did she? It figures. Good Neighbor Martin. Always ready with the valuable free advice."

"None that she ever took," said Martin. "And whatever she told me, I didn't pass it on to the police. If that's what's eating on you."

"What's eating on me is that she's dead!" Vic turned on him savagely.

"Dead, God damn it. I've lost her, I'll never see her again. My girl. Gone. Dead. Can't you understand anything?"

Martin had a sudden strong urge to yell back exactly how much he understood, and exactly why: Joyce too was dead, he too had lost his girl, they had suspected him—as he suspected Vic—of killing her, and with as much reason. He clenched his teeth against the words. What if he and Vic did happen to share a similar set of circumstances? That didn't make them soul mates. It was preposterous that he should feel so much as a second's rapport with this violent, jealous, bullying fellow. This murderer. Even Enid, who had once loved him, had recognized him as a menace. And Martin had seen for himself how full of tricks he was, what a manipulator.

"I understand plenty," he said. "She was the best friend I ever had. You can take that any way you want to. I know what it means, and so did she. If you were so damn much in love with her, why didn't you hang on to her when you had her, back there in Philadelphia?"

"Because I never do anything right! You got any more bright questions?"

They glared at each other in silence. Finally Martin said (because he was a little ashamed of himself, but not about to admit it), "You know, Enid once said the same thing to me. That she never did the right thing except at the wrong moment."

"She did?" Vic scanned his face hungrily. "Well, it was the truth. She had a way of belting you with things just when you were in no shape to take them... We fought like hell. Did she tell you that? And yet—we were happy. You're right, I shouldn't have let her go. It was a long time sinking in. But I've known for a year now that nothing was ever going to be any good without her. That's why I came to New York. I figured we'd run into each other, sooner or later. It had to be chance. Don't ask me who made the rules, but I wasn't allowed to call her. Sounds nutty, doesn't it? Like a superstition. If I tried to push fate I'd bollix everything up. You know?"

Martin nodded curtly. It had been the same with him and Joyce. The rigid taboos. The signs and portents: colors, for instance, he had always had the conviction that green was the color of disaster for them, long before that last night when she stormed out in her green dress. They too had fought like hell. And been happy. But then so had many another set of lovers. If Vic had any notions about working on his sympathies...

Could he have sensed, in some uncanny way, that tiny flicker of rapport between them and be trying now to fan it into a nice comfortable blaze for his own protection? It was impossible to tell. His face, for all its surface candor, was inscrutable; his hazy gray eyes seemed fixed on some private horizon.

"Didn't it ever occur to you that she might have changed her mind about you?" Martin asked. "After all, a lot can happen in four years. What made you think she was going to give you a second chance?"

"Because I couldn't stand it if she didn't," said Vic defiantly. The egotist's answer: I want it so, therefore it is so. "You've got to believe in something. All right. I believed in us. Enid and me. And I was right. The only difference was that this time around we weren't settling for what we had before." He banged his glass down. His voice grew louder, even more defiant. "We were getting married as soon as—as soon as possible."

"I see," said Martin. It wasn't the way he had heard it from Enid. More than two months ago, true; but since then she had mentioned Vic often, without ever once hinting at any such drastic switch in plans. Martin would have known if she had been dissembling—and anyway, why should she? As for the gap of ten days while he was away on vacation, she had written him once, a chatty little letter about inconsequentials. No. He simply did not believe in this projected, overemphasized marriage. Vic was lying—possibly because he was an egotist incapable of facing the unacceptable truth, possibly because he was a murderer bent on covering up his motive. Possibly both. "Do the police know all this?"

"They know we had an affair four years ago. And that we'd met again here in New York. But not about our plans. You see, Thelma—"

Martin finished it for him. "You hadn't broken it to her yet. And she hadn't guessed?"

"I doubt it. In fact, I'd be willing to bet on it. Thelma's like that. Inclined to dodge reality." She wasn't the only one, but Martin managed not to say it. "If she guessed anything at all, it was just—well, Philadelphia all over again. Which was bad enough, God knows. I told you before, I'm not proud of myself when it comes to Thelma."

"She's a charming woman," said Martin carefully.

"Very charming. Especially when she's on the wagon. No need to beat about the bush. Enid must have told you. Probably laid it on too thick, in fact. Thelma's sometimes a problem drinker, but that doesn't mean... Lulu's taken her on as one of her rehabilitation projects. She loves sticking people together again. Or trying to. It doesn't always work, of course."

"Not always with Thelma, you mean?"

"So far so good. Let's hope. One thing about Lulu, she doesn't give up easy. She'd still be spoon-feeding that worthless brother of hers if her husband hadn't put his foot down. He's one of The McGraths, Main Line, plenty of dough. Lulu was a hat check girl when he married her. So he calls the turns. Anyway, you can see why I held off telling Thelma."

"Yes. I suppose you'll never tell her now."

"Not much point to it. Not much point to anything, if you ask me." He fumbled with his glass. His face looked empty. Bereft. "Except I'd like to get the guy that did it."

"So would I," said Martin. "Not that it would bring her back. But I'd just like to know... When was the last time you saw her? It must have been after I did."

"Thursday. The Thursday night before it happened. We had dinner at her place. She didn't seem worried about anything, if that's what you're getting at."

You wouldn't know it if she was, Martin thought. Impervious bastard. And if that happened to be one of the nights when you fought like hell, you'd certainly keep it to yourself.

"She mentioned you," Vic added, grudgingly. "Said she missed you. You say she left you her books? In her will?"

"Her books and her jade ring." Martin straightened up; he had forgotten about the ring until now. "Only the ring seems to be missing. Anyway, Mrs. Nicholson and I couldn't find it. There was another one, but not the one she always wore—"

"I know. I ought to. I gave it to her."

"Yes. Well, I assumed that was the one she meant for me to have. But it's gone. We looked through everything. It's the only thing in the way of a clue I can offer. And a pretty damn thin one. Would a prowler take it and nothing else, not even her watch or her wallet? Maybe. If something scared him off before he had time... On the other hand, Mrs. Nicholson may be right and she was buried with it still on her finger."

Vic opened his mouth and closed it again. For what was surely a whole minute, he sat very still. Then he said softly, "I hope she was. I wouldn't want anybody else to have it. And that goes for you too, bud," he added, with a sudden, disarming smile.

"I don't blame you," said Martin before he could stop himself. He stood up. He'd better get out of here quick, before he lost his grip entirely and started telling Vic the story of his life. Enid had been right: this man was dangerous.

5

"I hope you don't mind my ringing your bell," Rosemary said, as she had planned in advance. "I happened to be in the neighborhood, and I just thought I'd stop by and see if you were home."

There was a noticeable silence before Martin—who was not behaving at all as she had planned—said, "Okay. I'm home."

"So I see." She produced a tinny, solitary laugh. "Don't let me interrupt you if you're busy."

"I'm not," he said. He did not open the door any wider. On the other hand, he did not close it.

"Well, if you're not even going to ask me in—"

"By all means." He gestured sweepingly. "I assumed you'd be scared to come in. How do you know you're not taking your life in your hands?"

"Don't be silly," she said, and stepped past him into the dusky living room. It had been slicked up since Saturday, but it still wasn't cheery. He couldn't have been reading; there wasn't enough light. Had he just been sitting here staring into space? "Look, I'm sorry about the other day. I didn't do it on purpose. I'm just stupid. If that makes any difference."

Personally, she thought it was quite a handsome apology. Martin ignored it. "How's your mother? I bet she doesn't know you're here." He stood beside her, exuding hostility. But misery too; she saw that when he switched on the lamp. "It must have given her quite a turn to find out this isn't the first mysterious death I've been mixed up in. Well? Didn't it?"

"I told you I'm sorry." She was conscious of an unpleasant little inner voice: Yes, and you thought that would fix everything, didn't you? Thought all you had to do was flutter the eyelashes and tremble the lip and he'd be eating out of your hand. And now it turns out you're not so irresistible, your nose is out of joint. "After all, it's no deep dark secret about Joyce. Plenty of people besides me know it. It would almost certainly have come out, one way or another."

"That's what I figured, with my usual low cunning. That's why I told the police myself, when they first asked me about Enid. As I expect you discovered when you went panting to them with the news."

"I did not!" she cried. "And neither did my mother, and neither of us ever will."

"Very kind of you, I'm sure. But doesn't it bother you, the possibility that you may be obstructing justice?"

"Oh, what's the use of trying to talk to you? You're impossible! Absolutely impossible!" She spun around and made for the door.

"Don't go," he said unwillingly. But urgently. "Please. Don't go, Rosemary." His hand touched her arm—for a moment only; she drew back instantly and stood still, in complete astonishment. So this was what had brought her back to his apartment. Not curiosity or a wish to apologize, but simply this, the good old basic drawing power that kept the human race in business. (Rosemary had no trouble recognizing it, in spite of her somewhat limited experience.) Never mind that he wasn't what she thought of as her type—that knobby, unhappy face; the personality that, beyond touchiness and a gift for sarcasm, was an unknown quantity to her. The spot on her arm still glowed and tingled.

"Stay and talk to me," he said. "Or— How about dinner?"

"I've already eaten."

"Yeah. Me too. A drink, then? Or coffee?"

"Coffee would be nice." She sat down, demurely smoothing her skirt, demurely lowering her eyelashes. Now that the first shock of surprise was past, she felt rather smug: at least the reaction seemed to be a mutual one, not all on her side.

The coffee was strong, the cups chipped, the sugar bowl on the sticky side. After a minute or two of awkward small talk, Martin said brusquely, "I don't see what's so impossible about assuming you'd go to the police. Seems perfectly logical to me."

"Well, it doesn't to me. What's the point in dragging up past history that's got nothing to do with Enid?"

"You'll have to admit it's an interesting coincidence, though. The police certainly thought so. A very interesting coincidence. Yes indeed. They'd have had quite a case against me, if it hadn't been for my dear little alibi."

"Without a motive? That's ridiculous. You had no earthly reason for killing Enid."

"How do you know? We could have gotten into a violent quarrel about—about horticulture. Anything. And I have this ungovernable temper. Just ask your friend Bill Dunning. He can tell you. He knows more about the quarrels Joyce and I had than I do myself. Especially the last one. He quoted it verbatim."

He was giving her the ferocious smile. She remembered it from Saturday. "Past history," she repeated doggedly. "It's no good brooding about it. All right. The Dunnings gave you a hard time. But they didn't get anywhere with accusing you of—of what happened to Joyce. The police didn't buy their story. They bought yours. You were cleared. It was three years ago, and it's finished, and the only thing to do now is forget it."

"I should forget it. How about you? You were the one that started all this."

She flushed. "And you're never going to forgive me for it, are you? You're going to hoard it up along with everything the Dunnings said. Another wound to lick."

"I forgive you," he said stiffly. "If it hadn't been you, it would have been somebody else. That's the thing, you see. I never know when it's going to happen again, I just know it will, sooner or later. It's not very—tranquilizing."

No, it wouldn't be. Rosemary could see that. "But it doesn't have to spoil your whole *life!* So somebody sees you or hears your name and says, 'Aren't you the Martin Shipley that et cetera.' So you say, 'Yes. Have you read any good books lately?' And that's that."

"God, you're wholesome," he said. "I find it simpler to avoid people whenever possible."

"Then why did you ask me to stay? You didn't have to."

"You didn't have to ring my bell, either. But I'm glad you did." He laughed. Really laughed. "I didn't start out as a hermit. It's just a form of protective coloration. I'm a self-made neurotic. That's what Enid used to call me."

"About Enid." Rosemary took a sip of coffee and went on rather nervously, "My mother may go to the police again. Not on account of you. Not that at all. But Enid's jade ring, to tell them it's missing. If it really is. I mean—"

"It is. You can tell her not to bother. I went back to them myself yesterday, so they already know. It wasn't buried with her."

"What did the police say? Do they think it's important?"

"Who knows? They didn't discuss the fine points of the case with me. She might have lost it, of course. Or, if it was a prowler who killed her, he might have stolen it. It wasn't particularly valuable, but... Did you ever meet Vic Holm? He's the fellow who gave it to her."

Rosemary shook her head. "Do you know him?"

"I met him once at Enid's, a couple of months ago. And the other day he asked me over for a drink. Enid had some of his books. That's why I called him. I don't really know him, no. Not of my own knowledge, as they say."

"What do you mean by that?"

"Enid used to talk about him now and then. They had quite a thing going at one time. But he was married—still is—so it sort of died on the vine." He looked at her sidewise. "Don't start getting ideas about Vic Holm. It's a waste of time. He's got an alibi too. Like me. Like everybody."

"Oh," she said, deflated. For she had started getting ideas: if only because of what seemed to her an oddly tentative note in Martin's voice. "Well, then, his wife..."

"I said everybody. And they don't just alibi each other, either. They had a guest that week end. The cops checked with her, too. Mrs. Lulu McGrath from Philadelphia. The three of them went to the beach Sunday afternoon, came back to the Holms' apartment, and spent a quiet evening there. One of them might be lying. Or even two. But three? It's just one too many."

"If she's a good enough friend of theirs, I suppose she might back them up," Rosemary said halfheartedly. "Or maybe they bribed her."

"She's rich. Her husband's one of The McGraths. I met her briefly—she was here again last week end—and she certainly didn't strike me as the type to carry friendship that far. After all, most people draw the line at murder. Judging by my own experience."

Brooding again, thought Rosemary; he would get no encouragement from her. "What are they like?" she asked. "The Holms?"

The telephone rang before he could tell her. Rosemary leafed through one of the magazines from the rack beside her to indicate that she was not listening; and listened for all she was worth. Nothing else to do, with the telephone right there on the table. She could even catch enough of the caller's mechanized voice to identify it as feminine. And voluble. Crackle, crackle, crackle.

"Oh yes," Martin said. "So that's where I left it... Well... If you're sure it's no bother... No, of course not. Awfully nice of you..." He hung up and cocked his head at Rosemary. "Stick around a few minutes and you'll see for yourself what one of the Holms is like. That was Vic's wife. Thelma. I forgot my lighter at their place the other day, and she's going to drop in and return it. Seems she'll be passing right by here, on her way somewhere else."

"Then maybe I'd better go," said Rosemary, and stood up.

It brought him (as she had hoped?) leaping to his feet. "No! You can't go!" he cried. This time his hand stayed on her arm. Glowing. Tingling. "Why in the hell should you go?"

"Well. In case you want to talk to her alone or something." There was no time to give him the inscrutable look or flutter the eyelashes. Even if she had remembered. The kiss intervened.

Then they sat down again and exchanged nervous little pleasantries while they waited for the doorbell to ring.

Thelma Holm came in talking, in a bubbly, cheerful voice that made Rosemary think of a fountain. A slapdash sort of woman: she looked as if she had thrown on her clothes, run a comb through her bangs, dabbed on some lipstick, and rushed out without more than a glance in the mirror. And none of it mattered when she smiled.

"You should have told me you had company, Martin. I didn't mean to intrude." Her hand reached out impetuously for Rosemary's. "So nice to meet you. No, really, I mustn't stay... Well, just a minute then, if you're sure, let me see if I can unearth your lighter..." She sat down and began rummaging in her purse. "Oh dear, I hope it hasn't sunk to the bottom. Never to reappear."

"Would you like a cup of coffee while you're digging?" Martin asked. "Or can I fix you a drink?"

She hesitated. "I'd love one," she said sadly. "But I'm still on this abstemious kick. Better make it coffee. That's the trouble, you see, it's never just one with me. I get carried away. Ah, here we are." She produced the lighter with a flourish. "It's very strange, I never used to be a problem drinker. That's what Lulu and Vic call it. Not a drunk. Not even an alcoholic. A problem drinker. I guess it does sound more genteel. Whatever it is, I'm tired of being it. Do you suppose I'll ever get off the wagon and back to civilization?"

"Why not?" said Martin. "Lots of people do."

"I know. Vic did. My husband," she explained, turning her clear, dark-blue gaze in Rosemary's direction. Apparently she had no more reserve than a child; it was as if she already accepted them, without question, as old family friends instead of the bare acquaintances they actually were. "He drank himself practically into the gutter at one point. Years ago. No sugar, thank you, dear. It gives me the shudders even now to think of it. What we both went through, before he pulled himself together and got back on the beam. That's what's so strange, that now I should be the one... But then it fits in with this theory I have about myself." She paused, showing for the first time a trace of self-consciousness.

"Theory?" Rosemary prompted her.

"It's sort of balmy. All the same, it's been happening all my life. I seem to take on other people's afflictions. People that are close to me, I mean. My mother's asthma when I was little. Later on, my brother's bronchitis. My girl friend's low blood pressure. Vic and the drinking. He quit and after a while I started. As if I'd drawn it out of him... Does it sound too, too balmy?"

Uncertainly, eagerly, she scanned their faces, waiting for her cue, ready to play it whichever way they took it—seriously or as a joke. It was impossible to tell whether she sincerely believed in her "theory" or was merely trotting it out as a conversation piece. Rosemary had the feeling that Thelma herself did not know. And if she was this susceptible to other people's reactions (even people she hardly knew), then why shouldn't she be a pushover for the illnesses of those who were really close to her? Not so balmy after all, thought Rosemary, and wondered if Martin thought so too.

"It's an interesting angle," he was saying cautiously. "The asthma makes sense, because it's one of those suspicious diseases anyway. Easy enough for an impressionable child to pick it up from somebody she loved."

"I didn't say loved. I said close to. As a matter of fact, my mother and I hated each other. We were ahead of our time. It wasn't fashionable then." Her laugh pealed out. Then she added hastily, "Vic, of course... I don't hate Vic. With my mother I might have been just grabbing the spotlight because I couldn't bear for her to have it. But not with Vic. How could it be that, when he's all right now, and has been for years?"

All right as far as drinking was concerned. And if the affair with Enid had died on the vine, to use Martin's phrase— But he had also mentioned meeting Vic at Enid's apartment a couple of months ago. So they must have been seeing each other again. That didn't mean an affair, of course. Even so, thought Rosemary, it wouldn't make Vic's wife jump for joy. Might well edge her into the fuzzy realm of problem drinking, whether or not she already had a predilection for absorbing the afflictions of people she loved, hated, was close to...

"Delayed reaction, maybe," said Martin. "Or maybe it's got no connection with the fact that Vic used to drink too much. You could have hit the bottle for some entirely different reason."

She thought this over. Then she said matter-of-factly, "I suppose you mean Enid. But that was four years ago. Another one of your delayed... Oh! Now I remember. You met Vic at her apartment, didn't you, the night he stopped in to help her with that job, so you're assuming he'd taken up with her again here in New York. That's it, isn't it?"

"It did cross my mind," Martin admitted drily.

"Naturally. Considering how attractive Enid was." She turned toward Rosemary with an air of bright apology. "Poor dear, you're probably wondering what this is all about. Did you know her? Enid Baxter?"

"I knew her. She and my mother were in business together."

"Oh, of course. Nicholson. I don't know why it didn't register with me before now. Well, then, no need to explain to you why Martin made the mistake of assuming..." After a moment's silence she added wistfully, "I couldn't really blame Vic. She was so stunning. And brainy besides. I used to think if he left me—well, at least it wouldn't be for somebody humiliating. That was another bad time, but we got through it too. He didn't leave me, and Enid moved to New York, and that was the end of it."

Martin shifted uneasily in his chair. He was careful not to look at her. Finally he said, "And now she's dead. Yes. It's all over now." Which was not quite the same, thought Rosemary. "Vic and I talked about her the other day, you know, after you and Lulu left for the theater."

"I know. That is, I took it for granted you would. It's made it harder for Vic, not to have anyone to talk to. He can't very well, with me. Or thinks he can't. I wish he would, you know, it isn't healthy to bottle things up. Is it?"

"It all depends," said Martin, without specifying on what. "He seemed—very much upset about Enid."

"Of course. Who wouldn't be? Even if she had been only a speaking acquaintance... And then to hear it like that, from the police. And all the questions they asked. It was a nightmare. At least Vic wasn't hung over that morning, the way I was."

"Oh?"

"Yes. Oh." She gave a reminiscent groan. "Didn't Vic tell you how stoned I got the night before? The day before, actually. I started early, while we were at the beach, and didn't stop till I passed out on the living room couch. By then Vic had gone to bed, so poor Lulu was the one that got stuck with me."

"No, he didn't tell me."

"Chivalry or something. Well, we didn't go into every last sordid detail with the police, either. No point to it. After all, a lady's hangover is her own business. I should have thought the one I had that morning would be visible to the naked eye, but apparently not. Ah, the good old days. I haven't had a drink since." She jumped up and held out a hand to each of them. "I must go now, I didn't mean to stay this long. Thank you for the coffee—and the company. I do hope you'll call and come over some time soon, both of you. We don't know many people here yet, and Vic's been working overtime a lot, so..."

When he had closed the door behind her, Martin leaned against it, peering at Rosemary. "Well?"

"She's certainly an uninhibited type. I liked her, of course. Nobody could help it."

"Enid could."

"That's different. Enid— She *was* involved again with Vic, wasn't she?"

"According to Vic, very much so."

"You mean he told you? He must be as uninhibited as Thelma."

"Oh no, he isn't. Not by a long shot." Martin crossed slowly to his chair and sat down on the edge of it. "But he figured I already had a pretty good idea of what was going on, from Enid. It wasn't safe to deny it to me. Don't worry, Vic knows what to bottle up and what not to."

"You're making him sound like a real foul ball. Doesn't he have anything to recommend him?"

"Plenty. Too much. I liked him in spite of myself. But I— Well, let's put it this way. I don't have Thelma's unquestioning trust in him."

"I wonder," said Rosemary thoughtfully. "I know what they say, the wife's the last to find out. But in this case it's the second time around. Thelma could know more than she's letting on. It would explain why she turned into a lush."

But Martin shook his head. "She had already done that before Enid and Vic ran into each other again. Enid told me. Anyway, if she knows, why would she pretend not to?"

"Pride," Rosemary said promptly. "And loyalty to Vic. If the reporters had gotten hold of this angle, when Enid was killed, they'd have had a field day with it. I don't know how much Vic told the police—"

"As little as possible. You can be sure of that."

"Why are you so snide about him? After all, *you* didn't tell them about the affair, either."

"No," said Martin. He closed his eyes. "I had my reasons, as Vic had his. And Thelma hers—either because she didn't know or because she wanted to protect Vic."

"She was protecting herself too," Rosemary pointed out. "If you want to get technical—as well as snide—Thelma's the one with the best motive for wanting Enid out of the way."

"Thelma? Not Vic?"

"Of course not Vic. If he was in love with her—"

"He was. That much I believe."

"Well then, why would he want to kill her?"

"Why indeed?" He began to laugh, in an almost soundless, secret, infuriating way. "Okay, okay, I'm sorry. It's all academic, anyway, isn't it? Motive or no motive, neither of them could have killed her. Thelma was stoned, and Vic was asleep, and Lulu was keeping watch over both of them."

"I don't see what was so funny," said Rosemary distantly. "I suppose that makes me not only wholesome but idiotic."

"It makes you lucky. And me a creep with a perverted sense of humor. There isn't anything funny about wanting to kill somebody you love. There isn't anything reasonable about it, either. All the same, it happens. But you don't believe that, do you, Rosemary? You're one of the lucky ones that never get love and hate mixed up. Or maybe you've never been in love."

"I guess I haven't," said Rosemary. "At least not that way." She took a deep breath. "You have been? You mean it was like that with you and Joyce?"

"I mean—" he began roughly. But he bit it off there. For a moment he glared at her, then buried his face in his hands. His voice came out, muffled but savage. "Why don't you get out of here? Beat it. Go home."

"If you want me to." She waited, but he did not answer.

She looked back from the door. He was still hunched in the chair, face hidden, fingers knotted in his hair.

6

Martin held out for two days: on Wednesday he called Rosemary and asked—oh, very casually—if she would by any chance be interested in having a drink with him after work.

"Fine. Where?" she said.

He was so effectively braced for a refusal that this answer threw him all off balance. "What? Oh. Good. About six, then?"

"Where?" she repeated, and he named The Peacock because it was a fixture in the neighborhood of his apartment and the first place that came to mind. As soon as he hung up, of course, he thought of any number of spots that would have been more glamorous or exciting. But if he called her back he might seem to be making too much of a production out of what was supposed to be an ordinary, spur-of-the-moment invitation. Better to let well enough alone.

He got there at five thirty, early enough to snag one of the tables outdoors; during the summer The Peacock went Continental with a sidewalk cafe. It was gritty but cheerful sitting there in the slanting sunshine behind the boxed shrubs that separated customers from passers-by. Yes, very cheerful to be waiting for Rosemary, who was still willing to see him again, in spite of his disgraceful behavior the other night. The waiting might be more pleasant than the actual seeing, he thought with his habitual pessimism: face to face with her, he might be too overcome with the shameful memory of their last meeting to enjoy the present one. For he had come within a hair's breadth of spilling the whole miserable business to her, had drawn back just in time. And then to pack her off like that, as if she were to blame...

The fact remained that she had agreed to come tonight. For whatever reason, time would tell. At the moment he refused to pick holes in the bright surface of the fact that remained. He sipped his gin and tonic and turned a benign eye on his fellow customers. Two of them were obviously also waiting for someone: the fellow with the profile and the drawing pad at the next table, who pretended to be busy sketching the passing scene; and, at the other end, the girl who alternated between nervous glances at her watch and clinical inspections of her face in her compact mirror. Others—like the two young couples, complete with babies and dogs; the pair of pretty boys; and the elderly man with his beer and evening newspaper—were settled for an hour's relaxation, absorbed in their own conversations or thoughts. As Martin and Rosemary would soon be: she would be right here, in the chair opposite him, with her butterscotch-and-molasses hair tethered in a topknot, and her round tanned arms and her summery dress...

This agreeable reverie was interrupted. "Pardon me, can you tell me the time?" It was the fellow with the sketch pad, openly restive by now. He turned toward Martin. His face, so handsome in profile, was unexpectedly ordinary when seen head on. The droop to his mouth now seemed less sensitive than weak; his hairline was no longer distinguished, but simply receding; the whole effect subtly coarsened. His smile was engaging, though, and his voice had vibrancy and depth. Almost an actor's voice, Martin thought. There was nothing theatrical—or artistic, either, when it came to that—about his clothes: gray summer suit, modest figured tie.

He gave a helpless little shrug when Martin told him it was a quarter of six. "Oh well, she's only half an hour late. No cause for alarm. There must be some punctual women in the world, but I don't know them. Do you?"

"I hope so," said Martin. The possibility of Rosemary's being late, which had not occurred to him before, instantly burgeoned into a near-certainty. With ramifications: she might not come at all. Probably wouldn't. Probably had seen his call as a heaven-sent opportunity to pay him back. "How long is cause for alarm? An hour?"

"Depends. I'm an easygoing type, myself. I always give them the benefit of the doubt. Could be I misunderstood the time, or even the place."

"There's only one Peacock. As far as I know."

"I was just generalizing. She picked the spot. I've never been here before. Nice, isn't it? I'm getting quite attached to it. And then I came prepared." He patted his sketch pad. "Something told me it was going to be like this. It's an ego-building device. Gives her a sense of power to keep me waiting."

Yes indeed. Martin decided to change the subject. "You're a professional artist?"

"Not with a capital A. Commercial stuff. Freelance. But I keep dabbling, just to prove I was meant for finer things. It's my ego-building device, I suppose. We all have them." He turned on the engaging smile. "Right?"

Maybe that was Martin's trouble. No ego-building device. Unless you wanted to count Rosemary, who could just as easily turn out to be very much the contrary. "Well," he began. But at that moment his fellow-philosopher sprang up, hand out-stretched. He at least had not waited in vain.

During their conversation Martin had been sitting with his back to the entrance; now he turned, mildly curious about what sort of girl it would be. The mental image he had built up—for no particular reason—was of a model-type, all bones and high style.

So it was with a double start of astonishment that he saw Thelma Holm threading her way between the rows of tables. She looked better put together than usual: the full skirt she was wearing was becoming to her slim figure, her bangs were brushed, the rest of her straight brown hair was pinned up smoothly, in a way that showed off her well-shaped head. But she was still a long way from high style.

She did not see Martin until he stumbled to his feet and gulped out a surprised "Hello." Then she stopped in her tracks, and her face flooded with color, the slow, painful flush of an embarrassment so acute that it communicated itself to him. If the table had been big enough, he would gladly have crawled under it. And if she had spotted him in time, she would have turned tail and fled. He was sure of it.

"You know each other?" asked the fellow with the profile. He sounded pleased and amused, not in the least embarrassed. Well, why should he be? Why should anybody be?

"Of course. Martin, how nice to see you!" After the first bad moment Thelma pulled herself together. A little too much chattering and exclaiming, maybe, but it was that kind of situation. What a coincidence. What a small world. She performed the introductions. Martin Shipley. Bob—White. Like that, with a definite pause in the middle, and a stress on the White, as if she had pounced on it. Or—more likely, thought Martin, observing Mr. White's slightly lifted eyebrow—plucked it out of thin air.

Martin hurried to explain that he was waiting for Rosemary. In other words, trapped; he did not want Thelma to think he was sticking around to spy on her, or to gloat over her discomfiture. Whatever its source, it was her business. By now she seemed to have talked most of it away. She was off that miserable wagon, hooray. Well, one foot off. Still in the experimental stage, but last night she had had one drink, only one, so she felt she could be trusted again tonight. Wasn't it wonderful?

She looked from one to the other of them, her face alight with hope and that other quality, the hyper-responsiveness that made her seem so vulnerable. (The word that had sprung into Martin's mind when he first met her. Here it was again.) Too susceptible to other people for her own good; she was bound to get hurt over and over again, in the future as she undoubtedly had been in the past. By Vic, Enid, perhaps in some mysterious way by this White fellow, possibly even by Martin himself...

He caught sight of Rosemary, and stopped worrying about Thelma or anything else. Not even ignominious memories could mar the moment of Rosemary's arrival on time. Pink dress, rose-fresh face, sunny hair. His head swam with jubilance. There was another spate of exclamations. Another set of introductions. Bob—White. (Again Thelma brought it out with that curious little pause-and-pounce effect.) Mr. White's inspection of Rosemary was thorough and appreciative. Also a bit surprised: he too must have built up a mental image of Martin's girl, and it didn't match with the reality any more than the model-type Martin had dreamed up for him. So he had expected a droop, had he? Ha!

Once more Thelma went into a fit of nervous talking. "Bob's going to do us some murals," she explained, a little feverishly. "At least I hope so. I'm counting on you, Bob, to come up with some ideas about what to do with those living room walls. If not murals then something else. They paralyze me. I mean it. When I look at them I lapse into a kind of coma." She took a swig of her one drink and glanced at her watch. "I don't want to hurry you, Bob, but I really would like to have you view the remains and see what you think..."

"Whenever you say. You're the boss," said Bob White with cheerful deference. He had been uncommonly quiet since Thelma showed up. Letting her run the show. Possibly waiting for her to feed him his lines. Now he added one of his own. "You and Vic, I should say."

"Oh, but I want to surprise Vic! I mean, he's not to know until it's all worked out. You mustn't breathe a word to Vic, any of you, about any of this." She made flustered, anxious gestures with her hands. The flush was back in her face. "You won't, will you?"

"Of course not," Martin assured her.

"Lucky I mentioned it," said Bob easily. "I might have let the cat out of the bag."

They left very shortly, Thelma with her head high, Bob carefully not taking her arm until they reached the corner.

There was a busy silence. Then Rosemary said, "Murals, my eye."

Martin had been thinking very much the same thing. But for some reason he resented hearing it put into words. "I don't know what you mean by that," he said stiffly.

"Oh come on, Martin. It was perfectly obvious what's going on. She made up the murals on the spur of the moment, just like she did his name. The Bob part may be okay, probably is, but I'll bet anything you like his last name isn't White."

"That may prove something to you. It doesn't to me. And I fail to see anything out of the way about Thelma's having a sociable drink with the guy, whatever his name happens to be. What the hell of it?"

"Nothing. My point exactly. I wouldn't have given it a second thought, nobody would have, if she hadn't gone into such a swivet. Don't tell me you didn't notice how jumpy she was. Guilty conscience. It was written all over her."

"What about him? He didn't act to me like a man weighted down with sinful secrets."

"I expect he's an old hand at the game," said Rosemary. "Actually, he's very good-looking from the side."

"Sure. He'd be great stamped on a coin."

"My, you're grumpy. I shouldn't think you'd begrudge Thelma a little fling of her own. Personally, I think it serves Vic right."

"So do I. If that's what she's doing." After a pause, he added reluctantly, "And I suppose she is. This White guy really is an artist, though. He was sitting here sketching while he waited for her. Look, he forgot his sketch pad."

It was still lying on one of the chairs at the adjoining table. Martin picked it up and flipped through the pages. Pretty undistinguished stuff. Well, Bob White had not pretended otherwise. His ego-building device.

"But if it was just a matter of murals," Rosemary began.

"I know. Why would she meet him here, instead of just having him come up to the apartment? And then that business about not telling Vic. That sounded fishy, I admit. In fact—" He looked across at her and lost the thread, simply let it sweep away in another flood of jubilance at the miracle of Rosemary's being here.

"I was so afraid you wouldn't come tonight," he said in a rush.

"Why on earth wouldn't I? I said I would."

"I know. But I thought maybe you— On account of the other night. You must have thought I'd gone crazy. Maybe you still do."

"No, or I wouldn't be here," said Rosemary. Her clear hazel eyes met his unflinchingly. "It was my fault for mentioning Joyce. But it seemed to me maybe you wanted to talk about her, and I thought if you did—"

"If I did you'd listen and pat my hand and feel sorry for me. Oh God, here I go again. Saying things I don't want to. Not saying things I... That's always my trouble. I'm not sure myself, I mean, about myself. Not sure about anything. I probably am crazy."

"Means nothing," said Rosemary briskly. "I'm not always sure about myself, either. And I'm so wholesome it's disgusting."

"I never said disgusting." He put his hand over hers; it was square and forthright, the kind of competent little paw Rosemary would have. So different from Joyce's hand—tapering, beautiful, useless—that it might have belonged to another species. Was that what drew him to Rosemary, the contrast between her and all that he had once loved and hated and agonized over? Or was it the contrast between his own nature with its endless convolutions and self-examinations, and Rosemary's straightforward approach to life? It was typical of him to be wasting this very moment, which ought to be pure enjoyment, in futile speculation. Futile and ludicrous: the really unfathomable mystery was what drew Rosemary to him. "And now I wonder if you're all that wholesome."

"Why?"

"Because you're here," he said. "That's what beats me. You're here with me instead of—"

"Hi, kids. Still here, I see." It was Bob White back again, alone this time, looking for his sketch pad. Think of the loss to posterity, if it had been swept out with the empty bottles! No no, he mustn't stay, he didn't want to muscle in... Well, if they were sure, and only if he could buy them a drink...

He sat down, beaming, especially at Rosemary, who said brightly, "Did you get the murals settled already?"

"Good Lord, I'm not that fast a worker! No, as it turned out, Vic got home early, so the murals will have to wait. Thelma and her surprises. Chances are she'll forget and let it out, if she hasn't already. She doesn't have the temperament for secrets."

"I shouldn't think so, from what I've seen of her," said Martin. "I take it you're an old friend of hers?"

"Well, not a close friend. I knew her and Vic slightly when they were living in Philadelphia. I put in a stretch there myself, several years ago. A brief stretch, mercifully. Hadn't seen either of them since, until just recently. Cheers. To the murals. I don't mind admitting, I jumped at the chance. Freelancing can be pretty poor pickings at times. But it still beats the old nine-to-five weekly pay check rat race. For my money. I don't know how you guys in the architecture racket feel about it, but—"

"Architecture? I'm with a publishing company. Where'd you get that idea?"

"Snatched it out of the air, I guess. Thelma said something about having met you through Vic, so I took it from there. No hard feelings, I hope."

"Of course no hard feelings. I only wish it were so. Actually, the way I met Vic—" He hesitated over Enid's name. But Bob White must already know, involved as he pretty obviously was with Thelma. Who didn't have the temperament for secrets. "Well. It was through Enid Baxter," he said, and instantly regretted it.

But why? Nothing happened, nothing in the least sensational. Very carefully, Bob White set his glass down. "Oh? You knew Enid Baxter?"

"Yes. Quite well. Rosemary knew her too. She and Rosemary's mother were in business together. Didn't Thelma tell you?"

"No. No, she didn't. I didn't realize..." He could hardly say anything else, of course, not and maintain the gentlemanly pretense that he and Thelma were only casual acquaintances. "A terrible thing. Terrible. Not that I really knew Enid Baxter. Just to speak to, back there in Philadelphia. But her name rang a bell, when I saw it in the papers, and then of course the picture of her. She had the kind of face you don't forget. It shook me up, but good. I can imagine what it must have done to her friends... They haven't found the guy that did it, have they? I suppose it was one of these crazy kids. Or maybe a junkie."

"Maybe," said Martin. "They haven't come up with any other answer. Or if they have they're keeping it quiet."

"They sure are. They must have gone through her private life with a fine-toothed comb, but there wasn't the slightest hint in the papers of anything suspicious. I should think, if there had been, the reporter lads would have gotten wind of it. They're a pack of bloodhounds. It's a wonder to me they didn't rake up all the old dirt—Sorry. I shouldn't have said that."

"If you mean about Enid and Vic," said Rosemary, "it's all right. We already know. So do the police. They questioned everybody in her address book, and the Holms were there, because she'd run into them recently here in New York. So of course it all came out."

"Yes. Bound to. Well, it never was much of a secret. The gossips had a field day. But then it all blew over. Enid came to New York, and that was the end of it." His smile, which could be so engaging, now seemed to Martin vaguely unpleasant. It was like the difference between his profile and full face: something about him that kept Martin swinging between like and dislike. "And a lucky thing for Vic. It could have been—well, let's say a little awkward, if he'd been mixed up with her at this stage of the game. He'd have had to come up with one hell of an alibi."

"Oh, we all had alibis," Rosemary assured him blithely. "Martin was on vacation, and Mother was at the movies, and I was in Connecticut, and the Holms had a weekend guest from Philadelphia. The three of them spent a quiet evening at home. So it couldn't have been anybody who knew her. That leaves a prowler, and if they ever catch him it will just be a fluke, I suppose. She wasn't robbed, so there's nothing to trace." Nothing except the jade ring, Martin thought; it must have slipped Rosemary's mind, or she'd spill that along with everything else she knew. He concentrated, willing her to get to work on her drink. At this rate they'd be stuck with Bob White for the rest of the evening. But—the perils of thought transference—she missed that message and picked up the other one. "Well, there was one thing missing, her jade ring. But that doesn't necessarily mean it was stolen. She could easily have lost it, it was too big for her."

"Funny she wasn't robbed, if it was a prowler." It was a perfunctory comment; Bob White's interest was obviously waning.

"Something scared him off," Rosemary explained. "Either that, or he just panicked and ran when he realized he'd killed her."

"Yes. Probably... Hey, it must be late, time I shoved off and left you to your own devices." He finished his drink and drew out his wallet. "No, no," he went on, as Martin started to protest, "this is on me. You can buy me a drink some time when I'm broke. I often am. No kidding, I've enjoyed this. Let's get together again—that is, if you'd like to."

Once more—partly because he was leaving?—Martin liked him, envied him his easy sociability and his poise under circumstances that might have been embarrassing, had been acutely so, to Thelma. He scribbled Martin's office phone number in his sketch pad (but not Rosemary's: another point to his credit); he himself was in the process of moving, so it would be simpler for him to call Martin. Which he might never do at all. Still, it was a nice gesture.

He shook hands with them both and was off, a brisk, average-looking fellow, neither young nor old, rich nor poor, handsome nor ugly. They watched till he reached the corner and, with a last wave in their direction, disappeared.

Then Rosemary sighed. "I wish I hadn't talked so much," she said.

7

"Mrs. Nicholson?"

He had a pleasant voice, and an air of tentative friendliness. He hesitated just inside the office door, not barging in the way some salesmen did. That was what Hazel took him for: a salesman of some kind. Furniture or rugs, probably. He had a briefcase under his arm; he was well dressed, in other words unobtrusively; and his profile reminded her fleetingly, very fleetingly, of John Barrymore.

"It's all right," she said when he apologized for interrupting her work.

More than all right; she was so frustrated by the problem living room she had been grappling with that any distraction would have been welcome. She pushed the plans to one side and gestured toward the chair opposite her desk. "Come on in. What's on your mind?"

"I'm Bob White, Mrs. Nicholson." He gave her a sincere handshake and sat down, smiling. "I met your daughter last night. Rosemary."

"Oh?" For some reason it gave her an odd little turn. Rosemary's friends often dropped in, and they were more often than not strangers to Hazel. College kids. Not that this fellow was old, exactly, but he was no college kid. No salesman either, apparently. "Rosemary's not here. I don't know whether she'll be back this afternoon or not."

"That's what I get for not calling first. Actually, it was all unpremeditated. I just thought I'd take a chance and pop in, as long as I happened to be in the neighborhood anyway."

"I see," said Hazel. Now that she was facing him, she decided she didn't care much for his looks. Definitely too old for Rosemary; not her type at all. "Well. I'll tell her you were here."

"What I wanted to ask her— You wouldn't by any chance know, would you? Where I can get hold of Martin Shipley?"

"You know Martin Shipley?" This also surprised her, and not just because he didn't seem like Martin's type, either. Rosemary hadn't mentioned meeting any friends or acquaintances of Martin's. Hadn't mentioned Martin himself, in fact, except to say that he had checked with the police about Enid's jade ring so Hazel needn't bother. It was Hazel's impression that this bit of information had been relayed via the telephone. No reason to get upset or hurt, of course, simply because Rosemary ("Please, Mom, I'm not a three-year-old child!") had neglected to give a complete, detailed account of how and with whom she had spent every single minute of the last few days.

"I met him and Rosemary last night," Bob White was saying, and then he launched into a complicated story that she didn't follow too closely. The name of Thelma Holm, which kept cropping up, didn't immediately register with Hazel; she paid more attention after it did. "I wrote Martin's office number down somewhere," he finished, "and now I can't find it. Don't even know what publishing company he's with. But I did remember Rosemary's saying you were Enid Baxter's partner—I knew her, you know, not well, but still—and as I say, I was in the neighborhood, so I thought I'd give it a try. I'd like to call Martin for lunch. Awfully nice guy."

Hazel had thought so, too; still did, in spite of that business about his wife. Which was another thing Rosemary hadn't mentioned since Saturday afternoon, when she had blurted it out, with such painful results. Not a word, though she knew how much it had disturbed Hazel. "I don't have his office number," she said, "but I can give you his number at home. He lives in the same house Enid did, you know."

"Really? I didn't realize that. Good Lord, then, he must have been right in the middle of the whole thing!"

"If you mean the night it happened, he wasn't. He was out of town. But he was a good friend of Enid's, probably as close a friend as she had." She caught the expression on his face, and added curtly, "I don't mean boy friend."

"No, of course not. Aside from the difference in their ages, Martin's just not... Well, she was quite a dream boat. Or so I gather."

"I thought you said you knew her."

"Only slightly. And it was several years ago, in Philadelphia. The Holms were living there then too." He paused, in case Hazel cared to comment. She did not. "I didn't realize they'd gotten together again here in New York. Enid and Vic Holm."

Hazel eyed him with cold distaste. There were several answers she could give him. *What makes you think they had?* Or, *I have no idea what you're referring to.* Or, *What of it?* But any of these could be twisted around into the confirmation he was fishing for. So could the silence she was preserving, she realized with a sinking sensation.

At least she had the satisfaction of staring him down. He was bright enough to know he had made a tactical error. And cowardly enough to turn tail. Fumbling with his briefcase, smiling abjectly, spilling over with thanks and other inanities, he scuttled out the door.

All right, he had gotten Martin's address and telephone number out of her. Big deal. If not out of her, then out of the phone book. That had been only an excuse, anyway. What he was really after... Rosemary? Possibly. Probably. In any case, Hazel decided, it was time for a word or two with that young lady.

She turned up shortly afterwards, and—as might have been expected—took a highhanded attitude about the whole thing. "Honestly, Mother, I don't know what you were thinking of, handing out Martin's phone number like that."

"It's a state secret? Anyway, look who's talking about handing out information. You must have given out with a few vital statistics yourself." Rosemary's face turned red, and Hazel pushed on. "To him, not to me. I didn't even know you'd been seeing Martin."

"Didn't I tell you he called me? How could it have slipped my mind, an earth-shaking news item like that? You'd think he was Richard Burton or something."

"Don't be fresh," said Hazel absent-mindedly. "After what happened

Saturday afternoon, I didn't think either of us would ever hear from him again."

"Oh well, all that nonsense." Rosemary fluffed her hair. "Matter of fact, Mom, I'm supposed to bring you down to his place for a drink tonight."

"Me? You're supposed to—"

"He likes you. I can't imagine why. You'll come, won't you? You're not doing anything else?"

"Not a thing," Hazel assured her. "I'll be delighted."

"Good. You can apologize for talking out of turn to Bob Whoever-he-is."

"All right, but I still don't—"

"And listen, Mom, you won't say anything about the Joyce business, will you? I mean, no use hashing over things like that. He broods too much, as it is. Forget I ever told you."

"I'll try not to disgrace you," said Hazel drily.

It was impossible, of course, to forget the Joyce business. All the more so with Rosemary in this much of a flap over Martin Shipley. But previous flaps had taught Hazel the weaknesses—indeed, the dangers—of maternal opposition. The folk singer, for instance, had stayed in the picture an extra month solely because she had not kept her mouth shut about him. She mustn't make that mistake with Martin. Wait and see. Play it cool. If push came to shove, then would be time enough to hash over the Joyce business, once and for all.

It could be worse, she told herself glumly on the way down to Martin's apartment. It could be Bob White or whatever his name was, instead of Martin. Besides, there was Enid's endorsement of Martin, the obviously genuine friendship between them...

Yes, and look at what had happened to Enid.

With a profound sigh, she heaved herself out of the cab, tucked in her blouse, and trudged after Rosemary. Who had bounced up to the door and was already ringing Martin's bell.

He looked quite spruce in his seersucker jacket, obviously primed for inspection by the older generation. Rosemary must have given him an advance briefing, too, thought Hazel; no wonder he seemed so nervous.

But that was only part of it. It turned out that he had another worry: a third guest, unexpected and uninvited, who had appeared ten minutes ago and whose dominating presence seemed to fill Martin's living room and imbue his little party with a color altogether different from that originally planned.

Vic Holm, master of all he surveyed, stood beside his chair waiting to be introduced. He was a big man (as Hazel preferred men to be), big and fair-haired and blunt-featured. He was not handsome, as Enid had been beautiful; but never mind non-essentials. Hazel, remembering those other shadowy "beaus," had no trouble recognizing that in him Enid had met her match.

"Oh yes, Enid's partner," he said as he shook her hand. His gray eyes met hers without self-consciousness; all the same, there was something disquieting about them. She thought of desert, wilderness, desolation.

Then he turned to Rosemary, smiling down at her, openly enjoying her fresh prettiness. And don't think she wasn't smiling back. Well, who wouldn't? "I've heard a lot about you too, Rosemary. Nice to meet you... Want me to tend bar, Martin? I'll be glad to."

But Martin was determined to hang on to at least this vestige of control over the proceedings. He set up a remarkable clatter with the ice and glasses, and when he served the drinks narrowly missed spilling Rosemary's in her lap. Nerves, no doubt. Or could it be repressed hostility toward Vic?

If so, it did not bother Vic. He downed his drink—a straight shot—at one gulp and plunged without delay into what did bother him. "You don't happen to know where Thelma is, do you, Rosemary?"

"Thelma? She's missing?"

"Lost, stolen, strayed. Last seen drinking." He caught Hazel's eye and smiled grimly. "My wife, Mrs. Nicholson. In case you're interested."

"But she was all right when we saw her last night. Wasn't she, Martin? She only had one drink."

"She went on from there. When I saw her last night, believe me, she was far from all right. I don't know where she went after she left The Peacock, but she must have taken the long way home. I didn't get in myself until after midnight, and I'd been there at least an hour before she came rolling in."

"After midnight? But I thought—" A look flashed from Martin to Rosemary, and she hastily shifted gears. "I mean, when did she disappear?"

"How the hell do I know? I gave up and went to bed about three, and when I woke up this morning she was gone. I've been calling everybody I can think of all day, and..." He pressed his hands against his temples in a sudden, brief gesture of weary despair. "I don't know what to do," he said quietly.

There was a moment of tense silence. "How about Philadelphia?" Martin asked. "That friend of yours, Lulu McGrath?"

"I thought of her first, of course. She and her husband are off on a cruise. Won't be back till next week. I wish to God Lulu was around. She's better at coping with these crises than I am."

"It's happened before?"

"In Philadelphia. Not here. If she doesn't show up pretty soon, I'll have to call the police. Or maybe I shouldn't wait, maybe I ought to—"

"Wait!" Martin cleared his throat and went on more calmly. "It's a little soon for that, isn't it? I'd give her another couple of hours. Did she seem upset about anything last night?"

"I suppose you mean did we have a fight," said Vic. "Thelma's always upset when she goes on a binge. Not about anything in particular. Just life in general. To tell you the truth, I don't pay much attention when she gets to maundering on. She seemed on the verge of passing out, so I figured it was safe for me to go to bed. My mistake. I remembered she mentioned your name a couple of times, that's why I came over here."

It didn't really answer the question of whether or not they had quarreled, thought Hazel. But she didn't like to press the point. Certainly there was nothing in Vic's manner to suggest evasion. He couldn't have sounded more candid. Or more tired. That was what impressed her most, and of course it made sense. No matter how devoted you might be to a drunk, in the end you just got tired. She wished she could think of something helpful. "You've checked with Bob Whats-his-name, I suppose," she said. "Bob White."

This harmless remark had a startling effect—at least on Rosemary and Martin. She caught her breath audibly; he stiffened. Both of them darted nervous glances at Vic, who merely looked blank and asked, "Bob who? Bob White? Who's he?"

Hazel, aware that she had somehow or other put her foot in her mouth, sent forth a silent plea for help. But neither of them even looked at her. There was nothing to do but blunder on. "Well, I understood, that is, I thought Rosemary said..."

"Rosemary said what?" Vic's voice crackled with impatience. "What is all this, anyway? I don't know any Bob White."

Rosemary remained dumb. After a couple of false starts Martin got it out. "He was there last night too. At The Peacock. With Thelma."

"You mean she wasn't by herself? Why didn't you say so in the first place? Who is this guy? Let's get hold of him and—"

"I haven't any idea where he lives. Probably in a hotel. I'm not even sure about his name. He seemed to know you and Thelma both, at least that's the impression I got."

"You're a big help," said Vic bitterly. "You were there too, Rosemary. What impression did you get, if any?"

"The same as Martin's," Rosemary snapped back. But then she smiled—a little too disarmingly, in Hazel's opinion—and switched to a tone of frank confession. "Oh well, it can't make that much difference now. Can it, Martin? Even though we promised. Bob's supposed to do some murals for your living room, only Thelma wanted to surprise you, you see. That's why we didn't mention him before."

"Murals? He's an artist?"

"Mostly commercial stuff. Freelance. I think he said he used to live in Philadelphia."

There was a silence. Under Vic's unnerving scrutiny Rosemary managed to hang on to her guileless expression. Martin, whose turn came next, shuffled his feet unhappily. "It still doesn't ring any bells with me," Vic said at last. "I wonder how many Bob Whites there are in the phone book."

A column and a half, it turned out, none of whom had chosen to identify himself as a commercial artist. And Martin pointed out, for the second time, that they were not even sure about the name. It was certainly the name he had given Hazel, but she refrained from calling any further attention to herself by saying so. After all, she too had sensed something fishy about the fellow.

"Maybe he's the mysterious phone caller I had after I got home from the office this afternoon," Vic was going on. "It happened twice. When I answered, nobody said anything. Just hung up without saying a word. If they were cooking up this mural surprise, I suppose it could have been him, trying to get Thelma. But in that case he can't know where she is either. I mean, if he expected her to be home— Oh God. I don't know. I just thought, if they did go on a pub-crawl together last night after they left The Peacock—"

"He came back by himself," Rosemary said. "Half an hour or so later, to get his sketch pad. He forgot and left it the first time. We were still there, and he had another drink with us."

"He could have met her again later, though," Vic persisted. "If he did, she might have hit some of the same spots when she went out by herself the second time around. It would at least give me something to go on." He sighed and stood up. "I've taken up enough of your time. I'll go home and start calling up Bob Whites. By the way, what did he look like?"

"Just an average sort of guy," Martin said. "I'd say about thirty-five. Medium brown hair and eyes. He was better looking from the side than head on."

Vic paused at the door, absorbing these meager clues. He did not comment on them. "Okay. If you hear anything, you'll let me know, won't you? Sorry to bother you with my problems."

As soon as he was gone Rosemary burst out like a faucet turned on full force. "Do you think he bought it, about the murals? I didn't see anything to do but tell him, once Mom let it out. Not that I'm blaming you, Mom, how were you to know? If I'd had any idea he was going to be here... And you just sat there like a bump on a log, Martin. Somebody had to say something. Besides, I felt so sorry for him."

"Oh sure," said Martin. "A very pathetic fellow. My heart bleeds for him."

"I don't know what you mean by that! Anybody could see how upset he was about Thelma. Absolutely distraught."

"He was upset, all right. The question is, why? You'll notice he didn't commit himself on whether or not they had a fight last night. For all we know, he could have beaten Thelma up and now he's worried because she walked out on him and he doesn't know what she might do next. It's just his word she was drunk, and somebody's lying, that's for sure. Vic says he didn't get home till after midnight, but according to Bob White he was already there when he took Thelma home from The Peacock."

"Oh well, Bob White! If you're going to believe what he said!"

"Listen, you two." Hazel took a deep breath. "Would you mind telling me what this is all about?"

"Don't be obtuse, Mom. We were keeping quiet about Bob White because we think Thelma's got something going with him. You know? An extra-marital affair. I don't believe that's his real name, any more than I believe the phony murals business. She's probably shacked up with him right now."

"Oh," said Hazel feebly. "Well. I never thought of that. I mean, she must be out of her mind. A husband like Vic, and she takes up with—" She remembered Enid, and realized she was being obtuse again. Was that why Martin was taking such an anti-Vic stand, because he resented the fact that Enid had once been in love with Vic? Had once been. Might well have been right up to the day she died. "That Bob White," Hazel said slowly, "or whatever his name is. Did you get the feeling there was something off-color about him? I don't mean because of Thelma. I didn't even know about that angle when I saw him."

"You saw him?" Martin asked in astonishment. "When was that? I thought you'd just heard about him from Rosemary."

"He came into the shop this afternoon. Claimed he'd lost your telephone number and wanted to get it from Rosemary. I apologize for giving it to him, by the way. He remembered I was in business with Enid, you see. I guess that's what put me off about him. He was so almighty interested in Enid."

After a moment Martin said, "Some people are like that. Morbid curiosity. No need for you to apologize. I gave him my phone number myself, last night. Now then. How about another drink? And then maybe a bite of dinner somewhere?"

"Not me, thank you," said Hazel, who had been strictly and thoroughly trained in the deportment proper for a parent. She was rewarded with a positive gust of grateful relief from both sides. "I've got to figure out that so-and-so living room some time between now and tomorrow morning. Don't be too late, Rosemary. Awfully nice to see you again, Martin."

She meant it. He was as nice a lad, Martin Shipley, as anybody could ask for. It occurred to her, on the way home in the cab he put her into—with alacrity, but also with a shy and surprising little kiss on her cheek—that she had not thought once about the Joyce business during the course of his little party. She wondered if she would have, without the distraction of Vic Holm.

8

When he came back from seeing Rosemary home, she was there waiting for him. Thelma. Sitting on the concrete slab that edged his four square feet of garden, so quiet and motionless that he all but stumbled over her.

"Martin?" she whispered. "It is you, isn't it? I thought you'd never come."

"Thelma! Are you all right? Vic was here earlier, looking for you. Nobody knew where you were."

"I don't know either," she said, and laughed dimly. "Can I come inside with you, Martin? Please? Just for a while. I don't know anybody else. I don't know many people here in New York."

She did not seem particularly drunk to him. No lurching on her way inside; no marked slurring in her speech. While he unlocked the door to his apartment, she stood close to him, peering fearfully up the shadowy flight of stairs. "She lived up there, didn't she? Somebody ran down the stairs. I read in the paper. The neighbor woman heard somebody running down the stairs."

"Come on in, Thelma." He flipped on the light and steered her inside. "Sit down. Would you like some coffee?"

"All right," she said docilely. "Thank you."

Last night she had looked unusually neat and crisp in her full skirt with the belt that cinched in her slim waist. Tonight her dress was rumpled and soiled; her hair straggled about her face, which looked drawn and shiny, devoid of make-up. She huddled in the corner of the couch, easing her feet out of her high-heeled pumps. He sat down beside her while the coffee perked.

"Have you talked to Vic? Does he know you're here?" She shook her head no. "I think we ought to call him, then. He was worried about you. So was I."

"Did he tell you I was drunk? He did, didn't he?" She seemed oddly pleased, almost as if she were proud of herself. "Shame on me," she said, and wriggled her toes.

Food, he thought; she's probably famished. But she only nibbled at the crackers and cheese he brought in with the coffee. "You're awfully good to me," she said. "I was afraid you'd be mad. But I couldn't think of anywhere else to go."

"You could go home, you know. Couldn't you?" She did not answer. Her eyes shifted away from his to a point in the middle of the rug. She sat still, knotted up with tension. "Why not? Are you afraid of Vic?"

"Of course not," she said quickly. "Why should I be afraid of Vic?"

"I don't know. I thought you might have had some kind of a quarrel last night. About your drinking, maybe. Or... Listen, Thelma, he knows you saw Bob White last night. I'm sorry. I didn't mean to tell him, but Rosemary and her mother were here and—well, it came out."

"Oh," she whispered. She did look at him now, out of big, unfathomable eyes. "Did he— What did he say?"

"Naturally he was anxious to get hold of the guy. But nobody knew how or where to reach him. The name didn't seem to mean anything to Vic. That was it, wasn't it? Bob White?"

"Yes. Bob—White." Again she wriggled her toes.

"It doesn't matter, I guess, now that you're back. If you won't call Vic, Thelma, I'm going to. Somebody has to. Otherwise he's going to report you missing to the police."

"No! Oh no!"

"Yes. Oh yes. He was threatening to do it while he was here." Seriously or not? Martin was still wondering about that, among other things—including what was actually at the root of Vic's concern and worry. But it wasn't safe to pooh-pooh either the threats or the concern: whatever had gone on between the Holms last night, Thelma's whereabouts could not be kept a secret from Vic. If she expected Martin to connive at any such goings-on she had come to the wrong place. "I talked him into waiting a bit."

"I see," she said gravely. "That was nice of you. It would have been awfully embarrassing, wouldn't it, to be plucked out of the gutter by the police. If that's where I was."

So that was to be her line: complete lapse of memory. Well, it was probably as good as any, as far as Vic was concerned. Martin himself was suddenly tired of the whole slippery conversation. Whatever she had turned to him for—sanctuary, moral support, a breathing space before she faced Vic—he was willing to supply, up to a point. But they could at least be honest with each other.

"Oh, come on, Thelma," he said. "You know perfectly well where you were. At least part of the time. So do I. Don't worry, I'm not going to give you and Bob White away. Or whatever his name is. You can save your blank mind business, and the phony murals, and all the rest of it, for Vic. Please. Don't waste it on me."

"What do you mean? What are you talking about?" She turned on him, shivering with anger, outrage, fear—he did not know what. "Do you think Bob White and I..." Her voice trailed off; her mouth remained a little open, and trembling.

"Of course I think Bob White and you," said Martin wearily. "It was written all over you when you walked into The Peacock last night and saw me. You looked guilty as hell. Ready to sink through the floor. Why would you act like that if you were just having an innocent drink with a casual acquaintance? You wouldn't. It simply doesn't make sense. I don't know how long you've been carrying on your little hush-hush romance, and I don't care, but you obviously need more practice when it comes to managing it."

"Oh dear," she said, in a stricken voice. And again her mood switched; a fit of giggles seized her, uncontrollable as hiccups. "Oh dear, and I thought I was being so clever ... I'm sorry, Martin, I just... Yes, of course. Doesn't make sense..." She leaned back, gulping and swiping at the tears that ran down her face. Watching her, Martin had to laugh too, though her lack of restraint made him a little uncomfortable. Drunks always affected him that way, and he realized now that she must be much less sober than he had thought at first. Eventually she pulled herself together and asked, with a fresh flicker of alarm, "Does Vic know? Is that why he was so anxious to get hold of Bob, because he thought we were together?"

"How do I know what Vic thinks? About anything? I certainly didn't tell him, but he may have guessed. You could have let it out yourself, when you saw him last night. Can't you remember anything you said to each other before he went to bed and you sailed out again?"

She shook her head helplessly. "I expect he was mad at me. Or not mad exactly. Exasperated. Disgusted. You can't blame him. And I usually get on a crying jag. Because I'm so ashamed... I remember bits and pieces before I went home. I remember about Bob going back to The Peacock after his sketch pad. I waited for him at this other place, this place with the pink piano. It was a mistake to leave me alone, I kept having drinks while I waited for him."

"So that's how it was," said Martin. "Rosemary and I were still at The Peacock when he came back, you know. He sat down and had another drink with us. His story was that he had taken you home, only Vic was already there, so naturally nothing could be done about the murals. But then Vic said he didn't get home till after midnight, and it was even later when you hove in. So I couldn't help wondering—"

"Wondering who was lying, you mean?" She gave a dreary laugh. "Vic's got nothing to hide. Nothing to lie about anymore. Not that he ever bothered to lie much, anyway. Everybody in Philadelphia knew about him and Enid, and he didn't care. Neither did she. They were past caring."

He hadn't left Thelma, though, thought Martin. How many times had he heard Enid say it? *Thelma won. He didn't leave her*. But would have this time—according to him—if death had not intervened. Not according to Enid, or Thelma either. Again, somebody was lying, and there was little doubt in Martin's mind as to who. The chances were that what Vic had to hide now would make the Philadelphia episode seem like innocent child's play.

"So why should I care if he knows about me and Bob?" Thelma was demanding belligerently. "Why should I lie to him about it? He'll find it out sooner or later anyway, the way he always finds out everything about me." Her eyes shifted to the telephone, and she shivered again. "If he doesn't like it, let him lump it. That's what I say. Isn't that right, Martin? Don't you think I ought to just tell him straight out?"

"Don't ask me, Thelma. You've got to tell him something, that's all I know about it. You can't put it off any longer."

"No. I can't, can I?" She stared at the telephone. Her hands remained locked in her lap. "I'll have to go home, won't I? I've got nowhere else to go."

"You could go to a hotel. I mean, if you're really that scared of Vic—"

"I'm not. Of course I'm not." Suddenly her hands unlocked; with a gesture of despair she snatched up the phone and dialed. Martin retreated to the kitchenette and clattered the coffee cups, to give her at least a semblance of privacy. He could still hear the murmur of her voice, and the click when she hung up. It was a very brief conversation.

"He's coming over to get me," she told Martin hopelessly. "Is that all right with you?"

"Yes, of course." Now that it was done—what he had urged her to do—he felt a surge of panic-stricken remorse. Who knew what Vic might do to her, once he got his hands on her? He was a violent man. A jealous man. And yet she would not admit that she was afraid of him. Wifely loyalty. Love. Yes, she must love him very much, in spite of all she had suffered on his account.

She sat there so quietly, as if resigned to her doom. For an instant her eyes met Martin's, and it flashed through his mind like a streak of lightning—the possibility that she too knew, or at least suspected, the truth about Enid's death. Suspected was more likely, because she had been drunk that night, and probably had only a hazy impression to go on. But that would be enough for Vic (who always found out everything about her). No wonder her drinking worried him: loyal though she was, she might, in her cups, drop the one word or two that could destroy him. And no wonder she was frightened...

Only Lulu McGrath had been there too. There was no getting around Lulu. She had not been drunk. No hazy impressions for her; Vic could not have gone out that evening without her knowing it. And no wifely loyalty or love, either; she had no reason for reinforcing his alibi if she knew it was false. Could even Vic be persuasive or lucky enough to have not one but two women willing to cover up for him?

"If only Lulu were here," murmured Thelma, almost as if she had read Martin's mind. Then the doorbell rang, and she shrank back into the corner of the couch.

Vic's first words, when he strode in, were: "Thank God you called. Are you all right?" If there was an edge of irritation to his voice, there was certainly nothing that sounded like menace. And he bent over his errant wife rather tenderly, patting her hand. But then came the other questions. Where had she been? Why had she come here instead of home? Finally, of course: "Who's Bob White? This guy you met at The Peacock? Who is he?"

"You don't know him," Thelma said quickly. It was her first coherent remark. She had burst into stagey, boozy tears at sight of Vic; had alternately clung to him and cowered away from him; had offered unintelligible sobs instead of answers. "He's just somebody I— Just because I was lonesome. Oh, I'm so ashamed! It's all over now, honestly, I promise you. I never want to see him again."

This information jolted Vic nicely. No doubt about it. His face stiffened. He blinked. "The murals? They said he was going to do some murals?"

"I had to tell them something. It was all I could think of. Silly of me. I shouldn't have tried to lie, it only made it worse." She gazed up at Vic pleadingly; it occurred to Martin that she might be hoping for an outburst of jealous rage, might be secretly enjoying the switch in circumstances that made her, for once, sinner instead of sinned against.

After a moment Vic said, "I see." He looked at Martin. "I gather you knew this all the time? You might have told me."

"Sure I might have. I don't happen to get my kicks out of running around tattling everything I know about other people's private affairs." And a damn lucky thing for you I don't, he added mentally. "I didn't ask to get in on any of this, and I'm sure as hell not going to take the blame for keeping my mouth shut or not keeping it shut, either one."

Thelma made wailing noises in the background. Vic had the grace to flush. "Okay. I shouldn't have said it." It was his version of an apology, delivered in clipped, imperious tones. Infuriating bastard. But then, with one of those weary gestures—could they be calculated?—that made Martin feel sorry for him, he rubbed his hand along the side of his face and turned back to Thelma. "It's late. Come on, dear. Don't cry anymore. We must go home."

Her chin trembled. "Vic, I didn't tell you, I took all the housekeeping money, and now it's gone..." By some miracle she still had her purse; she fumbled in it and drew out an empty billfold.

"It doesn't matter. Never mind the money, Thelma." Gently but inexorably, he urged her to her feet.

"All right. You don't have to help me. I'm not drunk. Haven't had a drink in hours. All Martin gave me was coffee." She lurched against the end table and giggled. "Not drunk. Just disorderly."

And scared, thought Martin. Snatching at any delaying tactic in sight, however tenuous or futile. And it was futile: with a resigned air, Vic took her arm again and headed her toward the door. His face gave no indication of what he might be thinking.

"What if I get sick?" she quavered.

"I'll hold your head," said Vic. "Come on. We're going home."

She gave Martin one last, big-eyed, entreating look. He could not get it out of his mind. Hours later he woke up, trying not to remember it, trying to convince himself that there was no reason for her to be afraid of Vic.

9

Next morning, bright and early, Bob White called Martin for lunch. Not unexpectedly: if he had talked to Thelma he must know about last night's session at Martin's apartment; if he had not talked to her he must be wondering where the hell she was. In either case, Martin would seem to him a likely source of information. And that was all right with Martin, who had similar designs of his own.

When he arrived at the modest French restaurant where they had agreed to meet, he found Bob already there, settled at a table and waiting for him. "Hi, Martin. Good to see you again." The sincere handclasp, the deep voice and consciously engaging smile—all were in good working order. Plus a certain rueful, man-to-man air that Martin had no trouble interpreting.

Sure enough. "I just talked to Thelma," Bob said, as soon as the greetings were out of the way, "so we don't have to do any hemming and hawing. She told me all about last night. Or anyway, enough. I know she let the cat out of the bag, to you and Vic both." He paused to adjust his expression, which he seemed to sense was veering unpleasantly toward the complacent. (Fancies himself as a lady-killer, thought Martin. No doubt figures he's irresistible, him and his profile.) "Naturally it shook me up. I didn't even know she was missing. When I couldn't get her yesterday, I just figured she was out shopping or something. If I'd had any idea she was going on a tear—"

"She was okay when you took her home Wednesday night?"

"Sure she was. It never crossed my mind she wasn't going to stay put. I swear she was okay. We had one or two, I admit it, it wasn't quite the way I told you and Rosemary when I went back to The Peacock after my sketch pad."

"So I gathered. She was waiting for you in the place with the pink piano. It's one of the few details she remembers. After that she more or less blanked out."

"She told me. Blanked out and came to on your doorstep. And that's another thing. Why pick your place? Why not go home? Do you know?"

Martin hesitated a moment. Then he said, "I think she was scared."

"Of Vic, you mean? Scared he'd be sore at her for getting drunk? Listen, he used to hit the bottle pretty hard himself, till she straightened him out. He's a fine one to be blaming her when she gets out of line."

"He didn't act sore." Well, and she hadn't acted drunk so much as exhausted. At least not at first; it was only after Vic's arrival that the staggers and mumbles set in. But then, if drunkenness was to some extent a matter of emotions, it might well have been the grip of fear as much as liquor. "No. I got the feeling she was scared of something else. Something connected with Vic, all right. She didn't want to call him. But we had to let him know where she was, otherwise he'd have called the police. I finally convinced her. Then, when he came over to get her, she tried to stall some more."

"She was scared to go home?" Bill licked his lips. "I mean, scared of Vic?"

"She said not. I asked her, before he got there. I thought maybe they'd had some kind of a scene after she got home Wednesday night and that was what had set her off."

"A scene. A fight? About what was going on with Thelma and me? You think he was already wise to us, before she told him last night?"

"He certainly didn't give that impression. No, I'm sure he was jolted. Good and jolted."

"Jolted," Bob repeated. "What interests me is how mad was he. How much hell is he apt to raise. Thelma didn't really go into that part of it."

"He didn't beat her up, if that's what you mean. Actually, he seemed to take it fairly calmly once he got over the first shock." True enough; it wasn't the infidelity angle that was responsible for Martin's night of dire forebodings, his feeling of having thrown her to the wolves, his relief when he called her this morning and heard her voice, remote but composed: yes, she was all right now, poor Martin, she hoped he would forgive her. What had he feared? Well, the same thing Bob feared—physical violence. Only for a different reason. Waiting for her to answer the phone he had conjured up an image of Thelma dead, murdered as Enid had been murdered—not because she was unfaithful but because she knew too much, sometimes drank too much, might have talked too much. But she couldn't know for sure, any more than Martin could! If there were any holes in Vic's alibi the police would have found them. Her facts must be as flimsy as Martin's, and facts were what counted. Never mind the emotional logic. Even so, it would be awkward for Vic if, in a moment of drunken disloyalty, she had spilled out her secret fears and fancies. Had she or hadn't she? Martin ought to be able to find some way of prying the answer out of Bob White. Or whatever his name was.

Apparently he had been busy with a different train of thought, namely, the preservation of his own precious petty skin. "Maybe he's saving his strength for me," he was saying. "Well, he'll have to catch me first."

"Yes, he will. Have you moved yet? I don't think you told me where your new place is."

"I'm not in it yet. A hitch in the paint job. It was supposed to be all set for this week end, but now I don't know. Ah, here we are. Food." He watched, in an abstracted way, as the waiter served their orders. "If I sound like a coward, okay, that's what I am. Put yourself in my place. Would you want to tangle with Vic Holm?"

"What makes you think he's such a dangerous character?" Martin asked, and for a moment they looked straight at each other. Bob's face was motionless, wary. But then his eyes slid away; he grinned a little.

"He's bigger than me," he said. "The way I look at it, anybody bigger than me is dangerous."

"You should have thought of that before you started playing around with his wife."

"True, true. On the other hand, how was I to know she was going to pull this confession act? And for no good reason. That's what gets me. Nobody was bugging her. Nobody pushed her into it."

"I suppose I did, in a way," Martin said. "Pushed her into telling me, I mean. Not Vic. That was her idea. But she had already given the show away at The Peacock, getting so rattled and giving out with the mythical murals business. So when she turned up missing I naturally assumed she'd been off somewhere with you—"

"So help me." Bob disposed of a forkful of veal and, chewing fervently, raised his right hand. "I took her home Wednesday night and that was the last I saw or heard of her till this morning."

"Okay. I believe you. After all, if you'd been off on a binge with her you wouldn't have had the time or energy for your little chat with Hazel Nicholson."

"Oh. She told you, did she? I lost your office phone number," said Bob easily. "Awfully nice woman. So anyway, getting back to Thelma..."

"There's nothing to get back to, really. That's it. I don't know if she meant it or not, but she said she didn't want to see you again."

"She meant it all right," said Bob without regret. Rather jauntily, in fact. He caught Martin's eye on him, and added, "Look, I'm sorry it's over. It was great while it lasted. But I never had any illusions about its lasting forever. I'm no home-wrecker. The last thing I wanted was to make trouble between her and Vic. She knew that."

"I should hope so," Martin said. But sometimes, when a woman was as vulnerable as Thelma, she managed to convince herself that even the sorriest little affair was love immortal. It didn't seem possible that she could have looked at Bob and seen anything but the weak, shallow opportunist he was. Yet if she had, it would explain the cheerful way he was accepting the end. Fun and games, yes. Intensity, no. More than he had bargained for. Made him nervous.

"I don't really understand Thelma," he was saying, and for once his candor seemed genuine. "Hell, for all I know, the only reason she took up with me was to get back at Vic. That could be the reason she told him, too. Because the circuit wouldn't be complete until he knew, the way she knew about him and Enid."

Ah yes, Enid. Her name had a way of cropping up in any conversation with Bob White. He was proceeding warily. "I can't help wondering whether it was really all over with those two or whether— You ought to know, as good a friend of Enid's as you were."

"That doesn't make me an authority on her personal affairs," said Martin curtly. If, by refusing to be pumped, he was forfeiting his own chances of pumping Bob—all right, so be it. He had no stomach for such a deal, now that he was faced with it. "The question is, not who was having an affair with Enid, but who killed her. Isn't it? So unless you're suggesting that Vic—"

"Who, me?" Bob leaned back and lit a cigarette. "With an alibi like his? Don't be silly. What's good enough for the police is good enough for me. A double-barreled alibi, no less. Oh no, I wasn't suggesting a thing. Any more than you were." Again their eyes met, and a smile crept slyly across Bob's face. It sickened and died under Martin's glare. But it had been there, it was still there for Martin, and would be from now on—of all Bob's expressions the unforgettable one, the essence of the fellow himself.

It was also what made Martin follow him when they left the restaurant.

He made no conscious decision to do so. In fact, he was a little surprised to discover that was what he was doing. If Bob had hailed a cab, or made for the subway, or caught a bus, Martin would in all probability have turned around and gone prosily back to the office.

But Bob walked. Downtown on Lexington, and behind him, like a toy pulled on a string, walked Martin. The lunchtime crowds made it irresistibly easy. All he had to do was dawdle or speed up, depending on the traffic lights, and preserve a comfortable chunk of humanity as insulation between him and his quarry. The trail took an eastward turn in the upper Thirties, the people thinned out, and at Third Avenue Martin decided he would be better off on the downtown side of the street and crossed over. He matched his pace to Bob's, which was brisk and purposeful, like that of a man on his way home. Yes, that must be where he was going; in the middle of the block he stopped at a cleaning shop and picked up a couple of suits.

Beginner's luck. It went smooth as silk all the way. Between the cleaner's and the corner Bob slowed down, fumbling for his keys; Martin crossed the street at his leisure (even the traffic lights cooperated) and eureka, the end of the trail, Bob's undisclosed address was undisclosed no longer.

For what the information was worth. Having watched Bob let himself into the basement apartment, Martin just stood there—at his shrewdly safe distance—feeling letdown and rather ridiculous. Now that the excitement of the chase was over, he wondered what its point had been. Certainly not any more conversation with Bob. Martin knew an impasse when he saw one, and that was what he had seen at lunch. Well then, what?

At least he could walk past the house and take a closer look at it. Its façade was of dingy, lumpy, weather-streaked stucco, with door and wood trim that had long ago, too long ago, been painted turquoise blue. The street-floor apartments were professional, semi-professional: there was a chiropractor's sign, and a dressmaker's. Combined office and living quarters.

And then there was the sign in the window of Bob's basement apartment. "Studio," it read. "Layout—Lettering—Creative Design." Below, in smaller letters, appeared the name. "Robert Black."

Martin was actually all the way past before it registered. The name was not "Robert White." It was "Robert Black." He took a second look to make sure. Thelma's voice came back to him, breathlessly performing the introductions at The Peacock. Bob—White.

It was typical of her, he thought as he headed back for the office. In a freewheeling way, it was appropriate that she should turn Black into White. Or try to. It would take more than a switch in names to sweeten the smell of that guy. How she could ever have taken up with him... Anyway, it was over now. If she had to go on a binge to shuck him off, okay, it was worth it.

Even if in her cups she had talked too much, blurted out what she suspected—what Martin suspected she suspected—about Enid's death?

All afternoon the question nagged at him, persistent as a low-grade toothache. He could not ignore it, any more than he could stop spinning his mental wheels in futile review of his own performance at lunch. What he had said, opposed to what he should have said. What opportunities he had failed to see, and saw now with belated brilliance. A busy afternoon: between bouts of rewriting the lunch scene, he examined the possibility—always present with him—that his imagination might be working overtime and that what had looked like skulduggery on Bob's part was nothing very sinister, after all, but only the kind of curiosity known as morbid. Lots of people reacted that way to murder, whether or not they knew the victim. And Bob had known Enid. Known of her.

The curiosity was there, all right. If any further proof were needed, Martin found it when he got home from work. At the street door he met Mrs. Klein setting out with her dog Bubbles for their pre-dinner walk. She was a dim little old soul, spry in her sneakers, dowdy in the gray silk raincoat she wore all summer long, regardless of the weather. Sometimes she interrupted the running conversation she carried on with herself or Bubbles to compliment Martin on "the posies" in his garden; at other times she passed by without noticing either him or his greeting. Tonight she was in touch with the outside world.

"How are you, Mr. Shipley? We were just admiring your posies. So pretty. Such a pleasure. As I said to the young man this morning, it's the little things that make all the difference. I thought I'd put in a good word, you know, in case he felt nervous about taking it."

Martin smiled and waited. It did not pay to rush Mrs. Klein, or try to pin her down.

"I'm not the least bit nervous myself. Bubbles is a wonderful watchdog. I never have to worry with him around. All the same, I'd rather it was rented again. And he was such a nice young man. So nice and polite."

"Oh. A prospective tenant," said Martin. At the thought of somebody else in Enid's place, he felt a pang of unreasonable resentment. "He was looking at Miss Baxter's apartment?"

"So friendly. After the real estate agent showed it to him we had a little chat. Bubbles and I were just going out. We met them in the hall. As I say, I thought I'd put in a good word. Not that he seemed to feel nervous, but some people might."

"Maybe he didn't know about Miss Baxter."

"They'll redecorate, of course. And I could tell, the terrace appealed to him. He's like you, he likes posies. Poor girl, so did she. I heard the footsteps, you know. Somebody running down the stairs that night. They kept asking me and asking me, but all I could tell them was just footsteps running, and of course Bubbles barking, the way he always does, a wonderful watchdog. Nobody gets past him." She and Bubbles exchanged a look of mutual admiration; he uttered a muted yelp to prove her point, and waggled his portly rear end. "Though generally speaking it's a quiet house, as I told the young man. Very quiet. She didn't have a lot of company."

"He asked about her?"

"It was in the paper. The address and all. Naturally I had no intention of bringing it up. He saw it in the paper. Her name caught his eye because he knows some friends of hers, you see. That's why he was so interested, he thought I might have seen them. And maybe I did, but I'm afraid I don't pay much attention." She peered at Martin apologetically, as she had no doubt peered at the nice young man this morning. "It didn't matter, of course. He just thought I might know them by sight. We had quite a little chat about her. Naturally he was interested."

"Naturally," said Martin. "What did he look like?"

"He didn't seem to feel the least bit nervous about it. Such a nice young man. Life must go on, he said. Terrible, a terrible thing, but life must go on. It's too bad he couldn't have talked to you instead of me. I didn't really know her that well. But you could have told him all about her. It would be so nice for you if he takes it. Another young man in the house. You'd have so much in common."

"I'm sure we would."

"The posies and all." Her gaze wandered off, as it so often did. Bubbles, whose attention span was perfectly attuned to hers, tugged at his leash. They started down the walk, with one accord slipping away into the hazy private world they shared. But before she lost contact entirely, Mrs. Klein had a final message. It drifted back to Martin like a wisp of smoke: "Such a nice-looking young man. Especially from the side. Like John Barrymore."

10

"He's up to something," said Rosemary. They were having dinner at The Peacock, and Martin had just finished his report on Bob White/Black. "Something about Enid, I mean. He's pumped everybody now. You, me, Mother, Mrs. Klein. Thelma too, I suppose. That's carrying idle curiosity too far. It's got to be something more. You think so too, or you wouldn't have followed him home."

Martin fidgeted with his coffee cup and tried to look like a man who was holding back nothing. It wasn't easy; his account to Rosemary had been artfully abridged to include all the facts and none of his own private unsubstantiated theories. It would have been safer to skip the whole subject. But impossible: she already knew, from their phone conversation this morning, that Thelma had turned up on his doorstep, and that he had a lunch date with Bob. Besides, he wanted to tell her, he had cherished the hope that with her fresh, straightforward eye she might spot some perfectly obvious angle—missed by him; he frequently failed to see the woods for the trees—that would reduce his theories to nonsense.

It wasn't working out that way. If the accusatory tone of her last remark was any indication, what she had spotted with her fresh, straightforward eye was the fact that Martin was holding out on her. And that crack about pumping Thelma too. That sounded as if she might be veering uncomfortably close to his own angle of vision.

"What's he after?" she persisted. "What's he trying to prove? It's not as if he and Enid were friends, or even acquaintances. Enemies? Could that be it?"

"How do you mean, enemies?"

"Well, supposing he made a play for her, and she brushed him off. She wouldn't bother to be tactful about it, you know, not Enid, so it's been eating on him all these years—"

"All these years? When did this happen?"

"Back in Philadelphia. He's never forgotten. It still rankles. So then he finds out she's in New York. From Thelma. Thelma could have told him. Anyway, he finds out, goes to see her, and... Martin." Rosemary's voice dropped; her eyelashes worked overtime. "Martin, he could be the one that killed her!"

"Sure," said Martin. "And the reason he's going around pumping everybody is that he's forgotten the details. Wants to refresh his memory." No need to be all that sarcastic, he thought, and reached for her hand. "Never mind. It was a great idea, I only wish it made sense."

"I'm not so sure it doesn't." Her fingers intertwined trustingly in his: a very pleasant arrangement. "It's the kind of weird thing murderers do. Like returning to the scene of the crime. Actually, the part he seemed most interested in was whether or not Enid and Vic were back together again. And that would fit."

"Would it?"

"Sure. Because it was on account of Vic that she brushed him off four years ago. Or so he figures. And he has this compulsion to know if it was Vic again, the second time around. He has to blame somebody, see. It would never occur to him that she was brushing him off for himself alone." After a moment's silence, she returned to her original tack. "There has to be some connection between him and Enid. Something he knows about her, or suspects, or— Could it be something he picked up from Thelma, do you suppose?"

Martin closed his eyes. He tried to keep his voice light. "Here we go again. A great idea a minute."

"All right. But it could be. I still think she may have known about Enid and Vic, that the affair wasn't over. Even if she didn't know for sure, she'd be worried, good and worried. Anybody would be, with a husband as attractive as he is."

"Okay. He's attractive. And maybe Thelma knew. And told Bob. I suppose that's what you're getting at. What of it?"

"I don't know exactly. If he wanted to do Vic some dirt, he could tell the police. They don't like having people lie to them, even when it's about something that doesn't particularly matter."

"Sounds pretty farfetched to me," said Martin. "I can see Bob as a trouble maker, all right, but he's also a coward. I doubt if he'd have the nerve."

"Well, he's up to something," Rosemary repeated stubbornly. "The least we can do is try to find out what. We've got his address now, and his real name. What are we waiting for?"

"You mean just barge in on him? Now?"

"Why not? If he's really going to move, now's the time." She broke up the pleasant hand arrangement and reached for her purse.

"Yes, but how are we going to— Look, Rosemary, he's a cagey guy. I didn't get anywhere with him at lunch."

"You didn't have me with you," she pointed out. "It's no use trying to figure anything out in advance. We have no idea what tack he's going to take. We'll simply have to play it by ear."

"Now just a minute. I can tell you one tack he's going to take. He's going to ask how the hell I knew where to find him."

"Tell him you got it out of Thelma. That's if you insist on lying. Personally, I don't see anything wrong with telling him the truth—that the name sounded phony right from the start, and then when he acted so peculiar at lunch, so cagey and all, you decided to follow him and see what was what. After all, he's the one with things to explain. Not you. You've got nothing to hide."

"Be that as it may," Martin murmured. He had to admit, the idea was appealing, in a bold, naive way. It might even work. Approached in this forthright fashion, caught completely off guard—as he almost certainly would be—Bob might actually be surprised into explaining what he was up to. And if Martin's theory turned out to be right?

Well, the test must come sometime. He could not just go on harboring his hunch—that Thelma shared his suspicions of Vic and had let them slip to Bob—without ever knowing whether it was true or false. He could not go on harboring his suspicions forever, either; sooner or later he had to know whether or not Vic had indeed been involved in Enid's death as well as her life. For his own satisfaction: no matter what he did with the knowledge. And promise or no promise: he had made no commitment about discovering the truth for himself.

He had to start somewhere. Why not here and now? Well, because...

He stared across at Rosemary, shocked by the strangeness and strength of what he was feeling. This was none of her business, it was Vic's and his, an intensely personal thing between the two of them, nobody's business but theirs.

She recapped her lipstick and snapped her compact shut. "Ready?" she asked. "Come on. Let's go."

"Rosemary, I don't think—"

"Listen, Martin. You can sit here and search your soul for the rest of the night if you want to. Or you can come with me. Because I'm going up there to Bob's. With you or without you. Take your choice." She stood up, eyes snapping, ready to switch her neat little rump out of there and up to Bob's.

She meant it. There was nothing to do but go with her.

The cab ride uptown was not sociable. Rosemary sat as far away from him as she could get, and kept her eyes trained on the back of the cabbie's head. Her profile looked purposeful, righteous, and contemptuous of soul searchers. Fortunately she was not a mind reader, or she would have been even more contemptuous: Martin was sustaining himself with the thought that Bob might not be there.

He was, though. And he already had a visitor. The sound of voices reached them through the open window of Bob's basement apartment; against the blind they could see two shifting shadows.

"Are they quarreling?" whispered Rosemary. She had set out, bold as a lion, down the half dozen steps leading to the basement door. Now she hesitated, wide-eyed and nervous.

"Sounds like it to me," said Martin. They stood side by side, listening. The voices were not loud, but there was a disturbing quality about them, a throb of underground violence. Furthermore, they were both familiar, the visitor's as well as Bob's.

"It's Vic, isn't it?"

Martin nodded. So of course it was a quarrel: the only kind of conversation possible between those two. The subject of the quarrel was what mattered.

Bob seemed to be trying a shaky kind of bluster. "Listen, you, don't try anything with me or I'll..." It was exasperating, the way his voice fluctuated, blurting and fading like a faulty sound track. And Martin did not trust his own ears; they were so strained to catch the name of Enid that they might hear it whether or not it actually turned up.

Vic sounded ominously pleasant: "You do that. Go right ahead. I dare you to. No? I thought not. That would be cutting off your nose to spite your face, wouldn't it? Remember, I've got a thing or two to tell myself. You miserable little bastard, trying to bluff me..."

There was an indistinct mumble from Bob. Sure enough, Enid's name leapt out at Martin. Seemed to leap out.

"Listen, you." Vic again, goading, bullying. "You and your methods. I've got mine too, and so help me, if I find out you ever so much as—"

"I didn't! You can't hang a thing on me, I can prove—"

The voices tangled unintelligibly. The shadows on the window blind suddenly shifted, in a menacing way. A scuffle of feet, a meaty smack, a muffled crash.

"He's killing him," gasped Rosemary. She was clinging to Martin's arm. "What'll we do? Don't go down there, Martin, he's killing him!"

"That's just a sample," Vic said, softly and viciously. "You'll get worse than that if you don't stay the hell away from Thelma. And from me too. Don't mess around. Understand? Just don't mess around."

The door flew open, even before Martin rang the bell. Beyond Vic's furious face and his solid, formidable bulk, they could see Bob propped against the overturned drawing board, his head hanging down, blood dripping from his chin.

"What's going on here?" Martin asked. The policeman's phrase, but without the ring of authority. It sounded as silly as he felt. Bob lifted his head and peered dully; Vic, after one arrogant glance at him and Rosemary, made as if to walk right past them, preferably over them.

But then he changed his mind. "What are you doing here, if you don't mind my asking? The way I heard it, you didn't know where Bob lived. Thought his name was White. How come you didn't say so last night, if you knew—"

"I didn't. I had lunch with him today and trailed him home."

Out of the corner of his eye he saw Bob's jaw drop, then with a resigned air he returned to mopping up his chin. A pathetic sight, at least to Rosemary; she went over to him. "Here, let me help you. Where's a towel?"

Martin and Vic stayed where they were, face to face at the door. "You trailed him home. I see. You just for the hell of it trailed him home. Do you often do things like that?"

"No. Do you often beat guys up?"

"Only when they start fooling around with my wife." A ringing husbandly statement, if Martin ever heard one. Vic delivered it with bravado, and watched to see how it went over. Well, it didn't. Not with Martin. His expression must have indicated as much, for Vic was falling back on the tried and true best defense. "That still doesn't explain what you're doing here now. Another sudden irresistible impulse, I suppose?"

"You can suppose anything you like," Martin said coldly. "I see no reason why I should explain—"

"Oh, stop being so huffy, Martin." Rosemary paused in her ministrations to the wounded long enough to toss this back over her shoulder. "We're here because we wanted to find out what he was up to, snooping around, asking everybody about Enid."

After a second of resounding silence Bob mumbled, "Who, me?"

"Of course you. You've been pumping everybody. Martin, me, Mother, even poor old Mrs. Klein."

"Mrs. who? Who's she?" asked Vic.

"Yeah, who's she?" echoed Bob. "I never—"

"You know perfectly well who she is," said Rosemary severely. "Come on, I'll help you clean up." She hustled him off to the bathroom. There was a businesslike sound of rushing water.

"Enid?" said Vic in a low voice. Almost as if they were conspirators, Martin thought; as if they were teetering together on the brink of that intensely personal thing between them that was none of Rosemary's business. Instinctively he shrank back—not now, not here, not yet—while Vic waited and watched.

"Enid," he said in the same low voice Vic had used. "She's in this, somehow or other. It's not just Thelma you were fighting about. Bob knows something—"

"He knows about Enid and me, that we were back together again," Vic said quickly. (Is this the way you want it? We don't jump now? Later?) "Suspects it, rather. God knows how he got on to it, or why he should care, one way or the other. Except that he's a troublemaker, a rat from way back."

"You did know him, then, in Philadelphia?"

"I knew who he was. His name was familiar." He paused a moment, curiously; when Martin made no comment he went on, with growing assurance. "I'm not sure I would have recognized him if I'd just met him cold. I am sure I don't want him messing around, stirring up trouble, getting Thelma in a twitch. That's what set her off the other night, him and his big mouth."

"I see. You threatened to do some talking yourself, if he didn't lay off. What was all that about?"

"Principally bluff," said Vic with his candid air. "I figured it was safe as long as I didn't get down to specifics. A rat like Bob is bound to have at least one smelly little episode in his past. Besides, he's a coward, one of those guys you can't resist bullying. Anyway, I can't."

The next moment nurse and patient emerged from the bathroom. "Of course it was you," Rosemary was saying irritably. "Mrs. Klein told Martin about it, that's how we know. He recognized you from her description. No use your denying it."

But that was what Bob persisted in doing. His hair was slicked down now, and the dull look was gone from his eyes. Except for a puffy lip and a plum-colored bruise on his jaw, he was back to normal. And sticking to his "who, me?" routine. Never heard of Mrs. Klein. Hadn't pumped her or anybody else about Enid. Couldn't imagine where they had gotten such an idea. Naturally he'd been interested, having known Enid, known of her. Was it his fault she was on everybody's mind?

"You mentioned her tonight to Vic!" Rosemary burst out. Her face was pink with frustration. "I heard you, I'm positive I heard you!"

"Tonight?" Bob lifted his shoulders, spread his hands helplessly. Martin had noticed before how his eyes kept shifting toward Vic, in apprehensive little bids for approval; now it was an open, insolent look, and with it came that unforgettably sly smile. "I give up. It's your turn, Vic. Maybe you can convince her."

"I never argue with a lady," said Vic promptly, and gave Rosemary the old razzle-dazzle smile. "If she heard it, she heard it. Good night. An ice pack might help. And don't forget what I told you."

There was no danger of that; he had accomplished his mission, and they all knew it. Evidently even Rosemary had given up all hope of getting anything out of Bob. "Let's go too," she said, and they followed Vic out the door and up the half dozen steps to the street.

He said good night as cheerfully and easily as if they were parting after a nice friendly get-together. But Rosemary had one more question. "How did *you* get hold of his real name and address? Did you pry it out of Thelma?"

"Beat it out of her, you mean? Like the brute I am? No, as it happens, I didn't have to. I remembered this quirk of Thelma's and figured it out on my own."

"This quirk?"

"She has a way of speaking in opposites. Especially when she's nervous. She'll say up for down, left for right, back for front. White for Black. Once I remembered that, it was elementary. All I had to do was look him up in the phone book. Good night."

Off he went. And after a moment off they went, in the opposite direction. They found a cab at the corner and rode uptown—Rosemary wanted to go straight home, no nightcap, thank you—in almost complete silence. Not unsociably this time; they sat close together, holding on to each other's hands. But thinking their separate thoughts. How separate only Martin knew. For his were focused on Vic and the private showdown they both knew was impending, the moment when they would shuck off subterfuge and take the perilous jump into truth.

Was it possible that Rosemary sensed he was still holding out on her? She was awfully damn quiet. And when they reached her mother's apartment she did not ask him in. At the door she said, in a subdued little voice, "It was a stupid idea, wasn't it? It wouldn't have worked, even if Vic hadn't been there. People don't tell you things just because you ask. Especially when it's a question of—of murder." She shivered. "And it is. Murder. It does make sense, what I said before, about Bob. You see it now too, don't you? Just the way he denied it to Vic—"

Bob. She thought it was Bob. They had overheard the same conversation; and come up with two entirely different translations. It was either very grim or very funny, Martin couldn't decide which.

"I'll call you tomorrow," he said, and kissed her gently. "Maybe we can dope it all out then."

11

"No egg?" cried Hazel. "But it's Saturday!" She set the glass skillet back on the stove and gave her daughter a sharp look. Weekend breakfasts were a tradition with them, and a treat: one of the few occasions when there was time for Hazel to revert to her native, country domesticity; time for them both to linger over extra cups of coffee and have a nice little gossip.

"I'm not hungry," Rosemary said wanly. She slid into her side of the breakfast nook and leaned her chin on her hand. Hazel decided she looked peaked.

"I didn't hear you come in last night. What time was it?"

"I don't know. Not late."

"Good time?"

Rosemary shrugged.

"You and Martin had a fight. Is that it?"

"Of course we didn't have a fight. For Pete's sake, Mom. Light somewhere and stop hovering!"

Stung into silence (hovering!) Hazel sat down too. She took another muffin and brooded about Martin Shipley. It was these nice quiet ones that did the damage. "Of course" they hadn't had a fight; nothing so vulgar or wholesome as that. She remembered the wolfish way he had smiled, that first afternoon, when poor innocent Rosemary had blurted out the business about his wife. His wife! Apprehension clutched her. How could she have forgotten, even for a moment, the ominous question of Martin's past? Yes, forgotten, brushed it aside, dismissed it as if it were nothing out of the ordinary, the kind of harmless scrape any boy could get into. A possible wife-murderer, that was all, and she had let him loose with Rosemary, who was a babe in the woods, never mind her sophisticated airs, and who now sat there moping and looking peaked and not eating her breakfast.

Their eyes met, and Rosemary said, with a pathetic little quaver in her voice, "The fact is, Mom, last night kind of scared me."

Hazel's knife clattered against her plate. She grabbed wildly for Rosemary's hand. "Baby! Tell me! What did he do to you?"

"Who?"

"That Martin of course. Who else? Oh, I could kick myself, I should never have—"

"Honestly, Mom! Simmer down. What's the matter with you this morning? Martin didn't do anything to me. Nobody did. Get your mind off rape and listen."

It hadn't been on rape so much as murder, and that—Hazel realized as she obediently simmered down and listened—was what had frightened Rosemary about last night. Enid's murder. It had hit her in a different, harder way. From the beginning, of course, it had been an indisputable fact. There was nothing hypothetical about it, as there was about the death of Martin's wife; it could not be glossed over as an accident. The only possible spot for a bit of glossing over (and Hazel and Rosemary had both snatched at it) was the identity of the murderer. They could not deny that someone had killed Enid, but they could deny that it was someone who knew her. It was more comfortable to believe in a panicky, anonymous intruder; it somehow kept murder at manageable arm's length. Last night had all but destroyed Rosemary's faith in the intruder. By the time she was through with her story, Hazel herself was aware of a few inner quakes and crumblings. But she was not about to admit it.

"Now look here, Rosemary," she said at last. "You're letting your imagination run away with you. Sure, Bob could have made a play for Enid, could even have killed her, I suppose. But there's not one single solid fact to prove it. No evidence that he ever saw her here in New York, or knew her better than he claims, or anything. All you know for sure is that he's been asking a lot of questions about her, and he had a fight with Vic. Who had a perfectly good reason for taking a poke at him, aside from Enid."

"They weren't just fighting about Thelma," Rosemary said mulishly. "It was about Enid too. Bob's mixed up in it somehow. If he didn't kill her himself he knows something—"

"Something Vic doesn't want him to tell," Hazel finished for her. "That's what you're suggesting, isn't it? Something that would implicate Vic."

"Well. Well, I guess so. Or maybe Thelma?"

"Or maybe Thelma. Something that would implicate one of the Holms." She let that sink in. She was feeling better by the minute; there was nothing like a few blunt statements to straighten things out. "And that really is pretty farfetched, Rosemary. I simply can't believe the police wouldn't have gotten on to it too, if there was anything to get on to. They checked the Holms' story backwards and forwards, and didn't find any holes in it. It's not just their story, remember. That Mrs. McGrath was visiting them the night Enid was killed. It's her story, too."

"I know it. I know the Holms couldn't have killed her. And I know I can't prove anything about Bob. All the same, that fight last night, it was about Enid. It was, it was!"

"But not necessarily about her death. Look. Why couldn't they have been talking about her affair with Vic? It would be like Bob to bring that up, under the circumstances. You know. Throwing it in Vic's face that he hasn't always been so faithful himself. That's certainly the angle Bob was working on when he paid his little call on me."

"Yes, but Mom, the very fact that he paid his little call on you means— Well, why would he bother? What's it to him if Vic and Enid had gotten together again here in New York?"

"Spite," said Hazel promptly. "Chances are he knew Thelma was about ready to chuck him, if she hadn't already, and he was looking for a way to get even with her and Vic both, make trouble between them. There are people like that and if you ask me he's one of them. Bob White, Black, Whatever." It was quite a convincing argument, at least to her own ears. She pressed on energetically. "Honestly, Rosemary, doesn't it make more sense? I know you were there and I wasn't, but— How about Martin? What does he make of all this?"

"I don't know," said Rosemary with a queenly air. "We didn't discuss it."

"Didn't discuss it! Why on earth not?"

Rosemary maintained a regal silence. But her chin trembled slightly, as if she might be on the verge of tears. That Martin. Fight or no fight, something had gone wrong. Didn't discuss it! Why, it was against human nature, they must not even be on speaking terms. And just as well too, with that big black shadow in Martin's past. If Hazel had a hollow, grieving feeling—yes, all right, she had—it was on Rosemary's account, poor child, but of course she would bounce back, all it took was time.

She had no sooner settled the matter in her mind, more or less satisfactorily, than the phone rang: Martin, she could tell from Rosemary's voice; obviously very much on speaking terms. The joys of motherhood, Hazel thought, in helpless agitation. What did she do now? Forbid Rosemary to see him again? Ha! Demand from Martin a yes-or-no answer: did you or did you not murder your wife? There was a limit, even to Hazel's bluntness. Yet to do nothing, to stand by, silent and inert, while...

"Thelma's invited us for lunch!" Rosemary called from the hall. "Martin says she asked him to bring us. Shall I tell him okay, Mom?"

A reprieve. Hazel's heart bobbed up like a balloon. More than a reprieve. A heaven-sent opportunity to meet Thelma Holm and judge her at first hand; to take another look at Martin, a cold, hard, maternal look this time, no nonsense about whether or not she happened to like him personally; and incidentally, to get his version of last night. That too, of course.

"Wonder how she happened to ask us," she said, when Rosemary came back, looking considerably less peaked.

"Vic's working—he puts in a lot of overtime—and I think she gets lonesome. She doesn't seem to have many friends here, they're all in Philadelphia. That's probably why she took up with Bob. Lonesomeness. Otherwise I can't see it, he doesn't seem her type at all. Martin said she sounded fine. Gay as a lark. Maybe she's celebrating Liberation Day from Bob."

"Does she know what happened last night?"

"She didn't mention it. So don't you, Mom, you keep your mouth shut, will you, for once in your life?"

It was the kind of slur Hazel was used to. She ignored it. "You know, Rosemary, I bet Dennis could give me a line on Bob Black, if I wanted to call him."

"Dennis?"

"You know. Enid worked with him when she was in Philadelphia. I sent her to him. He's lived there forever. Knows all kinds of people. And he's gossipy as an old hen. What do you think? It might be worth a try."

It was indeed worth a try. She didn't get Dennis right away; no answer at first, then a busy signal, at last—by this time they were ready and waiting for Martin to pick them up—Dennis' light, vivacious voice came on the line. In accordance with Rosemary's instructions, Hazel worked the subject around to Bob Black by an indirect route. After that she listened. Just as she hung up, the doorbell rang: Martin, on the dot of twelve thirty, with a cab waiting.

So she wound up giving them her report on Bob Black while they rode downtown to have lunch with Thelma Holm. There was no time to sort it out in her own mind first; not with Rosemary champing at the bit. Out it came, boom: "He's Lulu McGrath's brother. A ne'er-do-well, Dennis says, can't keep a job, never pays his bills, always getting into some kind of hot water and hollering for good old big sister Lulu to fish him out. She used to do it, all the time, till her husband got fed up and laid it on the line. Either she washed her hands of brother Bob or she found herself another husband. This was a couple of years ago, after Lulu had wangled a job for Bob in one of the McGrath enterprises. There are a lot of them. He's loaded. Dennis doesn't know exactly what happened, it was hushed up, but McGrath blew his top and booted Bob out, and nobody's seen or heard of him since."

"Including Lulu, I suppose?" Martin's voice, coming from the other corner of the cab, beyond Rosemary, sounded detached; he seemed to be gazing off into space.

"Especially Lulu. Naturally she's not going to break up her marriage for the sake of a black sheep brother. She came up the hard way, she knows a good thing when she's got it. Not many girls from the wrong side of the tracks are lucky enough to snag a McGrath."

"It connects him with the Holms, though," Rosemary pointed out. "How about Enid? Did she know Bob too, better than anybody's saying?"

"Not as far as Dennis knows. I certainly can't see her bothering with a fellow like Bob. Can you?"

"I can't see Thelma bothering, either. But she did."

"Well, but you said yourself, she's lonely. A lonely, neglected wife, and a semi-alcoholic..." Hazel had a confused feeling that she was floundering; in some obscure way the discovery of Bob's identity seemed to undermine the comforting, convincing argument she had evolved over the breakfast table. "It's not the same at all. And anyway. What's the difference how well he knew Enid, or whose brother he is? I can't see that it proves anything about the set-to he had with Vic last night. Do you, Martin?" That proved how rattled she was, that she should be appealing to Martin. "Rosemary's got this notion they weren't fighting about Thelma at all—"

"You're twisting it around, Mom! It was partly about Thelma, of course. But it was about Enid too. You know it as well as I do, Martin, whether you'll admit it or not!"

So there they were, both of them, appealing to Martin, and he continued to gaze off into space, shutting them out, refusing to commit himself. It came to Hazel that this was what had gone wrong between him and Rosemary last night: no quarrel but no discussion either; simply the chill of being shut out, without knowing why or from what. But Martin was miserable too. She saw it in his eyes when he turned toward Rosemary and put his hand over hers.

"Remember what you said last night," he said. "People don't tell you things just because you ask. You were right, they don't. Let's don't ask Thelma, and see what she tells us."

Which didn't strike Hazel as much of an answer. But then he wasn't holding her hand or giving her the soulful-eyes routine. She looked out the window and waited grimly for the tender moment to pass.

"Don't worry," she said as the cab pulled up to the curb. "Rosemary's already warned me about keeping my mouth shut."

"We go up these stairs." Martin guided them past the store window with its display of trusses and cervical collars. "It's kind of a weird arrangement, isn't it? But they have lots of space, the two top floors to themselves." He pushed the bell, the buzzer promptly sounded, and they started climbing the narrow, dark stairway, which smelled of Vitamin B.

The woman waiting for them at the top was smiling radiantly. Lonely? Neglected? Semi-alcoholic? Not so you could notice it. She was tall and willowy as a girl; standing like that, with her arms outstretched in welcome, she gave an effect of youthfulness and warmth that took Hazel completely by surprise. No one had told her that Thelma Holm was charming. But then it should have been self-evident. Only a charming woman could have held her husband against competition as stiff as Enid.

She had a breathless, impulsive way of talking, jumping from pillar to post, juggling two or three conversational balls at once, bubbling with pleasure in her own party. Such a small party, and made up of people drawn together by such ugly, shocking events... Yes, she must be lonely, after all. And her face, when seen close up, showed lines of strain, as if, with no one around to sparkle for, its basic expression would be one of sad bewilderment.

"No cause for alarm, Martin," she said as she handed around a tray of drinks. "I'm back on the ginger ale circuit. You heard about my fall from grace, Mrs. Nicholson? Good, I hoped Martin would tell you, otherwise I probably would, and it's not really very interesting... Poor Martin, what a nuisance I made of myself, and you were so good to me. Anybody else would have sent me packing."

"I did," said Martin, smiling. "Don't you remember? I made you call Vic, and then I sent you home with him, even though you obviously didn't want to go. I worried about it afterwards, you acted so scared."

"Who, me? That's how I am when I get drunk. I never want to go home. I had nothing to be scared of. You saw how Vic was, a perfect lamb about the whole thing." She patted her glossy bangs, and shot a quick glance at each of them in turn. "No point in pretending, is there? I can see everybody knows the worst. Should I be embarrassed? I'm not. It's a relief to me, having it out in the open like this. In a way, that's why I invited you. And I'm very grateful to you for coming. It was Vic's idea, actually. I was upset when he told me about last night, you see. That did embarrass me. Martin and Rosemary being there, I mean. What must you have thought!"

"So Vic said ask us to lunch and find out," said Martin drily.

"Of course not! How could you think— Well, yes, partly." Her laugh rang out, unself-conscious as a child's. "Naturally, I'm curious."

"So were we," said Martin. "And so was Bob. That's why we were there, why I tracked him down in the first place. Because he seemed so extraordinarily curious about Enid."

"I know." Thelma's eyes darkened slightly; there was no other sign that it had given her a turn. (As it had Hazel.) "He started in on me, too, trying to convince me that Vic and—that they were back together again. I know perfectly well it's not true, but all the same it bothered me. That was his point, I guess, he likes getting people stirred up. Especially me. He knew it would send me off on a binge. And it did. He's not really a very nice person, is he?" Her hands moved aimlessly, helplessly. "You said a minute ago, scared. Well, it's true. Only of course it wasn't Vic I was scared of, it was Bob. I was afraid to go home for fear he'd call me or—something. I couldn't bear the thought of hearing his voice again, not even over the phone. You wouldn't believe how spiteful he can be. Especially about Vic. It's frightening, the way he resents Vic. Almost as if he had a grudge."

That was all Rosemary needed. Up with the head, out with the chin. She was off: "Maybe he did have. Maybe he had a thing about Enid himself, back in Philadelphia, and feels he lost out on account of Vic. He might still have been after her, here in New York. It's not the kind of thing she'd mention to anybody, and neither would he. Certainly not after what happened to her."

Martin groaned. Hazel sighed.

But Thelma said quietly, "I've sometimes wondered myself. It might even be the reason he took up with me. To get even with Vic. He's capable of it. Capable of anything."

"That's going pretty far, isn't it?" said Martin.

"Not too far. Believe me. What a fool I've been, what a fool! The one thing to be said in my favor is that I see it now. Well, and I did have sense enough to know he was lying about Vic and Enid." Did she expect someone to argue with her? No one did. No one spoke at all. After a moment she rushed on. "Oh, I'm so glad it's over! I'm so glad I told Vic about it, the other night at your house, Martin. That's another thing I have to thank you for. I never would have told him, if it hadn't been for you."

"No, I don't suppose you would have," said Martin, in what struck Hazel as a rather odd tone. "As it was, you didn't tell him—or me either—who Bob really is, did you?"

"Oh, you mean the Black-White business. I just—"

"No, I mean the fact that he's Lulu McGrath's brother."

"Oh," she said. She covered her mouth with her hands—ringless, Hazel noticed, not even a wedding band—and shrank back like a smacked child. "Oh dear. I was so ashamed. I thought if I said White instead of Black nobody would ever find out. Only Vic caught on anyway, and now you— Who told you?"

"A friend of Hazel's in Philadelphia. I told you we were curious. Even more so after last night. We got the impression that Vic could make some trouble for Bob too, and would, if he was pushed far enough."

"Oh. Well, there was something a couple of years ago, I don't know exactly what, but it was the last straw as far as Lulu was concerned. I bet Vic doesn't know any more than I do. He must have been bluffing."

"So he said. I must say, it seemed to work."

She smiled, rather proudly, Hazel thought. The female primeval, pleased at being fought over, pleased too at the outcome. "That's why I didn't want Vic to find out, you see. It made it less ignominious, for both of us, to have him think it was nobody he knew. Just an anonymous somebody I'd taken up with when I wasn't entirely myself. I was ashamed to have him find out it was a—a good-for-nothing like Bob Black. Poor Vic, I might at least have picked somebody decent."

"How about poor Bob? He's the one that got socked."

"He had it coming. So did I, if you want my honest opinion. Only I was just foolish, not malicious like Bob. Funny, isn't it? He was doing his best to make trouble between Vic and me, and what he actually did was bring us closer together. There now. That ends today's episode in the Holms' soap opera. Another drink, everybody?"

She sprang up, head tilted, hands lifted in a gesture that for some reason made Hazel think of a magician's flourish. A trick? But everything she had said fit in with the facts, and furthermore with Hazel's own theories, which had seemed so comfortingly logical when she thought of them herself. She was not going to start picking holes in them now. Smiling—as Rosemary and even Martin were smiling—she accepted another drink and resolutely bent her mind to enjoying the party.

The phone rang while they were finishing their coffee and discussing the living room walls. ("I still think murals," Thelma declared, "only not please God Bob Black's.") She looked startled, maybe even panicky, at the peal of the bell, but when she came back from answering it her face was radiant again.

"That was Lulu!" she cried. "They're just back from their cruise, Mac has to get back to Philadelphia, but she's going to stay over till tomorrow, she's just around the corner— No, no, don't go, please stay. It will be such fun. A welcome-back party!"

There was just time, before Lulu's arrival, for her to add, with a shamefaced, pleading air, "You won't mention any of this? About Bob? Because of course Lulu has no idea... She never sees him anymore, hasn't in at least two years, after that last mess he got into she wrote him off as a bad bet. She doesn't even know he's in New York. So you won't say anything, will you? It would be too terribly embarrassing."

Lulu was a sleek little package of a woman: one of those durable, compact figures; expert maintenance all over the place—ash-blonde hair, flawless teeth, fingernails like perfect, rosy shells. Against her pecan-brown tan her white linen dress was dazzling, not a wrinkle in it. A modest fortune had no doubt been invested in her charm bracelet, another—not so modest—in her diamond. Yet there was something about her that took the curse off all this surface artifice—a quality of basic naturalness that refused to be polished away and that kept Hazel from begrudging her even her shoes, which were bright red, spike-heeled, sling pumps. Lulu's voice was husky and faintly raffish. Her eyes looked out at the world with a kind of zestful, astonished self-mockery, as if she were saying, Hey, look what's happened to little wrong-side-of-the-tracks Lulu, hey, how about that!

Thelma fell on her neck like a lost child restored to home and mother. "I've missed you so. Oh, Lulu, I can't tell you how good it is to have you back!"

Too true, she couldn't tell, thought Hazel. And like as not none of this would have happened if Lulu had been here to keep Thelma on the beam. For that was obviously her role: her manner toward Thelma was definitely managing, affectionate but firm.

"I hope you've been behaving yourself," she said. "How's Vic? Okay? Listen, dearie, you promised me you were going to get to work on this place and get it shaped up while I was away. I expected a transformation, and what do I get? The same old shambles. Six months, and you haven't even finished unpacking! You ought to be ashamed."

"I am," said Thelma, with a flickering half-wink toward her other three guests.

They stayed only a few minutes longer. Such a nice lunch, so nice of Thelma to ask them, so nice to meet Lulu. They must get together again, very soon. Goodbye, goodbye.

They trooped down the stairs, waving and smiling and not saying a single embarrassing word about Lulu's black sheep brother Bob.

12

Once they reached the street, of course, there was no holding back. Rosemary began it; the gleam in her eye made Martin think of a prosecuting attorney turning the tables on a hostile witness. "Well. Now try and tell me Bob Black had nothing to do with Enid. It's not just in my head. It's in Thelma's, too, the very same idea. I guess that proves it isn't so crazy, after all."

What it proved to Martin—though he refrained from saying so—was that Thelma had a remarkable talent for picking up other people's suggestions and making the most of them. Rosemary's suggestion, in this case, though she seemed to have lost sight of the fact. Not Martin. Indeed, it was during this particular part of the pre-lunch conversation, while Thelma was skillfully scooping up Rosemary's idea and tossing it back as her own, that he had experienced a revelation. Watching Thelma in action, he remembered his own conversation with her Wednesday night, and he saw, with flash-of-lightning clarity, that it was he, not Thelma, who had launched the idea of an affair between her and Bob. The affair that was now an accepted fact, unlikely as the combination had seemed at first glance. To everybody. Thelma herself had stared at him incredulously for a moment before she went off into that fit of hysterical giggles. What relief she must have felt, what gratitude to Martin for handing her this nice simple way of explaining the presence of Bob in her life! Then too there was the ironic touch, the inside-out logic (Thelma's favorite kind) of being most loyal to Vic when she was confessing her infidelity.

For Martin now realized that the key to everything Thelma did was just that: loyalty to Vic. She had pounced on the role of unfaithful wife gladly, gladly. Let everybody think she was a tramp. Just don't let anybody think Vic was a murderer. Better Bob as temporary bed-mate than as blackmailer. And trust Bob to pick her as his victim. Unlike Vic, she wasn't bigger than he was; she had neither the strength nor temperament to hit back. Suggestible, easily rattled—she sometimes drank too much, bless her heart—and above all devoted to Vic, ready to protect him no matter what she herself might suspect him of doing. Oh, she was the one, all right, the perfect customer for Bob's modest little racket. As to what he actually had on Vic, it was anybody's guess, thought Martin, pure speculation. The chances were all against Bob's talking now. Thanks to Vic. He knew how to handle rats like Bob; Thelma should have told him the whole story in the first place. But that would have meant admitting her own suspicions. Being loyal to Vic didn't keep her from being scared of him.

No wonder she was in buoyant spirits today. The Holms had squeaked through another tight spot, with only minor abrasions, and closer together than ever. No wonder, either, that she had snatched at the chance, so conveniently offered by Rosemary, to steer suspicion toward Bob, who was guilty of a worse crime than murdering Enid, the rotter, he had tried to make trouble between her and Vic...

"I never said it was crazy." Hazel's voice jolted him out of his own private reverie. She sounded defensive, as if Rosemary was making her feel like a hostile witness too, and she shifted uneasily from one space shoe to the other. "All I said was you've got no proof. You still haven't. Just because Thelma happens to agree with you—"

"You heard her. She was scared of Bob herself, scared of what he might do. Spiteful, resentful, capable of anything, she said. Anything. Including murder. She didn't say it in so many words, but that's what she meant. And she knows him, if anybody does."

"Better than his sister?" Martin asked. It was last night all over again; two entirely different translations. He had the same eerie, displaced feeling. "Yes, I suppose you're right, if Lulu hasn't seen him in the past couple of years."

The operative word, for him, was "if." But not for Rosemary. Or Hazel, either; she was saying, with an air of relief at finding one point of agreement, "She's given him up as a bad job too. Just as Dennis said. I'm not denying he's a real no-account."

"He's a lot worse than that, if you ask me." Rosemary looked flushed. Very pretty, and very obstinate. "I think the police ought to know about him. It's different when they ask questions. He'll have to tell them."

It figured. Martin should have known it was coming. But the knot of resistance that tightened inside him had nothing to do with knowing or thinking. It was instinctive. A great big panicky mindless No. Not the police. Not yet. Not before he and Vic had it out between them, the intensely personal thing that was nobody else's business. He said, quite calmly, "Now wait a minute, Rosemary. Before we go to the police—"

"You'll come with me, then?" Her eyes lit up.

"If you go I have no choice. They'll want my version of the fight last night, to see if it checks with yours. No getting out of it."

"No getting out of it," she echoed scornfully. "You'd like to get out of it. Why? Do you think I'm crazy too? Don't you want them to find out who killed Enid?"

Don't answer that question. Pick the easy one. "I don't think you're crazy. You've got a right to your opinion. But so have I, and I think it would be—all wrong to go to the police at this stage of the game." Thin ice. Watch your step. He glanced at Hazel, trying to judge how much of an ally she might prove to be. Her big, plain face showed worry. Uncertainty. A shade of mistrust? Oh Lord, the Joyce business. "I mean, stop and think a minute first."

"Oh sure. Search your soul. Drag your feet. That's you all over. It's a wonder to me you ever get dressed in the morning, what with making up your mind which sock to put on first, and then which shoe—can't have either of them feeling rejected, you know—"

"At least I don't go galloping off without looking where I'm going, or why. The police ought to know about Bob. Okay. Maybe. Let's be good citizens. Let's tell them about Bob. He deserves it. He's no good. A rat. But don't forget if we tell them about Bob it means telling them about Thelma too. I don't see any way of keeping her out of it. Do you?"

She didn't. And she hadn't thought of that side of it before. She gave a little gulp of dismay.

"Oh no," said Hazel, stricken.

"Oh yes. It would all come out. That she sometimes drinks too much. That she was foolish enough to get involved with Bob. Furthermore that there are still those who think her husband was Enid's lover, no matter what he and Thelma told the police before. That too. Once more through the meat grinder for both the Holms. With Bob directing every turn of the handle, and relishing it."

"They'd grind him through, too."

"True. They might even get something out of him. Then again, they might not. Your mother's right, Rosemary, you've got no proof, not even an honest to God connection between Bob and Enid. All you've got so far is a hunch, and I don't think that's enough. I think you ought to wait till—"

She was looking scornful again, half ready to bolt off on her own and leave him to his miserable soul searching. But Hazel put a hand on her arm. "Now calm down, Rosemary. Wait till what?" The look she gave Martin was both hopeful and suspicious. "You're hatching something, Martin. At least it sounds like it to me."

"As a matter of fact, I am." Could he leave it at that? No. He would have to improvise. "Call it a hunch of my own. Something I have to work out by myself. No use telling you about it yet. I have to think it through first, figure out the best way to tackle it."

"Naturally," said Rosemary. "A year or so of preliminary research, I suppose?"

"An hour or so. Sorry to disappoint you."

"Well? And then what?"

"Well. And then I tackle it. I test my hunch, find out if I'm right or wrong. That shouldn't take long, either. And after that... One thing I do know. The timing's got to be right. If you go to the police now you'll louse me up. Be a sport, Rosemary? Give me till tonight, tomorrow morning at the latest. Bob will keep till then. If it turns out I'm way off the track with my hunch, I give you my word, we'll go to work on yours."

She was wavering, he could see, but he did not realize what a total victory he had won until she spoke. "This test of yours. Won't it be dangerous?"

"Dangerous?" It was odd that the question should take him by surprise, odd that he should feel less like Vic's Nemesis than his fellow-conspirator. Surely Rosemary had a point? And such a flattering one; the temptation to play up to it was well-nigh irresistible. "I don't think so, really. Not if I play my cards right."

"Then see that you do," Hazel said, and promptly looked as if she wished she hadn't. "Come on, Rosemary, let's go home and let Martin figure out his tactics." He hailed a cab for them (no, he was not to come with them; he was to get busy figuring) and they said their goodbyes. "Take care. Be sure to call, won't you?" Rosemary whispered. She gave him a quick kiss. And at the last minute Hazel shook hands with him.

All very nice and ego-building, to use Bob's phrase. But the fact remained that Rosemary had pressured him into committing himself and Vic. They were in for it now; no more dodging or postponing the showdown. Dangerous or not, it was inevitable. Tomorrow morning at the latest. That meant tonight, this afternoon, the sooner the better. He stepped into a sidewalk phone booth, looked up the number of Vic's office, and dialed.

There was no answer. In his mind's eye he saw the Saturday emptiness, the deserted switchboard, one line left open for the benefit of extra-time workers like Vic—who was either not bothering to answer or had already left. Or might never have been there at all: "the office" might be a cover-up term for him, his explanation for the evenings he had spent with Enid, his escape hatch now. The thought conjured up another mental picture, sharp as an etching, of Vic tramping the streets, any streets, in a stupor of sorrow, as Martin himself used to do, after Joyce's death.

But this was the sort of thing he must stop, this imaginary empathy with Vic. There was no basis for it. Two totally different people, two totally different cases. Not comrades. Opponents. He was wasting his time, straying off on these dead-end paths, when he should be marching down the main road with his tactics figured out and his forces marshaled.

There was no help for it: he would have to wait till Vic got home and call him there. With some excuse prepared in advance, in case Thelma or Lulu answered the phone. In the meantime, what? He paused outside the phone booth, remembering Rosemary's scornful references to soul searching. Action, he thought nervously, up and at 'em. Don't just stand there. Do something.

He got on a bus and rode up to Bob's street, partly on impulse, partly because he remembered something else—a notion that had stirred briefly in the underground of his mind while Rosemary was making noises about the police. That threat of hers, which had forced a deadline on him and Vic, had throbbed for a moment with still another potential. Now it was stirring and throbbing again; by the time he reached Bob's house he saw how it could be used as a lever on Bob and, through him, on Vic.

But he was too late. (Typically, Rosemary would have said.) The "Studio" sign was gone from the basement apartment window; the name of Robert Black no longer appeared beside bell or mailbox. Bob had skipped out. Either that mythical new apartment of his wasn't mythical, after all, or—more likely—he wasn't taking any chances on a second visit from Vic.

In his new role of man of action, Martin rang the bell marked Superintendent. Presently the street door opened and a woman stuck her head out. A small head, like a chicken's, with dyed red hair and a pointed nose, perched on top of a withered neck. Her voice was like a chicken's, too, fussy, full of clucks and cackles. "Ain't here anymore," she said in answer to Martin's question. "Moved out last night, bag and baggage. Such as it was. Just like that, without giving me notice. Didn't say where he was moving to. Just up and left."

"You mean without paying the rent?"

She really did cackle at that. "Do I look like some kind of a nut? They don't pull that on me. Oh no. They pay in advance, or out they go. Including Mr. Black. You a friend of his?"

"An acquaintance." He was inspired to add, "I know his sister."

"That so? Mrs. Richbitch, to hear him tell it. It's one of the lines they try to pull on me, see, they've all got wealthy connections that are going to put a check in the mail tomorrow. Cuts no ice with me. Though I'll say this much for Mr. Black, his sister looked like she might be the real McCoy." Again she uttered her high-pitched, cracked laugh. "That's a good one. The real McCoy. Because her name's Mc Something, see, Mrs. Mc Something or Other."

"McGrath," said Martin. "She's been here? You've met her?"

"That's it. McGrath. I didn't meet her exactly. Just saw her the once—four, five months ago, soon after he moved in—and he told me afterwards it was her. No kidding, is she loaded like he said?"

"Her husband's wealthy."

"Yeah. He told me. She looked it, all right. You could get his new address from her. He'll keep in touch with her, don't worry, he knows which side his bread is buttered on."

"Yes, I'm sure you're right. I'll call her."

He had nothing to lose by trying, he decided on the way home. He was calmed down now, determined not to overestimate Lulu's visit to her black sheep brother four, five months ago. That didn't mean she knew his present whereabouts, or would admit it if she did. But she was the only lead in sight, his one hope of getting hold of Bob and putting his lever idea to the test. There was even a chance—slim, but still—that the lever would work on Lulu as well as Bob. And he had to call the Holms, anyway, since he had missed Vic at the office. Two out of three, he thought as he dialed the number: it shouldn't be Thelma who answered, but with his luck it probably would be. Okay, he was prepared. He would disguise his voice and ask for Vic.

"Hello?" It was Lulu's husky voice; luck was being a lady, for once. "Oh yes," she said, when he had identified himself. "Thelma's gone out to do some errands, and Vic hasn't come home yet. Can I take a message?"

"Actually, you're the one I wanted to talk to." Martin's mouth went dry, and with it his brain. Dry and blank.

"I'm all ears," said Lulu cheerfully.

"Well. It's about your brother. I'm very anxious to get hold of him."

"You are?" Not so cheerful now. Cautious. Defensive.

"It's a little complicated. I met him, you know. Or did you know?"

Silence. Once more drought had struck Martin's mind. Then Lulu said, with a show of impatience, "What is all this? I mean, why call me? I never see Bob anymore."

"Don't you? That's one of the things I wanted to talk to you about."

"What do you— Listen. Where are you?"

"Home." He gave her the address.

"I'll be right over." She sounded brisk and managing. "We'd better get this straightened out. Whatever it is. Frankly, it sounds pretty wacky to me. If I hadn't met you up here— You didn't act like such a screwball, either today or that first time. What's got into you? Never mind. Tell me when I get there."

Ten minutes later she arrived. He ushered her in, feeling nervous and inadequate—as he often did with small, bossy women like Lulu, no matter what the circumstances. And of course these were special circumstances; not that Lulu showed any sign of thinking so. She marched into the living room, appraised it with one shrewd glance, sat down on the couch, and cocked her head at Martin with an air of good-humored inquiry.

"Now then, what's with you and Bob? Incidentally, you don't need to watch your language. Thelma's already told me all, as they say."

It didn't surprise him. In spite of Thelma's plea for silence on the subject of Bob, he had had a feeling she was going to tell Lulu herself. But in her own way, and without an audience. "And what did you make of it?" he asked.

"What is there to make of it? I gave her a good talking to. That's what she expects from me. Poor Thelma, she's never grown up in some ways. Wants somebody to scold her for being naughty. I'm very fond of her, you know, and Vic's given her a pretty rough time... But that's neither here nor there. What I want to know is this business about Bob. My problem brother." She smiled wryly. "My no-good brother. Might as well admit it, I suppose. I don't give up easy, but he's too much for me. I checked him off a couple of years ago. Had to. It was either that or lose my happy home. Yes, and Mac was right. That's my husband, Mac. He gave Bob one last chance—against his better judgment, I talked him into it—and what does Bob do with it? Well, I won't go into details, but he was just damn lucky Mac didn't press charges or he'd have wound up in jail. I mean, what can you do with a character like that, even if he is your own brother?"

"Nothing. Check him off," said Martin. Only Lulu hadn't done that; she was too bossy and good-hearted to give up on anybody, ever. Scratch the Mrs. Richbitch veneer and you found a tough, misguided little missionary, incurably optimistic, and perfectly willing to lie—as she was doing now—if she had to.

"Right," said Lulu. "I don't know where you got the idea I could put you in touch with Bob. Surely not from Thelma. I shouldn't think from Vic, either." Her voice sharpened a little, on the name of Vic. No love lost between those two, Martin decided.

"As a matter of fact, it was from Bob's landlady. Former landlady, I should say. He cleared out last night. She said Bob talked a good deal about you, and that you were up there once, four or five months ago, to see him."

Lulu looked him straight in the eye and said, "Up where? She's mistaken, this landlady. I didn't even know he was in New York till Thelma told me."

"I see. I was hoping you'd know where he moved to."

"Well, I don't. Why are you so anxious to get hold of him? Don't tell me, let me guess. He put the bite on you and skipped out without paying you back. Okay. How much?"

"No, no. It's not that. I didn't lend him any money."

"Congratulations." She tried, gamely, to smile. "So I guessed wrong. Money isn't the problem. I'm assuming there is a problem, from the look on your face. But maybe I'm wrong again, maybe that's your natural expression."

"There's a problem, all right. The reason I want to see Bob is to—well, in a way, to warn him. Otherwise he's apt to find himself in kind of a jam."

She blinked. Her eyes were round and clear, sherry-brown in color; one of her best points. "How bad a jam?" she asked.

"Bad. He's going to be accused of murdering Enid Baxter."

The shock of it made her gasp. But her back stayed straight, and her voice crisp. "That's absolutely ridiculous. You must be making it up. Nobody in their right mind would accuse Bob of—of— Why, he hardly knew Enid!"

"Maybe not, but he seems to have an abnormal interest in her death. He's brought this on himself, with all the snooping he's been doing. Somebody was bound to start suspecting that he knew Enid better than he's saying, or rather that he wanted to know her better than she wanted to know him."

"Oh my God," said Lulu. She closed her eyes and pressed her fingertips along the edge of her ash-blonde coiffure. For a moment only; and when she opened her eyes again they were bright with purpose. "Somebody. Who?"

"Who do you think?" He hoped she thought Martin, and to urge her along in this direction he folded his arms and assumed a stern expression. "Nothing's going to happen before tomorrow morning. After that—well, it depends on whether or not I can get hold of Bob and what he has to say for himself. If I don't find him the police will."

"You mean you'd actually go to the *police* with this crazy story? Why, they'll laugh in your face!"

"Remains to be seen," said Martin. "It seems to me they'll at least check up on what Bob was doing the night she was killed. I'm curious, myself. Because I can't believe he'd be all that interested unless he was mixed up in it, somehow or other. I'm not saying there isn't some other explanation. I'm just saying I want to hear it."

"This landlady you talked to. Didn't he leave a forwarding address with her?"

"He didn't even tell her he was moving. Simply picked up and left. That was to dodge Vic, I suppose."

"Not to mention bill collectors," Lulu said wearily. "Listen. He may be a bum, but he's not a murderer. And I'm not going to sit with folded hands and let you or anybody else call him one. No matter what. If I knew where to find him, I would. Do you believe me?"

"Yes," said Martin truthfully. His heart was thumping with excitement and triumph. The lever was working—on Lulu, never mind Bob—working better and more easily than he had dared to hope. He knew he was on the right track now.

"All right. Then here's something else for you to believe—"

The damn doorbell rang. They froze, staring at each other: Lulu lifting her brows in inquiry, Martin shaking his head and signaling silence. He was not going to answer, whoever it was.

Unless it was Bob? Once the possibility sprang up in his mind, he could not ignore it. He crept over to the window and peered out—straight into the face of Vic Holm, who had stopped ringing the doorbell and was now gripping the iron window bars in order to peer in.

Martin heaved a sigh—of regret, relief, which?—before he went to the door and opened it.

13

Vic breezed in, authoritative as ever, completely unabashed by the less than enthusiastic reception. "Hi, Lulu. Have a good cruise?" He gave her a perfunctory hug. "I found the note you left for Thelma. That's how I knew you were here. Forgive me for barging in on your little heart-to-heart with Martin, but something tells me it involves the Holms. Husband's intuition, I guess you'd call it."

Murderer's intuition was what Martin would call it. Vic was no fool: he must have sensed Martin's suspicions from the beginning, just as he must know now that time was running out. He could not risk any unsupervised heart-to-hearts; he had to know where he stood—not only with Martin, with everyone else too—in order to know what to do next. If he could not dodge disaster, he could at least meet it with his eyes open. It was odd, how much Martin knew about him in some ways. And how little, in others. For instance, did Vic even want to dodge disaster? It might be what he had craved all along, the destruction of himself, his true motive for destroying Enid. When the showdown came, would he welcome it? Or turn on Martin and fight for his life? He was a violent man, never mind the surface effect of calm security. And, unless Martin was way off course, he would soon be a desperate man, with nothing to lose.

He may kill me, Martin thought. He may very well kill me.

Meanwhile, here he sat in Martin's easy chair, legs stretched out, hands clasped behind his head, looking comfortable as a cat. "It's a funny thing, Lulu," he said sociably, "but Martin seems to get in on all the Holm family crises. I don't know whether Thelma's had time to fill you in on the latest installment or not—"

"She has," said Lulu. "And Martin's gone on from there. Congratulations on your intuition. You're involved in it, kid. Up to your neck, if you ask me."

"Sounds ominous." Vic smiled lazily. "You going to sue me for punching your poor little defenseless brother in the jaw? He had it coming. Now he knows what he's in for when he starts messing around with somebody else's wife."

"You're a fine one to talk. But don't get me started on that. It's not the point, anyway. A punch in the jaw—what's a little thing like that, compared with being accused of murder? Yes, you heard right. Murder. Martin thinks he killed Enid, don't ask me why or how, and..."

"Martin?" said Vic incredulously. He looked ready to burst out laughing; his eyes flicked toward Martin and away again, as if they shared a private joke.

Martin cleared his throat. "Now let's keep the record straight, Lulu. I didn't actually accuse Bob of murder. But I do think he knows something about Enid's death, and I want to find out what. Time enough after I hear his story to decide whether or not I believe it and whether or not the police ought to hear it too."

"He might even tell you the truth," said Vic thoughtfully. "Scare him enough, and he probably will."

"That's what I'm counting on. The trouble is that so far I haven't been able to get hold of him. He moved last night, without leaving any forwarding address. Apparently one visit from you was enough."

"Yeah. I really fixed things, didn't I?" Again Martin caught the gleam of secret amusement in his eye. "Far be it from me to say a good word for a rat like Bob but honest to God, Martin, you're wasting your time trying to hang Enid's murder on him. I will admit, it's a lovely idea. Unfortunately, it won't work."

"Of course it won't," said Lulu. "I've been telling you the same thing. All right, I'm his sister, maybe I'm prejudiced, but Vic isn't. If he could help hang anything on Bob, don't worry, he'd do it. Nothing would please him more. You've got his word for it too. What more do you want?"

"Well, for one thing, I want to know how you can be so sure, both of you. If you haven't seen your brother in two years, how do you know what he's been up to? Same goes for Vic. He and Bob were barely acquainted, might not even have recognized each other if they'd met in the street. And that wasn't exactly a friendly call he paid on Bob last night. Yet he's firmly convinced Bob had nothing to do with Enid's death. So I want to know how Bob convinced him. It must have been a damn good story, and I want to hear it. One other thing, Lulu. I want to know what you were about to tell me when you were so rudely interrupted by the doorbell."

"You were about to tell Martin something?" Vic preserved his relaxed attitude. All the same, there was a difference, a sharpening of eye and tone. "Don't let me stop you. Or is it a secret?"

"Not from you," Lulu snapped back. "Are you going to tell him or am

I? Because that's how it is. Sure I was going to tell him. You would too, if it was your brother."

"You flatter me. If it was my brother I'd have smothered him at birth. But not you. Not do-gooder Lulu. No cause too lost for you, is there?"

"Yes, there is. People like you." Lulu was on her feet, hopping mad, and sputtering like a feisty little dog tackling an enemy twice her size. "You're too selfish to live, Vic Holm. I always thought so, and now I know it. There's not one single solitary thing you care about except yourself. Never was and never will be. Selfish. Ungrateful. I may be a dimwit and a do-gooder, but you know as well as I do where Thelma would be if it hadn't been for me. Did you ever lift a finger to help her? Ha!"

"Okay, you've been a good friend to Thelma. I'm not denying it, and I appreciate it, incredible as it may seem to you. But don't forget, it worked both ways. You used Thelma as a cover-up, took advantage of her hospitality—and mine, without my knowing it—to sneak in your damn fool errands of mercy. And that I don't appreciate. You knew I wouldn't stand for it, that's why you did it behind my back. Don't talk to me about being selfish. Look at the mess you've got everybody into with your big-hearted lies."

"My lies! What about you, telling the police there was nothing going on with you and Enid? You were lying your head off. I didn't think so then, and Thelma still doesn't, but—"

"But now you know." Vic waved his hand wearily. "Look, Lulu, you and I could go on sniping at each other forever and get no place. If you're going to tell Martin, tell him and get it over with."

"I'll be glad to." She whirled toward Martin, eyes flashing with tears, firm little front heaving. "All right. You want to know how I can be so sure about Bob. In the first place, it hasn't been two years since I saw him. As you've no doubt gathered. I meant to keep my word to my husband, but then Bob called me and I couldn't quite bring myself to cut him off... It was only money, and he swore he'd never ask me again. Of course he did. Thelma's known about it for quite a while, and after she moved here— It was her idea, she offered to. Bob would call her when he wanted to get in touch with me, and then she'd tell Vic we were going to the movies or something so I could nip off and meet him. She understood how I felt. It wasn't really hurting anybody, only I didn't dare let my husband know because he has this thing about Bob. Well." She drew a deep breath and burst out with it. "Well, the last time I saw him was the night Enid was killed. That's how I can be so sure."

"I see," said Martin. He looked at Vic, who was sitting forward in his chair now, staring at his feet. "And you didn't want your husband to find out, so you told the police you spent the whole evening in the Holms' apartment. In fact, all three of you lied to the police, because Vic and Thelma must have known you went out."

"Vic didn't," Lulu said quickly. "He went upstairs to bed right after dinner. We'd spent the afternoon at the beach, and the sun made him dopey. Besides, Thelma got started drinking, and when that happens he never sticks around if he can help it. Thelma did know. At least she knew I was planning to go out. We'd fixed it up between us to tell Vic our usual story, and then I'd leave her at the movies and slip off to see Bob. Only when the time came she was passed out. With Vic asleep upstairs, I figured it was safe, so I went anyway. It must have been about a quarter of ten when I left for 57th Street—Bob and I had arranged to meet at a bar up there—and I suppose it was about midnight when I got back. I remember Thelma was still laid out on the living room couch, but when I started undressing her she came to and reached for the bottle again. What a hassle! It's a wonder Vic didn't wake up."

"Not me," said Vic, with a one-sided grin. "I took a sleeping pill, just to make sure. I knew nothing about Lulu's excursion until Bob told me last night. As he'll tell you, if you still insist on tracking him down."

"But there's no point now, is there?" cried Lulu anxiously. "Bob's in the clear! No point in going to the police either. Surely you're satisfied now!"

Martin opened his mouth and shut it again. It was Vic who answered her, and he sounded not at all bitter—on the contrary, mild, even rather affectionate. "Lulu, Lulu, what about me and my alibi? It's blasted wide open."

"But nobody's accusing you of murder!"

"Nobody was. Maybe nobody will, but I doubt it. Our friend Martin isn't the type to shirk his civic duty. He's known all along that Enid and I were back together again. Now he knows I could have sneaked over here and killed her and sneaked back home with nobody the wiser. That's all he needs."

"I see," said Lulu. She sat down suddenly. "But I couldn't help it, Vic! I had to tell him!"

"Sure. Besides, he could be right. For all you know, he is."

"He can't be," she whispered. "If it had ever occurred to me, if I'd thought for one minute—I wouldn't have lied, no matter what."

"You didn't know then that I was back with Enid," Vic pointed out.

"All right, but I know now, and I still don't believe that you—that you—" She stared at him for a moment, then at Martin, then down at her sun-tanned, rosy-tipped hands. "Why should you?"

"Well, now, let me see. A lovers' quarrel, I expect. Right, Martin?"

Martin heard himself saying, explosively, "I want to talk to you. Alone." Nobody else's business. A private matter between him and Vic.

They both looked at Lulu, who stood up as suddenly as she had sat down.

"Yes. All right." There was a miniature clashing of charm bracelet as she fumbled for her purse. But once at the door she stopped, undecided, perhaps frightened.

"Don't worry," said Vic. "I'm not dangerous."

"I was thinking about Thelma. It will all come out, won't it, about her and Bob?"

"Unless I can head Martin off, yes. And about you and Bob. That's your problem. Thelma and I will have to cope with our own. If you don't mind."

"I get it. 'Lulu Go Home.'" Her husky voice roughened. Almost broke. "Nothing else to do, I guess. If Mac's going to hear it anyway, better from me than otherwise. The worst part is Thelma..."

"She'll find your note when she gets home. I left it there. She'd probably call Martin anyway. I told you he gets in on all our family crises. So long, Lulu. Good luck."

"You too." This time her voice really did crack. Nothing left of it but a squeak. She shoved the door open and rushed out.

"Now," said Vic. He leaned back, once more assuming the classical attitude of relaxation: legs stretched out, hands clasped behind his head. "Before we get down to business, congratulations on the way you wangled the truth out of Lulu. Very neat. You could make a fortune on the state, boy. Damn near had me believing you suspected Bob. How did you happen to hit on that angle?"

"Rosemary. She does suspect him. That's how last night looked and sounded to her. I had to do some fast talking to keep her from going to the police right after lunch. So it wasn't really an act. One way or another, Lulu was going to be pressured into blasting your alibi. Yours and Thelma's, if you want to get technical."

"Not much point, is there? Thelma was in no shape to know what anybody else was doing, let alone do anything herself. We can rule her out and concentrate on me. I've had your vote from the start, haven't I? May I ask why?"

"Because Enid told me you might kill her. She foresaw what was going to happen, and it did."

The slanting light of late afternoon—that hazy, sad, religious light—struck the lower part of Vic's face, leaving his eyes cavernous and shadowy. The backward tilt of his head now seemed defenseless; Martin saw the chords in his neck tighten and felt a corresponding strain in his own throat. He went over to the bar and poured out two shots. When he turned around Vic was sitting forward, head bent, hands dangling between his knees. "Thanks." He took the glass and stared at it absently. "But if she was afraid I might kill her..."

"I don't think she was afraid. She said if you ever did, it would be because she needled you into it." The words were Enid's own, and with them came an image of her in the brilliant-colored robe she had worn that night, preening herself like a bird, shamelessly playing Martin against Vic.

"She did?" Vic's eyes were fixed on his, searching, even now jealously intent on sharing whatever there was to be remembered about Enid. "When? How come she told you a thing like that?"

"The night I met you for the first time. Up at her place. You remember. You were going to the theater—" Vic nodded impatiently. "Well, that was when. We sat out on the terrace drinking brandy. She'd already told me a good deal about you. I don't know how come, maybe just because I was available. And lonesome, too. Anyway, we used to have these sessions. She'd talk about you, and I'd talk about Joyce."

"Who's Joyce?"

"My wife. She—died, a couple of years ago. Suddenly."

"Oh. I didn't know. Sorry. So you think Enid needled me into killing her."

"I think she refused to marry you. That was what you wanted. But she didn't, anymore. It was different from Philadelphia. When you told me she'd agreed to marry you, you were just wishing. Well, not just wishing. You were also trying to cover up your motive."

"Got everything figured out, haven't you?" Vic discovered the drink in his hand; very thoughtfully, he took a sip. "All right. Let's say I had a motive. As far as you're concerned, that must clinch the case. Enid's premonition, motive, and now—thanks to Lulu—opportunity. What are you waiting for? If I had that much on you, believe me, I wouldn't be sitting here talking to you. I'd have gone to the cops long ago. Why the hell didn't you?"

Why indeed? It was going to sound ridiculous to Vic; the mixture of candid curiosity and contempt in his face made that clear. Martin felt himself flushing. "Because I promised Enid," he said curtly. "I'm sure a little thing like a promise wouldn't stop you, you'd have told the cops anyway. That's the difference between you and me."

"One of the differences. I'd never make such a promise in the first place. Unless you didn't take it seriously, this premonition of hers, or whatever you call it—"

"I took it seriously, all right. If I'd had my way she wouldn't ever have seen you again after that night. She knew herself it was a mistake."

"That's what you say. She went on seeing me, didn't she? In spite of wise old Father Martin's advice."

"Unfortunately, yes." Martin's slow burn suddenly broke into a blaze. "Damn it, can I help it if she elected me father confessor? I never wanted any part of any of this. You and Thelma and your domestic crises. I didn't ask her to land on my doorstep the other night and take her hair down. No, and I didn't ask to get in on that hassle you had with Bob. But I did get in on it, and now I'm stuck with it. I know too much. My God, how can I back out now?"

"It's your kind face. Your sympathetic nature. People can't resist opening their hearts to you."

"Can't resist lying to me, you mean. I'm not quite the idiot you and Thelma take me for."

"Thelma?" Vic switched off his comfortably derisive smile; he took another sip of his drink.

"Of course Thelma. Just give me enough time, and eventually I get the pitch, even with an expert like Thelma. No, expert's not the right word. She's been lying out of desperation, frantically trying to cover up for you. Because she must have guessed it was you from the beginning and God help her she loves you. So she lied about herself and Bob. Actually, I fed her her lines. All she had to do was feed them back to me."

Vic waited, watching him steadily.

"The affair with Bob was a myth. It's perfectly obvious now what was going on between them. He wasn't romancing her, he was blackmailing her. In a modest way. He didn't dare push too hard, because it was to his own interest, as well as everybody else's, to keep his mouth shut about the night Enid was killed. He didn't want Lulu's husband finding out she was still giving him handouts; it would mean the end of the handouts, and in the long run Lulu was his best bet. On the other hand, he couldn't quite pass up the chance to put the bite on Thelma for a little extra, especially with the lifeline to Lulu temporarily disconnected while she was off on her cruise."

"Pretty shaky grounds for blackmail, if you ask me."

"Very shaky. He knew better than to try it on you. But it worked with Thelma. She was too scared to tell you—she couldn't bring herself to admit she suspected you of murder. And too scared to call Bob's bluff—she couldn't be sure it was a bluff, he might talk, out of spite if nothing else. She did what he counted on her doing. She panicked and paid."

"To cover up for me," Vic murmured. "Because God help her she loves me. You're right, you know. She does. God help us both." He got up and prowled aimlessly about the room. Finally he stopped in front of Martin. But what he said was, after all, a triviality. "You didn't tell Lulu. About the blackmailing business. Evidently Thelma didn't either."

"Nor you."

"No. She's not a bad little Indian, you know. In spite of everything."

"She should have been a missionary," said Martin, and there they were, smiling at each other in one of their flashes of comradeship. Once more he felt the inner swing, like a pendulum, between like and dislike, trust and mistrust, rapport and antagonism.

"I'm going to keep my promise to Enid," he said. "Whatever else I tell, it won't be that."

"I know it. What do you want, a vote of thanks?"

"No, I want you to understand. I want to explain..." The face above him, the deceptively open face, the strange, hazy eyes—friend or enemy, what was the difference? The bond between them remained. "It's because of Joyce."

"Joyce? Oh yes, your wife. How do you mean, because of her?"

"They said I killed her. Her family. They don't think it was an accident. They said I pushed her."

"I see," said Vic gravely. "So that's why. You know how it feels."

"I know how it feels. I know you can love somebody and still want to kill them."

Vic licked his lips. "Well. And did you? Kill her, I mean?"

"I don't know," said Martin, as he had said—how long ago?—to Enid; as he had almost said to Rosemary. "They said I pushed her, and I could have. I'm not sure I didn't. I simply don't know."

("That's impossible," Enid had told him irritably. "Of course you know. Of course you didn't kill her. You've worked yourself into a guilt complex brooding about it. It's exactly like you." Rosemary would have said much the same thing. You and your soul searching, Rosemary would have said.)

But Vic understood that it was possible. That was part of the bond between them: they both knew all about guilt. He nodded. His hand even reached out in what might have been a gesture of compassion. An uncompleted gesture. The next instant the pendulum took another swing, and he was turning away, once more arrogant and mocking.

"For a guy who doesn't know what he did himself, you're awfully damn sure about me. You get the benefit of the doubt but I don't. Is that right?"

"Right. I've stretched all the points I'm going to. I intend to keep my word to Enid, but that doesn't mean her murderer gets away with it."

"I could keep you from going to the cops, you know." Casually, Vic took a gun out of his pocket and put it on the end table beside him. There it lay, blunt-nosed and loaded with death, between the ashtray and Martin's breakfast coffee cup.

Martin swallowed hard. "You won't get away with killing me, either.

Too many other people know too much. Lulu, for one."

"I might figure it was worth it anyway. Did you ever think of that?"

"I'd rather not," Martin said, and—incredibly—a grin flickered between them. "There's the doorbell. Do I answer it or not?"

"It's Thelma." Vic's face suddenly looked haggard. Between urgent peals of the bell her voice reached them, excitedly calling Martin's name.

"Go ahead," said Vic. "Let her in."

14

"Vic!" She whipped past Martin and skidded to a stop in the middle of the room. Her bangs were plastered to her forehead with sweat; the rest of her hair, never very firmly anchored, straggled about her face. She was out of breath—she must have run all the way—and her eyes looked like a frightened horse's. "Lulu told me," she panted. "She was there when I got home, she came back for her bag, and she told me— It's not true? Martin? You're not going to—"

"It's true." Vic got up and led her over to the couch. Then he went back to his own post. Beside the gun. Had she seen it? No. She had eyes for nothing but Vic. "You did your best for me, Thelma, but it's no use lying anymore. Martin's got everything figured out."

She doubled over, as if in physical pain, pressing her head against her knees; Martin saw the ridges of her knuckles as she gripped the edge of the couch. When she straightened up, the miracle had been achieved: she was in control of herself. "I'd like a cigarette," she said, and Martin sprang to light one for her. "Thanks. Sit down and listen to me, Martin. I can't let you do this. It's terrible. A terrible mistake. First of all, there's a difference between lying and just not mentioning something. Isn't there? Well. That's all Lulu and I did when they asked us, you know, about that night. We just didn't mention that she went out to meet Bob. Not on Vic's account, believe me, but on Lulu's. It never even crossed our minds that—"

"I said it's no use." Vic seemed to be speaking between clenched teeth. "He knows you weren't having an affair with Bob. It was blackmail. Lulu doesn't know it, but he does. I told you, he's got everything figured out."

Her eyes closed briefly, then opened wide. They looked deep and dark as the ocean. "All right. Yes. I did lie about that." Her face trembled into a smile. "You gave me the idea, Martin. Just as you gave Bob the blackmailing idea. You and Rosemary. When he went back to The Peacock to get his sketch pad and you were still there. That's when it started, that's when he got off on the Enid project."

"But you were there with him earlier. He must have already made his pitch for money."

"For a loan, a nice, innocent little loan to tide him over while Lulu was away. That's all it was when he called me the first time and I agreed to meet him. I couldn't let him come to the apartment, you see, because Vic didn't know about his arrangement with Lulu. Then we ran smack into you and Rosemary and I had to say something, so I made up the murals, Bob White instead of Black, don't tell Vic, it's a surprise." She pulled dreamily on her cigarette. "But it was a different story, after he went back to get his sketch pad. He had something else in mind. Oh no, it wasn't just an innocent little loan anymore."

No, it wouldn't be, thought Martin. He remembered the careful way Bob had set down his glass when Enid's name was mentioned; his own obscure alarm at having mentioned it; Rosemary's sigh: "I wish I hadn't talked so much." What a package of goodies they had handed Bob! How his heart must have leapt when he heard about everybody's alibis and realized what he could do to two of them! He had not made the connection before; why should he? The newspaper accounts of Enid's death named no names. Lulu, the Holms, Martin—all had been lumped together as "the dead woman's friends," who had produced no leads when questioned by the police.

"He didn't come out with it right away," Thelma was going on. "Not until after he'd tried pumping everybody he could think of. All he did that first night was drop a few hints. About Vic and Enid. It was enough for me. I knew what he was working up to and I couldn't face it. All I could think of to do was have another drink, get lost, disappear, not be there next time he called. It didn't work, of course. You always have to come back and face everything. I took the long way round, I stopped here first. Crazy, isn't it, but I had this notion that I might even be able to tell you the truth. Only—"

"Only I gave you the idea for another lie, so you told me that instead."

"And you sent me home with Vic. And Bob called the next day and I pawned my jewelry and paid him. Yesterday? It seems so much longer ago." She looked down at her outstretched hands. Her diamond, and her wedding band, which had been missing at lunch, were now back in place. "I redeemed them this afternoon. That's where I went after Lulu came. After lunch. It was fun, wasn't it? We had a good time, didn't we?"

"You had a good time lying," said Martin. Too good a time. She would have done better to omit the innuendos against Bob. For they had precipitated this crisis. Without them to trigger Rosemary into action—threatened action—and through her Martin, he might still be dragging his feet and searching his soul. But surely not for much longer? No, of course not. The pressure of all he knew and suspected would have forced him (even him, a reluctant hunter if there ever was one) into cornering his quarry, one way or another. No escape, for either Vic or him.

Or for Thelma. What could she do but go on lying? That had been the point of the luncheon party—to find out what Martin and Rosemary made of the night before and tailor her lies to fit. It must have given her a nasty shock to learn that they knew who Bob really was. But she had carried on. Was carrying on now. Would continue to carry on, as long as she had the breath left to lie with.

"Lying, yes. But in a good cause," she said, and sent a glowing look across the room to Vic.

He received it impassively.

Martin felt his temper rising. "A good cause. For God's sake, Thelma! You must have suspected Vic yourself or you wouldn't have paid Bob off."

"Why must I? Why couldn't I have been looking out for little old me? Vic wasn't the only one that would be left without an alibi if Bob talked. And when it comes to motive, I had more reason for wanting her dead than Vic had. He loved her. I—hated her." She lingered over the word, cherishing it. "I knew, of course. Vic didn't have to tell me. When I saw her at that press party, I knew how it was going to be. And it was. Oh yes, if anybody had a motive it was me."

"It's not quite that simple," Martin began, "because Enid wasn't—"

But Vic cut in unceremoniously. "This is all beside the point. Nobody's going to take you seriously, Thelma, motive or no motive. You were falling down drunk that night. In no shape to do anything yourself or know what I did. How many times do I have to tell you it's no use trying to convince Martin? He won't believe a word you say. Neither will I."

"No?" She smiled off into space. "You don't believe I hated her? Your beautiful little brainy little bitch?"

"So you hated her. I said motive or no motive."

"Yes. Falling down drunk, you said. That isn't like you, Vic. You always used to call it my drinking problem. My dear departed drinking problem. I was in unusually good form that night, wasn't I? It was an inspired performance."

There was a brief, twanging silence. Then Martin said, "So that's your pitch, is it? You weren't really drunk. Just putting on an act."

"You think I couldn't have?" She sprang up, smiling mischievously. For a moment only: all at once her face sagged into drunken vacuity, her eyes went bleary, her legs rubbery. She lurched and mumbled and finally melted back onto the couch, head lolling, toes up, wrists boneless. No doubt about it, she looked plastered. "Just a sample. I can do even better when I put my mind to it. Sometimes, of course, it was for real. It always was, at first. But then I discovered how easy it was to fake it, and how convenient... You see what a terrible mistake you're making, Martin? It doesn't have to be Vic. It could just as easily have been me."

"Maybe the police will buy that. I won't," said Martin stubbornly.

"Neither will I," Vic said, but after a noticeable pause. And he was watching her with peculiar intensity. Suddenly, violently, he smacked his hands down on the arms of his chair. "Stop trying to help me! Do me a favor and stop this crazy lying! Martin thinks I killed her and that's the end of it. He knows more than he's told you—"

"What? What hasn't he told me? I have a right to know."

"For one thing, he knows you can want to kill somebody you love. For another, he knows—he's figured out a whiz of a motive, especially for me. And just to make everything perfect, he knows that Enid halfway expected me to kill her. She had no secrets from wise old Father Martin. He had none from her. And they always kept their promises to each other."

"She told him you were going to kill her?" Thelma gave an ugly laugh. "Yes. Typical. Exactly like her, to frame you in advance."

"That's not true." Martin and Vic said it in unison, once more trapped into uneasy collaboration. Vic went on, in a withering-cold voice. "Nobody's interested in your views on Enid. You don't know a damn thing about her or how she felt about me."

"Oh, don't I!" The color blazed up in Thelma's face. "It's beyond my ken, is it, this immortal love of yours and Enid's, too sacred for the likes of me. She wasn't going to marry you! That's how much she loved you. She wouldn't have you as a gift! If you want to know how..." She gulped into silence, like a child frightened by the force of her own tantrum. Her brief, costly triumph was turning visibly into terror. Vic had risen deliberately, and now towered over her; she shrank back against the couch cushions as if she expected him to hit her.

"Yes," he said softly, "I'm very much interested in how you happen to know that. I never told you."

But he must have. Must have confessed everything to her, knowing that he could count on her loyalty, even in the face of murder. No wonder she was terrified at having lost her temper and blurted out the confirmation of what Martin knew anyway, the "whiz of a motive" he had figured out for Vic.

"Martin told you, didn't he?" Vic demanded, still softly. "It's his theory. Of course. That's how you know. Thelma?"

She had never looked more vulnerable, more openly at the mercy of her feelings than in that long moment of hesitation while she stared up at Vic, loving him, fearing him as much as she feared for him. Then her eyes shifted to Martin, and the scales were tipped. She shook her head. "Enid told me," she whispered. "Now will you believe it was me, not Vic?"

Without a word Vic turned on his heel and went back to his chair. He sat down heavily. He waited, poker faced.

"I don't—I—" Stop stuttering, Martin told himself. You knew it was coming. Knew she was going to pull a phony confession act if she couldn't find any other way to clear Vic. It is a phony. She's lying her head off. As usual. And Vic's letting her. The bastard. "You tell me, Vic," he said. "Should I believe her?"

"No!" Vic himself seemed startled by the one vehement word he had loosed. His voice sank to a murmur. "No. Of course not. Impossible."

"Why is it impossible?" cried Thelma. "You were sound asleep upstairs. Lulu left without your hearing her. How do you know I didn't go out too?"

"Are you saying you did? Because if I thought you killed her, Thelma, so help me, I'd—"

"Kill me?" she began to laugh hysterically. "Yes, kill me, I'd wind up like her, murdered, it's been happening all my life, I take on other people's afflictions... It's such a funny word to use for being murdered, isn't it? Affliction? Like calling war the recent unpleasantness..."

"Sh," said Martin. He gave her a little shake, and she subsided. "Okay, maybe it's not a physical impossibility. You could have faked the drunk act and gone to see Enid that night. You've got no more of an alibi than Vic has. But you've got no motive, either. If what you claim is true—that she told you she wouldn't have Vic as a gift—then why on earth should you kill her? You had nothing to fear from her. She wasn't going to break up your marriage. So why—"

"No, she did that four years ago," said Thelma bitterly. "I wouldn't admit it at the time, but she did, she reduced it to rubble, and even that wasn't enough for her. This time it was going to be Vic himself. I couldn't stand it, I couldn't—I'd do anything for him, I'd even give him up, and all she did was sneer. Don't you see? It wasn't just sneering at me, it was Vic too, it was everything I've lived for." She paused, and finished in a different, hushed tone, "So cruel. Oh, she had such a mean tongue."

And that at least was true. Martin could imagine the scene—fictitious though it surely was; look at the glaze of self-hypnosis in Thelma's eyes—in all its galling detail. Enid would have shown no mercy; she had a sure instinct for the word that would cut deepest. A way, as Vic had said, of belting you with things just when you were in no shape to take them. And Enid herself: I never do the right thing except at the wrong moment.

All right. But it took some doing to go on and imagine Thelma snatching up the knife and ramming it home. Violence was Vic's native land; Thelma lived in a world of devious side steppings and labyrinthine lies. This last tale was only more of the same. No matter how adroitly she twisted the facts, Vic's motive remained stronger than hers. She had said it herself only a moment ago: she would do anything for him. Even to giving him up. Even to confessing to his crime. And there he sat, not only letting her do it, but threatening to kill her if she made it convincing enough.

It was probably an idle threat, intended as clinching proof of Vic's innocence. One more stroke in the image he was trying to project of himself as Enid's avenger instead of her murderer. And yet...

As if he sensed the trend of Martin's thoughts, Vic switched on the table lamp beside him, dispelling the shadows of dusk. The gun sprang into view; Thelma saw it and stiffened.

"I'm prepared, you see," he said. "I have been, ever since Enid was murdered. I don't care what she was or what she was going to do to me. I just want to get my hands on whoever killed her." He caught Martin's eye on him, and smiled his sudden, warm smile. "No exceptions. Not even myself. But then I've never suspected myself. I leave that to you, Martin."

Martin sat silent and unsmiling, reminding himself that he had invited this sort of double-edged crack (and a pretty good one, too) when he chose to confide his own secret guilt to Vic. Chose? He had no choice; circumstances, and the fitful, ghostly comradeship between him and Vic had combined to draw it out of him. The ultimate in foolish futility: he had experienced no healthful catharsis, and Vic had certainly not responded with an outpouring of his own. But then Martin had not expected anything like that. Vic was too cagey. And too arrogant even to bother denying his guilt. This was as close as he had come to it.

"I'm not afraid, Vic," said Thelma with calm assurance. "You won't kill me. Because—"

"Because he knows you didn't do it," Martin broke in. "Nobody better. No. That would be carrying the bluff a bit too far. Even for him."

Neither of them took any notice; once more Vic was watching her with that strange fixity. It did not unnerve her. She met it with a steady, challenging stare of her own. "Because I'm the one you really love. Me. Not her. If I hadn't known that, I would have let you go, four years ago. Because I'm the one that really loves you too. She didn't. You were just the Great Might-Have-Been to her. That's all. She couldn't forgive you for staying with me. She was going to get even with you if it killed her. And it did, it did. Martin's right, you know. If I hadn't killed her you would have."

"No!" Again Vic loosed the single violent word. It throbbed and died away. He went on hoarsely, "You're lying. That's where Martin's right. You're lying to get me off the hook. It's all a lot of—"

"You want me to prove it? All right then, I will." She sprang up, so white-faced and trembling, with such a wild blaze in her eyes, that Martin and Vic jumped to their feet in alarm. "You think I didn't hate her enough? You don't know, oh, you don't know... I'll show you. Look. Come on. Both of you." She darted across to the window sill where three of Enid's potted plants still sat, waiting to be transplanted. Snatching up the begonia, she turned and thrust it at Vic. "Here. See for yourself."

"See for myself? It's just a plant of some kind, a what-do-you-call-it—"

"Oh, is it! Is it! You don't believe it's special, the only one of its kind. It doesn't show till you pull it up. You think I'm crazy, don't you? So humor me. Pull it up."

"Oh, what the hell," said Vic, and wrenched the plant free of its pot. Dirt crumbled to the floor from the packed roots. Impatiently he gave it a little shake, and there was a different sound, a muted, metallic rattle.

They stared down at Enid's jade ring, missing no longer. After a moment Martin stooped and picked it up. He looked from Vic's drawn, blank face to Thelma's, which was set in a smile of terrible triumph. Above the roaring in his ears he heard her saying, "Now will you believe I killed her? You gave it to her. That's why I took it. I hid it here the night you came and got me, after Bob... I thought it was all up with me then. It never occurred to me anybody would suspect you. Or that you wouldn't... Vic!" Her voice rose sharply; she began stumbling backward in jerky, clumsy steps. "It was for you, Vic! I did it for you!"

Too late, Martin saw Vic's face, the ponderous lowering of his head, like a bull getting ready to charge. Too late, he made a grab for the gun; Vic's arm shot out and spun him halfway across the room to crash against the couch. When he picked himself up the gun was in Vic's hand and he was moving deliberately toward Thelma, who stood frozen in piteous, incredulous panic.

"Don't!" yelled Martin, and hurled the footstool. It smacked against Vic's shoulder. Harmlessly, but in the moment that he was off balance Thelma whirled and scrambled out into the hall. Instantly noise erupted: a dog's shrill barking, and a thready old voice vainly demanding quiet. Through the open door Martin saw the familiar figures of Bubbles and Mrs. Klein—the one rotund and fuzzy, the other frail and raincoated—just coming in the street door, blocking Thelma's way out.

That left the stairs; she fled up them at breakneck speed, as she must have fled down them that night—very fast, Mrs. Klein had reported, very hard—accompanied then as now by Bubbles' frantic racket.

It was hopeless, of course. Vic was already after her. Martin felt himself shoved aside and heard the thick, labored breathing and then the other, heavier footsteps. He watched from the foot of the stairs, rooted there in nightmare fascination. For he seemed to be not only spectator but actor. His own chest ached with the fury of pursuit; the stairs he was looking at dissolved into the rough, moonlit path to the quarry, along which he pounded, oblivious to everything but Joyce up ahead, in her disaster-green dress... Did it matter that there had been no gun in his hand? He could still have had murder in his heart.

"No," he whispered, and the path, the quarry, vanished; it was two other people on a stairway.

At the landing Thelma stopped running and turned to face Vic and the gun. In despair? She knew the stairway was a blind alley and she would be trapped at the top if not before. Or was it in hope? She might still believe that he loved her too much to kill her. Love her he must; or he would not have struggled so long and obstinately against the fact of her guilt. For unlike Martin, he knew that he himself was innocent. Yet he too had insisted she was lying. For his sake. Everything had been for him. If he could still kill her, knowing that, then...

Then the basis of her whole life was delusion, and Enid was the winner, after all.

For whatever reason, she stopped running and turned. Vic stopped too, arrested in mid-step; with one hand grasping the banister and his head tilted back, he seemed, illogically, the more defenseless of the two. On the landing Thelma waited, poised in unearthly tranquility. In the instant he fired, she lifted her arms, as if to embrace him and death, the two together. Then she toppled and slumped down in a graceless heap.

Behind Martin, Bubbles abandoned himself to complete hysteria, while Mrs. Klein offered a quavering obbligato: "Mr. Shipley, Mr. Shipley..."

He started up the stairs; Vic was already at the landing. "Don't come up here." He still had the gun; he gestured with it imperiously. "Stay away from me."

Martin stayed where he was.

"She's dead. I killed her. Martin, I—"

"I know," said Martin.

"Yes. All right. Then don't try to stop me." There he crouched, a murderer at last, but peremptory as always, a little contemptuous of Martin, and a little admiring. Behind the desolation in his eyes Martin caught the old flicker; once more they were drawn together in unlikely, unwilling rapport. “Don’t try to stop me,” Vic repeated.

“I won’t,” said Martin. He would have promised, even without the gun. There ought to be something more to say. But there wasn’t. He went back down the stairs.

The second shot came before he reached the door of his own apartment. He stopped, shivering, but not with surprise. He had known Vic was going to do it.

It was what he would have done, too, if he had killed Joyce.

THE END

The Troublemaker

Jean Potts

1

The cook had quit again that day, so it was once more unto the breach for Bax, who, after eight years as owner of Seaview Inn, was still frequently pleased and surprised at his own versatility. Cooking was the least of his hitherto unsuspected talents. He wouldn't go so far as to say he fully understood the plumbing and electrical systems, but he had come to terms with their idiosyncrasies. Most of the time he could keep them working. More or less. He was also fairly proficient at carpentering, plastering, general housework, even accounting....

Anyway, there he was, shucking corn outside the kitchen door, enjoying the afternoon sunshine, when he heard this voice behind him. "Any idea where I can find the manager? There's nobody at the desk."

Susie must have sneaked off again, as she so often did on fine days, especially now that she had caught the eye of one of the lifeguards at the beach. The handsome one. But then she didn't need the job, she was only filling in as a favor until Bax found a replacement for the original clerk, who had turned out to be a drunk of spectacular proportions.

"I'm the manager. Baxter Knight, at your service. Minor crisis in the kitchen, so I'm lending a hand." He stood up and smiled his genial host smile. It was genuine; he was predisposed to like people. If that turned out to be impossible, he still found them interesting. Some instinct warned him that the present specimen might fall into the latter class. Not that the man was unprepossessing. Quite distinguished, in fact. He looked to be about Bax's own age—mid-forties—a tall, well set up fellow with graying hair and beard. He wore dungarees, a T-shirt, moccasins. So far so good. Was it his smile that was off-putting? A forced, brief baring of teeth that did nothing to dispel the bleakness in his eyes.

Still, a customer was a customer. Bax twitched off his apron, brushed the corn silk from his hands, and started for the stairs that led up to the wide verandah with its porch swing and rocking chairs, all empty at the moment. "Sorry if you've been inconvenienced. Susie's probably just stepped away from the desk for a minute. Let's see what we can do about fixing you up with a room. I can give you a nice one on the front, with a view—"

"Wait," said the man. "That is. I mean. They told us down at the cove that you might possibly need some extra help."

"Oh? Oh, well, that's a different dish of tea, then, isn't it?" And a damn unexpected one, too, Bax might have added. He was used to the kids who came around looking for a job to tide them over till time for the next check from home. And to the handful of native "summer workers," who when they got fired from the other hotels and restaurants drifted his way because—his wife Janet was probably right—he was known as an easy mark. But this guy was neither a kid nor a local incompetent. He had the air of one used to authority. A business executive? Possibly, except for what must be his car, parked under the pines at the end of the driveway—a beat-up old Volkswagen with North Carolina license plates. Something in the academic line was more likely, Bax decided, and he ought to know: during the winters he taught drama at a small Connecticut college. He also decided to stall. That smile, or whatever it was about the man, that smacked of trouble.

"Well, now, let's see. What kind of work did you have in mind?"

"Anything," came the answer, so curt with embarrassment that Bax felt a pang of sympathy. He repressed it sternly. "You said a crisis in the kitchen. I could help out there. Or at the desk. Or yard work." He cast a disparaging glance at the stretch of weedy, stony lawn sloping down from the big old house. "My name is Quentin Leonard, by the way."

"Nice to meet you, Mr. Leonard," Bax said automatically. Then he got back to the stalling which should lead, as painlessly as possible, to the turn-down. "It's a minor crisis in the kitchen. Really. And I take care of the yard, not too well, maybe, but still. So I just don't ..."

His voice trailed off as he saw the girl who had gotten out of the Volkswagen and was coming up the drive. She seemed to glide along, after the unearthly fashion of a lady in a hoop skirt. Not that she was wearing anything of the sort. Tattered knee-length jeans, and a sad, crocheted garment on top. She was very slight, with long, boneless-looking arms and legs and a fragile, lily-stalk neck. The sun brought out muted gleams in her hair, which was long and pale brown; she wore it parted in the middle, twin loops against her round forehead, drawn back into a shining, straggling coil. There was a dreamlike quality about her, something legendary, haunting, that transcended the ordinary criteria of beauty. No, she was not beautiful. Yet Bax discovered that he was holding his breath. Snatches of long submerged poetry rose in his mind. He thought of enchanted princesses, of Helen and the topless towers of Ilium....

Then the moment, a strangely memorable one, was over. He became aware of Quentin Leonard's cold hawk eyes watching him, and of his voice saying, "Lisa dear, Mr. Knight. My wife, Lisa." Again the teeth-baring business, as if he knew the exact blend of surprise and skepticism with which Bax received this announcement, and were daring him to reveal it.

"How do you do, Mr. Knight," she said and held out her hand. It felt as languorous as it looked. Warm, though; a real, live hand. Amberish eyes, shallowly set between the roundness of forehead and cheekbones. A vague, fixed smile. By no means a flawless face. And yet. And yet.

"You were saying, Mr. Knight?" said Quentin Leonard. "If the kitchen and yard are out, how about the desk?"

"Well, you see, Susie—" I shouldn't be doing this, he thought helplessly; Janet's going to give me hell. "Well, as a matter of fact we might be able to work something out. Come to think of it, Susie's only filling in temporarily, so I suppose ..."

He picked the cocktail hour as the most favorable time to break the news to Janet. She had had a good afternoon with her sketch book out on the rocks, and was in an unusually mellow mood. Even so, she let fly with a certain amount of fireworks.

"Honestly, Bax. Honestly. I don't know what you could have been thinking of!" She cocked her neat dark head at him. Her eyes were snapping. "I met them on the stairs when I came in. There's obviously something eating on him. And that girl with him. She's his wife?"

"His wife," said Bax firmly. "Lisa. Her name's Lisa. I don't see why you're so sure he won't work out. Just because he's broke at the moment. It could happen to anybody, a run of tough luck like that, the car breaking down and all. I didn't have the heart to turn him down. After all, a fellow teacher."

"Doesn't he have any friends back there in North Carolina to help him out?" A good question. One that had occurred—but fleetingly—to Bax himself. "And anyway. Anyway, *them*, you said. You hired them. What's *she* going to do, pray tell?"

"We can always use somebody extra in the dining room. She's had experience, while she was in school, waiting tables during summer vacations. Uh. How about another martini?"

"Another thing," she said, holding out her glass. "You didn't have to give them the best room in the house. One of the best. People always want to be on the front, with a view. Paying customers, I mean. Look at the money we're losing. A cheaper room would have done them just as well."

"I know, but you see I'd already mentioned the front one, before I got the pitch on them. They seemed to take it for granted...."

"And you let them, of course. Couldn't bring yourself to disappoint them. A back room's good enough for me. And for you." They were in Bax's room at the moment; she flashed a withering look of disapproval around her. The place did seem a bit cluttered. Narrow to begin with, it had become more tunnel-like with each passing year's accumulation of furniture in varying states of disrepair (the broken-armed wicker rocker, the four-poster bed minus one post); books, magazines, theater programs; odds and ends (the bird cage, the stuffed raccoon, the coconut lamp) that were sure to come in handy some day. A disgrace, said Janet, whose own room next door was a model of orderliness. But then her closet was twice as big as Bax's; she had no need of the clothesline he had strung up between bed and transom. That made a difference. Sure it did.

He refilled their glasses and said hopefully, "We can switch them later, if we get jammed up with business. As long as the room's vacant anyway, it doesn't matter. He teaches literature. I can't remember the name of the college. I'm not sure he mentioned it. He's expecting a check—"

"Yes, you told me. He's not the one that worries me."

"Uh. You mean the girl? But dearie, you haven't even talked to her. You've just barely seen her."

"One look is all it takes," said Janet crisply. "I know a troublemaker when I see one. What's more I know you. I ought to, by this time. So don't bother with the wide-eyed innocent stare, Baxter, my boy. It's wasted on me."

"Jannie, you've got it all wrong...." But it was no use arguing with Janet; once she got hold of a notion, she wasn't going to let go, come hell or high water. Granted that she knew him—too well for everybody's good, he sometimes thought. Granted too that there had been a couple of little episodes in the past that probably justified this particular notion. All the same, it was an oversimplification to equate Lisa Leonard with those other "troublemakers." His reaction to them had been direct and single-minded; to Lisa it was far more complicated, ambiguous, even in an odd way impersonal. Try explaining that to Janet!

"Poor Bax," she was saying, with one of those lightning changes of mood that still took him by surprise. The sudden smile, too, as dazzling now as the day he first laid eyes on her. "And you had to cook again, too. While I was off having myself a fine afternoon. How about if I help in the kitchen now?"

He talked her out of that: she didn't always hit it off with the waitresses, too efficient herself to put up with their scatterbrained college-girl ways. "Everything's under control," he assured her. "I'll nip down in a minute or two, keep an eye out during dinner. Nothing to it."

So that was the extent of the fireworks. She had let him off fairly easy, he thought comfortably as, drink in hand, he made his way down the back stairs. All right, so there might be something eating on Quentin Leonard; they still had nothing to lose by taking a chance on him. God knows Susie was no bargain. As for Lisa being a troublemaker, well, check that off to the primeval distrust of one female for another. Bless them, incidentally, one and all. He paused to sip a solitary toast and felt the last of his own misgivings melt away in the sunny optimism that was the prevailing climate of his mind.

2

"I can't get over how lucky we are," Lisa said, as she had said—how many times?—during the course of the evening. "You know? Such a nice place. Such a nice room." She turned from the window, where she had been looking out at the water, rippling with lights from the cove, once more to gaze in wonder at their room. As if it were the ultimate in luxury, thought Quentin, instead of an ordinary bedroom in a seaside inn: iron bedstead, pink chenille spread, skimpy curtains, floor bare except for a worn little rug beside the bed, college dorm furniture spruced up with a coat of green paint, chipped washbasin in the corner.

Well. It beat sleeping in the Volkswagen. As for their luck, he had been watching Baxter Knight's face when Lisa got out of the car and came up the driveway. He knew why the job market at Seaview Inn had suddenly opened up.

And the knowledge rankled. It wasn't enough that he had had to grovel for work—yes, grovel; any kind of work, he had said, and the words still stuck in his throat—he had then been reduced to capitalizing on Lisa's appeal. Pimping. Or the next thing to it.

"I don't know about lucky," he said curtly. "It was your doing, really."

"Mine?" Her eyes went wide. "But I didn't do anything." True. It was never anything Lisa did. It was what other people did because of her. This whole fantastic trip was his idea, not hers; whatever came of it he had no right to blame her. Yet in the last couple of weeks he had become aware of resentment smoldering in him like an underground fire, resentment at the very quality—her passivity, her effortless, aimless way of gliding through life (as against the chatter and bustle of Grace's presence)—that had drawn him to her at first.

He was aware of it now. She looked so innocent, standing there in the sleeveless white shift she had put on for dinner, so innocent with her wistful smile, her quaint, high forehead and smoky-amber eyes. She was watching him rather anxiously, as if she sensed the resentment without in the least understanding it. As of course she did not, and never could: the humiliation their day's "luck" had cost him was totally beyond her comprehension. So was, or would have been if she had known about it, the joint account with Grace, which he would rather die than dip into.

For reasons that were as self-evident to him as they would have been baffling to Lisa.

The generation gap, he thought bitterly. Kids nowadays saw nothing wrong with begging on the streets, taking anything anybody was willing to hand out. They didn't have his age group's hang-ups on pride and self-respect.

And then there was that other shopworn phrase. Failure of communication. "You know?" Lisa was constantly saying, and sometimes he did know, but not because she had been able to tell him. She had no feeling for words, no skill in using them herself, no appreciation of the way other people used them. She did not read for pleasure. Did not read at all, if she could get out of it. Language was not a means of expression to her, it was an obstacle. She might not even think in words, but in music, color, sensation....

She had been singing the first time he ever saw her, sitting under one of the campus elms with a group of other students. Somebody was strumming the eternal guitar, and Lisa was singing one of those phony folk ballads. "There'll come a day, there'll come a day, when the wind blows through the grass."

Her light, soft voice, nicely suited to the simple-minded tune and words; the mellow haze of the autumn afternoon; his own pensive mood—all had combined to make him pause. He walked on at last, taking with him the image of her face. He found himself watching for her. She was in none of his classes, so he had to depend on chance glimpses of her. In those days she and Carlos Verdell were always together, strolling the campus, love-struck, absorbed in their private dream world. During their romance—it was Carlos's first and, if his mother had her way, his last—his grades plunged from straight A's to barely passing. When it ended, in February, he dropped out of college, and a month or so later all but dropped out of everything. Poor Carlos, no more able to cope with death than with life. He had been one of Quentin's favorite students, the kind of son he would like to have had. But by then the spell was cast for Quentin, too; chance glimpses were no longer enough, he was caught in the now-familiar pattern of lies and deceit, too enchanted with Lisa even to feel guilty. That was how he thought of her, as a kind of unwitting witch who had changed him from the reserved, steady college teacher he used to be into—

Into whatever it was he had become. Or might still become.

Yet he must have been ripe for it. Must have harbored unconscious yearnings for escape from the safe monotony of his life. Not always unconsciously: he remembered moments of near panic at what was happening to him, no heights or depths left, no challenge or excitement, nothing but the dead-level round, the predictability, the pettiness. Yes, he had sometimes felt as if he were trapped in a vacuum, with Grace forever burbling along in the background. He seldom listened to her anymore, and occasionally she realized it and did not seem to mind; she called him, fondly, the absent-minded professor. Emptiness, emptiness. An obscure hunger that could usually be eased by the lonely pleasures of books, music, his woodworking shop in the basement.

Lisa had shattered the vacuum. Was that at the root of his resentment?

The touch of anxiety was still there in her face. Now she put out her hand. A timid, futile gesture. "Is there something wrong?"

"Not a thing," he said between his teeth. "We're very lucky. God's in his heaven, all's right with the world."

"Yes. It's so nice here. You know? They're so nice, Mr. Knight and his wife. Everybody."

"Very nice." Though Baxter Knight was clearly none too sure about Seaview's new desk clerk. And Janet Knight—like any woman with a lick of sense—was all too sure about the new waitress. They were to take over their duties tomorrow. Tonight at dinner they had been guests at the Knights' table. Introductions all around, much friendly chitchat among the Knights and their other guests, a cheerful clink of silver and china. The dining room was big and many-windowed. Outside, in the tranquil, fading light, the trees trembled and sighed; a muted accompaniment to the sounds of dinner. Ah, dinner. Their first square meal in three days. Corn and chicken. Homemade relishes. Lemon pie and coffee. Lisa had come near to wolfing hers. In that comfortable atmosphere even Quentin had felt lulled, almost at ease for a little while.

"It's great, being so near the cove," Lisa said, as she kicked off her sandals. "That little drawbridge, and the art shops and all." They had walked down there after dinner, across the bridge to the cluster of lobster pounds, fishing shacks, hotels, restaurants, gift shops. Swarming with tourists and bicycles and cars. He had noticed a couple of North Carolina license plates. It figured, of course. Even this far north. Someday, any day, he supposed, they might run into someone who recognized them. One of those small-world episodes that happened all the time. That would set tongues to wagging back home. Maybe they were wagging already.

Not to Grace, though. At least, not up to the time of his last phone call to her. She had nattered on as usual, exactly as usual: her bridge club, her golf score, the latest round of cocktail parties. So far he had managed to be vague—but plausibly so—on the subject of addresses. He was moving on tomorrow. Destination undecided. It was true enough, as far as it went: he and Lisa had stayed no longer than a couple of days at any one place, and they had no fixed itinerary.

But now, thanks to the breakdown of his trusty old friend the Volkswagen, there was no money left for "gipsying." (That would be Grace's word for it. "Quentin's off gipsying. Yes, by himself. Getting it out of his system at last, he's been talking about it since I don't know when....") Now he would have to specify his whereabouts for the sake of the check which he had not expected to need at all, much less this desperately. Almost two weeks before it was due, so the Seaview business had damn well better work out. Meanwhile, he could still hold back the address for a while. Could, and would, until the last minute.

The address itself meant nothing—unless, of course, word somehow got around that Lisa happened to be there too. And there was no reason why it should, barring the always possible chance encounter with someone who knew them. Or ...

Lisa too made her weekly duty calls. Collect, like his to Grace. She had made one of them tonight, during the course of their stroll around the cove.

He took a step toward the window, where she was standing again, drinking in the view. His voice came out stiff, not as casual as he would have liked. "I forgot to ask before. Did you get through to Aunt Mabel all right?"

"What? Oh." She turned, her face still half-bemused. And guileless, guileless. "Oh, yes. No trouble at all." Another pause. Then she added, "She sounded kind of down. You know? I guess her arthuritis is bad again."

She always pronounced it that way. Arthuritis. It kept Aunt Mabel confined to her wheelchair out there in California, and it was one of her reasons for deciding to send Lisa to college in North Carolina, where Aunt Mabel had grown up. There had also been a boy friend, Quentin gathered, someone Aunt Mabel—who was Lisa's guardian, all the family she had—considered undesirable. As undesirable as Quentin himself? Possibly. He did not care to hear the details.

Once, at the beginning, he had asked Lisa what account of her trip she was putting out for Aunt Mabel's weekly consumption. He remembered her airy answer: Oh, just that she and a couple of other girls were driving up north, looking for resort jobs along the way to cover their expenses.

It was no more of a lie than the abridged version he produced for Grace. Surely he hadn't expected her to tell Aunt Mabel the truth? No. But he hadn't expected her to be quite so glib, either. And just now, when he asked about tonight's call—her blank expression, the momentary pause. Like one called back from a private dream world.

It was the phrase that had come to his mind before, the way Carlos and Lisa used to look, wandering the campus hand in hand. Absorbed in their private dream world. This time it conjured up an even sharper image of Carlos. Handsome. Lithe. Young. Soulful-eyed. Eating his heart out over Lisa. Not wanting to live without her. She had not seen him since that near-fatal bit of business. So she said. It would never have worked, anyway—so she said—not with Carlos's mother breathing down his neck.

"You okay, Quentin? You look so—"

"Did you give Aunt Mabel our address?"

She was silent a moment, searching his face for a clue to the right answer, the one that would meet with his approval. Not to be confused with the truth.

She shook her head No. A lie. He was sure of it.

"You told me not to," she explained virtuously. "Except the name of the town, of course. The operator always says what town, when it's a collect call." She gave him her dreamy half-smile and turned with her back to him. "Unzip me, please?"

What other lies might she be telling him? He had never heard her make any of her purported calls to Aunt Mabel. They could be to anyone. To Carlos. A weekly telephone rendezvous arranged between the two of them before the start of her secret excursion with Quentin. Surely it must be a secret from Carlos; he would never tolerate the truth. Was she deceiving both him and Quentin, then? Feeding Carlos her glib little story about the other girls, the resort jobs? It would work as well for him as for Aunt Mabel. They might be scheming their separate escapes—he from his mother, she from Quentin—waiting for the right moment to take off for whatever meeting place suited them best. Why not? Quentin was there to be used. Poor old Quentin, obsessed with her and his summer's idyll, he would not dare expose how he had been gulled. He had too much to lose.

Yes. No. Possible. Impossible. He watched his own hand grasp the zipper of her dress and slide it down. How fragile she was! The knuckles of her backbone showed; her shoulder blades were like rudimentary wings.

She is destroying me, he thought with cold detachment. And I still cannot leave her, I cannot let her go. What am I going to do?

She gave a sudden little shiver. Her head turned on its stalk, and their eyes met; hers were luminous, alive with what seemed to him an animal awareness.

"Lisa, Lisa," he whispered. He released his grip on her shoulders.

Later, in the sway-backed bed, she curled herself against him as she always did, warm and cat-cozy. When he shifted his arm to enclose her, she lifted her mouth to his. A tentative kiss that offered but did not insist. Tonight he did not respond: the thought of Carlos made it impossible, an open invitation to defeat.

She did not seem to mind. She settled back, stretched contentedly, and was presently breathing in the deep, purring way that meant she had dropped off into the enviable sleep of youth.

She could not be feigning that. Could she?

Quentin himself lay sleepless and tense, staring at the ceiling where shadows trembled and shifted, listening to the night sounds. The whispering of the trees. Footsteps in the hall. The slam of a car door. A muffled peal of laughter.

When he closed his eyes the image of Carlos was there waiting for him. Carlos and Lisa, Carlos and Lisa. Round and round they circled inside his aching head, sometimes fast, sometimes slow; either way he was powerless to turn them off.

3

Yes, Grace told the waitress in the coffee shop, Mr. Leonard was still away. Off gipsying. "He was some place up in New Hampshire when he called last week. No telling where he is by now. It's what he's always wanted to do, you know, just take off by himself—he's not like me, he likes being alone—just take off without planning where or how long or anything else for sure. You couldn't pay me to make such a trip." She laughed indulgently. "But there. That's what makes horse races. As I said to him, 'Quentin,' I said, 'I'm tired of hearing you talk about it, I wish to the Lord this summer you'd do it and get it over with.' Let me see, iced tea and—I know I shouldn't, but I just can't resist; I'm going to treat myself to a piece of cake, no, not the chocolate, the coconut layer...."

It was delicious. And she would make up for it tonight. Salad and Melba toast. For once she had no dinner engagement. This past month, since Quentin left, everybody had rallied around with invitations to keep her from being lonesome. She still missed him, of course. Quiet as he was, and getting more and more absent-minded—she declared, sometimes she wondered if he listened to a single word she said—all the same, it seemed strange without him to cook for, fuss over, talk to. But it was probably all for the best, this separate vacation of his, much as the idea had hurt her feelings at first. She was glad she hadn't let on how much. Hadn't tried to talk him out of it. It might be just what the doctor ordered. Quentin hadn't been all that easy to get along with this winter. So moody and irritable, even more so than usual, and—oh, she didn't know—remote, as if he didn't care about anything anymore. He needed a change, that was all. Things were going to look mighty good to him when he got back—job, home, friends, their whole comfortable way of life. Personally Grace saw very little wrong with it. Neither would Quentin, once he got his perspective back.

She lingered over her iced tea. It was nice sitting here in the air-cooled dimness, resting her feet after her afternoon of shopping. She still had half a mind to go back and take the beige linen, even if it was a trifle snug, maybe it would spur her on to watch her diet. The color was perfect with her new hair shade, and then it was marked down, such a bargain....

She didn't pay much attention to the three girls when they first came in, except to envy them their slim waists and flat behinds. But then, after they were settled in the booth in front of hers, she caught the name of Carlos Verdell. Naturally she pricked up her ears. Not that she was likely to hear anything she didn't already know about Carlos, not with his mother using Grace as a wailing wall the way she did. But the angle would be different: the girls were Carlos's age, college students from the look of them. As he was. Or used to be. Before he went all to pieces over Lisa and his broken romance.

That was the next name to crop up in the conversation on the other side of the partition. Lisa. "Just because Lisa's not around this summer, you think you've got a chance with him? Forget it. He doesn't know any of the rest of us are alive. When she hooks them, she hooks them good. It wouldn't surprise me if that's where he's gone, off looking for her. He'd do it in a minute if he had any kind of a line on where she is."

Grace could have told them different. Carlos was up in his cabin in the mountains, his favorite retreat when things got too much for him. A few days away from home and mother—no question about it, Rhoda could be wearing—seemed to have a calming effect on his nerves. He had always been high-strung. A brilliant student, until Lisa came along and took his mind off of everything else; such a handsome boy, too. But he was never one to mix much with the other kids. Certainly not with girls. That was probably why it was taking him so long to get over Lisa.

She missed the next few lines of conversation. A joke of some kind, judging from the giggling that was going on. "Stop, I can't bear it, it's too much," gasped one of the young voices. "No, I mean it, you shouldn't say such things. Nobody knows for sure. It could be just a coincidence."

"Yeah. A planned coincidence." This was the smart-alecky one. "Don't underestimate the old boy. It's the quiet ones that blow their tops.

Besides, I've seen him watching her. Don't try to tell me that gleam in his eye was academic. And I'm not the only one, I didn't start the talk that's going round. His wife may not have heard it, but everybody else has. I'll bet you anything you like they're shacked up together, Lisa and the honorable Mr. Leonard...."

After a while, when the twanging in her ears had let up a little, Grace collected her parcels, paid her check, and left. She did not glance at the girls, and maybe she only imagined that a thunderclap of silence struck them as she passed their booth. On the other hand, they may well have recognized her. It didn't matter.

Now she had heard it, too, the talk that must have been going round all month. The wife. Always the last to know. No wonder her friends had been so lavish with their invitations. Pity. Plus morbid curiosity: Did she honest-to-God not suspect, or was she just putting up a front? The coffee shop waitress, the salesgirls in the shops, the boy who delivered her groceries, the mailman—all with their friendly inquiries about Quentin, they too had been sounding her out, no doubt comparing notes behind her back.

Her face burned at the thought of how she had prattled on about Quentin's summer of gipsying. Her eyes felt dry and hot. The twanging in her ears—"Lisa and the honorable Mr. Leonard, Lisa and the honorable Mr. Leonard"—built up to another peak of electronic volume, sank and rose again. It was a moment before she could remember where she had parked the maroon convertible. (Hers. Quentin still clung to the beat-up old Volkswagen.) But the drive home, up the hill and past the campus, went all right. And there was the house, solid and reassuring, a pale green ranch-type with picture window and patio, in its neatly landscaped setting. The late afternoon sunshine slanted across the grass in tranquil shafts. For once even the mountain looming up in the background looked benign, veiled in heat haze.

She stepped inside, into her living room—avocado and chocolate brown, pimiento accents—and said aloud, "It's a lie. Not a word of truth in it. Quentin's my husband, I know him better than they do, those silly girls, I know him better than anybody. It's simply not true."

She made herself a Tom Collins. Refreshing. Relaxing. Why, she could practically feel her nerves unkinking, one after another. But when the phone rang she went rigid. Quentin. Reporting in, as he did every week: Hello, how are you, fine, fine, moving on tomorrow, call you again, goodbye. She found she wasn't up to talking to Quentin; or anybody else, when it came to that. Not just yet. Later, when she'd had a chance to get over the jolt, because of course it had been a jolt, even though she didn't for one minute take it seriously....

She stayed where she was, bolt upright, willing the phone to hush its noise. As at last it did, after eight rings. Cautiously she leaned back and took a sip of her drink. He might try again. All right, let him. He could keep trying from now till morning, for all the good it would do him. Give him a taste of his own medicine, for a change. Let him do a little worrying about where she was and what she was doing. See how he liked it.

And if by any chance it wasn't Quentin but someone else, well, that was all right too. She had ignored the phone once; she could do it again.

But the doorbell was something else again. No use pretending she wasn't at home: she had left the light on in the kitchen, her car was in the driveway, and furthermore the door was unlocked, so that there was nothing to stop her caller—most likely Rhoda or one of her other neighbors—from walking in on her. As Grace herself would have been apt to do.

Yes, it was Rhoda. "Yoo hoo, anybody home?" she called out as she opened the door. "Oh. There you are. Grace honey, I don't want to bother you if you're busy. But I just felt I had to talk to somebody, either that or go out of my mind—"

Carlos again. Another crisis, real or imagined, it didn't matter which. Rhoda suffered as much over the one kind as the other. A smothering mother, Quentin called her, and he was probably right. But then, as Rhoda was always pointing out, her son was all she had. Her husband had died when Carlos was a baby. Of drink, so the story went. She hadn't married him until she was in her thirties, after her parents' deaths. One of the old families of the town, kept themselves very much to themselves. As Rhoda still did; maybe not an out-and-out recluse, but the next thing to it. Apparently Grace was one of the few friends she had ever had in her life.

"No, I'm not busy. Just sitting here having a drink. Join me?" Once in a great while Rhoda broke down and had a sherry. Not tonight. Though God knows she looked as if she could use one, thought Grace.

She was wearing tattered sneakers and one of those sack-like garments (where did she get them?) that gave her the look of a prison inmate. She did as little about her hair as she did about her clothes—it was streaked with gray, and she wore it long, wadded up in a straggling knot on top. Yet she must once have been as handsome as Carlos; the same high-arched nose and great dark eyes. And there was still a flicker of elegance about her tall, angular figure. Funny, that behind that rather regal exterior she should be so—well, so helpless.

She perched tensely on the edge of her chair, as usual too absorbed in her own troubles to notice anybody else's. For a moment Grace considered turning the tables on her, seeking a little sympathy for herself. She was entitled. But no. Rhoda wasn't built to dispense comfort—above all, not in this case, with Lisa involved. Besides, she had already plunged into her tale of woe.

Grace didn't really make head or tail of it at first. All about a phone call from Mabel Somebody-or-other out in California, who for some reason seemed to have gotten the wind up about Carlos. Eventually, though, she took in a basic fact or two. She remembered those girls in the coffee shop again, something else they had said. And she began to listen in earnest.

4

Rhoda had been out in the yard, weeding her flower bed, when the call came. Carlos, she thought instantly. An accident with his motorcycle. A fire up in that sorry little shack in the mountains. The other terror, the nameless one that she never put into words but never forgot, either. Fast as she was about getting up the porch steps and into the house to the phone, there was time for all the bloody, brutal visions.

"Mrs. Verdell? Rhoda?" A woman's voice, leisurely and soft. Surely not the tone of disaster? "I don't know if you remember me or not. Mabel Fitzroy? We were in the same class in high school, way back when...."

Mabel Fitzroy. Lisa's aunt. Rhoda heard her own guarded, hollow voice. "Yes, of course. I thought you were out in California."

"Sure enough that's where I am. And not about to leave, either, not with this plaguey old arthritis. Well. I'm sure you must be wondering why I'm calling, out of the blue like this. I'm not quite sure myself, like as not I'm just making a muchness. You probably know all about it already."

"All about what?"

"About him calling me the other night. Carlos. Your son. He's all right, isn't he?"

"Certainly he's all right. He's gone up to his cabin in the mountains for a few days."

"Oh. Well, that's fine, then. I wouldn't have bothered you, except he sounded a little upset to me. But there. That's young folks for you. They're either up in the clouds or down in the depths. Nothing in between. It's like my daddy used to say—"

"Lisa," Rhoda cut in. Across the wire came the sound of a breath drawn in sharply. "That's why he called you. To find out where Lisa is. Did you tell him?"

"Maybe I shouldn't have. But he sounded pretty much all right at first. And I knew he was a friend of Lisa's, she used to mention him real often. So I didn't see the harm in telling him. Only then he kept going on and on, not like he was drunk, but—"

"Carlos doesn't drink," said Rhoda curtly.

"I said not like he was drunk. He just sounded—peculiar. I don't know how else to describe it. Peculiar. All kind of disconnected, and most of the time just barely above a whisper. That was Friday, three days ago, and it's been nagging away at me ever since. Couldn't seem to get it off my mind. So tonight I just decided to pick up the phone and call you. It's a relief to know he's all right. I suppose what happened was, they had a little tiff, you know what they say about the course of true love...."

There was a good deal more of that sort of maundering. Plus the inevitable reminiscing. But when it was over Rhoda (like Carlos) knew where Lisa could be reached.

The house seemed to press in on her; she went back outdoors, to her flower bed. Though the sun was almost down, the heat still held, not a breath of air stirring. When she stooped to pinch off a dry leaf or two—salvia, zinnias, the hot, gaudy flowers of August—her head went queer and giddy. She sank back on her heels to keep from tipping over.

Friday. Three days ago. The night he had left for the cabin—on the spur of the moment, the way he was always doing, she ought to be used to it by now, was used to it, she never said a word anymore, though it was beyond her what he saw in the place. Nothing but a shack: no telephone—had he already called Lisa's aunt when he left, or had he stopped somewhere on the way?—no electricity or running water; only the fireplace to cook on, and his sleeping bag for a bed. "It restores my soul," he once told her, and true enough he usually did seem calmer after a few days up there. "I should think you'd understand how I feel about getting away from the human race. You're not exactly a mixer yourself."

There was no answer to that. Sociability was not part of the pattern of her life. Her garden; her home, the big old house where she had been born, yes, and her mother before her; above all Carlos himself, her son—these were enough. She felt no need for the friends she had never had, anyway. But sometimes, in the last year or so, she found herself wondering what sort of person she might have been with a different background—if she had had a couple of brothers and sisters, say, or if her parents had been more sociable and outgoing. That was the word you heard nowadays. Outgoing. Without them to set the mold for her, Rhoda might be like Grace Leonard, full of bustle and chitchat, her life a round of parties, luncheons, committee meetings, shopping expeditions, beauty parlor appointments....

The surprising thing was that, different though they were, they should have grown to be such good friends. And not just different in temperament; Rhoda was a good ten years older. Yet somehow, in the seven years since the Leonards came to town and moved in next door, Grace had managed to get past the wall of reserve that shut Rhoda off from her other neighbors. It was a mystery to Rhoda how, or for that matter why. She felt toward Grace the way she used to feel toward the lively, popular girls in her class at school. The same mixture of fascination, envy, and boredom (sour grapes, mostly, because she herself was so much an outsider). Except that those other girls, unlike Grace, had never had time for her; and she had been too shy to reach out to them. Or maybe just not desperate enough. She did not know, she literally did not know, how she would have gotten through the past year without Grace Leonard to turn to.

Friday. Three days ago. Peculiar, according to Lisa's aunt. Not like he was drunk. She didn't know how else to describe it. Just peculiar. It was a relief to know he was all right. A little tiff. That was young folks for you. Carlos. Your son.

As if he needed to be identified to Rhoda. She straightened up cautiously and stood still, waiting for the giddy spell to pass, staring at the blaze of her flower bed. It seemed to be doing a slow-motion dance.

Then she was not there anymore, she was in Grace's living room, and Grace was saying in that flat-out way of hers, you wouldn't think it would be comforting but it was: "So what you're scared of is that he's gone tearing off after Lisa. Where did you say she is?"

Rhoda told her again. The resort town in Maine. Seaview Inn. "She's got a job there, waiting tables or something. That's how they've been paying their way, she and these girl friends of hers, picking up whatever work they can find."

"Yes. I've never heard who her friends are. Have you?"

Of course Rhoda hadn't. She didn't even bother to shake her head. "I thought he seemed better here lately. Not so keyed up and jumpy. I thought for sure he was getting over it—"

"It's not much of a drive up to the cabin. That's the only way to find out whether or not he's there. If he is, all well and good. If he isn't—well, at least you'll know, one way or the other."

"He *must* be there," quavered Rhoda. "Carlos wouldn't lie to me."

"Then what are you fussing about? Everybody lies, Rhoda. Everybody." Grace took a swallow of her drink and added, as if to herself, "When she hooks them, she hooks them good."

"What?"

"Nothing. Just something I happened to overhear this afternoon. Some girls. Talking about Lisa."

"And Carlos? Lisa and Carlos?"

After a little silence Grace said, "Yes. Lisa and Carlos. Well. How about it? Do you want me to drive you up to the cabin or not?"

"You mean right now?" She felt a clutch of alarm, crueler, sharper than ever. Grace wasn't the kind to agitate over nothing. Maybe she knew more than she was telling, maybe those girls had said something else that she was holding back.... Because Rhoda herself never heard any gossip; how would she, living the way she did?

"No time like the present," said Grace briskly. She got to her feet and hitched down her girdle. Ready for action.

By the time they reached the cabin it was almost full dark, and cool enough so that they were glad of their sweaters. Grace had said they would need them. She had thought of the flashlight too, and a good thing, since the trail that led up to the cabin was too narrow for the car. She led the way, between the bushes and undergrowth that crowded in on either side. The path was slippery with pine needles. A starless, windless night. Off in the woods the rustle of night creatures, the gurgle of the creek.

"Here we are," said Grace, and she trained the flashlight beam on the door. "Hi! Carlos?"

There was no answer. Of course not. Rhoda saw now that the door was padlocked. He wasn't here. Wasn't here. She had known he wouldn't be.

But Grace said he might be out in the woods somewhere, communing with nature. "We might as well take a look inside, as long as we're here. Where's the key?"

"The key? Oh. Under the rock. The flat one, to the right."

The door creaked open, and they stepped inside. The air was musty and dead. No sign of Carlos's sleeping bag, food, books, any of the things he would have brought. Mouse droppings on the rough wooden table; a span of cobwebs across the shelf of dishes; the fireplace stone cold. It was obvious that no one had been staying here recently. Rhoda sank down on the one chair and covered her face with her hands.

"Now, now," said Grace, and then, with more conviction: "Come on, honey, let's get out of here. You hold the light while I lock up."

But on the way back to town, for once in her life, she had very little to say. As for Rhoda, she was past words, or even tears. She huddled in the corner, her dazed eyes fixed on the darkness stroking by outside the car window. After a while the darkness changed to lights, buildings, houses, the Leonards' house. She stumbled out of the car and across the flagstones into Grace's living room. Back where they had started from.

"What am I going to do?" she said. "I don't know what to do."

"Actually, you have several choices." Grace sat down on the couch, but not leaning back, very straight and businesslike, as if she were chairing a meeting. "I was thinking it over on the way in, and here's how I see it. First of all, you can do nothing. Just sit tight. Let him go find Lisa—if that's what he's up to, and I see no reason to doubt it—find her and work things out for himself."

"But he might do something terrible! To himself, to her, to both of them. Besides, she's not *right* for him, he's too young, she'll be the ruination of him, that Lisa, either way, if she takes up with him again or if she doesn't. I can't just stand by and let her destroy my boy!"

"All right, then. That's out. Second of all, you could call in the police."

"The police!"

"Well, he's a missing person. He's not where he told you he was going."

Rhoda stared at her aghast. Admit to the police that her son had lied to her? Expose her private terrors for outsiders to gloat over? She would rather die. "That's no reason why he should be tracked down like a—like a criminal! It would be different if I had no idea where he is. But I do know. At least I know where Lisa is. I could get her on the phone up there at Seaview Inn, and if Carlos is there ..."

"Would she tell you if he is? It's up to you, of course. You know Lisa better than I do. If you're willing to take her word for what's going on, okay, fine and dandy."

"It's not a question of being willing!" cried Rhoda. "You know good and well, I wouldn't trust her as far as I could throw her. It's just that I've got no alternative!"

"Not unless you want to go up there and find out for yourself," said Grace calmly. She inspected her fingernails. Brushed a speck of ash off her skirt. "You could, you know. I might even go with you. Because you don't drive, and a car would be the best way of getting around. We could fly to Boston and rent a car there. I've heard of the place; it's not very far up in Maine."

"You can't be serious, Grace. I mean, just to pick up and—"

"Sure I'm serious. All you have to do is say the word. I haven't been away all summer. Why shouldn't I do some gipsying myself?" She gave a sharp little laugh. "And as far as you're concerned, what have you got to lose?"

Inside Rhoda's head a roller coaster seemed to swoop, plunge, soar. Fly to Boston and rent a car. She had never in her life been in a plane. Had not been away for decades, never mind this summer. To her a trip downtown was a memorable event, not to be undertaken lightly. Yet here was Grace, offhand as you please—serious, though, no mistaking that—suggesting a jaunt that might, after all, be a wild goose chase. And at a moment's notice. Rhoda was supposed to say the word, yes or no, right here and now. That was all she had to do. Say the word.

She sprang up, hands pressed to her temples. Then, at the crest of panic, her mind went miraculously cool and steady. She heard herself saying, almost as calmly as Grace, "Yes. All right. What have I got to lose?"

Their eyes met, and for a ghostly moment it was as if they were girls again—the sort of girl Rhoda had never been—trembling on the verge of giggles over some secret lark.

"Good for you," said Grace, and reached for the phone. "Just let me check the flights, that's the first thing, and then ..."

5

The day, Wednesday, began like any other at Seaview, with the usual after-breakfast interlude on the verandah. For a half-hour or so the guests collected there to inspect the weather, exchange pleasantries, and smoke, read, or knit—according to their inclinations—while the blueberry muffins and scrambled eggs settled and plans for the day crystallized. The youngsters perched on the railing or steps; their seniors creaked back and forth in the row of rocking chairs.

Margaret Robinson, who was neither one nor the other, compromised by leaning against one of the verandah posts. She felt fuzzy-headed from lack of sleep. Somehow she hadn't been able to settle down again, even after the fuss in the room next to hers was over. Fuss? It didn't seem like the right word. Too trivial-sounding for what had awakened her in the middle of the night: the two voices, one cold with rage, the other no more than a murmur, sad and soft as the call of a mourning dove; and at the end the ominous, muffled thump—though that might have been her imagination, keyed up for violence as she was. Anyway, whatever had gone on in the Leonards' room last night had not been trivial.

Yet they were both at their posts this morning, with no dramatically visible aftereffects. Lisa, drifting between dining room and kitchen, her tray at a perilous angle, her face set in its dreamy half-smile, had upset no more than the usual quota of cream pitchers. And when Margaret stopped at the desk to cash a traveler's check, Quentin had seemed pretty much the same. By now she was used to his tense air, his nervous preoccupation with efficiency, his haggard look. The unhappiest face she had ever seen, she thought. Haunted. And haunting. It flickered before her mind's eye now, and with it came the echo of his voice last night. Low-pitched, but charged with fury. Strange, her own lack of surprise at such a tone from him. She had never before heard him speak with anything but the utmost civility and reserve. Good morning, Miss Robinson, how are you today? That sort of thing. This morning, come to think of it, he had skipped the pleasantries. Just as well. She couldn't have looked him in the eye and told him she was fine. She wasn't; the episode had shaken her, probably out of all proportion....

"Another lovely day, isn't it?" said the lady from Canada. "You look a little pale, dear. I hope you had a good night's sleep."

Could she have been awakened too? No, Margaret decided; on the other side of the Leonards' room was the linen closet, then the stairs. It hadn't been enough of a commotion to reach any ears but Margaret's. She felt an odd, protective pang of relief.

"I can imagine how much you must miss your mother," the lady from Canada was going on. "I remember her from last summer, that was our first time here at Seaview. Oh, yes, we had many a good visit, your mother and I, right here on this verandah."

And would have had today, thought Margaret drily. Mother would have gotten a lot of mileage out of the Leonards, even without last night. A man his age. Old enough to be her father. Not that such things didn't happen, of course. But it did seem a little funny, a professor, if that's what he was, coming all the way up here from North Carolina to work as a desk clerk while his wife, if that's what she was, waited tables in the dining room. Buzz, buzz. By this time everybody at Seaview would know that neither Margaret nor Mother had gotten a wink of sleep, for reasons that would have grown more lurid with each retelling.

No one was ever going to hear about it from Margaret. But she could not forget it, either. It hung in her mind like a thundercloud, swollen and dark, all the more menacing because so much of it was a blur. The general import had been unmistakable, but she had caught few of the details. Aside from the name Carlos. That she was sure of. That had emerged sharp and clear. Carlos.

"Her heart, I understand?" the lady from Canada inquired. "Such a shock. So sudden."

"Yes. Very," said Margaret. There hadn't been time to change her vacation plans. Their vacation plans; though Margaret sometimes daydreamed about two exotic weeks by herself, Mother took it for granted that she would be included, and of course she always was. Seaview Inn was her choice: such an easy drive from their home in Boston, not fancy, but comfortable, oh yes, it suited them both, Margaret worked hard in the office all year, what she needed was a good rest.

Personally, Mother didn't care for the beach. So crowded, and too much sun was dangerous. Not that she minded being left alone. Not in the least. She just didn't want Margaret spoiling her vacation with a bad sunburn, that was all. A little walk along the rocks would be nice. And after lunch maybe they could drive down the coast for a browse through the antique shops....

She missed Mother, yes. A shock, yes. The shock of freedom.

A guilty flush rose in her face at the thought. She began edging past the lady from Canada—in full spate—toward the screen door, which at that moment slapped open and shut behind Lisa. No doubt setting out for the secluded spot, down on the rocks, where she spent her mornings. Margaret had caught a glimpse of her there once or twice, secret and still, gazing out to sea.

Now their eyes met—Margaret's sober and brown behind the harlequin glasses that were supposed to give her a piquant look; Lisa's dazed, amber, revealing nothing. She had exchanged her white nylon waitress's uniform for faded shorts and what appeared to be one of Quentin's old shirts. She slumped inside it bonelessly. The shining loops of her hair were as insecurely anchored as ever.

Margaret, watching as she glided on her way, was acutely conscious of her own shorts and matching top—like all her clothes, in such good taste that hardly anyone ever looked twice at them—of her expensive haircut; her face that was neither plain nor pretty; her straight back and compact figure. And, she thought, those were just the externals. In all Margaret's thirty-one years (to Lisa's what? Twenty? Twenty-one?) there had been no memorable romance. The schoolgirl crushes didn't count. But neither did the beaus—Mother's term—who had turned up from time to time to take her to the movies or concerts or church affairs. A tepid lot, on the whole, and they had dwindled away as the years went by, until now the one man in her life, if anyone cared to put it that way, was her boss, who noticed her absence far more than he did her presence.

Whereas Lisa—

"Such a strange girl, isn't she?" murmured the lady from Canada.

Without answering, Margaret ducked through the screen door. Halfway up the curving staircase, she glanced back toward the office. Quentin stood there at the window. Watching Lisa go down the path to the rocks. Loving her? Hating her?

And Carlos. The recurring name in last night's scene. It had been a scene of violence; overt or not, it made no difference. That was why Margaret could not forget it. And the reason she was shivering was that the violence was unresolved. Still pending.

Yes, she was shivering. In broad daylight. Too ridiculous.

Downstairs at the window Quentin watched and waited.

When she was out of sight, beyond the last curve in the path that led to the rocks, Quentin went back to his desk and opened the folder of bills. The figures shimmered in front of his eyes; back of them the ache peaked to another crescendo, like cymbals crashing.

The kitchen door swung open and Mrs. O'Boyle, the housekeeper, charged through it. She was breathing heavily, and her eye had the fractious roll that almost always appeared when she surveyed what went on "out there." Quentin, however, met with her approval; she flashed her dentures at him. "Morning, Mr. Leonard.... Are you all right? You look kind of peaked."

He admitted to a slight headache and turned down her offer of aspirin. "Thank you, I've already had some. It'll wear off."

Aspirin, he thought, when she had bustled away to raise hell with the college-girl chambermaid crew. Aspirin. Like applying a Band-Aid to a mortal wound.

He had found the note from Carlos last night, when he came upstairs to fetch Lisa's sweater. Typical of her to toss her shoulder-strap bag down on the dresser like that, with its big frog mouth gaping open and half its contents spilling out.

Yes, of course he had read it. No power on earth could have prevented him from doing so, once he recognized the handwriting, which was cramped, stiff, and very familiar to him from the days when Carlos had been one of his students.

He read it through several times, including the superfluous signature. A short note, undated and hand delivered (meaning that Carlos was here, on the scene), imploring Lisa to meet him down by the rocks "tomorrow evening."

So there it was, confirmation of the suspicions that had been clawing at him for the past week. At first he even found a certain grim relief in knowing that he was through teetering between yes-no, possible-impossible. It didn't last long. After all, Carlos's note posed as many questions as it answered.

They remained unsettled, in spite of Lisa's so-called explanations. The memory of her soft, glib voice—explaining, explaining—set off another explosion of cymbals in his head. He had left Carlos's note where it was when he went downstairs to join her for their after-dinner stroll. And he had held off asking her about it until hours later. (Who knew why? Maybe in the fatuous hope that she would mention it herself.)

The holding off was probably a mistake: just that much extra time for the questions to rankle. They still did. He could not let them alone, and the more he picked at them the more they festered.

Take, for example, Carlos's phrase "tomorrow evening." Whenever that might be. Last Friday, according to Lisa, no, Saturday, the note had come on Friday, someone had stuck it in her bag during the breakfast hour. The appointment on Friday, no, Saturday? Of course she hadn't kept it; she spent all her evenings with Quentin. How did Carlos know she was here? He must have found out from Aunt Mabel. And, since there had been no further word from him, he must now have given up and gone back to home and mother. Poor Carlos, he was always getting these wild ideas that didn't work out. She hadn't thought it was worth mentioning to Quentin.

Such neat little explanations. But they were not to be believed. Once again Lisa was giving him the answers he wanted to hear instead of the intolerable truth. He had seen the panic in her eyes last night; he knew he was terrifying her into lying. Knew and still could not stop. That degrading abomination of a scene! (Which Margaret Robinson had all too obviously overheard; couldn't look him in the eye this morning, and no wonder.)

No wonder, either, that Lisa was terrified of him. After last night he was terrified of himself. But he hadn't followed her just now—

"What's the matter?"

He lifted his head from his clenched hands—when had he assumed that posture of despair?—and saw Bax standing in the archway between office and hall. He looked, as always, dapper and fresh; surrounded by sunlight that, even filtered through the screen door to the verandah, seemed dazzling to Quentin. "Nothing. Just a headache."

"You look like hell," said Bax cheerfully. He came on in for a better view. "How about taking a break? I'm not doing anything constructive, I can mind the store. Go ahead. Get yourself some fresh air and sunshine. That'll fix you up."

Quentin, who knew better, hadn't the strength to argue.

The verandah was deserted by now. Without permitting himself so much as a glance at the path that led to the rocks, he made for the side steps and took off in the opposite direction, toward the woods.

It was all he had left, the one last shred of self-respect that kept him from following her, spying on her. He clutched it to him. All right, he had watched her from the window earlier this morning. But he had not followed her. Was not following her now. Or any other time. Never. For his own sake. And for hers. Because if he ever did ...

He clamped his mind shut against the thought and strode on, away from disaster.

6

The two new ladies checked in at Breezy Point Inn—down the road from Seaview—on Wednesday morning. They had driven up from Boston and had no reservations; the best Breezy Point could do for them was two small rooms, neither with a view, and on separate floors. Of course if they cared to try some of the other hotels ... They had already tried, and took what they could get.

Their arrival was duly noted by Emerson, who missed very little that went on at Breezy Point and its environs. He was a great favorite with the ladies, many of them elderly, who constituted the backbone of Breezy Point's clientele. Such a charming little boy, they told each other and his doting parents. So intelligent and polite, so considerate. Not like the general run of children nowadays; nobody seemed to teach them any manners any more. A perfect little gentleman.

True enough, there was not much of the child about Emerson. He was slight, fair, and very neat, with blond hair brushed straight forward over his brow in bangs, and below that a little beak nose, bird-bright eyes, and a practiced smile. He spoke in measured cadences, like a miniature clergyman. The ladies listened with flattering attention while he explained, in his clear, piping voice, the workings of his binoculars—a permanent fixture, hung on a strap around his neck—or described the bird-watching expeditions that took up most of his time.

He listened to them, too, far more than they realized. In the evenings, when they sat on the porch, rocking and reminiscing, Emerson remained indoors, curled up with his book in a chair near one of the windows. Sometimes he heard some very interesting things.

The newcomers struck him as promising material. In the first place, they were younger, less decrepit, than most of the other guests. And then they were so different from each other, not at all the ordinary combination of traveling companions. The younger one, the one who did the talking (and plenty of it too, Emerson observed for future reference) was a familiar type—stylishly dressed, a bit overweight, full of bustle and self-assurance. But how to classify the other one, with her dazed, helpless air, her scarecrow frame and limply hanging clothes? Emerson had an orderly mind: here was a challenge.

Instead of setting off on his usual solitary ramble, he lingered near the desk, unobtrusively watching while the busboy unloaded the ladies' luggage from the car and escorted them upstairs to their separate rooms. Twenty minutes or so later, which was less than he had figured on, they reappeared. In search of a telephone, according to the gabby one. At once Emerson slipped into the little sitting room next to the public phone booth; he had discovered some time ago that its acoustics were excellent.

The silent one waited outside, looking anxious, while the managing one took care of the conversation. It started off briskly: "Hello, I'm trying to locate a friend of mine, a friend of a friend, really, and I understand she may be working there at Seaview. A girl named Lisa? I wonder if you could tell me.... What? Who? Lisa and her husband are there?" In the little sitting room Emerson hugged himself in excitement. Just the name Lisa would have been enough. But on top of that there was the change in the voice he was listening to, the break, as if its owner had suddenly run out of breath. "Oh. I see. Who am I speaking to, please? ... Mr. Knight? Thank you very much, Mr. Knight.... A message? You might just tell him Grace called. Yes, if you would, please. That's right. Grace. He'll know. Oh, one other thing, if it's not too much bother. Is there a Carlos Verdell staying there, a young man from North Carolina? He's a friend of Lisa's, and ... You haven't. All right. Thank you again, and goodbye."

It was a moment before she emerged from the phone booth, and Emerson could not see her face. But it must show something because, how about that, the silent one had at last found her tongue. "What is it, Grace? What's the matter? You look as if you'd seen a ghost."

Emerson missed Grace's answer. He did catch a brief glimpse of her, though. Under the makeup her prettyish face, with its incipient double chin, was pale and set. Then they both moved out of sight and earshot. Very frustrating.

The little sitting room had served its purpose. Casually he strolled out into the lobby. There they were, back at the desk conferring with the clerk, who was shaking his head and saying, "No, I don't recall seeing anybody of that description. Not here at Breezy Point, anyway. We get more of an older crowd. Of course down at the cove, or on the beach, that's a different story. Lots of young folks around there. A good looking young fella, you said? Yeah, and a motorcycle with North Carolina license plates. Black turtleneck sweater. I wish I could help you, but..."

Emerson made a quick decision and stepped forward politely. "Excuse me, ladies, I couldn't help overhearing, and I think I may know the person about whom you were inquiring. One of my interests happens to be bird-watching, you see, and—"

"Carlos? You know Carlos?" The tall one bent over him, her eyes wild with hope.

"He's never mentioned his name. And I can't say that I actually know him. It's just that I keep seeing him at this place on the way down to the rocks where I go on account of the birds. So we say hello to each other. Sometimes we chat a little." Quite a little on Monday, the day before yesterday, when Emerson had agreed to deliver the note to Lisa, but that was something he preferred to keep to himself for the present. "I do know he's from North Carolina, I guessed from his accent—that's another of my interests, accents—and checked it out with him to make sure I was right. He came up here on his motorcycle. So you see why I took the liberty of speaking to you."

"It has to be Carlos! Where is he staying?"

"Nowhere special. Just on the beach, or maybe in the woods."

"My poor boy! Sleeping on the beach!"

"Now, Rhoda. Calm down." Grace had pulled herself together; she was once more the manager. What was Emerson's name? What did this acquaintance of his look like? And this place on the way to the rocks, exactly where was it? Would Emerson take them there?

"I'll be glad to," Emerson assured her suavely. "But he's never there in the mornings. The best time to find him would be after lunch. Just a suggestion, of course. It's up to you." He paused, secretly holding his breath.

He was safe: they decided on after lunch. One o'clock. Here in the lobby. Profuse thanks, which he acknowledged with a self-deprecating smile. Then he nipped off, his mind happily abuzz, to spread the word to Carlos, who was always there in the mornings, and who might very well wish to be elsewhere at one o'clock this afternoon.

Dinner at Seaview that evening was more of a flurry than usual because they were short one waitress. No Lisa. But such unexplained absences among the staff were routine; Bax accepted them philosophically. Somehow or other the guests had all been served, and now Bax was comfortably ensconced among the artifacts in his room, enjoying a restorative highball while he waited for Janet to join him.

The knock at the door was not quite peremptory, but determined sounding. Now what? On his way to answer it he took a good swig of his drink as a preventive measure in case it turned out to be a major crisis.

There stood Quentin, strung up to concert pitch. As was his wont, thought Bax; as was his wont. However. "Come on in, Quentin," he sang out cheerily. "Join me in a drink?"

"Thank you, but I—" He stepped inside and stopped, momentarily jarred out of his personal distractions. A good many people reacted that way to Bax's room, particularly when they saw it for the first time.

"Straight ahead. Through the tunnel." Bax led the way, to dump the contents of the wicker rocker onto the floor and whack its broken arm back into the socket. "There. Just don't lean too heavy on your left elbow."

"Thank you. I'm sorry to intrude like this, but—"

"Not at all. Not at all. Gin? Scotch?"

"All right. A little Scotch, please." Even seated, and with a glass in his hand, Quentin gave the impression of a man standing at attention. Against a firing wall. "I want to apologize for Lisa. She wasn't feeling well enough to work at dinnertime. And I didn't realize she hadn't let you know. I'm very sorry. It won't happen again."

He delivered these lines rapidly and without expression; as if he had memorized them. They sounded remarkably hollow to Bax. Now that he thought of it, he didn't remember seeing Quentin at dinnertime, either. "Don't worry about it," he said. "The other girls filled in for her. I hope it's nothing serious."

"What? Oh. No. Nothing serious. You can count on her for breakfast."

"Good. Fine." The silence began to get on his nerves, and he added, "Did you get rid of your headache? Oh Lord, that reminds me. I never gave you the message. I knew damn well I'd forget if I didn't write it down, only then the phone rang again and I had to leave before you got back...."

"A phone message for me?"

"This morning. When I sent you off for a walk to get rid of your headache. A woman called. She asked about Lisa first. A friend of a friend, she said. I'll think of her name in a minute." He shut his eyes and concentrated on working his way through the alphabet. "It began with G. Gladys? No. Grace. That's it. She said to tell you Grace called."

"Grace," repeated Quentin. He set his drink down very carefully.

"I'm sorry, but it slipped my mind completely. She didn't leave her number. Just her name. Said you'd know. Oh. And she asked if Carlos Somebody was staying here. A young man from North Carolina. A friend of Lisa's." He needn't have tacked that last bit on. Wished to God he hadn't. But it was too late now.

"I know," said Quentin curtly. That fierce, cold smile of his.

Another unnerving silence fell, and this time even Bax—ordinarily so ready with the small talk—could find no way of breaking it. If only Quentin would finish his drink (but he had barely touched it) and go! If only Janet would show up and rescue him! Where was she, anyway? What could be keeping her?

Oddly enough, in view of her misgivings at the start, Janet and Quentin seemed to hit it off very well together. But then of course most of her misgivings had been focused on Lisa. Still were. And give the devil his due, Quentin was efficient, conscientious, far and away the best desk clerk they had ever had. It was just that he put Bax off, somehow....

There he sat, locked in his private hell, arrogantly refusing to open up to anybody, least of all to Bax, who, after taking one look at Lisa, had found it in his heart to hire them both. Okay. So be it. Let silence reign.

"She asked about Lisa first," said Quentin abruptly. "Wasn't that how you put it?"

"Why, yes. Yes, it was. Said she understood Lisa might be working here. So then I said you both were, and—" Bax broke off, with a sinking sensation in the midriff. What had seemed perfectly natural at the time now revealed itself as a glaring piece of indiscretion on his part. It was he, not Grace, who had mentioned Quentin. He cast his mind back, trying to recall her reaction. Surprise? Not exactly. But a definite quickening of interest. No doubt about that. Quentin alone had been singled out for her message. He would know, she had said; and she had been right. "Look here, Quentin, I'm sorry if I talked out of turn. I thought she was just—uh, you know—an acquaintance passing through or something. That's how she sounded to me. A nice, chatty sort."

"Yes. Very chatty," said Quentin. He hesitated a moment, and then went on, with the air of one who has made up his mind, come what may, "The truth is, Bax, and I should have told you this in the first place, only I was too—"

He got no further with his moment of truth. There was a rush of footsteps in the hall, a frantic wrenching at the door, and Janet burst in. Her face was white and pinched. When Bax got to her—on the run—she clung to him, literally clung to him. And as if that weren't un-Janet-like enough, she was damn near whimpering.

"Down on the rocks" was all she could get out at first. The whimpering had eased off into gasps, but she was still clinging, and Bax could feel her shivering like a wet puppy. "I went back to get my sweater, I'd left it down there this afternoon, and ... the police are downstairs, I called them first, oh Bax, I found her, she's ..."

"Found who, Jannie? Take it easy, dearie, tell me what it is."

Behind them Quentin said hoarsely, "Lisa."

Bax had forgotten he was there; Janet had clearly not noticed. Her teeth clicked together, and her eyes went wide and round. Quentin was on his feet, very straight, swaying only a little, like a pine tree in the wind. "Lisa," he said again. It was not a question.

After the first shock, the sight of him seemed to steady Janet. She stepped away from Bax; almost herself again. "She must have slipped and fallen. Probably from the path. It runs quite close to the edge of the cliff there, on the way down to the rocks. The water's not deep at that point, but—"

For an instant Bax saw her drowned face, the amber eyes staring at nothing, black weeds tangled in the long mermaid strands of her hair. But the other, crueler image was there too—the sheer drop to the jagged rocks, Lisa broken and battered. In either case, an accident, death by misadventure. Just what sort of misadventure was something for the police to determine.

"Who is it downstairs? Peck?" he asked in a low voice, and Janet nodded yes. Her eyes remained fixed on Quentin, who still stood there, silent and somehow forbidding. Maybe she could think of the right thing to say to him; it was too much for Bax.

"Go ahead, Bax," she said, as if she had read his thoughts. "Tell him Quentin will be along shortly."

Relieved, he headed for the door. But even before he opened it he heard the voices in the hall. Peck's was tuned to its customary holler: "Now just a minute, Ma'am, let's not—" The woman's, though not so loud, was way out ahead on both speed and staying power. A regular whirlwind of words, from which Bax was able to snatch only the two phrases "I have a right" and "I'm his wife."

Which made the sudden hush that fell when she caught sight of Quentin all the more dramatic. She stopped in the doorway, all her words spent, a well-turned-out woman whose lower lip was caught between her teeth—like a child trying not to cry, Bax thought—and whose face was mottled in a painful flush. A pretty face, round as a baby's, with a pert nose and thick-lashed, deep blue eyes.

Quentin made no move toward her. His eyes closed briefly. "Hello, Grace," he said at last. He sounded mortally tired.

7

"Took a lot longer than I figured," said Chief of Police Peck in a voice that was, for him, unnaturally subdued. "If it wasn't for this fellow Carlos ..."

It was midnight. He and Bax were alone in Seaview's office. The guests had been thanked for their cooperation and had straggled off upstairs, no doubt to group and regroup in each other's rooms for the inevitable, endless speculation, the comparing of notes, and airing of theories. They were far too stirred up for sleep, of course; even if it turned out to be accidental, Lisa's death was sensational enough to keep them simmering for the rest of the summer.

And there was no getting away from the fact that it might not be accidental, much as Bax would like to think otherwise. Chief of Police

Peck, too: he was an easygoing man, inclined to believe the best of his fellow human beings, and furthermore unaccustomed to dealing with anything more complicated than traffic violations and complaints about the hippies who nowadays descended on the beach in droves. It had not taken him long to realize that he was out of his depth. The sheriff had been called in on the case and was off with his men, beating the bushes for Carlos.

"Chances are he's still in the neighborhood," said Peck uneasily. "They've already found his motorcycle, out there in Jug Lane. That's the first thing, to get a hold of him, and then—" He sighed.

Bax knew how he felt. It would all have been so simple, except for Carlos. But there was the note from him in Lisa's purse, which had been found with its shoulder strap broken, halfway down the steep slope between the foot path and the rocks. There was his distracted mother carrying on all over the place; and with her—just to complete the cast—her good friend and neighbor Mrs. Quentin Leonard.

Every last one of them, thought Bax despondently, with a valid reason for pushing Lisa to her death. Including Quentin, who might be pretending more nonchalance than he felt on the subject of Carlos. He knew Carlos was up here, yes, knew about his note to Lisa; it had been slipped into her purse on Friday. But that was impossible: Carlos had not left North Carolina until Friday evening. Not to mention Emerson, the oily little bastard of a kid who had delivered the note. On Tuesday, he declared in his piping voice. Yesterday. Thus specifying Carlos's ambiguous "tomorrow evening" as tonight.

So who was lying about the note? Lisa to Quentin, or Quentin to the police? "As I recall it, she said Friday. I could be mistaken. She had no intention of seeing him again of course ..."

Maybe not. But Bax could not help remembering Quentin seated here at the desk this morning, clutching his head in his hands, or the haggardness of his uplifted face. It must have been one hell of a headache to make him look like that.

Besides, Lisa had skipped dinner tonight and gone out by herself, and whatever her intentions about meeting Carlos, she had wound up at the place named in his note. No one seemed to know exactly when she had gone. All Quentin could say was that she was in their room at about six, when he came downstairs, and not there at eight, when he went back up. For the first of those two hours he had been on duty at the desk. After that, deciding against dinner because of his headache, he had sat out on the side patio; it was a very pleasant place at dusk, cool and quiet. When he learned—from Mrs. O'Boyle—that Lisa had failed to show up for the dinner shift, he was not so much worried as annoyed at her lack of responsibility. She must have drifted off somewhere, he thought, and lost track of the time. Meanwhile, he did his best to cover up for her (they needed their jobs) with his story to Bax about her not feeling well. And then, while he was still in Bax's room ...

"At least she wasn't under age," said Peck. He finished off his nightcap and moved toward the door. "That would have put Mr. Leonard in the soup but good. Funny, the way things happen. He don't seem like the type, if you know what I mean. Last guy in the world I'd pick to go looping off like that. And poor kid, she was such a skinny little thing, you wouldn't think anybody would ever look at her twice."

After a moment Bax closed his mouth, which seemed to have dropped open. "Well. Uh. No accounting for tastes."

"You can say that again." Some of the boom was back in Peck's voice. "So long for now. Be seeing you."

Bax didn't doubt it.

He took the back stairs up to his room. Janet was there, sitting on the four-poster, sipping gin. She was still pretty big-eyed, and when Bax sat down beside her she hung on to his hand gratefully.

"If I hadn't gone back for my sweater," she said after a while, "she might never have been found. Probably wouldn't have been. The tide would have washed her out to sea, and nobody would have known what happened to her."

"We don't know now," Bax pointed out. "That is, uh, whether she drowned or whether it was the fall that did it. Peck says they won't have the report till tomorrow." He paused and added, "She looked so—" But the right word for Lisa, in death as in life, would always elude him. There had been a bruise on her temple; otherwise her face was unchanged. And changeless now: forever young, forever enchanted and enchanting. To him, that is. To Peck a skinny little thing not worth a second look. And to Janet a troublemaker.

She let go of his hand and said drily, "All right. I'll never forget Lisa, either. And the big thing we don't know about her is who killed her."

"If anybody," said Bax.

"Ha," said Janet.

"Well then, Carlos. That's where Peck's money is. Find Carlos, and they'll have all the answers."

"Carlos's answers, yes. He'll lie, like everybody else."

"Everybody? I didn't lie to the police."

"No need for you to. I hope. But I bet you didn't mention, any more than I did, what we've both felt about Quentin and Lisa right from the beginning—that there was something wrong. Not just that they weren't really married. I doubt if anybody believed they were, and who cares, let the old biddies buzz, it keeps them happy."

Bax nodded. "I told you, he was about to come out with it tonight. Would have, if you hadn't charged in just when you did."

"He figured he had to, I suppose. With Grace on the scene. And don't tell me she didn't have at least an inkling about him and Lisa when she decided to come up here with Carlos's mother."

"Well, what if she did?" said Bax defensively. He rather liked Grace; in spite of her non-stop talking and her bossiness she seemed vulnerable to him. And God knows Carlos's mother needed somebody to take charge. A fey type. Too feckless ever to have managed such a trip on her own.

"Nothing. Except that it proves my point. Nobody tells the police the whole truth. Including that horrid child from Breezy Point, what's his name, Emerson. Especially him. Snooping around with his bird-watching glasses. He might even have seen the whole thing."

"You mean he's protecting Carlos?"

"Not out of the kindness of his heart. That's for sure. Anyway, who says it has to be Carlos? Peck, on account of the note. And you, simply because you've never met Carlos. You don't like to think it could be anybody you know."

"That's not it at all." It was, though. Trust Janet to hit the nail on the head. "At least Quentin's in the clear. Margaret Robinson saw him out on the patio while she was having dinner. Her table's on that side, right by the window. Mrs. O'Boyle, too. She went out and told him about Lisa goofing off. Mad as a wet hen. As usual."

But neither of them, now that he thought of it, could have kept Quentin under surveillance every single minute. It wasn't much of a walk to the path above the rocks. Ten or fifteen minutes. Less, for someone in a hurry. Quentin might conceivably have nipped down there and back, with no one the wiser. Mrs. O'Boyle was a staunch supporter of his. And Margaret Robinson ...

Everybody lied to the police, according to Janet. He stole a glance at her. She was gazing off into space. After a moment she said, "For all we know, Carlos could be dead too. I gather he's a bit on the unstable side. Maybe he leapt in after Lisa and drowned himself. One of those murder-suicide things."

"You could be right." The idea had a certain appeal for Bax. Tragic, of course, but in a romantic, star-crossed-lover way. Whereas the other possibilities were too grim to bear thinking about. "If so, they may never find his body."

"Don't get your hopes up," said Janet sadly. "They may never find him if he's alive, either. And even if they do—Well. It's not going to be easy to prove. Somebody killed her. I'm sure of it, yes, and so are you." She shivered and reached once more for his hand. "Oh, Bax. Supposing we never find out for sure who?"

"Please, Rhoda. Try to calm down a little. You're only wearing yourself out, carrying on like this." There was a slight edge of irritation to Grace's voice; she wasn't in the best of shape herself—who would be, after the session she had just put in with Quentin?—but of course Rhoda was too wrapped up in her own misery to be aware of anybody else's. Grace had known when she tapped on Rhoda's door half an hour ago how it was going to be. And it was, only more so.

"I can't help it, I can't...." Back and forth Rhoda paced, back and forth. Grace had managed to get her into her robe, which was like all her other clothes, no-color and limp. Huddled in its dismal folds, hugging her arms against her scarecrow body, she wept, wailed, paced.

"You're not trying," said Grace, this time with real sharpness. "And if you don't stop pacing the floor I declare, Rhoda, I'll—After all, you're not the only one with troubles. I've got my share too, you know."

It permeated at least partway: Rhoda stood still and peered at her dully. "You've been crying," she said.

"Of course I've been crying. Quentin drove me over here from Seaview. We talked awhile. That is, I talked." Most of the time Quentin had stared at the rug in silence, listening (or maybe not listening) while she raged at him. She had said it all, several times over. "He hardly opened his mouth, except a couple of times to say he was sorry. Sorry. Very sorry. As if that made up for everything. It doesn't even explain anything! When I think of how I trusted him, and all the time that girl, Lisa—How could he, oh, how could he!"

Nothing was settled between them. At the end, defeated by Quentin's silence, exhausted by the futility of her own words, she had cried out to him to go, leave her alone, get out.

"Poor Grace." But Rhoda said it absently; after the one brief flicker of sympathy the glazed look was back in her face. "Yes. That girl. Lisa. Just like it was with Carlos. My son, my son...."

"Please, Rhoda. Sit down. And take one of those pills the doctor left you. You won't be worth shooting tomorrow if you don't get some rest."

"Even now that she's dead." Her glittering eyes fastened on Grace. Her voice sank to a whisper. "They think he killed her."

"Here. Take your pill."

"That's why they're so anxious to find him. Hunting him down. They think he killed her."

"All the more reason why you should pull yourself together," said Grace bluntly. "He's going to need you."

After a moment of staring silence, Rhoda said in the same hushed voice, "You think so too, then. Yes. Of course. That's how they knew about what happened last spring, after Lisa—when he—All that pack of lies. It wasn't Quentin. It was you. You told them."

Grace, who had been sitting on the edge of the bed, stood up and faced her squarely. "All right. I told them the truth, Rhoda. It's not a pack of lies, and you know it. What's the use of pretending it didn't happen? It did. And anyway, attempted suicide's nothing to be ashamed of. Don't you see how much worse you were making it for Carlos, trying to hush it up?"

"No. No. It was an accident."

"Nobody slashes their wrists by accident. If Carlos had gotten the kind of help he needed at the time, all this might have been avoided."

"You told them," Rhoda repeated. "That's where they got the notion, how did they put it, mental instability, kept on at me about mental instability. If you hadn't told them—"

"They'd have found it out from someone else," said Grace matter-of-factly. "Naturally they have to check up on him on account of his note to Lisa. It doesn't mean they think he did it. Or anybody else, for that matter. She could have missed her footing, slipped, and fallen.... But they have to investigate. It's routine in these cases. Just a routine investigation."

Rhoda got back to her pacing. "And that boy, that Emerson. I don't trust him, either."

"What? Why, Rhoda, he's a nice little fellow. A perfect little gentleman. Why, if it hadn't been for Emerson we wouldn't have had the least idea of where to look for Carlos!"

"So we wasted the whole afternoon waiting where he said, and Carlos didn't come."

True enough. A nerve-racking afternoon, and when at last Rhoda was persuaded to come on back to Breezy Point, she had been too distraught to eat a bite of dinner. Grace, with her own problems to grapple with (she had kept the news about Quentin to herself, out of pity, or maybe shame) had left Rhoda holed up in her room, while she tried, and failed, to relax over a couple of drinks. And after that ...

"No. I don't trust him. He's sly. There's only his word for it that he ever saw Carlos there at all."

"Well, but—" It was near the spot where Lisa's body had been found. Very near.

There was a pause, while they eyed each other warily. Then Rhoda burst out, "You're against him, too. Quentin, that's all you care about. I wasn't born yesterday. I know why you talked me into coming up here. Making out to be such a friend of mine, letting me think it was a favor to me. The real reason was Quentin. You knew all the time he was up here. Oh, it's so plain now, the way you finagled things. It doesn't matter fiddlesticks to you what happens to Carlos or me, no, and never did, you were just using us. You still are. Oh yes, you are. Undermining him, turning them against him just to save Quentin's skin—and I thought you were my friend!"

Grace gave her a long, measuring look. "All right, Rhoda. If that's the way you feel about it, there's nothing for me to do but go away. And stay away." She moved purposefully toward the door. "We probably won't be seeing each other again. At least, not if you can help it. So goodbye, Rhoda, and good luck."

She had her hand on the doorknob when Rhoda broke. "Wait!" It was a breathless, terror-stricken wail. "Don't leave me, Grace, please, I didn't mean it, I didn't know what I was saying, I'm not myself, please, I can't bear it if you leave me, you've been the best friend in the world, the only friend I've ever had...."

There were tears in Grace's eyes when she turned around. She held out her arms, and they clung to each other, sobbing.

When the police were through asking questions Margaret fled to the patio. She wanted no part of the talkfest that was sure to occupy her fellow guests for the rest of the night. Let them chew it all over to their hearts' content; she had no further comments of her own, and was not interested in theirs.

Moonlight drenched the driveway, but here in the dense shade of the trees it was dark, deserted, safe. The questions were over, and the answers. She had told them what they asked. No more and no less. That was all that was expected of her. Wasn't it?

Huddled in one of the lounge chairs, she observed the departure of Chief of Police Peck. She had caught a glimpse of him and Bax in the office when she slipped out to the patio and had heard him (naturally, with a voice like his) saying that the first thing was to find Carlos.... Now his figure loomed briefly in the moonlight as he crossed to his car. He did not glance toward the patio. The car door slammed. He was gone.

She could still tell him, of course. Maybe that was what she should do—get in her car right now, follow him to the police station, march in, and speak her piece. Let him make what he would of the fact that she had overheard Quentin and Lisa quarreling last night. He might make nothing of it, might dismiss it (and tale-bearing Margaret along with it) as of no significance whatever. On the other hand ...

On the other hand, Quentin already had a bad enough name as far as the police were concerned—a married man, a college teacher, gallivanting around the countryside with a girl young enough to be his daughter. The quarrel, which he had also neglected to mention to them, would be one more black mark against him. And they would be all too ready to connect it with Lisa's death. Try to connect it, rather. At the time of the accident, or whatever it turned out to be, Quentin was out here on the patio. Margaret herself had seen him.

She had not hesitated to pass that bit of information on to Peck. Surely it canceled out the business about the quarrel. Did it? Didn't it? Yes? No? Either way, what right had she to judge?

On the verge of tears—except that she hardly ever cried anymore, she had almost forgotten how—she clenched her hands against her aching temples.

There was a crunch of footsteps on the gravel. Quentin. His head was down, he was clearly absorbed in his own thoughts. She could easily have shrunk into the foliage and let him pass her by. Instead, she sprang up and choked out his name.

"Who ...? Oh. Miss Robinson. Margaret."

He moved toward her tentatively; Margaret's feet of their own accord carried her forward to meet him, and her hand reached out in a gesture of silent, unpremeditated sympathy. She realized, from the grateful way he seized it, how few such gestures had come his way tonight. Because he did not deserve them? Possibly.

And now, having instigated this encounter, she could find nothing to say. The questions swarming in her mind were all unaskable. The truth about himself, Lisa, Carlos, for instance she could not possibly ask him for that. They were strangers to each other, hardly acquaintances, let alone friends. By the purest happenstance she had stumbled on a bit of information about his private life, which she had chosen to keep to herself tonight. For her own obscure reasons; certainly not at his request, probably not even with his knowledge. If it bothered her conscience, not knowing whether, by remaining silent, she had protected an innocent man or aided and abetted a guilty one—well, that was her problem, not his. Neither conscience nor chance information gave her the right to pry any further into what was none of her business in the first place.

In the end it was Quentin who broke the silence. He put the small canvas zip case he was carrying down on the grass and said, "I'm on my way to Janet's little studio. She was kind enough to offer me the use of it until—for the time being."

"Oh. I see." He wouldn't want to stay on in the room he had shared with Lisa, of course. Or in any other room at Seaview, for that matter. Too many avidly curious stares from the guests, who had done plenty of speculating about him and Lisa even before tonight. Janet's studio, a converted lean-to just around the bend in the road, would give him some measure of insulation. "They're very kind people, Bax and Janet."

"They are. Kinder than I deserve. After all, I wasn't exactly forthright with them when we first came here."

"Well, but they must have known all along that you and Lisa weren't really married," she said bluntly. "Or at least suspected it. Everybody else did."

"Yes, I suppose so. Does that make it any less of a lie?"

A good question. The question of a good, forthright man. Then she remembered the other lies he must have told his wife. And tonight. He hadn't mentioned the quarrel with Lisa, either.

She stared up into his face, trying to read his expression. But it was all shadows. His dark figure, silhouetted against the moonlight, seemed eerily elongated.

He said painfully, "I keep thinking if I had followed her—"

If he had followed her, thought Margaret, he might very well be in jail. Aloud she said, "But you didn't know she was gone until Mrs. O'Boyle told you." She remembered Mrs. O'Boyle with relief. It wasn't just her own one or two glances through the dining room window, in the intervals of chatting with her waitress and the lady from Canada, at the table next to hers. There was Mrs. O'Boyle's word for it too: she had come out here on the patio to tell him that Lisa was missing. "And even then you didn't know where she'd gone. Not for sure."

"Not for sure." Perhaps he smiled. She caught the gleam of his teeth. "I could have made a pretty good guess. I still didn't follow her. It was a point of order with me, never to follow Lisa. You might almost call it a point of honor."

"Please." In a spasm of nervousness Margaret twisted her head aside. "You don't have to explain. I mean—"

"I know what you mean," he told her quietly. "You heard us quarreling about Carlos. I thought you must have. Except you didn't come out with it to the police tonight."

"They didn't ask me." And if they had? All right. They hadn't. "They knew about Carlos, anyway, on account of the note."

"I should have torn it up. I wish to God I had."

"What do you mean, you wish you had? If she really did go down there to meet him—"

"Of course she did," he said bitterly. "The quarrel didn't stop her. And it wouldn't have made any difference if I had torn up the note. The kid who delivered it would have piped up. Not to mention Carlos's mother. No, they were bound to get on to Carlos, note or no note."

"I should hope so," Margaret said with some asperity. "If they're ever going to find out what happened to Lisa, he's their best bet. Or so it seems to me." There was a longish pause, long enough for her to think over the reasons why Quentin might not be overanxious to have Lisa's death cleared up, and to feel again the cold stir of doubt.

"To me, too," he said at last. "We used to get along very well, Carlos and I. He was one of the most promising students I ever had. Brilliant but erratic. Too much mother, that was one of his problems. And then of course Lisa." His tone was remote, impassive. He added, "He's about her age. And handsome."

In her mind's eye Margaret saw him roaring all the way up here, the handsome, love-struck youth, perhaps not knowing about Quentin in advance, perhaps only suspecting, in either case crazily bent on a rendezvous with Lisa. She saw him on the path to the rocks, waiting tensely in the dusk until the slight figure glided into view. Reaching out for an embrace that somehow—through despair, rage, panic, whatever—turned into a deadly thrust.

It could have been like that. Brilliant but erratic, Quentin had said. Too emotionally disturbed to realize that he could not hope to hide out indefinitely. Wherever he had fled to, sooner or later, they were sure to track him down.

And, for all Quentin's bitterness and jealousy, he might still feel a pang of regret at the waste of a life with so much potential. Maybe even an underground sort of empathy. After all, they had both loved Lisa. She had left her mark on them both.

Possible. Possible too that Margaret was picking and choosing her explanations, discarding—for the sake of her own conscience—those that did not fit in with what she wanted to believe. What she had to believe. Otherwise how could she justify the information she had withheld?

"You see, Margaret," he began in a different, urgent voice. "The strange thing is—"

Footsteps sounded on the gravel. Mrs. O'Boyle, immune to the glamorous flood of moonlight, marched toward them. "Oh, there you are," she sang out. "I thought you'd be in the studio by now. It's going to need airing out, you know. I've got your sheets and towels here. And a blanket, just in case. I'll make up the couch for you, and you'll be all set. Evening, Miss Robinson."

There was nothing more to be said but good night. Whatever it was that Quentin meant her to see was left dangling, along with all the other loose ends.

He had started to tell her, though. It had been like a current between them, the impulse to communicate. Unfulfilled, but still there. She paused on the verandah, watching the two figures—Quentin's tall and angular, Mrs. O'Boyle's chunky—making their way up the road.

Loose ends, she thought. Including the matter of her conscience, which was not really any easier now than before. Yet out of the welter of doubts, one certainty rose up solid as a rock.

They might not be exactly friends, she and Quentin. But they were no longer strangers to each other.

8

Emerson woke early next morning. His sleep had been briefer than usual, but deep and dreamless; now he lay in his bed, as neatly arranged as a body in a coffin, once more savoring the richly satisfying flavor of yesterday. It had been the most delightful day of his life. True, there had been the fiasco of the afternoon. But the evening made up for that. His first (but not his last) taste of glory. He hugged himself at the memory of his own matchless performance as a key witness, no less, in what was obviously a murder case, whether the police were ready to admit it or not. An accident? Hardly, in view of all the people who had a motive for doing Lisa in. And all more or less on the scene. Emerson ticked them off in his mind: Carlos, Quentin, Rhoda, Grace. Four bona fide candidates; more than enough to make accidental death the father and mother of all coincidences.

No, it was a murder case, and he was a key witness, the only person who had actually seen Carlos, talked to him, acted as his messenger by delivering the note to Lisa. After having read and resealed it—a bit of information which, along with a few others, he had not mentioned to the police. Let them do some of the detecting themselves. They needed the practice. Emerson was already at least two jumps ahead of them.

Cautiously he slid out of bed and tiptoed over to the window. His parents occupied the room next to his; the slightest sound from him, and they would be up and fussing. They were responsible for the fiasco of yesterday afternoon. Except for them and their stupid excursion to Yarmouth, he might well have reached even more spectacular heights as a witness. Certainly he would have been down there at the rocks, watching from his hideaway to see whether or not Lisa turned up for the rendezvous.

The drive to Yarmouth shouldn't have loused up his plans. Under ordinary circumstances they would have been back in plenty of time for early dinner at Breezy Point and his customary evening stroll. And of course it wasn't his parents' fault that the car kept stalling on the return trip. Nothing serious, according to the mechanic at the garage where they finally stopped; just a minor adjustment. A minor adjustment which took one and a half mortal hours to make.

Even so, he might still have managed to get to the rocks on time if—and this was where he did blame his parents, doters that they were—he hadn't had to eat dinner first. There was no getting out of it. He knew from past experience the commotion that was sure to arise over a missed meal. Emerson darling, you're not hungry? You don't want any dinner? There must be something wrong, you're coming down with something, let me feel your forehead, poor lamb, you're flushed, you're running a temperature ...

It was either eat dinner or be tucked into bed before dark with a hot-water bottle. That was the ignominious fact of the matter.

Still, a couple of rather interesting observations had come his way. And afterward, last night, the glory.

Today ought to be every bit as delightful. Maybe even more so. From the window he could see the cove, shimmering in the early morning haze, the boats gently rocking, gulls gliding and wheeling on the bias against the sky. The haze would burn off. It was going to be another bright blue day. Like yesterday. And just as full of goodies. He knelt there until the breakfast bell rang, caught up in a daze of happy anticipation, mulling over the thrilling permutations of what he knew and how to use it to the best advantage.

Half an hour later, immaculate in white shorts and striped T-shirt, his fair hair shining from the brush, his eyes modestly lowered, he entered the dining room with his parents. Once his mother was seated—as always, he attended to this ritual—he took his own place and permitted himself a glance toward the table assigned to Rhoda and Grace. Just as he had foreseen, it was vacant. The spotlight was all his, and he made the most of it. In an unobtrusive way: when his special friends among the Breezy Point ladies stopped on their way in or out for a little chat about last night's drama, he let his parents do most of the talking. They could be depended upon to give proper emphasis to his role in the affair, which Emerson himself minimized. It was everyone's duty to cooperate with the police, he explained with becoming gravity. He only hoped that the information he had been able to supply would be of assistance.

Again and again he repeated, by popular request, his impressions of Carlos Verdell. No, not a hippie type, in spite of the motorcycle and the beachcomber life style. Quiet. Always by himself. But friendly enough, once the ice was broken, and well-spoken. There had been something about him ... Tense? Yes, Emerson thought that was the word. Tense. Not in the least frightening, though. Emerson had seen no harm in delivering his note to Lisa. If it seemed a roundabout approach, well, that was Carlos's business, not his. Far be it from him to pry. Of course not, the ladies chimed in, right on cue. Emerson was much too mannerly a boy to go around asking impertinent questions. As Carlos had no doubt realized. To think of it, said the ladies, taking advantage of an innocent child, capitalizing on his trusting, helpful nature.

It was all very gratifying. But Emerson had other matters to attend to. Surfeited with flattery and hot cakes, he made his polite excuses and headed for the door. "Now not too far," his mother cautioned. "Remember, darling, the police haven't found him yet, he's still at large."

"Only down to the cove," he assured her. And indeed the cove was his first stop. For half an hour or so he dawdled in and out of the shops and lobster pound and along the water's edge, picking up whatever gossip was available. The one topic of conversation, of course, was Lisa's death and its exciting aftermath. There was a wide selection of rumors about Carlos. The police would never find him. They would find him before nightfall. He was dead too. Suicide. He had been seen in half a dozen different places, north and south along the coast. He was on his way to Canada by bus. He was holed up with the hippie colony. He had gotten away in a boat. In a plane. In a stolen car.

No one mentioned what seemed to Emerson the most logical hideout for Carlos. But then no one else had actually talked to him. Only Emerson, who preferred to keep his ideas to himself for the present. No one spent much time or breath on the other possible suspects, either. After all, Carlos was a fugitive; a fact which automatically established his guilt, for those of only ordinary intelligence. Even for Emerson, it pointed that way. But it did not completely eliminate the others: Quentin, who had an alibi, of sorts; Grace who, so she said, had gone straight from Breezy Point to Seaview, intent on a showdown with her errant husband; Rhoda, who claimed to have spent the late afternoon and evening in her room deep in doped sleep.

From the cove Emerson made his way back across the bridge and, circling to avoid Breezy Point, on up the hill to Seaview. Halfway up the steeply climbing path there was an open stretch where he could look down and see Lisa's favorite spot on the rocks, the spot where she had met her death. There were some people milling around down there. Curiosity seekers, or maybe some of the sheriff's bright boys, still on the alert for clues. The sea galloped up, foaming white against the darkly jutting rocks, then stretched out in its endless swell and glitter to meet the sky.

Carlos too had had his favorite spot there, a particular rock from which he could watch Lisa without being seen. There he had been yesterday morning, when Emerson showed up, breathless with his news. "My mother? She's here? Oh, Jesus!" Blank despair. But the report of Grace's presence as well had worked a subtle change in his expression—a queer, sly half-smile at the thought of Quentin's wife tracking him down. Emerson had made a mental note. No love lost between those two. Naturally. Lisa and the sex bit.

At Seaview the atmosphere this morning was subdued. No sign of Quentin. Bax himself was manning the desk, and he was not in his usual talkative mood. One after another, Emerson's conversational shoots were left to die on the vine. He diagnosed a hangover and left the patient to suffer in silence. But all was not lost. Just as he was starting down the side steps of the verandah Chief of Police Peck drove up. Taking no notice of Emerson, he lumbered out of his car and up the front steps into the office. Whatever he had to say would of course come through loud and clear; by edging closer to the open window Emerson might be able to catch some of Bax's lines too.

"Quentin around?" boomed Peck.

Mumble mumble. Very frustrating. But then Peck obligingly filled in the blanks. "Janet's studio? Oh. You mean the lean-to up the road. Okay. We've got the results of the autopsy. I just wanted to let him know."

He had no inhibitions about letting Bax (and Emerson) know, either. Lisa had not drowned; she had died of a broken neck. But that didn't rule out foul play. Not by a long shot, according to Doc. There were some bruises on her shoulders that looked mighty suspicious to him. Peck couldn't remember the technical terms, but they weren't the kind of bruises she'd get just from the fall. More like thumb marks. Doc was pretty well satisfied somebody had grabbed a hold of her and shoved.

Another mumble from Bax. A hearty "Poor kid" from Peck. And after that: "No. Not yet. But we've got a lead on him that sounds like the real McCoy. From up north on the coast. We'll find him, don't you worry about that."

A few moments later he came out again and drove off in the direction of Janet's studio. Emerson waited until his car had disappeared around the bend in the road. He gave some thought to following, but decided against it. No use pushing his luck. Peck had already given him a nice little windfall. And whatever might be forthcoming from Quentin—not much, if Emerson was any judge—it could wait. First things first. He struck off, his bird-watcher's binoculars swinging against his chest, for the path known as the old mill road.

It led through the woods, and Emerson had covered it many times before in his solitary rambles. Maybe in their hunt for Carlos the police had covered it too. He had a mental picture of them crashing through the undergrowth, advertising their presence at every step, and smiled to himself. Any fugitive they caught would have to be blind, deaf, and even thicker in the head than they were. Which would make him too dumb to run in the first place.

Emerson's own progress was almost completely silent, thanks to his sneakers and the thick layer of pine needles that cushioned the path. An old hand at creeping up on birds, he knew how to avoid the snapping of twigs, the dislodging of stones. He also knew exactly where he was going. Unlike the police, who, if they tore themselves away from the coast and searched the woods at all, could do little more than thrash around at random. The chances were all against their discovering the crucial spot; Emerson had stumbled upon it only by the merest accident. Literally stumbled. One day, two weeks or so ago, when he was clambering over an outcropping of rocks far off the beaten path, he had missed his footing and landed right in front of it. And even then it was a while before he saw what it was.

The air was stifling, still, heavy with pine scent. Here and there the summer sun struck through the trees in fierce shafts. A jay screeched. Insects whirred. Emerson's T-shirt grew sticky with sweat. The going was even hotter and rougher when he turned off the trail. And much slower, now that the need for silence was really pressing.

Most of all, he was slowed down by his thoughts. For it occurred to him as he inched along that—assuming his theory was right—Carlos might already have spotted him and be lying in wait, the hunted turned hunter. With the outcropping of rocks in sight, he came to a full stop, heart thumping, midriff hollow with qualms. His original plan, to approach Carlos under the guise of friendship and capture him single-handed, now revealed itself as a piece of foolish, idle daydreaming. Plan? Sheer fantasy. Kid stuff.

At least he had come to his senses in time. He hunkered down with his back against a tree and concentrated on what to do instead. Another plan, this time a real one. Another, workable way of trapping Carlos without risk to himself. And without appealing to the police for help. That bunch of dopes. What an anticlimax, after last night's taste of glory, to go wagging tamely to them. They would only botch it up, anyway.

All right. No police. No more daydreaming, either. That left him face to face with the cold, hard facts. One, he had a theory, neither proven nor unproven so far, as to Carlos's whereabouts. Two, Carlos was possibly a killer and certainly twice the size of Emerson, who would therefore do well not to tackle him personally. Three, someone else must be maneuvered into undertaking this project.

The question was, who? Rhoda was of course ruled out: she would go to any lengths to shield her son, no matter what he might be guilty of. (Or she herself, when it came to that. After all, Carlos was not the only one with a motive for killing Lisa.) By the same token, Grace Leonard was no one to depend on. Ah, but Quentin.... Now there was a different breed of cat. Quentin too might have killed Lisa, but if so he had done it in a jealous rage. And who had sparked his jealous rage?

Carlos, that was who. Quentin, guilty or innocent, would jump at the chance to get back at his rival, possibly through official channels, possibly not. It would be very interesting to see which.

Why, it was perfect, perfect, the tailor-made solution to Emerson's problem. He hugged his knees in a transport of triumph. All he had to do was drop a few hints, and Quentin would be hot on the trail. They hated each other, bless their hearts, they were natural enemies, just waiting for someone like Emerson to pull the strings and set them one against the other. He had it made. He had it made.

In mid-flight—for there he was, off on the fantasy trip again—he jolted himself back to fact number one. His theory was only a theory. If by some unlikely chance it turned out to be false, then the whole beautiful business fell apart. So the first step was to test out his theory—rigorously, without bias, and of course from a safe distance.

Once more he concentrated. Presently he smiled a secret smile and, taking care to make no noise, rose to his feet.

9

After Chief of Police Peck's visit, Quentin stood for awhile in the doorway of the studio, and after another while he stepped outside and drifted around to the rear, out of sight of passers-by. Aside from an aversion to being stared at, he felt nothing, nothing at all. It was as though he had had an anaesthetic of some kind. The numbness of exhaustion, no doubt; and like an anaesthetic it would no doubt soon wear off. Meanwhile, not a twinge.

Lisa was dead of a broken neck. One thing about it, it was quick, according to Chief of Police Peck: never knew what hit her. Or who. Because of those bruises, which indicated to the doctor that she had been pushed. Grace had discovered his infidelity and was here. Rhoda Verdell, who never went anywhere, was here too. Carlos had disappeared.

And Quentin, probe though he might, felt nothing about any of them.

There had once been a garden back here. Grown up in weeds now. It was another pretty day. The sun beat down. Time passed. Getting on toward noon. He found a shady spot and sat down on the ground. Stared at a tough little clump of marigolds that had survived the weeds. Watched an ant laboriously scale the slopes of a fist-sized rock beside him. Then down again. For reasons of its own. Maybe because the rock was there.

"Morning, sir. I hope I'm not disturbing you." A child's voice, polite and piping. Where had he heard it before? He looked up at the face above him—a non-child's face—and remembered. The kid from last night, what was his name ... "Emerson, sir," said Emerson. "I won't take up much of your time. I wouldn't dream of intruding at a time like this, except that it might be important and—the fact is, sir, I feel a bit out of my depth."

That would be the day, thought Quentin. Though on closer inspection Emerson did show signs of wear and tear. He had seemed supernaturally tidy last night. Now, with his smudged face, scratched knees, and torn T-shirt, he looked more like a real human boy. Except, of course, for his expression.

"Yes?" said Quentin warily. "What is it?"

"Do you mind if I sit down?" He waited, head deferentially inclined, for permission before he arranged himself in a neat cross-legged pose not too close to Quentin. "Please excuse my appearance. I'm sorry it's not more respectable. But I was afraid if I took the time to clean up first—"

"Never mind. What's this all about?"

A pause for deliberation. "What would you say if I told you I've discovered where Carlos is hiding?"

So that was it. Boy Detective Cracks Case. "I'd say you were spinning me a tall tale."

"But is it actually so unlikely?" Emerson asked reasonably. "After all, I seem to be the only person who had any social contact with Carlos. No one else talked to him or even saw him. I don't mean to sound conceited, but I've always been a rather keen observer. For example, this idea of looking for Carlos along the coast—it simply doesn't make sense to anyone who knows anything about him. He's not used to the seashore. Doesn't know one end of a boat from the other. He's not even much of a swimmer. The woods is where he'd head for. Not the coast."

"You've got a point there," said Quentin. And a good one: Carlos's mountain cabin back home was his favorite refuge, had been for years. On the run, under stress, he would instinctively make for a kind of terrain that was familiar to him. "But according to Peck they've searched the woods too. No luck."

"Of course not. That doesn't mean he's not there. All it means is they don't know the right hiding place."

"And you do, I gather." The kid really was pretty insufferable. Not stupid, though. "In that case, don't you think you ought to give the police the benefit of your superior intelligence?"

"They'd only say I was spinning them a tall tale," said Emerson, and permitted himself a small, prim smile. "I couldn't tell them, anyway. On account of my conscience."

"Your conscience?"

Emerson nodded solemnly. "We were friends, in a way, Carlos and I. I mean, we might have been, in time. He's not the gregarious type and neither am I, but.... No, I couldn't turn him in to the police. They don't want him just for questioning, you know. They think he killed her. Just because he cut and ran. That's no proof."

"No." And there it was, the first, premonitory throb that Quentin had been waiting for. He sat very still. Gone now. All the same, a warning. The anaesthetic was beginning to wear off.

"I had a feeling you'd agree with me," said Emerson. "That's why I came to you."

"Is it?"

"Of course, sir. You know Carlos, too. Much better than I do. If the police got hold of him, he wouldn't have a chance. They're not interested in finding out what really happened. They've already made up their so-called minds. I don't have to tell you—"

"Well then, don't," snapped Quentin. More than a throb this time. A pang. And the kid, tactfully looking elsewhere. But not before Quentin caught the flicker of sly triumph in his eyes. "This discovery of yours. How sure are you about it?"

"If you mean did I see Carlos, no, I didn't. But he knows about the place because I told him. I found it by accident a couple of weeks ago, up on the old mill road. It's terrific, sort of a cave, where a trestle used to be, only now it's half fallen in and all grown over. You have to be right on top of it before you realize what it is. Terrific. I bet I'm the only one that's poked around in it in years. Or even knows it's there." For a moment his born-old face glowed, his voice rang with a genuine boy's love of secret places, hideaways that defied detection. "Before I told Carlos, I mean."

"But if you didn't see him, I don't see how you can be sure he's there."

"I took a good look through my binoculars. That's how I tore my shirt, climbing the tree so I could get my sights right. Somebody's been there, all right. I marked the entrance with a rock—look, I made a map, it's right here, a fish-shaped rock—and it's been moved, it's not quite the way I left it. Almost, but not quite. There was a bush, too, and it's gone. I could squeeze past it, but he's too big, he had to pull it out. It couldn't have been the police. If by some miracle they found the place, they'd rip it all apart; it would have looked as if a herd of buffalo had stampeded through there."

"Probably. But all the same—"

"Well! There you are!" Mrs. O'Boyle came sailing around the corner of the studio, in her usual state of agitation. "I couldn't think where you'd gotten to. Brought you over a bite of lunch and—" Her eye fell on Emerson. "And you, young man. Are you going to catch it! Your mother's tearing up the pea patch looking for you. I saw her just now in the office with Mr. Knight, and take my word for it, you better get on up there before she calls out the National Guard."

Emerson said a word his mother would not have approved of. (Under his breath, so that Mrs. O'Boyle did not hear.) Then, grimly resigned, he scrambled to his feet. "That means I'm stuck for the afternoon. Here, Mr. Leonard, you keep this. And you think it over. I'll be in touch." He thrust his map into Quentin's hand and dashed off.

"There's soup," said Mrs. O'Boyle accusingly. "It won't be fit to eat if you let it get cold."

Over lunch Quentin studied the map. Trust Emerson, even within the space limits of a page from his bird-watcher's notebook, to be precise. Each landmark had its neatly printed label, distances (approx.) were indicated, likewise variations in elevation. X marked the spot where Carlos was hiding out.

Might possibly be hiding out. Because of course it was all wild surmise, probably nothing to it, just a kid's soap-bubble dreams of adventure. Though Emerson didn't seem the type....

Not at all the type. And one or two of the points he had made were undeniably logical. Whatever else he might be making up—the shifted fish-shaped rock, for instance, and the missing bush—his reasoning on Carlos's choice of a hiding place was sound. And his arguments against telling the police?

Quentin expended a good deal of thought on that question without arriving at an unqualified answer either way. But he was not exactly surprised to find himself, in midafternoon, setting out for a walk in the direction of the old mill road, with Emerson's map in his pocket, available for easy reference. After all, there was no harm in doing a little reconnoitering. If he happened on anything significant, well, time enough then to decide what to do about it.

In his pocket he also carried the gun which—again after due

consideration—he had removed from its customary habitat in the glove compartment of the Volkswagen.

He had always been fond of the woods. But today he had the feeling that the trees were closing in on him; the hush and the burnished twilight seemed less like a cathedral than a prison. Or maybe what oppressed him was the mental image of Carlos on the run, fleeing in panic along this narrow path. Oppressed him and at the same time drew him on: nothing could have induced him to turn back. Never mind that the Carlos-image might be false. It might also be true. He had to know.

The map remained in his pocket. Its details were apparently imprinted on his brain. Here were the three lightning-struck birches, his cue to leave the path and strike off at right angles. There, after he had covered the prescribed approx. distance, was the outcropping of rock. This must be the tree Emerson had shinnied up in order to get an unimpeded view of Spot X. Quentin pressed on cautiously, eyes alert for the fish-shaped rock, which—shifted or not—in due course appeared. The one detail Emerson had neglected to mention (but then he had been interrupted) was the sound of water. It reached Quentin's ears now, the faint gurgle of a little brook meandering along to itself. The spring that fed it must be fairly close by. An added attraction, from the fugitive's point of view. Eventually, of course, food would present a problem, but long before that the need for water would have driven Carlos into the open. The fugitive. Carlos. Again the image flicked past his mind's eye, the hunted figure, desperate, beaten.

He took another wary step forward, and another. Then he froze. Something was moving in the bushes that sloped downward beyond the fish-shaped rock. Some creature, a bird or chipmunk perhaps, scuttling about its own business of staying alive. There was almost no sound, only the stealthy stirring of leaves to mark the passage of whatever it was. Too big for a bird or chipmunk. Too ...

A moment later, thanks to a stretch where the bushes thinned out, he saw what it was. The man was hunched over in a dead run for the next patch of cover; and he couldn't have caught sight of Quentin, else he would have gone to ground instead of coming on as he was doing.

Of the two of them, Quentin was closer to the fish-shaped rock. He reached it in half a dozen steps, passed it, and found himself face to face with Carlos. A Carlos haggard, panting and—yes, cornered, back up against a shoulder-high thicket that cut him off from escape as effectively as if Quentin had planned it that way.

Carlos spoke first. A hoarse, tense warning: "Keep away from me. I mean it. One more step and I'll let you have it." His hand rose, quick and smooth; the knife in it gave off a wicked glint.

"Listen, Carlos—"

"Listen? To you? If it weren't for you, you bastard, she'd be alive. You want to talk about that? No. I thought not."

"If it weren't for me ..." Quentin set his teeth. Well. He had known he wasn't going to get off with a mere throb, one isolated pang. "How about you? I'm not the one she went down there to meet. You are."

"Right. So you had more reason for killing her than I did."

"Possibly. But less opportunity. Don't try to tell me you weren't there, too. You were, if only to see whether or not she turned up."

"I'm not telling you anything. You or anybody else. So don't waste any more of your time. Hustle back and tell the police where I am. Was. Because I'll be somewhere else by the time they get here."

"And stay on the run for the rest of your life? They're sure to catch up with you sooner or later."

"Maybe I don't intend to live very long." Carlos patted the knife. As one might pat the shoulder of an old friend.

But it would be just his luck, thought Quentin, to bungle the job this time too. Just his luck ... Yet what an aura of bright promise had once surrounded him! In those days, before Lisa, the treasures of life had been all his for the taking. Lost, wasted, for the sake of a girl who had no capacity of her own for intensity of feeling, and therefore no notion of what she was doing to him.

Or to Quentin. Or to Quentin. That was the maddening thing about Lisa: not that his passion for her was unrequited, but that it was uncomprehended; not that she destroyed, but that she did so unwittingly. You could not even call her wanton. Acquiescent, rather, pliant, bending like a flower to whatever wind blew her way.

Dead now. And because she was dead Carlos stood here, a fugitive, patting the knife that would insure his escape from the forces of law and order. Personified, as it happened, by Quentin. Mortal enemies, yes, but at the same time ... It was only by a quirk of fate that their roles were not reversed. Luck. Chance. A hair's-breadth shift the other way, and Quentin, not Carlos, would have been on the run.

"I'd just as soon kill you first," said Carlos.

Quentin took the gun out of his pocket.

For an instant they stared into each other's eyes. Carlos's were sunken but fever-bright; his face had the scooped-out look of utter fatigue. He drew in his breath and moved forward in a desperate, jerky spasm, knife at the ready.

Quentin's hand came up automatically to deflect the blow. The knife caught him on the arm, a shallow bite, hardly more than a sting, and he brought the gun down sharply on Carlos's wrist. Once, twice, and then a brief, fierce struggle before Carlos crumpled at the knees and dropped the knife. Of the two, Quentin was the stronger, taller, better coordinated. And he had the gun. But did not fire it. All right, could not, he had been bluffing. Carlos was sagging in his arms, a dead weight. He eased him to the ground, picked up the knife and put it in his pocket. There was a trickle of blood from the scratch on his arm; he mopped it with his handkerchief. Then he said, “Come on, let’s get going.”

Carlos got to his feet, groggy but still defiant. “So that’s why you didn’t kill me when you had the chance. You aim to haul me in to the police alive. Listen. If you think I’m going to—”

“No, that’s not why. You goddam fool, I’m not going to turn you in. But you can’t stay here. The kid tipped me off; he’ll like as not tip them off too.” He paused, and repeated curtly, “Come on. I’ll sneak you into the studio. They won’t look for you there.”

“You mean you—” Carlos swallowed. His eyes went wide, then narrowed suspiciously. “Why should I trust you?”

“The way I see it, you haven’t got much choice,” said Quentin and gestured with the gun. “I didn’t use this before, but I might change my mind. Meanwhile, start moving.”

10

“You’re not at the beach today?” Bax looked up from the desk, where he was sorting the mail, to give Margaret an abstracted smile. He had a rather harried look these days; in addition to all the other complications arising out of Lisa’s death, there was the minor inconvenience of being short-handed.

“My car’s on the blink. Something with the transmission, the repairman said. It’s supposed to be ready later this afternoon. Maybe when I pick it up I’ll go on to the beach. I’m going to be around anyway, if you want me to spell you at the desk.”

“You’re a good girl to offer, but there’s no need, thanks. Tell you what you might do, if you don’t mind, is take Quentin’s mail up to him. I’m late sorting it, and Mrs. O’Boyle’s already brought back his lunch tray, so—”

“No, of course I don’t mind.” She had not seen Quentin since the night of Lisa’s death, night before last. But their conversation on the patio was still green in her mind. Green and thorny. “Any news yet about Carlos?”

“Too much, according to Peck. They keep getting these reports from all over the map, people who think they’ve seen him here, there, everywhere. All false leads so far, but they can’t afford to pass any of them up. They're holding off on the inquest, but if they don't nab him pretty soon they're going to have to go ahead without him."

"Maybe he's dead too," said Margaret. "I mean, he doesn't sound any too stable, coming up here the way he did."

"That's what Janet thinks, that he took a running jump into the ocean. If she's right, there's not much chance of their finding his body. In which case we'll never know for sure...." Bax let his voice trail off into a sigh. "Well, anyway. At least Mrs. O'Boyle's in a better humor today—Quentin's appetite has picked up. She says he ate a good breakfast *and* a good lunch. She'll find something else to stew about, of course, but meantime let's be thankful for small favors."

Quentin didn't look like a man who had eaten two good meals, Margaret thought when she reached the studio a few minutes later. As haggard as ever. He was out in the yard, and Emerson was there too; as she approached she heard his precise, piping voice: "Yes, you weren't here when I came back again later yesterday afternoon, so I assumed you were taking a walk. Quite a long walk, wasn't it? I waited as long as I could, but you still—"

"Hello there, Margaret," Quentin cut in. His manner struck her as both embarrassed and relieved. "Oh, you've brought me some mail. That's very kind of you."

"Good afternoon, Miss Robinson," said Emerson, with his usual suave courtesy. "Mr. Leonard and I were just talking about what interesting walks there are around here. Did you take the one I suggested yesterday, sir? Through the woods?"

"Yes, that is, more or less. But I—" Quentin flushed slightly, and Emerson's eyes sharpened. "Here. Here's your map."

"If you're sure you won't be needing it." After a moment's pause Emerson took the slip of paper and tucked it in the pocket of his shorts. "Excuse me, sir, but your arm. What happened to your arm?"

"Nothing." Quentin flushed again, started to put his left arm behind him, thought better of it. "Just a scratch. I must have scratched it on the bushes or something."

"It looks pretty deep for a scratch," said Emerson solicitously. "You ought to put something on it. You don't want to let it get infected. Well. I'm sorry if you didn't find your walk as interesting as I thought. Or maybe you didn't go far enough. I'd like to hear more about it some other time. We don't want to bore Miss Robinson with the details now."

"No, we don't. And as far as I'm concerned, we've already exhausted the subject. There's no point in pursuing it any further."

"I see." Emerson's smile was knowing; under his bright-eyed gaze Quentin shifted uneasily from one foot to the other. "If you'll excuse me,

Miss Robinson, I'll be on my way. What's the latest word on Carlos? Anything new?"

"Just that they're still looking for him," said Margaret. She cleared her throat nervously. Though what she had to be nervous about—Quentin. The way he was acting. The queer undercurrent of something more than simple antagonism toward Emerson. She didn't care much for the child herself. If you could call him a child, and you had to because of his size. But Quentin seemed not just annoyed but constrained, almost as if he were on the defensive.

"Strange they haven't found him yet. But I'm sure they will. That is, if he's still alive. Right, Mr. Leonard?"

Quentin nodded curtly, and did not bother to say goodbye.

Into the silence that followed Margaret said, after another clearing of her throat, "I'd better be getting on back too. I have to pick up my car later on and—"

"Don't rush off. That kid," he added apologetically, "gets under my skin."

"Yes, I noticed."

"All that stuff about walks, and his map. A lot of nonsense. Just a notion of his. You know how boys are."

"Emerson's different," said Margaret quietly. "He hardly seems like a boy at all."

His eyes flicked away from hers. "Let's forget about him. How about a beer? There's some in the refrigerator, if you'd like one." As she moved to follow him inside, he added quickly, "I'll bring it out here, where it's cooler. The studio gets pretty heated up in the afternoon."

So she waited outside, and in a couple of minutes he was back with the beers and a folding campstool for her. They found a patch of shade back of the studio and settled down, Quentin on the ground at her feet. He took the letter she had brought him from his pocket and said, "This is the check I've been waiting for. And, I expect, my walking papers. Excuse me, while I ... Just as I thought. 'It is with deep regret. Under the circumstances.' Et cetera, et cetera. It's a Baptist college. Cheers."

"Cheers. I mean, I'm sorry—"

"Don't be. It doesn't matter. I asked for it."

His expression seemed no bleaker than it had been before. Probably he was past caring. What would happen to his life from now on? More to the point—again Margaret felt the clammy chill of doubt—what was the real truth about his life up to now?

Even if she could have put the questions into words, and of course she couldn't, this was not the moment: he was making small talk. "What's with your car? You have to pick it up, you said?"

She told him about the problem with the transmission. He told her about the breakdown of his Volkswagen on the way up here—unprecedented, a great little old car, seven years old, and still running as good as new, no, he wouldn't turn it in, not even after the trouble it had given him this summer. After all, one breakdown in seven years. It was entitled.

"I can drive you into town to pick yours up," he offered. "I'll be going in anyway, to cash my check at the bank." He paused and added stiffly, "Unless of course you'd rather not—"

"Thank you. It's quite a long walk, and I'll be glad of a ride. If you want to go to the bank, maybe we ought to start now."

"No, no, plenty of time. It's only two."

They smiled at each other and went on with their small talk, the kind of conversation suitable to the occasion—two acquaintances, friends, whatever they were to each other, having a beer together on a summer afternoon. Margaret's qualms receded, she almost forgot them. And then ...

At the garage, where they stopped first, the repairman was profuse in his apologies. The job on her car was taking a little longer than he had figured; it would be ready tonight, absolutely, word of honor, six thirty, well, seven, seven o'clock without fail. They left him crossing his heart and drove on to the bank.

Margaret stayed outside in the Volkswagen. Trusty it might be. Beat-up it certainly was. Dented outside, and threadbare within. The window on her side wouldn't wind all the way down, and the door to the glove compartment was bent and out of line. She gave it a little push to straighten it. It sprang all the way open; she sat rigid for a moment, staring; then she slammed it shut. There was nothing she could do about the image of its contents, permanently imprinted on her mind's eye. The knife. The bloody handkerchief. The gun.

She could not bring herself to look at Quentin when he came out of the bank and slid into the seat beside her. "Okay, all set. Would you like—Margaret, what's happened? What's the matter?"

"The glove compartment," she croaked. "It came open, and I saw, I saw ..."

"Yes. All right. I know what you saw." He started the car and headed back toward Seaview and the studio. She did look at him at last; his profile was stony. So was his silence. Stony and arrogant, she thought with a flash of anger. Did he really think she was going to let him leave it at that?

"I'd like an explanation, please," she said crisply.

"Yes, of course. I owe you an explanation."

"Not a made-up one, if that's what you're working on. The truth. There's something going on, I could tell the way you acted with

Emerson. And now this—"

"And now this," he repeated. They were off Main Street by now, rattling sedately along under the trees past houses, shops, strolling tourists. "The truth, and let the chips fall where they may. Okay. The gun is mine. So's the handkerchief. The knife belongs to Carlos."

"Carlos! You've seen him? You know where he is?"

"He's holed up in the studio. I sneaked him in there last night. Without informing the police. Which puts me on the wrong side of the law too. We have a good deal in common, Carlos and I."

"But I don't understand—"

"No, and maybe you never will. However. It all began with Emerson. He gets around, that kid, he keeps his eyes and ears open, no flies on Emerson. He figured out his own theory about where Carlos was hiding, and he figured right. I'm not sure why he chose to tell me instead of the police. No doubt he had his reasons, he doesn't operate on impulse. Anyway ..."

He told his story tersely, in a matter-of-fact tone: Margaret could take it or leave it. There were no dramatic embellishments to sway her one way or the other. She wanted an explanation. He owed her one. Here it was. The walk along the old mill road with Emerson's map (and his gun) in his pocket. The encounter with Carlos, who had a knife. The skirmish, which accounted for the cut on Quentin's arm and his bloody handkerchief. The march back to the studio.

On the surface, Margaret supposed, it was a satisfactory enough explanation. Dig a little, and it was no explanation at all, a bare recital of facts that settled none of the really crucial questions. Brought them, instead, to a full rolling boil—in her mind, if not in Quentin's.

Having spoken his piece, he now lapsed into silence. Margaret herself was momentarily tongue-tied, immobilized by the sheer volume of all that he had left unsaid. Finally she struck out blindly.

"But if you're protecting him then—then—what about Lisa? He didn't even see her that night? He wasn't even there? But then why is he hiding?"

"If I knew that—" He clenched his hand on the steering wheel. Clenched his teeth, too, from the sound of his voice. "I don't know. He's told me nothing. Nothing whatever. Not one word. The stubborn bastard, he won't even admit he was there, waiting for her."

"And you still haven't turned him over to the police? They'd pry it out of him. He wouldn't be able to hold out against them."

"Possibly not."

She said tremulously, "There's nothing to stop me from going to the police, you know."

"I realize that. And I realize the trouble I'll be in if you do. After all, harboring a wanted man—it's not the sort of thing the police are apt to brush aside."

Nor could Margaret. She closed her eyes, but the qualms were still there, the implications, spreading like ripples from a stone flung into the water. The wanted man was someone Quentin hated, and with good reason. Why harbor him, then? Why take the risk he was taking to keep Carlos away from the police? Unless Quentin himself was guilty, and Carlos knew it....

There was the quarrel, the quarrel which she had overheard and chosen not to report. And it was barely possible—though she had seen him on the patio that night—just barely possible that he had slipped away long enough to kill Lisa. With Carlos watching from the sidelines? Fleeing afterward, not from the police but from Quentin?

One ripple led to another.

"Margaret?" She turned to face him. His eyes had an aching look. "I know it doesn't make any sense. But I can't do it. Turn him over to the police. I couldn't shoot him yesterday, either. I know he was there, waiting to meet her. I think he may have killed her. But I still can't do it. Because—"

She sat motionless, her eyes fixed on his, waiting.

"Because there but for the grace of God go I. It might just as easily have been me instead of him. If I had followed her, for instance. I didn't dare follow her. I knew what might happen if I did. So who am I to come down on Carlos?"

"I see," said Margaret, and she did. Yes. This much at least was the truth: he was capable of murder. Hardly grounds for reassurance. Yet she did feel a surge of returning confidence in him. And she remembered the poor job he had made of trying to dissemble with Emerson. Surely that was something else to his credit, proof of how little aptitude he had for lying.

"How about Emerson?" she asked. "He knows enough to get you in trouble, too."

"That's another chance I have to take. There's no telling what either of you will do. Not to mention Carlos himself. At least I've managed to convince him that I'm not going to turn him in."

"What are you going to do with him? You can't go on hiding him forever!"

"No. But I don't think he can go on refusing to talk forever, either. And he's less likely to lie to me than to the police. That's only my opinion, of course. You must do whatever you think best."

What Margaret thought best for the time being was to keep her eyes straight ahead and her mouth shut. They made the rest of the trip in tense silence.

Back at the studio, he got out of the car and came around to open the door for her. "I should have asked you if you'd rather I dropped you off at Seaview," he said. "I didn't think of it till now."

And then, before Margaret, who hadn't thought of it either, could get out a word, he took off like a shot for the rear of the studio. A moment later—she still sat there, open-mouthed—he reappeared, hustling Emerson along by the scruff of the neck. "You damn little sneak, what's the idea, you've got no business snooping around here.... No, don't give me any more of your 'Sir' stuff, I've had all I can take." Here it was again, his middle-of-the-night voice, cold with rage, the one Margaret had heard once before; now she saw the face that went with it. Cold too, pinched and white, except for the red vertical streak in his forehead. "Now get out of here and stay out. Any more of your snooping around, and I'll break your neck." He gave Emerson one last shake and then let go of him, with a contemptuous little shove that sent him scrabbling to his knees.

An ordinary boy would have blubbered, kicked back, hollered insults and threats to tell his father. Not Emerson. He took his time about getting up and brushing himself off. "If that's the way you want it. Sir." He did not even sound much out of breath; his departure was calm and deliberate. But the look he gave Quentin before he left was unmistakable: this indignity would not be forgotten.

Perhaps Quentin did not see it. Though he was obviously embarrassed by his fit of temper, now that it was over, he seemed less concerned about its consequences than he should have been. In Margaret's opinion. As she got out of the car and started toward him he said, "I'm sorry. But damn it, the kid's too nosey for any good use, and on top of that smarmy. If there's anything I can't stand—I locked up before we left and we got back just in time. Otherwise he'd have found a way inside. Well. He'll think twice before he tries any more of his weaseling tricks with me."

"All the same," said Margaret soberly, "you made a mistake, throwing him out like that. I wish you hadn't done it." She realized as she spoke that she was committing herself, once more taking her stand with Quentin, not against him. When had she decided?

"I can't believe it's all that much of a disaster." He flushed a little, defensively. "Just because I blew my top...."

Margaret did not argue the point. But it was ominously clear to her, if not to him: he could not afford an enemy like Emerson, and that was what he had bought for himself. The price was going to be high. Emerson would see that he paid it.

11

Once his inner boiling subsided, Emerson took stock of the afternoon's events, methodically sorting out plus from minus. There was a nice balance between the two.

Quentin was responsible for the minuses, and Emerson had every intention of getting even with him. First of all, and worst of all, the humiliation—and with an audience; Margaret Robinson had been watching from the car. But there was also the collapse of Emerson's scheme, his perfect, seemingly sure-fire scheme. Down the drain. A fizzle. Instead of cooperating in the capture of Carlos, as he should have done according to any sensible prospectus, Quentin had broken all Emerson's rules and rung in a whole new set of his own.

Why? Emerson could think of only one answer to this question: Quentin had taken the law into his own hands and was either holding Carlos captive (pending permanent disposal) in the studio or was hiding Carlos's already murdered body there (again pending permanent disposal). Either way, it was an intriguing answer; and furthermore it offered a chance for getting even that thrilled Emerson to the marrow of his bones. It was the big plus that, properly handled, might make up for everything.

Explained everything too—Quentin's failure to cooperate, his clumsy attempts at evasiveness, and the clincher, his fit of rage. (All right, Emerson had let himself in for that; next time he would be more careful.)

There would be a next time, if only to satisfy his own curiosity. The more he thought about it—and he thought long and hard on the way back to Breezy Point—the less need he saw for any actual proof of his latest theory. A few well chosen words in the right quarter would do the trick. The realization of how easy it was going to be to do in Quentin, with no risk to himself, set off in him a shooting star of jubilation.

It died with a whoosh when he saw his mother and father waiting for him on the porch at Breezy Point. They were full of glad tidings: friends had called from their summer home fifteen miles away and invited them to drive over for dinner, Emerson was particularly urged to bring along his bird photographs, hurry dear, they were already late getting started. The story of his life, he thought bitterly. They were always springing these traps on him. There was no way out. He had had his own plans for the evening; now they would have to be postponed. He swallowed his disappointment, produced the enthusiastic noises that were expected of him, and obediently ran upstairs for his slides.

And then, after he had checked the evening off as a total loss, his luck turned. It was about ten thirty when they got back. Which was most likely too late for Emerson's purposes, but not too late for his parents to get involved in a bridge game. Bless them, bless them. Their instructions to go to bed could be safely disregarded; for the next hour at least he was his own man.

There just might be a chance, after all, that he could put his project into operation tonight. He nipped upstairs, telling himself that it was too much to hope for, of course it was, the odds were all against ...

But a line of light showed under the door of Rhoda Verdell's room, he could hear someone stirring inside, and when he took a deep breath and tapped he got a prompt response. "Yes? Who is it, please?" Grace Leonard's voice. Well. It figured. Might be all to the good, in fact.

"Emerson, ma'am. I'm sorry to disturb you at this hour, but there's something I—"

The door opened. He stepped inside. The too-much-to-hope-for was actually happening. For a moment his mind went blank with stage fright; he could not remember a word of his lines.

"Hello there, Emerson, how are you?" Grace was cordial but subdued, no longer so full of cheerful bustle. The last couple of days seemed to have diminished everything about her; she didn't even look as tall as he remembered. Neither she nor Rhoda had made any public appearances at Breezy Point since Lisa's death. They took their meals in their rooms, and according to the grapevine Rhoda was being kept under sedation. Doctor's orders.

She spoke from the bed, where she lay propped up with pillows, ghostly gray except for her eyes. They had the glitter of jet, and they were fixed on Emerson; they impaled him. "Carlos," she whispered. "It's something about Carlos."

"I think I know where he is." It came out in an undignified gulp. And he had meant to be so cool and assured! Those eyes of hers. Unnerving.

"What? What did you say?" sputtered Grace, and he turned to her with relief.

"I'm not positive. That's why I decided not to go to the police. I don't want to make trouble for Quentin, in case I'm wrong. On the other hand, I felt it was my duty to tell somebody because—"

"Quentin!" Grace again. Dead silence from the bed, and Emerson did not tempt fate by glancing toward it. "What do you mean, you don't want to make trouble for Quentin?"

"I think that's where Carlos may be. In the studio. With Quentin." He let that sink in, and went on briskly, "I'd better begin at the beginning."

The beginning, of course, was the cave. He worked his way straight on from there, and by the time he was halfway through, his self-confidence was restored. If the story, as he told it, made him sound a bit ingenuous—well, what of it; he was, after all, only a boy, with a boy's imperfect grasp of the adult world. Grace heard him out with goggle-eyed, speechless attention. The only interruption came from Rhoda, when he reached the part (a rather tricky stretch) about how he had confided in Quentin.

"But why didn't you come to me then?" she broke in. "If you were so sure Carlos was in the cave ... To tell Quentin! Quentin, of all people!"

He found he could face her glittering stare now without getting rattled. His explanation rolled out smoothly. "I didn't want to get your hopes up until I was absolutely sure. I'm sorry if I did the wrong thing. I realized I wasn't going to be able to handle it on my own, and Quentin—he sort of drew it out of me, I guess. The way it seemed to me, I thought we could go to the cave together and talk to Carlos, get him squared away. It's only because he panicked and ran that the police are after him. Nobody that knows him at all could ever think he was guilty. Well, anyway. I couldn't figure it out at first, why Quentin should be acting so funny about the whole thing ..."

His account of Quentin's peculiar behavior was full and accurate. But he was something less than candid about his own conclusions as to its cause. It was better, he had decided in advance, to stick to his image of boyish naïveté and leave the sinister inferences to his audience. All right. He suspected that Quentin, having gone off to the cave on his own and found Carlos, was now harboring him in the studio. That was all. Emerson didn't blame him. Given the chance, he would have done the same. The police, though—naturally the police would take a different view. So naturally Quentin couldn't afford to let anybody, not even Emerson, in on his secret. At the same time, it didn't seem right not to let Carlos's mother know....

There was no immediate response from Carlos's mother. She had sunk back against her pillows and lay with her eyes closed and her long, narrow hands resting palms up on either side. Like a stone image on a tomb. But then, unexpectedly, she spoke. "Thank you, Emerson. I appreciate your telling me."

"Rhoda," said Grace sharply. She brushed past Emerson, who had all but forgotten her in his concentration on the other half of his audience, and bent over the figure on the bed. "Rhoda honey, I hope you've got better sense than to take this nonsense seriously."

Nonsense? His mouth dropped open in astonishment. He had taken it for granted that Grace would be solidly on his side, if only because she was the type—they were a dime a dozen, dear ladies—who knew a perfect little gentleman when she saw one. Not to mention the fact that she had even more reason than Emerson for wanting to pay Quentin back. Or so one would think. Well. One would think wrong.

"That's all it is, nonsense. Personally, I don't believe a single word of it, not one single syllable, and I don't see how anybody in their right mind—" She gave up on Rhoda and whirled to face Emerson again, her eyes snapping. "I'm surprised at you, Emerson, a nice boy like you, making up such a story. You ought to be ashamed of yourself. It's cruel, that's what it is, with poor Rhoda worried sick the way she is, you know good and well she's in no shape to judge between true and false!"

"No, that's not fair," he cried, jolted out of his customary aplomb. "I'm trying to help her and Carlos! And I'm not making it up, it's not a lie, it's—"

"All right then, not a deliberate lie. Let's just say you let your imagination run away with you. You knew about the cave, and that set you off. But you've got no proof that Carlos was ever there, much less that he's in the studio now. That part of it's just plain crazy. No. If Quentin found him in a cave or anywhere else, take my word for it, he'd turn him in like a shot."

This was more like it. Emerson widened his innocent eyes and faltered, "He would? But I thought they were friends. Carlos told me they were. So did Quentin. At least he gave me that impression...."

"They used to be friends, yes. Before Lisa came along and hacked us all up." She swallowed hard. "If you were trying to help Carlos, Quentin's the last person in the world—" She stopped short. Her eyes darted toward Rhoda, who remained motionless, apparently sealed off. Could she really be as impervious as she seemed? Emerson was inclined to think not. He sincerely hoped not.

"I didn't realize. I do now, of course." He let his head droop abjectly, injected into his voice a tremor of remorse. And he quoted Rhoda's phrase. "To tell Quentin. Quentin, of all people."

"No need to lay it on that thick," said Grace. "You make it sound as if Quentin—" She decided not to finish that sentence. With Grace as an opponent, who needed allies? "I can't see what difference it makes that you told him, as long as he didn't buy your story. And he obviously didn't, or he'd have gone right straight to the police."

"Yes, I expect he would have," said Emerson humbly. "But I still don't understand why he acted so peculiar this afternoon."

"Quentin's like that. Prickly. And good Lord, boy, what did you expect? I'd boot you out too, if I found you snooping around my place." Then she softened a bit and gave him a friendly little push toward the door. "Now run along to bed. You've gotten into enough mischief for one day."

"Yes, ma'am. I'm sorry if I did the wrong thing. Truly I am."

"Just so it doesn't happen again. You're not fixing to tell anybody else this yarn of yours, I hope."

He assured her that he would not dream of doing any such thing—as indeed he would not—said good night, and left.

Outside the door he lingered for a couple of moments, but the murmur of their voices was mostly unintelligible. Rhoda did speak out once, clearly and passionately: "He's my son. Not yours. You don't know, you don't know!"

Satisfied, Emerson went back downstairs. After checking unobtrusively on the card room where his parents sat in grim absorption, he slipped out the side door. He still had half an hour to himself; without making any conscious decision about how to use it, he found that he was heading for the studio.

The night air was a little chilly, and there were only occasional brief glimmers of moonlight through the scudding clouds. On his way past Seaview, he glanced in at the office window and saw Quentin there, talking to Bax. Ah. Ah. That meant the coast was clear, if he wanted to have another go at getting into the studio....

After one heady moment, he rejected the idea as not only foolhardy but pointless. Why risk being caught again when he already had conclusive evidence—Quentin's fit of temper this afternoon—that his theory was right? If Rhoda felt that further proof was needed, let her get it for herself. She had the facts. The next move was up to her.

Meanwhile, since he was this close anyway and had the time, he might as well take a quick look at the studio before going back to Breezy Point and bed. He moved ahead cautiously, sticking close to the side of the road where he could dive into the bushes in case of emergency, and keeping his ears pricked for footsteps behind him. He heard none. The only sound was the wind sighing through the trees. It made him feel a little spooky.

All the same he crept on, past the bend in the road. With the studio in sight, he kept his distance, hunching down behind a rock. If there was anything to see, he could see it from here. Not that there was likely to be anything of interest, except possibly Quentin's return. From across the road the studio seemed to stare back at him, dark, quiet, self-contained, hugging its secret. Or so Quentin thought. Emerson knew better.

He was on the point of leaving when he saw, thought he saw, a flicker of movement at the corner of the studio. His imagination? A trick of wind and shadow? No. The moon broke through clouds for a moment, and he saw it again, this time for sure. The figure of a man flattened against the studio wall, stealing forward step by step, out of sight now, behind Quentin's Volkswagen, which was parked in front of the door. Emerson waited, frozen in a half-crouch, holding his breath. There was nothing to be done about the hammering of his heart. Slowly, warily, the figure detached itself from the Volkswagen—it was like watching ink blots spread on a blotter—and the next second streaked across the road, whizzed past the rock, so close that Emerson could see his face, Carlos, no doubt about it, could even feel the rush of air as he passed.

Once the first shock was over, Emerson recovered his wits, his breath, and his powers of locomotion. In that order. A stirring in the roadside bushes told him which way Carlos was heading. Toward Seaview. But surely not to meet Quentin; on the contrary, the stealthiness of his performance could only mean that he was bent on escaping from Quentin. Emerson had a fleeting impulse to call out, identify himself, offer his assistance.... The notion died a-borning. He had already set too many other wheels in motion; the friendly approach was no longer feasible. Besides, though he had revised his theory since yesterday, and shifted his basic aim—what mattered most to him now was getting even with Quentin—nothing had happened to change his view of Carlos. A desperate, hunted man. A possible killer. And twice as big as Emerson.

But not necessarily twice as fast, and of course not as smart. For one thing, he did not know he was being followed. Emerson, slipping along behind, began to wonder if he even knew where he was going. Could he just be striking out at random, with no specific destination? The general aim still seemed to be Seaview, by way of a shortcut through the scrub. Emerson knew it well; it gave him no trouble, even in the dark. Once through it, Carlos halted, no doubt to reconnoiter. The clearing lay ahead: Seaview, with lights gleaming in its windows, its cluster of parked cars, but with no bustle of arrival or departure, no sound of voices on the verandah. Wherever Carlos was going, now was the time.

There. He was off, bent low for the sprint across the open stretch and veering toward the side of Seaview's white bulk. It was clear enough now what he was up to. Not a bad idea, either; Emerson himself could hardly have picked a better hideaway. There was no need for further pursuit. He stayed where he was, watching and thinking.

The evening's events, though unexpected in some ways, were not at all unsatisfactory. He was still two jumps ahead of everybody else. And the wheels he had set in motion would still work, possibly even better.

He set off for Breezy Point, at peace with his world.

12

Carlos was gone. Quentin knew it as soon as he stepped inside the studio. Sensed it. Had perhaps expected it.

He gave the little bobwhite whistle they used as a signal—which was as near as they had come to comradeship in the last day and a half—and got no answer. Then he climbed the rough steep flight of steps, more ladder than stairway, leading up to the storage area that had served Carlos as a hidey hole. Not anymore. The blanket he had slept on was rolled up neatly. There was, rather to Quentin's surprise, a note: "Thanks anyway, but it's no good. Don't try to find me. That's no good, either."

He read it over several times. Took it downstairs and read it several more times. Finally he put it away in his billfold. The sensible thing to do with it, he supposed, was to destroy it; if the police ever got hold of it they would take it, and rightly so, as evidence of Carlos's presence here, with his knowledge and consent. (For reasons more easily explained to Margaret Robinson than to the police.) But then the sensible thing would have been to turn Carlos over to the police in the first place. They had their methods; they would have pried Carlos's story out of him. Or anyway a story. Whether or not it would have been the truth....

Quentin had gotten nothing out of him at all. "It's no good." No good trying to re-establish contact with Carlos; there could never be anything but bitterness between them, after Lisa. Whatever Carlos knew about her death, he had taken it away with him, locked up tight in that desperate, storm-racked brain of his.

Desperate. Quentin stepped outside to the Volkswagen and checked the glove compartment. His gun was gone. So was Carlos's knife, his old friend, his escape route.

The night was full of restless movement—wind-chased clouds, black shadows, fitful gleams of moonlight, a handful of raindrops that made a pattering, rustling sound. Like footsteps, he thought.

Then he caught sight of the hurrying, wispy figure on the road. The footsteps were real. The next second, and he recognized her. Carlos's mother.

He started toward her, and at once she made her breathless demand: "Where is he? Don't lie to me. I know he's here. My son, my son!"

No need to ask how she knew. Oh, Margaret's prophetic soul. Though he doubted if she had foreseen the exact nature of Emerson's revenge. Nobody could have, except maybe Machiavelli.

Meanwhile, Rhoda was brushing past him and on, into the studio. She stood there like a gaunt tigress, her eyes raking the cheerful little room with single-minded intensity. Up the steps she went, down again.

"Where is he? What have you done with him?"

Quentin had never liked her; he saw too clearly what the destructive force of her love had done to her son. But it had ravaged her too. Was ravaging her now. The pang of fierce pity he felt for her made him speak with more than his usual curtness.

He gave her the facts, stripped down to the bare, hard bone.

There was a longish silence. Then: "He was here, and you didn't let me know?"

"It was too risky to let anyone else know. On account of the police. We both—"

"Not Carlos! No! No! He wouldn't do that to me. He would have found some way of getting a message to me. You're lying to me! You've killed him, that's what you've done, murdered my boy...." She wheeled wildly, and he caught hold of her wrist; it was hot and dry to his touch, as if she were burning up with fever. "For God's sake, Rhoda, you don't know what you're saying. This is crazy. Why should I kill Carlos? Why?"

"Because of her. That girl. You had more reason for killing her than he, she went down there to meet him and you hated them both for it. And now you're trying to make yourself out a friend of his, hiding him here, shielding him from the police—You were shielding yourself! You had to get to him first for fear of what he might tell them!"

"You're accusing me of killing not only Carlos, but Lisa too? Is that it?"

"You had more reason than he," she repeated stubbornly. "If he was there and saw you—"

"Well, he didn't. I wasn't there to see. Which is more than can be said for Carlos. Whatever else he did or didn't do, he must have been there."

"Did he tell you he was? I have a right to know. What did he tell you?"

"He told me nothing, Rhoda. Nothing at all. But if he's not guilty, why is he so hellbent on dodging the police?"

"Guilty. You think he's guilty...." And she burst out again: "That's why you killed him, then! Hunted him down, dragged him here, murdered him without giving him a chance. Lynch law. You're not going to get away with this, Quentin Leonard. Not without killing me too." She wrenched free of his hold on her wrist, stumbled against the couch, and sank down on it, her blazing eyes hidden by her hands, her thin shoulders heaving with sobs.

Again he felt the stab of pity. "Listen to me, Rhoda. I don't know whether Carlos is guilty or not, and I don't know where he is. But I do know he left here tonight under his own power and—" He remembered the note (thank God undestroyed) and drew it out of his billfold. "And I can prove it. Here. Here's the note he left me. Does this sound as if I'd murdered him?"

She caught her breath and after a moment reached out hungrily. She seemed not so much to read the note as devour it. At a gulp the first time, then more slowly, running her finger along the cramped lines as if to assure herself of their reality.

"It's not signed," she whispered at last.

"No, but you know his handwriting."

"Yes. Yes, of course I know his handwriting. My boy, my boy.... He was overwrought when he wrote it. I can tell. The size of the loops. And the way it all runs downhill." She looked up at Quentin. Her eyes went narrow and hard. "You could have forced him to write it."

"Possibly. But I didn't."

"Why should I take your word for anything? Look at the way you've treated Grace. Lying to her. Chasing off with a girl half your age."

He set his teeth and kept his eyes steadily on hers. "All right. But that doesn't make me a murderer."

"The police aren't going to be satisfied with just your word for it."

Again there was no denying it. Even if the police did not take this crazy notion of hers seriously—and they might, they might—he would still be on the spot. For impeding justice. Harboring a fugitive.

He snatched at the only straw in sight. "How about Carlos? If you go to the police, you'll be doing me in. Yes. But you'll be giving them a red-hot lead on Carlos, too. The best they've had so far. Is that what you want? To turn him over to the police? They'll put him through the meat grinder. They'll—"

"No. No!" She spoke in an impassioned whisper. "I want to see him again, see for myself, with my own eyes. My son! Carlos!"

Yes, of course. Her son. Carlos. The impossible dream: to have him back again, all hers; somehow to return to the never-never land of their life before Lisa.

"Then give me a chance to find him, Rhoda." The proposal seemed to leap out by itself. None of his doing. Yet he recognized the voice as his own. Matter-of-fact. Even. "Give me a chance to prove I haven't murdered him. Could anybody have a better motive for finding him than that? And I'm as anxious as you are to keep the police out of it, for my own sake as well as Carlos's. So what's to lose by letting me try?"

She closed her eyes and sat silent, squeezing her hands together until the knuckles stood out, shiny and taut. At last she said, "Yes, but you found him before and didn't tell me. How can I trust you not to do the same thing this time? If you haven't killed him already, you might—"

"Don't be ridiculous," he said irritably. "I wouldn't dare. Even if I had any reason to kill him, which I haven't." He pushed to the back of his mind the thought of his missing gun, and the knife. If there was going to be any killing, it wouldn't be done by him. "As for finding him and not telling you, that's ridiculous too, now that you're calling the turns. Don't worry, if I find him, you'll see him all right. That's the whole point of the deal."

"Deal." She echoed the word tentatively. Then she looked up at him. Those great dark eyes of hers. Flickering between hope and fear. But her mouth was set in a firm line of resolve. "All right. A deal. I'll give you two days. Till Sunday midnight. If you haven't found him by then I'm going to the police."

Two days. It wasn't much time. But he was damned if he was going to plead for an extension. As he had pointed out to her, she was calling the turns. She held out her hand, and he took it. The bargain was sealed. For better or worse.

"I'll drive you back to Breezy Point," he said. "Or don't you trust me that far?"

"I trust you that far," she said, as drily as he.

Neither of them spoke again until they reached Breezy Point. He saw her up the porch steps to the door. There they exchanged brief good nights. To hers, Rhoda added an equally brief good luck.

He was going to need it, he thought as he went back to the car. Two days. And not the first notion of where to start looking. Would Carlos head for the woods again? Or would he switch his tactics this time and ...

He paused with his hand on the Volkswagen door, watching the car that came bucketing up the driveway. It pulled to a stop. Grace leaned out and called his name.

No getting out of it. With a sinking heart he crossed over to her. "Rhoda," she began at once. "Is she back here? She's been to see you, hasn't she? I thought I'd talked her out of it, Lord knows I did my best, but then when I went back to her room and found her gone I knew good and well that's where she must be, poor soul, I realize she's half out of her mind with worry, but all the same ..."

"Yes. I just brought her back." Warning signals flashed in his brain: Grace already knew too much for comfort; he was going to have to watch every word he said.

"I never heard of such foolishness in all my born days. I told her so, and Emerson too, though of course he's only a child, you can't expect him to realize. All that rigamarole about some cave, and Carlos holed up with you in the studio; why, it's plain as the nose on your face Emerson was just storying."

"He's an imaginative boy," said Quentin.

"I might have known Rhoda wouldn't wait till morning, the way she promised me. No. She had to go looping off on her own, this time of night, and the shape she's in, and all for nothing, just a wild goose chase, as if she weren't upset enough already—" She caught her breath, on the brink of tears.

"Never mind, Grace. I managed to calm her down. And at least now she knows Carlos isn't at the studio." Not a lie. An evasion. He felt the familiar wave of self-loathing. It had been the pattern of his life for the past six months: evasions, half-truths, outright lies. He could not break out of it even now, with Lisa dead. "It's the only way she was ever going to be satisfied," he added. "To see for herself."

"That's so. But—" Again there was the tremor of tears in her voice. The porch light, falling on her face, showed it still drawn, uncomforted. "What if they never find him? What if he's dead too?"

"I hope not," said Quentin. Sincerely, for once.

"Well, but he could be. He could have done away with himself. Rhoda keeps trying to make out it was an accident, that other time, but she knows herself it wasn't any such thing. So does everybody else. Who knows but what this time he's pulled it off? And if he has, God forgive me, I can't help thinking it might be the best way out. Because don't tell me the police just want him for questioning. They're fixing to charge him with murder. Can you imagine what that would do to Rhoda? Nothing could be as bad. Nothing."

She was crying in earnest now. He reached through the car window and patted her hand. It was plump, well kept, a pretty little luxury kind of hand. Complete with narrow, diamond-set wedding band. He had a mental image of Lisa's long, limp fingers, often none too clean, and always hung with at least four rings. Lisa, Lisa. Her hand separating his from Grace's. The memory of her forever between them.

"Look, Grace, this is only guesswork on your part. Whatever happens, Rhoda's going to have to face it herself. All you can do for her is what you're already doing, being a friend to her, standing by her."

"I wasn't being a friend to her when I put it into her head to come up here. Because I didn't let on to her that I had a reason of my own for wanting to come. It wasn't just to help her find Carlos. But I couldn't bear to tell her. I was too ashamed, and I still couldn't quite believe that you ... Oh, Quentin!"

How to answer that cry of reproach and betrayed trust? He stood in guilty silence, trying not to flinch when she lifted her drowned face.

"It's no use saying forgive and forget," she whispered. "I can't, I can't. No, it's all fallen apart now, no way to pick up the pieces, nothing left.

Daddy warned me before we got married. He had a feeling it wasn't going to work out. But I was too much in love to listen."

"I was in love too."

No, it was not another half-truth. Through the blur of time he could still see them, those two bygone, ghostly figures—the fresh, vivacious, sociable girl and the young man who had courted her with such quiet intensity.

She was going on, as if to herself, "The whole town laughing at me behind my back. Common gossip. They all knew, everybody but me, everybody talking and sniggering over what a fool you were making of me; oh, when I think of it—" She had stopped crying; she gave him a long, unwavering look and shook her head with bleak decision. "No, Quentin. I can't ever forgive you for this, no use pretending different."

No use. Nothing left for her now either. For Quentin their marriage had gone hollow long before he ever set eyes on Lisa. And just now Grace had provided the fitting epitaph, he thought sadly: the deepest hurt, to her, was not that he had been unfaithful but that everybody in town knew it.

Which of course did not excuse the wrong he had done her. It would be on his conscience for the rest of his life. Whatever Grace's limitations, she did not deserve such treachery from him.

"I can't ever forgive myself either," he said stiffly.

"Lisa." She hissed the name; the venom in her voice, and in her face, startled him. "It's all her doing, she's to blame for everything. You and me. Carlos. Everything. I'm glad she's dead! She got what was coming to her!"

13

"Sunday midnight," Margaret echoed. "That's not a whole lot of time."

It was now early afternoon Saturday. After last night's rain and a morning of fog that kept Seaview's guests drooping on the verandah, the sun was out again and everybody had taken off for the beach. Everybody but Margaret, who had spent the last half-hour on the side patio, worrying and waiting. A premonition? That would have been Mother's word for it. Anyway, she was not surprised when Quentin showed up—he had done so as soon as the coast was clear—or when he told her the bad news, either.

"Thirty-odd hours," he said dispassionately. "Time enough, I suppose, if I'm ever going to find him at all. It's just a matter of sheer blind luck. I've got nothing to go on, really."

“Except that he can’t have gotten very far. He wouldn’t dare try to hitch a ride or take a bus anywhere. And if he stole a car the police would have nabbed him by now.”

“I thought they were off on a false scent up near Bangor.”

“Yes, but they’re still watching all the roads around here. Bax told me this morning. He gets all the dope from Peck.”

“Okay, so he hasn’t gotten very far. It’s still like looking for a needle in a haystack. I ought to know, I’ve been beating the bushes since dawn. The trouble with the woods—and I’m assuming Emerson was right about that being the best bet—is that there are just too many hiding places. Good ones, too. I could have been within arm’s reach of Carlos twenty times and never known the difference.”

He looked ready to drop from weariness and discouragement. But Margaret steeled herself; pity was of no practical use to him. The facts must be faced in all their bleakness. “Are you sure he’ll cooperate if you do find him?” she asked bluntly.

“Of course I’m not sure,” he snapped back. “He may shoot me on sight. Or himself, provided he hasn’t done it already. While we’re on the subject of cheery possibilities, let’s not overlook that one. But if he’s still alive and if he’ll give me a chance to explain, I think he’ll get me off the hook with Rhoda. For his own sake, if not for mine.”

“That’s right,” said Margaret with relief. “And after all, the reason you’re in this fix is that you didn’t turn him in when you had the chance. It’s not much of a favor to ask in return.”

“I’m glad to hear you testify. That leaves me with only one minor problem. All I have to do is find him. From then on I’ve got it made.”

“Don’t be so sarcastic,” she said absently. There was a longish silence before she spoke again. “Emerson ...”

“All right. I shouldn’t have chewed him out. You said at the time it was a mistake, and it was. I don’t see what’s to be done about it now.”

“Nothing. I wasn’t thinking about that part of it. I was thinking—well. He figured out where Carlos was hiding before. Both times. He’s a pain in the neck, but he’s bright. And a natural born spy. No amount of chewing out would stop him from snooping. Just the opposite, in fact. If anybody’s got a line on Carlos, it’s Emerson.”

Quentin straightened up a little, and a gleam of hope showed in his eyes. “You might have something there. You just might. He thinks the police are a bunch of dopes, so he wouldn’t tell them this time any more than he did before. Plus he’s still got dreams of glory. Boy Hero Captures Desperado Single-handed.... Yeah. But he wouldn’t tell me, either. Especially if he knew how bad I need to know. I really blew it yesterday. For good and all. Because I have the feeling it’s once an enemy always an enemy with Emerson. If he's got a line on Carlos, he's not about to confide in me."

"No. But he might in somebody else. Me, for instance."

"You!" After the one startled, disparaging word, he said brusquely, "There's no reason why you should get mixed up in this."

"I already am," she pointed out. "Between what I've picked up by chance, and what you've told me, I'm mixed up in it plenty."

"Yes. I've told you too much. Part of it because I had no choice. But I could have kept today's installment to myself. I guess I just—" He paused, eying her curiously. "Well, anyway. Emerson wouldn't open up to you, either. He knows we're friends."

"Does he?" To herself she added, Are we? "He knows I brought you your mail yesterday, and you gave me a lift into town because my car was on the blink. That doesn't make us bosom companions."

"No. No, I suppose not. But you've never taken any particular notice of him before. He's going to smell a rat if you suddenly get interested in him now."

"Don't forget, I was there yesterday when you threw your tantrum. A grown man, jumping all over a poor defenseless child. Disgraceful. Shocking. Why would anybody put on such a performance? Unless, of course, they had something to hide...."

"So that's to be the pitch, is it?" The little laugh he gave sounded both surprised and admiring. Which was pretty much how Margaret felt about it herself.

"There's no guarantee he'll buy it," she said modestly. "And even if he does buy it, he may not have any ideas about Carlos. But I can't see what's to lose by trying."

"Nothing whatever to lose." Quentin heaved a sigh and stood up. "Let's just hope to God he does know something, and that you can pry it out of him. And listen, Margaret, if you change your mind about trying—"

"I won't," she assured him. And she wouldn't, she thought helplessly. Never mind what Mother would say. Never mind her own doubts about Quentin—no use pretending she was rid of them; she wasn't—but never mind, she was still on his side. "There's a phone in the studio, isn't there? It's better if I call you from the cove or somewhere in town, because there's only the desk phone at Seaview. No privacy. And with Emerson snooping around, the less we see of each other the better."

"That's right. We're not supposed to be friends anymore, are we?" He stood for a moment, looking down at her. Hesitating. Perhaps trying to puzzle her out. As well he might. But in the end all he said was, "Okay, then. Let me know how you make out. Good luck. And thanks."

She watched until he disappeared around the bend in the road. As straight-backed as ever under the load of this latest misfortune. One more link in the chain of disaster, she thought, and the name of the chain was Lisa.

All right. The root causes were none of Margaret's concern. The immediate problem was as much as she could hope to deal with. She gave herself a little shake and focused her mind on Operation Emerson.

He was nowhere in sight around Breezy Point, which seemed to her the logical place to start. If she asked for him.... No. It must be an apparently chance encounter; otherwise Emerson would know at once that something was afoot. She strolled casually past the rocking-chair brigade on the front porch, circled around to the rear, and headed back toward Seaview. No need to start worrying yet: her car was working again, she had most of the afternoon to cruise both town and back roads, she was almost sure to come across him somewhere or other, why, he was always popping up out of the background with his sanctimonious smile and his binoculars. There was absolutely no need to start worrying yet.

All the same, she kept having to wipe the sweat from her forehead as she hurried along. And when she caught sight of him mousing around the side driveway at Seaview, her heart gave an almost painful leap of relief. His back was toward her; at the sound of her footsteps on the gravel he turned, and she had the fleeting impression that he might be slightly rattled. A comforting notion, if an unlikely one.

"Hello there, Emerson. Sorry if I startled you."

"No, no, not at all. I was just looking for something. My bird whistle. I've lost it, and I thought I might have dropped it when I came past here yesterday." He gave the gravel a final scuffle with the toe of his sneaker, and assumed a sad, brave smile. "I guess not, though. It probably would have gotten squashed here, anyway."

"What a shame," said Margaret. "How about up around the studio? You could easily have lost it there, when Mr. Leonard was raising such a fuss. And by the way, what was that all about? What on earth possessed him? I haven't gotten over it yet, the way he lit into you. And for no reason, as far as I could see. As if it was a criminal offense for you to be up there! You've got as much right as he has. It's not even his studio; it belongs to the Knights."

After a quick glance at her, Emerson fixed his bright, abstracted gaze on the contraption of trellis that served as a screen for Seaview's underpinning—a narrow strip under the verandah, widening here on the downward slope of the hill to the height of a door, with stacks of firewood showing through the trellis openings. He said carefully, "Yes, he seemed extremely upset, didn't he? But then I expect Mr. Leonard has a lot on his mind these days."

"Well, but even so. To jump on a kid half his size, he knocked you down, Emerson, he could have injured you seriously!" She paused, wondering if she might be laying it on a bit too thick. But no, the smug expression on Emerson's prissy little face reassured her. And he was edging her unobtrusively toward the lounge chairs on the patio. "I don't care how much he has on his mind, that's no excuse for taking it out on you. I don't mind admitting, Emerson, it scared me. I mean, he's always before seemed such a quiet sort, why, it was as if he'd suddenly gone crazy!"

"Crazy? I don't think so, really. Though I can see how it might strike you that way—shall we sit down a minute, Miss Robinson? If I'm not intruding on your time—being a friend of his."

"I wouldn't say friend exactly. After all, I hardly know the man." How restful it was to be honest, if only for a moment! The trouble with lying—not that she had had much practice until now—was that it was such a nuisance, having to watch every word, every gesture and intonation. Aside from the ethics of the thing, of course. Odd, how that angle seemed to have gotten lost in the shuffle. "If he hadn't been the desk clerk, I probably never would have exchanged two words with him. He was good at the job, you know, very conscientious and obliging. And then the business about Lisa. I couldn't help feeling sorry for him, winding up in such a mess, even though he had only himself to blame. And he does blame himself, I'm sure. That's one of the things he has on his mind, the feeling of guilt—"

"But he couldn't have had anything to do with what happened to Lisa." Emerson hitched forward in his chair, alert and beady-eyed. "You saw him yourself out here on the patio. At least that's what you told the police."

"Certainly I saw him. Several times. Whenever I happened to glance out the window."

"Yes, I remember," said Emerson thoughtfully.

"I didn't mean that he *is* guilty. Just that he *feels* guilty. If he hadn't brought her up here in the first place—anyway. I never was what you'd call a friend of his, and after yesterday's episode, believe me, I never will be. He knows it, too. I was too shocked to say a word while it was going on, but after you left I told him exactly what I thought of his performance. Accusing you of spying on him! Where would he get such an idea? And even if it were true, why should it matter that much? Unless ..."

Emerson waited, rocking slightly on his chair edge and pressing his hands between his knees. As if he were hugging himself, she thought. A horrid little specimen. All right. She still had to find a way of getting at him.

"But that's too ridiculous," she said. "What could Mr. Leonard possibly have to hide? He's in the clear himself as far as Lisa's death is concerned. And if he had any information implicating anybody else—no, of course he wouldn't hide it, he'd be only too glad to hand it over to the police. They've already raked over his entire life history, nothing more to lose in that department. It simply doesn't make any sense."

"Except that he didn't act like a man with nothing to hide." Emerson rocked some more and smiled a secret smile. "It was obvious even to you. Forgive me, Miss Robinson, I didn't mean that in a derogatory sense. We're not all keen observers by nature, and I don't suppose you've made a point of training yourself along those lines. So it's interesting that you and I should reach the same conclusion about Mr. Leonard."

How she would have enjoyed smacking his conceited, patronizing face for him! She mastered the impulse—after all, she had not undertaken this project for pleasure—and said humbly, "Only you reached it way ahead of me. Didn't you, Emerson? Yes, and I bet you're way ahead of me on the rest of it, too. Because I still can't see—"

"There's always an answer. Like working a puzzle," Emerson explained kindly. "Just a matter of putting the pieces together in the right combination. Of course you have to have all the pieces first. That's where the keen observer bit comes in. If you don't mind my saying so, Miss Robinson, you seem to have lost sight of one of the key pieces."

"Have I? Yes, I must have." She blinked. Chewed her lip. Poor muddle-headed Miss Robinson, struggling to grasp what was of course elementary to a superior intellect like Emerson.

"You seem to have forgotten Carlos. I consider him rather a key figure. Don't you?"

"Carlos! Yes. Yes, of course I do. If anybody knows the truth about Lisa, it's Carlos. He must have been there that night. The question is, where is he now? It's not just me that's lost sight of Carlos, it's everybody!"

"Well ..." From under his smooth blond bang Emerson eyed her slyly. "Well, maybe not quite everybody."

"What did you say? I don't know what you mean." She gave him the wide-eyed astonished stare he expected; actually what she felt was excitement. So he did know! But no, not necessarily; he might think Carlos was still in the studio. Might not realize that Rhoda had already acted on his tip. And might be hanging around now, waiting for the fun to start. It wasn't like him to miss out on that much of the action; on the other hand, it would be just Quentin's luck....

"I said maybe not quite everybody. Just because the police haven't found Carlos that doesn't mean nobody else has."

"You, for instance?" And she laughed. "Come on now, Emerson, you don't really expect me to believe that. It's not just the local police, you know. There's a statewide alarm out for him."

"Five states," said Emerson. "And Canada."

"All right. Five states. And Canada. And you found him all by yourself? Why, you're only a boy. It's too much. I simply can't believe—"

"I don't see what's so incredible about it." His face had gone red; he sat bolt upright, no longer rocking. "I may be only a boy, but I know how to use my head. Yes, and my eyes and ears too. Once I bent my mind to it, I didn't have any difficulty figuring out where Carlos was. Nothing to it."

"All right, then. If you know where he is—"

"There's no if about it," he said sharply. "You think I'm kidding? You don't believe me? Listen. I've known where he was, all three places, right from the start. I could have turned him in any time I wanted to. I'm not ready to yet, but when I am—just you wait. I'll show you, wait and see if I don't!"

"I'm not saying I don't believe you." She did, of course. All three places. All three places. But now that she had found the way of getting at him, she must make the most of it. "I just don't see why you haven't told the police."

"That bunch of dum-dums. Why should I do them any favors? Let them do their own hunting. Besides, if I told them at this stage of the game they'd only louse things up. The case is settled as far as they're concerned. Carlos ran for cover, therefore he's guilty."

"And you don't think he is?"

"Let's just say I'm not closing my mind to the other possibilities. He's not the only one with a motive for killing Lisa, you know. But that's how the cops are. They like things simple. Well, they have their methods. I have mine, and I don't want them messing around with Carlos till I've worked things out myself. They'll get the whole story when I'm good and ready to give it to them. Not before."

He had very nearly talked himself back into his normal state of impervious complacency. She snatched at the first straw in sight. "Supposing they find him without your help?" No good. Emerson disposed of the notion with a scornful laugh. "Or how about me? There's nothing to stop me from telling them what you've just told me. Is there?"

"That's up to you. But if you do, it will be your word against mine. I'll deny it, I'll say you're lying. And I won't tell them where he is, no matter what they do to me. Them and their rubber hoses. They still won't get it out of me."

"Well then, supposing Carlos gives you the slip? You may know where he is now, but there's no guarantee he'll stay put. He didn't before. Or so I gather. Unless you're planning to stand guard on him every single minute...."

"No reason why I should. This time it's different. No. He'll stay put. He'd better, if he knows what's good for him."

He hadn't shown much talent in that direction so far, Margaret could have said but didn't. Silence was sometimes the most forceful comment. After a moment of waiting, Emerson went on, "And anyway, it's only for another day or so. Just till I get my plan all laid out. Because I'm not taking any chances. It's got to work and work the first time. Otherwise—"

"Yes. Otherwise. I wonder if you realize, Emerson, how much of a risk you're taking. Here you are, a boy—now don't get huffy, I'm not belittling your brain power, I'm talking about the physical part of it—a boy, planning to tackle a grown man on your own. A man on the run, for whatever reason remains to be seen. I don't know about you, but to me it sounds like a pretty dangerous proposition."

"I told you I'm not taking any chances," said Emerson stiffly.

"You'd better not. Because as I understand it Carlos is only the half of it. Quentin Leonard is mixed up in this somehow or other too, and judging by yesterday's little episode he's nobody to fool around with. He's a violent man, Emerson, and I hope for your sake you haven't got any ideas about taking him on single-handed."

Emerson sat motionless, staring at the toes of his sneakers. Finally he said, "I know it. I know I may need help."

"Yes, I think you will. Have you talked to anybody else about this? I mean, anybody besides me?" He shook his head No. "Well, then ..." The hook hung there, untouched. Not tempting enough. "I'm a fair shot. And Bax has a gun. I know where he keeps it." The last part wasn't a lie. Well, maybe the first part wasn't either. She might be a crackerjack of a shot. You never knew till you tried.

And she had hooked him. Up came his head. His bead-eyes fastened on her in a look of cool, deliberate speculation. "Good," he said. "I think I'll take you up on that."

He was still playing it cagey, though. Afterward, when she called Quentin from the drugstore phone booth, the report she gave him seemed woefully full of gaps—the most glaring one being Carlos's whereabouts. "He knows, all right. But he's not telling. Not yet, anyway. And I didn't dare push him too hard for fear of tipping my hand."

"Of course not." Quentin's disembodied voice sounded surprisingly cheerful. "Just so he opens up before tomorrow midnight."

"I know, I know." And she repeated the only firm commitment she had been able to extract from Emerson: that he would get in touch with her tomorrow evening, between eight and nine. By then he would have his plan thoroughly thought out and be ready for action. "But whether or not he'll actually open up even then—"

"Don't worry. He will. He needs help, and he knows it."

It was something to cling to. Not much, but something. "I'll let you know the minute I hear from him."

"Good girl," he said, and then they hung up.

14

"Oh! It's you! I was beginning to think you weren't going to call." Miss Robinson's voice came through breathless. Anxious sounding, thought Emerson. And she had picked up the phone herself, on the first ring, so she must have been right there at the Seaview desk, waiting.

"It's only eight thirty," he said. Then, warily, "Are you alone?"

"Yes, it's all right. Bax and Janet aren't back from their cocktail party yet, and everybody else is at the movies or out on the sun porch, playing bridge."

Like Emerson's parents, bless their hearts, who sat glued to their chairs in Breezy Point's card room (he had checked before stepping into the phone booth to make his call), safely out of the way for the next three hours. Early dinner on Sundays at both inns, so that on the kitchen front too the coast would be clear by now. That was something else he had taken into account when he figured out the timing.

"Good," he said. "Then I think we're all set."

"I'm ready any time you say." Too, too casual. "Just tell me where."

Yes indeed, just tell her where. So she could relay the information to Quentin Leonard? Emerson rather thought so. In fact, he rather hoped so. He had constructed his plan with this contingency in mind—two plans, really, Number One in case his suspicions proved groundless; Number Two in case they did not—and of the two the second was his favorite. More brilliant. And at the same time more decisive.

"Emerson? Are you still there?"

"Don't rush me. I'm thinking." He had of course done all his thinking long ago; had applied the finishing touches while attending divine services with his parents this morning. But let Miss Robinson simmer a bit longer. She would find out where Carlos was hiding soon enough. In due time. When Emerson was good and ready to tell her. Not before. "Can you meet me in twenty minutes? The side driveway at Seaview? I'll whistle when I get there. Don't come out before."

"Where? What? Yes, of course. The side driveway...."

"We'll go on from there," he explained gently. "Remember, stay in the office till you hear me whistle. And don't forget to bring, you know, what you promised."

He needed the gun. Nothing else would have induced him—mistrusting her as he did—to accept her offer of help. With the gun, he had no doubts about being able to pull off his coup. Without it, he did not even dare try. But at least it would cut both ways. If she didn't come through with the gun when he saw her tonight, then he didn't come through with the dope on Carlos. She stood to lose as much as he.

Meanwhile, twenty minutes. Long enough for her to alert Quentin Leonard, if that was her game; and long enough for Emerson to take one last look before the action started, just to be sure his memory of the layout was exact.

He slid out the door of the phone booth. Nobody in the lobby except for the desk clerk, nodding over the Sunday paper. From the card room a clipped, tense bid of four hearts. From the front porch the creak of rockers, a murmur of voices. No time for eavesdropping tonight, or for chitchat either. He had just let himself out the side door when he saw the two of them coming down the stairway: Grace Leonard and Rhoda Verdell. He hesitated, but only briefly. No time, even for them—curious though he was about the repercussions, if any, of his visit with them on Friday night. Since then his taps on their doors had gone unanswered. Now here they were. Exasperating. He could spare only a minute to watch through the screen door as they came on down the stairs and went into the little sitting room next to the phone booth. Then he took off, at a brisk trot, for the other, more pressing business at hand.

He circled around to the rear of Seaview, past the door to the sun room with its flickering TV screen and cluster of absorbed watchers. Next to it was the dining room, where all was quiet and dark; through the tall windows the rows of tables, set for breakfast, gave off a ghostly glimmer. The door was unlatched, as doors at Seaview were apt to be. He stepped noiselessly inside and tiptoed toward the kitchen. A roundabout route to where he was going, but tonight he preferred it to the approaches he had always used before—the outside entrance to the kitchen and the trellis door—because they were both on the side driveway. It wouldn't do for him to be seen ducking into either of them at this juncture, and Miss Robinson might well be on the lookout for him in the area of the side driveway.

He was wearing sneakers, so it didn't matter that the dining room floor was uncarpeted. But it was also alarmingly creaky; no amount of caution could prevent the series of squeaks and pops that rang out as he felt his way across to the swinging doors.

And there was still the kitchen. An even trickier stretch: only a short passageway separated it from the office, where Miss Robinson was presumably waiting, her ears pricked for his whistle. Not only that. The ice machine was in the kitchen, and at any moment somebody might come barging out for a bucket of ice. To Emerson, already shaken by his unexpectedly noisy trip across the dining room, it was an unnerving thought. Surely, though, he would have advance warning, enough time to dodge out of sight behind some piece of equipment. He couldn't expect to carry out his plan if he refused to take any risks at all. There was simply no way of ruling out the element of chance. It was always there, lurking around the next corner, the unforeseeable happenstance, the fluke, the little accident of time or place that could foul everything up....

He eased one of the swinging doors open a crack and peered in at the off-hours kitchen. Deserted, full of cavernous shadows and obscurely gleaming knobs, smelling of coffee and soap and fried shrimp. The refrigerator hummed comfortably to itself. A tap dripped. The pilot light on the stove flickered blue. Directly opposite him, beyond the long worktable, gaped the black-on-black rectangle that was his goal, the doorless exit to the pantry. That was where the outside door was, the one that opened onto the side driveway. That was also where the back stairway started, the one that led down to the cellar.

All right. Now or never. He slid through the swinging door and stole forward. Speed and stealth, in equal parts. No creaking floorboards here. Linoleum. Still, it seemed a long way across; and by the time he reached the pantry, he had no breath left and his heart was knocking against his ribs like a stir-crazy prisoner trying to get out. He leaned against the wall, waiting for it to quiet down. The tricky stretch was behind him, safely traversed. Miss Robinson had heard nothing that called for investigation. Nobody had chosen these few crucial moments for a visit to ice machine. And he was running right on schedule: a glance at his luminous wrist watch showed that he had ten minutes, exactly as planned for his reconnoitering expedition.

There were two sections to the cement stairway. The first was short, only four steps down to the outside door at the landing; there the second section, steeper and longer, angled off sharply to the cellar below. Emerson paused at the landing for a quick look out at the side driveway. A couple of cars were parked under the trees on the far edge of it. Otherwise it stretched empty and quiet, its gravel glinting dully in the starlight. Apparently Miss Robinson was obeying instructions and waiting inside for his signal. And Quentin? If she had alerted him, he might be waiting too, skulking somewhere out there in the shadows, ready to follow when the time came.... Well, let him. Because when the time came, Emerson would be in charge—either through possession of the gun or, if Miss Robinson failed to deliver, through possession of the information which was his and his alone. No gun, no deal. It was as simple as that.

He was just about to move on when he caught the gleam of headlights turning in at Seaview. At once he stepped to the side of the door, where he could watch without being seen himself. A good thing, too, because the car—he recognized it now, Janet's little convertible—swerved around from the front and drew up only a few yards away, beside the other entrance to the cellar, the lattice-like door in the underpinning. Janet, who had been doing the driving, hopped right out; Bax, after a little difficulty with the door, stepped forth with stately tread, extended his arms, and declaimed:

> "How sweet the moonlight sleeps upon this bank!
> Here will we sit and ... something or other, I forget.
> Sit, Janetta. Look how the floor of heaven ..."

"Okay, Bard." Janet began propelling him gently toward the side steps of the verandah, meanwhile launching into poetry herself: "'Bare ruined choirs, where late the sweet birds sang...'"

"No, that's something else. Another part of the forest. You're just trying to confuse me, Jannie, this one winds up something about ... Ah. Here we go. 'But in his motion like an angel sings, still quiring to the young-eyed cherubins...'"

It must have been a good cocktail party, thought Emerson. And got back to his own business.

The lower stretch of the stairway, though dark as a pocket, was familiar to him by now; cautiously but confidently he proceeded to the point, halfway down it, which served as his observation post. From there, crouched behind the cement block which supported the guard rail, he peered down. The territory below was also familiar to him. He had explored it some time ago, for the same reason he explored any cellar or attic he could get into—because such places fascinated him.

Actually, he had stumbled upon Seaview's cellar without realizing what it was. Mousing around the side driveway one day, and noticing that the lattice-effect door had been left unpadlocked, he naturally pushed it open and entered. It didn't look particularly interesting at first—just a space for storing fireplace logs—but what it led to was great.

A dream cellar, full of thrilling possibilities. Off to the left, in addition to the stairway on which he was now perched, were the hot water heater, a couple of derelict laundry tubs, a delightful jumble of discarded furniture, tools, leftover paint cans, and two closed doors—one, as he had soon found out, to the freezing room, the other to the canned goods pantry. All feebly lit by a dangling bulb. (It was burning tonight, as usual. For those, unlike Emerson, who needed real illumination, there was a switch at the top of the stairs.)

But what he had found most exciting, even on that first day before fantasy turned into fact, was the gradually narrowing space, secret as a tunnel, straight ahead, beyond the wood storage area. Back and back it ran, between the cellar floor, roughly hacked out of solid rock, and the wooden beams above, dwindling at last to nothing.

He had spent a blissful afternoon scrambling about in those black recesses, looking for the treasure he imagined might be hidden there. Nothing, of course. And then, a day or two later, his discovery of the cave had crowded everything else out of his mind.

But this was a better hiding place for Carlos than the cave. As a matter of fact, he could hole up here indefinitely. Why not, with the contents of the canned goods pantry and the freezing room at his disposal? Nobody was going to notice a few missing items. There was a good deal of traffic up and down the stairway during the day, but again, nobody was going to go poking around in the far reaches of the cellar. All Carlos had to do was lie low in his crawl space and wait for night; once dinner was over and the kitchen staff had cleared out, he could safely emerge to forage at leisure. Not much chance of interference from the police, either. Having searched all of Seaview, in their half-baked way, right at the start—before Carlos was there to be found—they weren't likely to come back for a second look when it might do them some good.

He might not know that, though. Might not realize just how lucky he had been two nights ago, when he dodged in here on the run from Quentin and the studio. Emerson had not actually seen him since then; he was only operating on the assumption that Carlos was still in the cellar. Supposing he wasn't? Supposing something had happened to scare him off and he was on the run again....

Always before, Emerson had been able to brush this possibility aside. Now, huddled behind the rough, damp-smelling cement block, he had the sinking feeling that it might not be so remote after all. But then what of his plan, his brilliant, intricately constructed plan? He knew what of it, all right. He could forget it.

And then, still shivering at the mental image of disaster, he caught a slide of movement in the murky depths below. He held his breath and waited. There. Again. At the pantry door—hardly more than a shifting shadow as it opened and closed. Another moment, and the shadow materialized under the dim bulb, in fact, stopped there. Carlos, no doubt about it. Cadaverous, shaggy-haired, still wearing his black turtleneck sweater, and apparently in no hurry to get back to his hidey hole. Having inspected the label on the can he was carrying—that must be why he had stopped under the light, to see what kind of a haul he had made—he took out his knife and jabbed a couple of holes in it. Juice of some kind. He tilted the can to his mouth and gulped thirstily.

Watching, Emerson felt something almost like fondness for him. Good old Carlos, right here where he was supposed to be, on the spot; and how obliging of him to show up just when Emerson was beginning to get the jitters. Not that he really, seriously believed, even for a second, that his plan might fail. After all the time and brain power he had spent, working everything out to the last little detail? Of course not. Why, if he had the gun, he could nail Carlos right now; a few minutes of being shut up in the freezing room and he'd be only too happy to answer any and all questions about Lisa. The same went for Quentin Leonard, in case he was hanging around hoping to get to Carlos first. Once in the freezing room, Quentin would talk too. Plenty. And Emerson would take his own sweet time about letting *him* out, no matter how cooperative he might be in helping to solve the case.

The gun. If he had the gun—

The overhead light came on without warning. One second he sat, secure in the darkness; the next he was caught, transfixed in that blast of light. And Carlos with him. He stood down there, blankly staring and motionless, the can halfway to his mouth. Tomato juice, Emerson had time to notice before the paralysis passed and he was able to turn his head.

It was Bax at the top of the stairs. "Hey, what goes on?" He spoke in a tone of genial interest. A little befuddled. Not in the least alarmed. He had taken off his shoes and came padding down the steps in his socks. "Emerson? Yeah. Emerson. What the hell are you doing down here? And who—" Then he gave a sudden gulp and reached for the stair rail, visibly remembering the police description of the man wanted for questioning in connection et cetera.

"Never mind who," said Carlos. "Just get on down here and be quick about it. You too, Emerson. Both of you."

That wasn't a can of tomato juice in his hand any more. It was a gun. But I'm supposed to have the gun, Emerson thought as he scrambled to his feet. I'm supposed to be in charge.

"I said get on down here." Carlos took a step or two toward them, with the gun leading the way; and Bax, who had half turned, as if to make a dash for it up the stairs, abruptly changed course.

"Now look here," he began. He still had his genial, bumbling air, like someone willing to go along with a joke, even if he didn't get the point yet, and even if it turned out to be not a very good joke. "I mean, let's not—"

"Hurry up. And shut up." Again the gun moved purposefully. Above it Carlos's face was hollow, smudged with dirt and a two days' growth of beard. His eyes had the wild sheen of a woods creature's. "Do as I say and you'll be all right. Otherwise you're going to get hurt."

Hurt? Killed was what he meant. He'd just as soon kill us as not, thought Emerson, and came down the stairs fast. Bax followed more slowly, silent now except for the whispering sound his socks made on the worn steps.

"Back here," said Carlos and herded them out of the glare of the light, past heater, laundry tubs, clutter of tools and furniture. And away from the freezing room; only Emerson had been shrewd enough to think of that. His plan, his beautifully worked out plan! All brought to nothing by a flick of Bax's finger on the light switch.

"Okay," said Carlos. "This is far enough for now." He jerked Bax's tie loose and handed it to Emerson. "Here, make yourself useful. Tie his hands behind him. Good and tight. I'll check it later, so don't try any tricks."

Emerson did as he was told. With the gun trained on him, he went back for the clothesline, several lengths of it, beside the laundry tubs. That was for Bax's ankles. There was his handkerchief for a gag.

Then it was Emerson's turn. Something was thrust into his mouth, he would rather not know what. Wrists, ankles, bound with one piece of clothesline; Carlos did a quick, thorough job on him. It only hurt when he tried to move. Ignominy upon ignominy: Carlos picked him up as if he were a turkey trussed for the oven and carried him deeper into the blackness, wedged him into one of the niches he had explored a lifetime ago, and left him there.

Went away and left him. To check on Bax, presumably; presently there were some dragging sounds, as if he were stashing Bax away in a corner of his own. Wherever it was, it was nowhere near Emerson.

He struggled a bit at first. No use; in fact, worse than useless. He gave up and lay still, shivering with disbelief and outrage.

It might be hours before they found him. Hours before they even missed him. The thought of his parents back there at Breezy Point, impervious to everything but their bridge game, was too much for him; tears squeezed out of his eyes, bubbles out of his nose. An abject snivel—

that was all he was capable of, and he was past caring.

He just wanted somebody, anybody, even a dum-dum cop, to come and get him.

15

Nine o'clock, and still no sign of Emerson. Deep in the shade of the lilac trees, Quentin waited and watched, now and then shifting cautiously from one foot to the other. When Margaret called—almost half an hour ago now—he had picked this spot because it gave him an unimpeded view of Seaview's side driveway. Where the action was supposed to start.

But where so far the only action had been the return of Bax and Janet, a bit smashed, from their cocktail party. Could that have disrupted Emerson's schedule? No, they had made their entrance and their exit, on wings of poesy, well before the appointed hour.

Ten minutes late. It wasn't really anything to get uneasy about. Even someone as punctilious as Emerson might get hung up for that length of time. Circumstances over which he had no control. Some little happenstance popping up to delay him. Or ...

Or the whole thing might be a hoax. The idea was not a new one to Quentin; he faced it stoically. It hadn't been a hoax before—Emerson's story about the cave. All the more reason, in a way, that he should be fabricating now. Why not capitalize on his record as a sleuth and, just for the fun of it, cook up a fresh, false lead on Carlos? Tricky little bastard, it would be right up his alley. Tricky and bright: he might well have seen through Margaret's anti-Quentin act and realized that anything he told her stood a good chance of getting back to Quentin. In which case, it was almost certainly a hoax, especially designed to pay off the grudge rankling in Emerson's bosom.

Well. No use speculating about the convolutions of that busy little brain. They were endless. True or false, Emerson's story was the only lead in sight, and Quentin was in no position to pass it up. Beggars couldn't be choosers. He checked his watch again. Five past nine. Not quite three hours till deadline, and if he thought Rhoda wasn't going to hold him to it—well. No use dwelling on that, either.

What, then? Margaret? She had sounded fairly calm over the phone. But by now she must be in a fine old state of jitters. He saw her, sober-faced and tense, sitting on the edge of the couch in Seaview's office, clutching her tote bag with Bax's gun inside it. Counting the seconds as he was doing. Waiting for the overdue signal, not daring—any more than he—to make a move until it came. And most likely asking herself how on earth, why on earth, she had gotten mixed up in any of this. As well she might. Because Quentin knew she wasn't all that sure about him. There was a certain look that came into her eyes when she was remembering his quarrel with Lisa, his dealings (ambiguous, to say the least) with Carlos. Even though she had not reported the quarrel to the police, had accepted his explanation about Carlos—even so, she was not absolutely, unshakably sure about him. But all the same, committed to his cause. He would have gotten nowhere trying to pump Emerson himself; she had done it for him. Not only that.

If tonight's action had gone as planned, she would have played the leading role, at least at first. It had sounded quite simple: her rendezvous with Emerson, who really knew where Carlos was, and who—once he was satisfied that she had brought the gun as promised—would lead her there. With Quentin following, keeping well out of sight until the time came for him to take over. Wherever and whenever that might be. Not until the gun, Bax's gun, was in his hand. Never mind whether or not he would be capable of using it this time, he had to have it; Carlos was armed, and he must be too. And he would be. If Margaret (Fair Shot Margaret) still had it she would pass it to him. If Emerson had insisted on toting it himself, the transfer might take a little longer....

Simple or not, the whole business could be forgotten now. Because it was fairly obvious the kid wasn't going to show. Had never intended to. Was no doubt chortling to himself over the success of his hoax.

All right. It had been a flimsy hope at best; the wonder was that Quentin should feel so lost without it. He must have been banking on Emerson's purported lead more than he realized. For want of anything else to bank on. Now there was nothing. Nothing. He hadn't a hope in hell of finding Carlos before midnight, or of preventing Rhoda from going to the police with her story, or of convincing the police that it wasn't true. He was well and truly in for it. Before morning he would be under arrest and probably charged with murder. And maybe that was what he deserved. Lisa, he thought. Lisa.

Meanwhile? One thing sure, there was no point in waiting any longer, and the least he could do for Margaret was tell her so. She may already have given up. He didn't think so, though. She seemed a bit on the stubborn side.

Even now, he felt an odd reluctance about openly crossing the side driveway, choosing instead to stick close to the shrubbery that bordered it and after that to the shelter of Seaview itself. He had almost reached the outside entrance to the kitchen when he noticed the light in the cellar. It rather surprised him. Enough so that he paused. The next instant it flicked off, and he stayed where he was, expecting whoever it was—somebody coming up from the cellar, he assumed—to turn on the kitchen light. But no light showed, no sound of footsteps came from the kitchen. Presently he went on, past that door and the other, trellis-effect one that led to the wood storage space. As usual, it had been left unlocked. Again he paused, hearing, thinking he heard, a stealthy stirring from within. Maybe a raccoon; according to Mrs. O'Boyle, they sometimes got in there, stared out at you, oh, spooky, she wouldn't go down in that cellar, not for love or money. Must be a raccoon. Except that the business with the lights was a little peculiar, too.

"Quentin?" From the bottom of the verandah stairs, Margaret leaned forward to peer at him through her harlequin glasses. Her voice was low and tremulous; she moved toward him jerkily. "Where is he, Quentin? Twenty minutes, he said, and it's almost nine thirty. What could have happened to him?"

"I doubt if anything has. This is probably his idea of a joke."

"You mean—"

"I mean he was having us on, making out he knew where Carlos is. It wouldn't surprise me if he was watching us right now, laughing his damn little head off. Emerson's like that. Never a dull moment with him around."

"But he really did know about Carlos before," said Margaret. Stubborn. Just as he had suspected.

"That's what made it so easy for him the second time. He simply couldn't resist. Besides, it gave him a chance to even the score with me. Well, he's evened it. I'm only sorry you had to be dragged into it. A fine evening you've had, sitting around waiting, all keyed up and nowhere to go."

"It wasn't so bad at first. Only then Bax and Janet came rolling in, and I couldn't quite think what to do. Because I was still expecting Emerson, you see, it hadn't occurred to me yet that he might not come. Bax kept saying I must have a drink with them, and I knew I'd have to, if I stayed in the office the way I was supposed to, but then what if the whistle came—Well, anyway. Finally I got my wits about me enough to tell them I had a date and ducked out onto the verandah. That's where I've been for the last twenty minutes or so, hunched down back of the rocking chairs, praying nobody would come along and notice me. And wondering if it was safe to—" She cocked her head, listening. "What was that? Did you hear something?"

He had. The same furtive scrabbling as before. "Sounds like somebody's in the cellar. Bax or Janet, probably. Did you see either of them go down there?"

"No, they were both starting upstairs when I came out on the verandah. They could have gone down later, of course. If they used the back stairs I wouldn't have heard them. But then why isn't the light on? They wouldn't be prowling around down there in the dark."

"Animals get in there sometimes. I expect that's all it is." But the animal theory didn't explain the peculiar business of the flicked-off light. No point in worrying Margaret with that, he thought, and added casually, "I might just take a look. See what's going on. I've got a flashlight."

"But supposing—" She was wearing slacks and a sweater, both dark-colored. Only the pale triangle of her face stood out, and her hand, fumbling with the tote bag she carried over her arm. "Here. You'd better take this too." And she handed him Bax's gun. "As long as I won't be needing it."

In her quiet way, she could be a pretty cool customer.

"I don't think I'll be needing it either, really," he said. "But all right. If I find Bax in there, I can return it to him."

She uttered a polite little laugh. Finally, after a moment of fidgeting with the buttons on her sweater, she turned and headed back toward the side stairs to the verandah.

"Margaret," he began. But she kept right on going, head down, one more shadow blending in with all the others. He wouldn't have known what to say to her, anyway, so maybe it was just as well.

There were no more sounds from the cellar. Not so much as a rustle. Quentin eyed the trellis door with its padlock dangling open, considered briefly, and snapped it shut. On his way back to the kitchen door, he realized that he had not checked it; if by some miracle it was locked—it wasn't. He let himself in quietly and paused, trying to get his bearings. He had been in Seaview's cellar only once before, with Bax, helping him tinker the water heater out of one of its seizures and back into action. His mental picture of the place was vague: a couple of storage rooms, a good deal of clutter, and in the unused part a sharp uptilting of the rocky foundation, an impression of black, cavernous passages. Spooky, as Mrs. O'Boyle had put it. Whoever it was down there, whatever, might already have heard him and retreated to those dark recesses; would certainly do so if he switched on the overhead light. He was better off without it, and without his flashlight too, for the present. Save it for later.

He found the guard rail and started groping his way down the stairs. Halfway down there was a cement block; peering cautiously around it, he saw that the cellar was not in complete darkness, after all. In the yellowish glimmer from the dim bulb, maybe fifteen watts, hanging from the underside of the stairway, he could make out the shape of his old acquaintance the water heater. And beyond it the two doors to the storage rooms....

After the one lurch of recognition, his heart steadied. Yes, recognition: he knew it was Carlos, even before the figure materialized into anything more than a formless blur. Carlos, coming on fast from the wood storage space—with its door padlocked now—making for the only other exit. At the foot of the steps he pulled up short, as if sensing Quentin's presence, possibly caught up in his own flash of recognition.

"Okay. It's you. I'm getting out of here. Don't try to stop me." He had the gun in his hand. His voice sounded hoarse, with a panicky edge to it.

"I'm not trying to stop you. But I have to talk to you. Listen, Carlos—"

"No! Shut up and get out of my way." He started up the steps, menacingly.

"Don't be a damn fool. You take a shot at me, and you'll never get out of here. Everybody in the house will be down here on your back." The gospel truth. But was Carlos in any shape to see it? "I helped you before. You owe me something for that."

"I don't owe you anything for tonight. If it weren't for you I'd be long gone. I was all set to make it out this way when I turned off the light. Only you had to come along. Not only that, you locked the other door on me."

"I didn't know it was you in here. And I still say you owe me something for helping you before. Give me a chance and I'll do it again. You're going to need help; don't kid yourself. All at once you're in a sweat to get out of here for some reason—"

"That's my business."

Quentin thought he knew the reason. He wouldn't have been able to stick it out for very long down here, either. A cave in the woods was one thing; a black dungeon of a cellar, something else again.

"Right. Your business. Have you figured out where you're going? Or how to get there without being seen?" Carlos was only a couple of steps below him by now. He could smell the sweat on him, hear him breathing. "I can sneak you back to the studio again. Unless you've got a better idea."

"Why should you?"

"My business. We'll go into that later. Come on if you're coming." And if he wasn't? Better not to think about it. Quentin turned, more or less steadily, and started up the stairs. It seemed like a hell of a long time before he heard the whisper of Carlos's footsteps coming along behind.

"I never asked you to do me any favors. So even if I do owe you something ..."

"Later," said Quentin. "It'll keep till we get to the studio." He had a chance now, a middling to good chance; and the thought of blowing it threw him into a fever of anxiety. From the kitchen door he looked out at the side driveway. Only three cars were parked there—two under the trees at its far edge, and Janet's, close to the house. But at any moment others might drive up. Somebody coming back from the movies. Somebody inquiring for rooms. At any moment, furthermore, somebody might pop out of the kitchen. And that would be it. Because Carlos looked exactly like what he was—a fugitive. Begrimed, hollow-eyed, shaggy-haired, tense. And armed: the gun was still there in his hand. Next time he might be foolhardy enough to use it. Or he might suddenly decide to skip the studio and light out on his own. I'd have to shoot him, thought Quentin; so help me, I'd have to.

He felt Carlos stiffen. Then he too heard the sound and recognized it as the squeak of the door between office and kitchen. There was no time to waste. He reached for the door with one hand, for Carlos with the other, shoved him outside and slipped through himself. And none too soon; the next moment the kitchen light flicked on. They stayed where they were, flattened side by side against the outside of the house, listening. A thump. A snatch of "O Solo Mio," whistled off key. Clattering sounds.

"Just somebody getting ice," whispered Quentin. If Carlos heard, he gave no sign. Eyes straight ahead, rigid as a robot, he waited until the light flicked off again. Then he let his breath out and sagged bonelessly against the wall.

There was no more stalling from him after that. Whatever ideas of his own he may have had to begin with, they were gone now, drained out of him by those few final moments of tension. (Such a small crisis, compared with all the others he had been through in the past week; but one small crisis too many.) It was more than Quentin had hoped for, this mood of dazed obedience; and on the theory that it wasn't going to last, he made the most of it.

"This way," he whispered. "Stay close to the house. After that the bushes. If you hear a car coming, hit the ground."

Luck was with them. One car did come, but they had already reached the lilac trees—Quentin's waiting place of an hour ago—and stayed there, safely screened, until the car's headlights went out and its occupants disappeared up the side steps of the verandah. From there on no problems: after a short sprint up the road they were inside the studio.

Quentin closed the door behind them and pulled the drapes shut across the window. The little wall lamp was already on; he left it at that.

When he sat down he realized that his legs were trembling, and when he went to light a cigarette the match wobbled embarrassingly. According to his watch it was only ten thirty. A good hour and a half till deadline. Or maybe a bad hour and a half. Depending on one thing and another.

Across from him Carlos slumped on the couch, his head in his hands. It was hard now to remember being jealous of him, hard to think of him as handsome or even young. His abject, beaten attitude—more than cellar dirt, tangled hair, or scruffy clothes—made him seem like a derelict, broken-spirited, with no fight left in him.

But then he lifted his head, and Quentin knew better. They stared at each other, enemies once more. "So you're in some kind of a bind," said Carlos. "And I'm supposed to do you a favor. Like what?"

"Like talking to your mother when she phones—she'll be calling before long now—so she'll know I haven't murdered you."

"What did you say?"

Quentin said it again. "She found out you were here in the studio, and she's made up her mind I killed you. She's not going to believe otherwise until she sees you, or at least talks to you."

"Until she—" Carlos went off into what seemed to be a fit of wild, silent laughter. It left him sounding choked but positive. "All right. Let her believe it. I'm not seeing her. Or talking to her, either."

"Not even to keep her from going to the cops?"

After a moment of silence Carlos said, "She wouldn't do that to me. Never."

"Not if she knew you were alive, no. To me she'd do it. Any day."

"In that case why hasn't she done it already?"

"I showed her the note you left me. Even so, she had some reservations. She seemed to think I might have forced you—"

"I know how her mind works. She's my mother." The silence this time was quite long. When Carlos spoke again, it was as if the words were being pulled out of him, against his will. "Is she—How is she?"

"For God's sake, how do you think she is? You're her only son, the one person on earth she cares anything about, and you're in trouble, bad trouble. She doesn't know where you are, or even if you're alive. You expect her to be feeling great?"

Carlos closed his eyes. "Okay, okay. I owe it to her. Maybe I owe it to you too. That doesn't mean I'm going to do it." He snatched up the gun and sprang to his feet. "I don't have to stay here. I can walk out that door any time I feel like it. You can't stop me."

"No, but I can try. And I will. You're going to have to kill me first. I mean it, Carlos, you're going to have to shoot me dead."

He might be panicky enough to do it, too, Quentin thought. Then so be it. He rose deliberately, crossed to the door, and stood in front of it. For his own part, he knew that he still could not kill Carlos, and he was not going to pretend otherwise. Let Bax's gun stay where it was, in his pocket; he was not about to use it, even as a threat.

Which made him as crazy as Carlos, he supposed. Pretty crazy, judging by that gray, tight face of his, and the glare in his eyes. But it seemed to Quentin that the longer Carlos hesitated, the less likely he was to shoot. And if he tried to bull his way out without shooting, or made a break for the back door, Quentin had no doubts about being able to handle him.

For another couple of moments they faced each other, deadlocked; then, with a gesture of defeat, Carlos tossed the gun on the couch. "All right. I'll talk to her. Damn you, damn you...." His voice was dull with fatigue, and he was swaying on his feet.

Quentin felt a bit drained himself. He can't kill me either, he thought. It's the same as it was with me. Much as he hates me, he can't kill me either.

"There," he said, as the phone rang. "That must be her now."

16

After a while, with the inevitable fading of the glow, Janet's mellow mood began to go a little sour. Just a little; not enough to make her snap at Bax when he trundled back up here to his room—as he ought to do any minute now—with the makings of the festive snack they had decided to have instead of dinner. Her share of the preparations was done: she had cleared off the marble-topped table (the clutter that man could collect!), had laid out the paper plates, the glasses, and plastic forks and spoons. Bax had volunteered for the foraging expedition. Plenty of goodies in the cellar. Let not poor Jannie starve, he had said. He would be back in a jiffy.

A pretty long jiffy. But that was how Bax was. Time meant nothing to him. He sauntered through life at his own easygoing, meandering gait, and no amount of snapping was going to change him. She didn't want to change him, really. If he were any different, he might not put up with her.

She brushed her hair, repaired her lipstick, lit a cigarette. Mustn't be impatient. That was probably him she heard right now.... No, the footsteps went on past.

Dammit, she was *hungry*. And if he wasn't, he ought to be. Let not poor

Jannie starve, indeed! Oh, she knew what was keeping him: he had found somebody to have another drink with and had forgotten all about her and their festive snack. Was no doubt sitting down there spouting poetry, while she waited in this junkshop of a room of his—well. She would give him ten more minutes, no more and no less; and if he didn't show up by then, she would go down and do her own foraging. And, incidentally, tell him what she thought of him.

The trouble was that she couldn't find him to deliver her speech, which by this time was honed to razor-edge sharpness. That was another exasperating thing about him, his habit of disappearing at crucial moments. Just dropping out of sight and then bobbing up, relaxed and gently surprised to find that anybody had been looking for him.

Smiling her "mine hostess" smile, Janet made the rounds. Out on the sun porch the TV watchers unglued their eyes from the screen long enough to shake their heads when she asked if they had seen him. She got the same response from the card players in the sitting room. The library was deserted except for the retired teacher from Providence, who sat bolt upright and fast asleep with her copy of *Pride and Prejudice* open in her lap. Still on page 47. Janet left her undisturbed and moved on to the front hallway. Mrs. O'Boyle was there on the love seat, looking more than usually put upon because she had been delegated to listen for the office phone, and knitting up a storm. "Haven't seen hide nor hair of him," she stated, with satisfaction. "Why would I, if he used the back stairs? I can't keep tabs on everything. The phone hasn't rung but once. Wrong number."

There was no one in the office, of course. Or in the kitchen. And the light wasn't on in the cellar, so he couldn't be down there. He hadn't driven off into the night; both the station wagon and her convertible were still parked outside.

Janet, pausing to peer into the kitchen refrigerator, decided she was no longer hungry. Blast him, where could he have gotten to? Plenty of other places. Too many. Just for openers, it was entirely possible that he had never even come downstairs. He was always getting sidetracked. A chance encounter with some convivial soul in the upstairs hall, an invitation to come in and have a quick one—that was all it would take to switch him off course. In which case, he could stay there all night; Janet had no intention whatever of going around tapping on every bedroom door that had a light under it.

She wasn't going to scour the grounds for him, either, if by any chance he had decided on a nice little head-clearing walk. The verandah was as far as she cared to carry that particular line of investigation. As she stepped through the screen door, she remembered that he had taken off his shoes in his room. Would he set off for a walk in his sock feet? The answer was that he would. And never notice the difference.

The line of rocking chairs stood empty. She lingered a moment at the top of the front steps, hugging her arms against the night air, listening to the forlorn sound the wind made in the trees. She hadn't really expected him to be out here. And he wasn't. No use brooding about it. As she turned back toward the door she caught sight of a figure huddled on the side steps.

"Bax?" she called out sharply. Hope, relief, annoyance—equal parts. "Bax, is that you?"

"No," said Margaret Robinson. "It's me." She rose, rather reluctantly, it seemed to Janet, and started across the verandah.

"Oh. What are you doing out here? I thought you had a date."

"So did I. But I guess—I seem to have been stood up."

Poor girl, she sounded a bit on the teary side. And Janet hadn't helped any, blurting it out like that. "That makes two of us," she said. "Bax was supposed to bring us something to eat, we were going to have a spread upstairs, only now he's pulled one of his disappearing acts and I can't find him anywhere. I'm not even hungry anymore. Just mad."

"Can't find him?" Margaret echoed foggily. "But where—I mean—"

"Yes. Where. He started off to raid the storage pantry in the cellar, but it's anybody's guess where he actually wound up."

"The cellar!" Margaret sounded more than foggy now. Practically strangled. And she reached out and clutched Janet's arm. It wasn't at all like her to make such a gesture. New England reserve personified. Not to mention a lifetime of being put down by that mother of hers. "Listen, Janet, I think we ought to ... I think maybe there's something wrong."

Had the girl's mind suddenly cracked? Janet peered up at her, trying to make out the expression in her eyes. But the light was too dim; Margaret's face was no more than a whitish blob glimmering between the darkness of her high-necked sweater and her forelock.

"Wrong? It's just the way Bax is, especially when he's had one or two. I don't see why—"

But Margaret, again uncharacteristically, cut in. "The cellar, you said. Did you actually go down there to look for him?"

"Well, no. No, I didn't. But he wouldn't go down there without turning on the light." Unless, of course, he had slipped and fallen and was lying at the foot of the stairs, senseless, maybe even lifeless.... Surely, though, Margaret had no reason to jump to such a conclusion. That couldn't be what she meant by something wrong. "What is this, anyway? What's going on?"

"I didn't think about the light. Of course Bax would have turned it on. You're right, of course. He's somewhere else. Not down there at all. I don't know how I could have been so stupid. Getting you all upset over nothing. I'm sorry." She let go of Janet's arm and pushed nervously at her glasses. "Terribly sorry."

So much for the alarm that had been Margaret's immediate—and genuine—reaction. Quite a switch, thought Janet; now that she was supposed to believe otherwise, she found herself more convinced than ever that something was wrong. And whatever it was, and whether or not Bax was involved in it, its focus was obviously the cellar. Because that had been the triggering word for Margaret. "The cellar!" she had choked out and grabbed Janet's arm.

"I'm not so sure it's over nothing," said Janet. "Those stairs are steep. Bax might have taken a header down them before he had a chance to flip the switch. It didn't occur to me before. Now that it has—well. There's only one way to find out." She set off briskly for the side steps of the verandah.

"Wait! I mean—" A pause. Then Margaret said in quite a different voice, cool and decisive. "Wait for me. I'm coming with you."

Down the steps they went, side by side. Past the trellis door, padlocked for once in its life, and on to the kitchen entrance. It was only when she reached for the light switch that Janet realized just how anxious she was; how tensely braced for the sight of Bax sprawling on the cellar stairs, broken, bloody, or—even more dreadful—like Lisa, unmarked yet unmistakably dead.

Her finger fumbled, flicked. The breath rushed out of her. And out of Margaret beside her. They smiled at each other wanly.

From down below came a muffled thump. And another. After that a waiting silence.

No need to ask if Margaret had heard it too. The cock of her head showed that she had, and her eyes, round and unblinking. "Who is it?" Janet called out. "Bax? Is it you?"

The thumps started up again, quite a little volley of them this time. Not in the least furtive-sounding. Urgent, rather. Like a signal. It sent Janet flying down the stairs. Even so, Margaret got to him first. And a good thing too, because she set to work ungagging him, very businesslike, while Janet could only goggle at him—disheveled, trussed, helpless as a bug on its back—and ask simple-minded questions.

"Bax! What in the world! Are you all right? What happened?"

He couldn't talk yet, of course. When the gag was out, and after he had worked his tongue around to get the juices going again, he managed to croak, "About time you came and got me! Is there a drink in the house?"

She dashed to the laundry tubs, found a jelly glass on the shelf, dashed back with it half full. Not what he had in mind, and the water was probably brackish. But wet; he drank it gratefully. By this time Margaret had his hands untied—his poor wrists, cruelly chafed—and he was able to sit up. He even produced, for Janet, a dazed, dim version of his sunny smile. Bless him, bless him; she burst into tears.

"Carlos," was the next word he said.

Margaret, who had been busy unknotting the cord that bound his ankles, was electrified into jerky speech. "Carlos! He got away? Where? Did Quentin—"

"Quentin. Yeah." Bax nodded, in a bemused way. "It was his voice. I think. I didn't have my glasses on, so I couldn't hear very well. Well, and it was after the light went out anyway, so—I wasn't all that sharp, the whole business, none of it's any too clear in my mind...."

He had dozed off for a while after Carlos finished tying him up. It seemed the only sensible thing to do under the circumstances. The more he tried to loosen his bonds the tighter they got, and somebody was bound to come down here eventually, no use fretting about how soon. Admittedly, he had grown a bit impatient after he came to, until he discovered the technique of thumping himself along, inch by inch. Uphill work, but it helped to pass the time, and it had, thank God, attracted their attention. He gave them another befuddled smile. "I might really have gotten discouraged if you'd gone away without finding me."

They helped him to his feet and brushed him off. He was covered with grime, stiff, full of kinks and scratches and bruises. But he made it up the stairs and into the kitchen. There, knees buckling, he folded onto a stool; Janet poured a good hooker of brandy for each of them; and Margaret said, in an odd, challenging voice, "I suppose you're going to call the police?"

Of course. Naturally. Peck must be notified. "Only let's keep it as quiet as we can," said Bax. "If Mrs. O'Boyle gets wind of it there'll be no holding her. She'll have the whole house in such an uproar Peck wouldn't be able to hear himself think. They'll know soon enough. In the meantime—"

"I'll take care of her," said Janet. She was pretty much recovered by now, once more capable of coping. "Then I'll call Peck."

"I've got a better idea," Margaret announced. Cool and decisive, the way she had sounded back there on the verandah. "What about Quentin? If he was there and talked to Carlos, he must know something. Probably more than Bax does. The least we can do is check with him. And even if he's not at the studio, we can call the police from there. A few more minutes won't make that much difference. Or, if you'd rather, I'll go by myself—"

She would have, too. Bax might not know it—he was blinking at her like a dazed owl—but Janet did. After a moment she said quietly, "Why no, Margaret, we'll go with you. Anyway, I will. Bax? Okay, drink up. Off we go."

17

They had the little sitting room to themselves. The other guests at Breezy Point, those who had not already retired, preferred the main living room for their card playing and socializing. Rhoda sat in the platform rocker, fixed for the moment in one of her trances, her long hands idle in her lap. Grace had laid out a game of solitaire and was burbling along as usual, expecting no answer, and getting none.

"There now, isn't this nice and cozy? I've said all along, haven't I, it wasn't healthy, holing up in that room of yours, nothing like a change of scene.... You look better already, dear, really you do, just our little outing for lunch yesterday, it did you a world of good.... Once you've made the effort, and I know what an effort it was for you, believe me, I know, even though I'm supposed to be such an extrovert...."

Against this background of chitchat—as gentle and undemanding as the plashing of a fountain—each was free to pursue her own thoughts.

Rhoda's were focused, with fanatic intensity, on the phone call she was to make later tonight. Eleven o'clock, Quentin had said; if he was going to fulfill his part of their bargain at all, he should be able to do it by then. That was the sum and substance of last night's bulletin, delivered in the same laconic style as the earlier, no-progress report at noon. No trace of excitement over the lead—yes, fairly promising, the details could wait—that had developed in the interval. No pretense of sympathy or comfort. It would have been pretense, all right. He couldn't abide her; nor she him.

Eleven o'clock. One final call, and they would be through with each other, and with the deal forced upon them, him as much as her, through stark necessity. Either he would have found Carlos or—

But that was forbidden territory. She slammed the door of her mind on hope and dread alike and concentrated instead on how she was going to get away from Grace long enough to put through her final call. She had managed handily enough yesterday. A purported visit to the ladies' room during their luncheon outing—let Grace take the credit for persuading her out of seclusion if it made her happy—and the first call was accomplished. No problem with the second one, either: she had slipped downstairs to the public phone booth in the lobby while Grace was taking a pre-bedtime stroll. It might work out that way again tonight. But she couldn't count on it. She must be ready with some excuse in case one was needed when the time came. Eleven o'clock. By then, he had said. So she could take a chance on pushing the time up a bit. Ten minutes, maybe even fifteen. How long from now? She could only guess; she was not allowed to look at her watch until Grace finished her game of solitaire. That was the rule she had laid down for herself, one of the countless, senseless rules that had made it possible for her to get through the last two days.

"Oh, sugar," said Grace. "Where is that jack of diamonds? There. Only one card away, and I would have made it." She scooped the deck together and began shuffling.

No doubt about it, she was thinking, Rhoda was up to something. The way she kept looking at her watch, for instance. Shaking it, holding it up to her ear to make sure it was still going. She was doing it now. And there she went again, rocking away for dear life, one hand clamped on the chair arm, the other fidgeting with the cameo pin at her neck. Another spell of twitching; it was either that nowadays, or the trance business, the times when she sat motionless, only the glitter of her eyes to show that she was still alive.

Nowadays. Yesterday and today. Since the Friday night session with Quentin, when he claimed to have calmed her down. Not so Grace could notice it.

Something else peculiar: Rhoda, who before Friday couldn't be budged out of her room no matter what, had agreed to yesterday's excursion with a minimum of urging. And tonight she herself had suggested coming downstairs. Why the switch all of a sudden? Of course it might be just coincidence. Or Grace might be making something out of nothing; she wasn't quite herself these days, she knew that, it was one of the few things she did know for sure.

But the very fact that she knew so little about Friday night was significant. They were purposely keeping her in the dark. Both of them. Rhoda with her: "You were right about Emerson's story, Carlos wasn't there," and not another word to be pried out of her; Quentin with his sketchy assurances.... No, there had to be more to it than that. There had to be some reason for Rhoda's erratic behavior, her air of tense, urgent waiting. For what? For what?

Something to do with Carlos, of course. So he was alive, not a suicide, as Grace had assumed. And Quentin really was involved in some kind of shady compact with him. She had been so sure that Emerson was just fabricating, so determined not to believe a word of what he said. But she couldn't have it both ways. If there was more to Friday night's session than anybody was saying, then there must be more to Emerson's story than she wanted to admit.

She stole another glance at Rhoda, who had stopped fidgeting and was once more locked in that unearthly stillness. Yes. As if she were waiting for something.

She came out of it with a snap. "Why are you watching me like that? I declare, Grace, I don't know what's got into you the last couple of days!"

"Into me! You're the one that's been acting funny. Ever since Friday night. And you still haven't told me what actually happened. I can't help wondering why you're being so hush-hush about it."

"And I can't help wondering why you're being so inquisitive about it. Unless Quentin—Is that it? Something he said? Something he told you?"

"You don't need to worry about Quentin. He knows how to keep a secret. Especially from me."

"Oh, for pity's sake! There's no secret to keep." She caught her breath, as if startled by the sharpness of her own voice, and went on tremulously. "Please, Grace. This isn't like you. I know I went against your advice Friday night. Yes, and I broke my word to you, I promised to wait till morning—I shouldn't have promised. Only you kept at me and at me. It was too much to ask of me, I couldn't possibly wait, surely you don't blame me for that. If there was the slightest chance of finding him, my boy ..." She closed her eyes, trying to hold back the tears.

The familiar pattern. Automatically Grace made the consoling sounds that were expected of her. Tired. She was so tired. And, yes, homesick. If only she were back where she belonged, if only she had stayed there instead of coming up here, and not just herself, she had finagled Rhoda into coming too. Lisa. It was Lisa's fault. Lisa was at the root of all the trouble.

"He wasn't there, of course." Rhoda's eyes were open again, bright with suffering. "You were right. I shouldn't have let myself hope; it only makes it harder. If I've been acting funny, that's the reason. And if I haven't talked much about it—"

"All right, Rhoda. We won't talk about it." After a few moments of silence she said with forced heartiness, "Maybe what we need is a breath of air. Do you feel like taking a little walk down to the cove?"

"I don't think so, really. But you go ahead. Don't let me keep you."

"No. I just thought it might appeal to you." She picked up the cards and began laying out another hand—this time without the customary accompaniment of small talk. Somehow she couldn't get out a word. The consciousness of Rhoda's presence—waiting, still waiting—and of their near-quarrel weighed on her like a stone.

In the end it was Rhoda who broke the silence. All at once she sprang up, like a jack in the box. "It's time for my pill. I'll just run up and take it. Be right back." Lickety-split, she scuttled out the door.

Usually Grace had to remind her about her pills. And why come back, when it was practically her bedtime?

One more little puzzlement to add to Grace's collection. Thoughtfully she placed the red seven on the eight of clubs. Then she heard the voice and sat stock-still, her hand poised in mid-air.

It was Rhoda's voice, slightly muffled but unmistakable. "Hello, yes ... He is? He's there, oh, please God, let me talk to him, let me ..." For a while after that there was nothing intelligible, only a blur of sobs that ended in the one hoarse, wrenched word: "Carlos!"

By now Grace had remembered the phone booth next door and was past the first jolt of being able to hear with such eerie clarity. Some trick of acoustics, and a lucky one for her; otherwise she would still be floundering around, trying to make out on her own what Rhoda was up to. Now all she had to do was listen.

Rhoda was talking again, and talking fast. It was as if she didn't dare slow down for fear of losing control. "No, it's not enough to hear you, no, I will not leave it at that. How do I know he's not standing over you with a gun, dictating every word.... You don't sound like yourself, you think I can't tell, I have to see you, I have to.... I know what the bargain was. So does he. If I don't see you it's all off.... Yes. Yes, I do insist.... Of course I can. I can be there in ten minutes...."

She did break down then. Grace missed the rest. But she had heard enough. She was there, waiting, when Rhoda stepped out of the phone booth.

"I'll drive you, Rhoda, wherever it is you're going." She spoke gently, and her hand, closing on Rhoda's wrist, was gentle too, gentle but firm; if the desk clerk should happen to look up from his newspaper he would see—as so often before—one staunch friend supporting another.

"You were listening!" Rhoda's eyes blazed. She made as if to wrench free of that kindly grip. Changed her mind when it tightened. And for all its fierceness, her voice had not risen above a whisper.

"It wouldn't do to make a scene, would it?" said Grace.

As if on cue, the desk clerk—it was the talkative one—sang out, "Evening, ladies. Nice to see you downstairs, Mrs. Verdell. Feeling better, I hope?"

After a moment Rhoda said faintly, "Yes, thank you."

No. It wouldn't do to make a scene. Even so, Grace kept her hand where it was. "We were just thinking about taking a little drive."

"Good for you. Nice night for it." Out he came from behind the desk, bent on sociability.

It was five minutes before they got away from him. Rhoda's face was glazed with tension; now and then her arm jerked convulsively. But not in resistance. Grace had no trouble edging her toward the door and when she said, "Come, dear. We'd better be going," Rhoda turned on her a look of wild relief.

"Yes. Please...."

"Night, ladies," the clerk called after them. "Have a nice drive."

18

"I knew it," Carlos said bitterly. He hunched over the phone, which he had just hung up. "I knew she wouldn't be satisfied, just hearing me. That's not good enough. How does she know you weren't holding a gun to my head, feeding me my lines?"

If I had been, Quentin thought, I'd have made a better job of it. Carlos's half of the conversation had consisted mostly of monosyllables, delivered—either out of constraint or utter exhaustion—in a lifeless monotone. Guaranteed not to reassure, in Quentin's opinion. But all he said was, "So I gathered. What happens now?"

"Yeah. What happens now. She's coming over here, of course. To see for herself, with her own two eyes. And she's got some scheme that's supposed to keep the cops from catching up with me—" He swallowed convulsively.

"It's something you're going to have to think about, you know," Quentin said. "Unless you're aiming to give yourself up."

"Never." The word flashed out, fierce and swift as lightning. "They'll never take me alive."

Quentin sighed. The old suicide threat bit again; the weapon Carlos had been brandishing ever since that first unsuccessful try.

"I know what you're thinking," said Carlos. "If I really meant to kill myself I'd have done it by now. I wish to God I had! Except that if I had, then—then—"

Then, for one thing, Lisa's death would be a closed case. The police already had enough reason to suspect him of murdering her; his suicide would clinch the matter. Was that what had stopped him? Or was it simply a failure of nerve, the same spineless streak that had kept him tied to his mother for much too long?

"Well, you didn't," said Quentin drily. "And I didn't kill you, either, or turn you in to the cops, when I had the chance. If I had I wouldn't be stuck with you now."

"I never asked you to do me any favors! It's your own doing if you're stuck with me. Your own damn meddling fault!"

"Listen, you bastard. I couldn't care less what happens to you. The only reason I've done you any favors is—Lisa. I thought I could get it out of you, the truth about Lisa. I couldn't, but I had to give it a try. And after that I had to get myself off the hook with your mother. Otherwise, believe me, I wouldn't have lifted a finger to find you; you could have stayed in that cellar till you rotted, for all of me."

"So what else is new?" Carlos eyed him stonily.

"Just this. You want to stay out of jail. Okay. Then whatever your mother's scheme is, you'd better listen to it. Because you're going to need help, and plenty of it. So when she gets here—"

"When she gets here you get the hell out! You've conned me into this; now you can do me one last favor and get the hell out!"

"I intend to," said Quentin. "But not until she gets here. I'm not taking any chances on you. You might take a notion to skin out without seeing her—I wouldn't put it past you—and if you did I'd be right back where I don't want to be. On the hook." He sat down and lit a cigarette. "You won't have to put up with me much longer. She'll be here any—"

"Sh! What's that?" Carlos sprang up and grabbed the gun, and then stood rooted, his eyes wild with alarm.

There wasn't much traffic on the road, more of a lane really, that ran past the studio. Only the people who lived in the scattering of houses beyond, or an occasional tourist. But the car they heard now was not going past. It was slowing; it was stopping. Rhoda? No, she didn't drive.

"Quick," whispered Quentin. "The back way." He grabbed Carlos, still rooted in panic, by the arm and hustled him back into action. His own heart was hammering. Once outside, he took a deep breath of the cool night air; it cleared his head.

All right. He wasn't rid of Carlos yet and wouldn't be until he handed him over to Rhoda. But he wasn't giving up yet, either. She was due here at any minute, alone, on foot, and as anxious as Carlos to keep their meeting a secret. The sight of an extra car at the studio would give her pause; surely she wouldn't just barge in without some preliminary reconnoitering. So with any kind of luck Quentin should be able to intercept her, bring her face to face with her perishing precious son and leave them to it. Outside the studio, or inside, who cared? Meanwhile ...

"Who is it?" Carlos breathed in his ear. "The cops?"

If so, of course, things were likely to get complicated. The cops would search not only the studio—for the life of him, Quentin couldn't remember whether or not he had stubbed out that last cigarette—but the environs as well. And if they found him and Carlos together, that would be that. That would also be that if, in trying to run away from the cops, he failed to keep his bargain with Rhoda. So there was no sense in running, at least not until he knew for sure it was the cops. After all, it didn't have to be.

Motioning Carlos to stay put, he slid cautiously to the corner of the studio and sneaked a look at the car parked on the road in front. Not a police car. But—Margaret? He felt an ominous inner lurch. She wouldn't betray him, not Margaret. He knew it: never mind how. Yet something must have happened to bring her here; and here she undoubtedly was. Her car, her cream-colored Pinto. He could even make out Margaret herself behind the wheel, leaning out the door, which stood open.

At the same moment Janet's voice rang out clearly: "Quentin! Anybody home?" There was a man's voice too, Bax's, saying something incomprehensible. They were knocking at the front door of the studio, out of Quentin's range of vision.

Friends though they were—up to a point—they couldn't just be paying him a social call. Not at this hour of this particular night. It was odd, to begin with, that they should have driven so short a distance instead of walking, as they usually did. And then, of course, Margaret's presence.... Something had happened to bring them here; some urgent something to keep them knocking so persistently. The door was not locked, and it was Janet's studio; there was nothing to prevent them from walking in. From the sound of it, that was exactly what they were doing.

He heard Carlos move up beside him and whispered, "Not the cops. The Knights. From Seaview."

It seemed to him that Carlos tensed up another notch or two at the news, but he had too much else on his mind to pay much attention. What now? He could hear Janet and Bax moving around inside the studio, talking in low voices; and he tried to imagine himself walking in on them, greeting them with pleased surprise, pretending that all was normal with him. It would be one way of finding out what was going on. But far too risky a way, one that might well kill his chances of meeting Rhoda's deadline. If only she would show up now, right now, so he could turn Carlos over to her and get the hell out! She must be on her way, maybe even nearby, waiting across the road, scared off by Margaret sitting out there in her car.

Margaret. She was his best bet. She not only knew what was going on with the Knights; she knew what had gone on with him up until an hour or so ago. Two minutes with her would make all the difference. Two little minutes, before the Knights got tired of doing whatever they were doing in the studio and came out....

He heard Bax's voice, startlingly close: "Maybe he's out in the back yard. I'll just take a look." With one accord he and Carlos melted around the corner and ducked into the bushes beside the studio. The back door snicked open. After calling Quentin's name a couple of times, Bax gave up and went back inside.

Then came Janet's voice, at the front door. "There's nobody here. You coming in, Margaret?"

And Margaret's, "No, I'll wait out here."

"Jesus," whispered Carlos. "Somebody else. Out there. In the car."

"It's okay." He wasn't going to waste any of his two minutes—and he had them now, he had them!—explaining the whys and wherefores. "Look. Here's my chance. Don't blow it. Just sit tight. Stay where you are till I get back. Okay?"

He could hear Carlos breathing, a quick, ragged sound. "But how do I know—"

"You don't. You have to take my word for it."

And he had to take Carlos's, he thought as he rose from full to half crouch. God help them both. He paused, steadying himself with one hand braced on the ground, mentally plotting his course. The yard was all shadows, except for two rectangles of muted, mellow light from the studio windows, where the drapes were still drawn. The night wind rustled in the bushes, sighed high up in the big shady maple. His Volkswagen was parked under it, off the road, a blunt, homely shape. Comforting. All he had to watch out for was that one outcropping of rock near the front path, and beyond it the brick-edged petunia bed.

From Margaret's car came a muffled thud as she pulled the front door shut; he took off like a runner at the starter's signal.

She gave a little gasp as he slid into the seat beside her. Then she said quietly, "They're calling the police. I couldn't stop them. Where's Carlos?"

"In the bushes. The police ...?"

"He tied Bax up—Bax walked in on him, down in the cellar—tied him up and gagged him. Didn't he tell you?"

"Son of a bitch," said Quentin mildly. "No. No, he didn't tell me."

"So I couldn't stop them from calling the police. We found Bax down there, Janet and I, he's not really hurt, just stiff and kind of dazed. He heard you, that is, he thinks it was you, talking to Carlos. That's why we came over here. It was the best I could do, to stall them off on calling the police until we tried to find you. I didn't tell them anything about Emerson or Carlos's mother. But I couldn't—"

"Of course you couldn't. We're still okay. Maybe. If Rhoda gets here before the cops. And she might. She ought to." But in the back of his mind there lurked the other possibility—unthinkable, but there it was—that she might be somewhere close by, sitting tight like Carlos, waiting for the crowd to clear out. It wasn't going to, as she would realize when the police made the scene. And by then it would be too late, all over but the shouting.

"Somebody's coming," said Margaret. "I hear a car."

So did he. They both turned around to look out the rear window. The police already? He glanced at Margaret; her mouth was a little open, defenseless looking. The headlights rushed at them. Their heads swiveled as the car approached, slowing down, then picking up speed as it swerved past them. But not far past; at the entrance to the old mill road the driver turned, expertly if rather too sharply for safety, and came back. This time the car cruised past them very slowly. For a long, numb moment Quentin stared into the faces of its occupants.

Rhoda had not come alone? Grace was with her?

Rhoda had not come alone. Grace was with her, at the wheel of the car, which had now pulled to a stop a few yards ahead of them. Grace....

All right. Leave that part of it. Concentrate on Rhoda. She was here. Before the cops. There was still time. He opened the car door and started to get out.

There was a harsh, wordless cry, hardly human, from the car ahead. And Margaret stammered something, he didn't know what; her head was turned away from him, toward the studio yard, where the other car's headlights cast an eerie glow as far as the maple. The pattern its leaves made on the Volkswagen was shifting, tricky. But then his eyes caught a different, purposeful kind of movement, a shape too dense to be only the tremulous dance of shadows. The Volkswagen coughed apologetically—yes, he had left the keys when he parked it there in the afternoon—as it always did when it started up, and the next instant shot out past Grace's car and off down the road.

Carlos. Too many people for him, too many pressures. He had panicked and bolted. Well. It figured.

"Come on," said Margaret. "Hurry up." She gave him time to get back inside, but just barely; before he had the door shut she was off for the old mill road turn-around. Driving like a parking lot attendant. They were still rocking when they whizzed back past the studio. He caught a glimpse of Bax and Janet, gaping at them from the front door.

Grace had wasted no time, either, and she had been headed in the right direction to begin with. Already her tail lights were disappearing around the curve. By the time they reached the cross road beyond

Seaview there was no sign of either her car or the Volkswagen.

To the left the road ran into town; to the right along the coast. Margaret braked to a stop. "Any idea which way he'd go?"

"It's anybody's guess. I doubt if Carlos knows himself." But after a moment Quentin added, "Somehow I don't see him heading for town."

They were off again. And they didn't have far to go, or long to wonder about whether or not Quentin had guessed right. The Volkswagen stood abandoned, its door swinging open, beside the road close to the spot where it joined the footpath leading down to the rocks. Grace's car was a little farther on. Nobody in sight there, either.

So Maybe Carlos had known where he was going, after all. Quentin sat still, staring out at the straggling footpath. Lisa's path, the one she had followed so many times before that last night when it led her to her death. The scene of the crime, he thought; could chance alone have drawn Carlos back to this place?

He opened the car door. "Please," said Margaret. "Please don't leave me. I mean—"

She meant she was scared. It jolted him: Margaret the intrepid, the demon driver, the cool customer. But now she was peering at him anxiously. "All right, then. Come with me," he said. When she had scrambled out—and she lost no time about it—they both paused, listening. There was only the endless surging sigh of the sea. Overhead the sky arched, immense, with a lopsided, in-again out-again moon and a few stars twinkling through the gauzy racing clouds. Off to the left they could see the white glimmer of the drawbridge, lights gleaming on either side.

The path was too narrow for them to walk abreast; Quentin went ahead, picking his way carefully. It sloped downward more and more steeply, uneven and stony, edged with tough scrub that thinned out gradually. A sharpish turn, and all at once there were the rocks down below, jutting up at awesome angles, massive, somber, rooted in churning foam. Straight ahead was the overhanging ledge, flat as a table, from which Lisa had fallen to her death.

Quentin stopped so abruptly that Margaret bumped against him. "Sorry," she murmured automatically. Then she saw them too—the two figures standing on that ledge. She caught her breath and stood as still as he.

19

Bax and Janet were out front waiting when Chief of Police Peck, with a second official car in tow, pulled up at the studio.

"Quick," said Janet, hopping right in. "I'll explain on the way. Come on, Bax. They must have taken the shore road. Otherwise you'd have met them. You didn't, did you?"

"Who?" asked Peck. But he was already negotiating the turn at the old mill road and signaling his men to follow. When Janet projected crisis, the message got across.

She told him who. "Quentin's Volkswagen. Then the car with the two women in it. Then Margaret. They all took off. Bang, bang, bang. Just like that. Didn't they, Bax?"

Bax nodded dreamily. His mind seemed mildly out of focus, nothing to worry about, rather restful in fact, and certainly not to be wondered at in view of the evening's commotions. Well, and possibly the drinks, though he was never one to blame the liquor.... He made a stern effort to concentrate. "There was somebody with Margaret. I think. I'm almost sure. And whoever it was in the Volkswagen, he came from back of the studio. Like a blue streak. All I got was a glimpse of him. It could have been either Carlos or Quentin. I'm sorry, I just don't know."

"Let's hope it was Carlos," said Janet. "Because if it wasn't him in the Volkswagen, then it has to be him with Margaret, and he's got a gun.... I didn't see him at all, myself. I'd just finished phoning you, I was still sitting on the couch, across the room from the door. I didn't even know about the two women until I heard this sort of screech, and then Bax—"

"Give it to me from the beginning," said Peck patiently. "The cellar."

The cellar. For an instant Bax almost had it, whatever it was that kept bobbing around just below the surface of his consciousness. Then it slipped away again, out of his reach. He settled back and let Janet do the talking. No use trying to force these matters. After all, the feeling that he had forgotten something was not exactly a rare phenomenon. Usually it turned out to be something trivial, not worth remembering in the first place. He might as well save his strength.

Janet's brisk voice rose and fell, rose and fell. By the time Peck turned on to the shore road she was winding up her story: "I did get a look at the two women, the one that was driving, anyway. Grace Leonard. So I suppose it was Carlos's mother with her. That's it, all I can think of to tell you. Bax? Did I skip anything?"

Bax flipped his eyes open. "Not that I noticed," he said truthfully. After a moment he added conversationally, "Is that Margaret's car up ahead? Looks kind of like it."

"By George, it's all of them," boomed Peck and slowed down suddenly enough to send them cracking against the windshield if they hadn't been wedged in too tight. There was a squeal of brakes from the car behind. Sure enough, all of them, caught in the headlights' glare as Peck swung over to the side of the road and stopped: Margaret's Pinto, Grace Leonard's rented job, and the Volkswagen with its door hanging forlornly open. All of them here—Bax's mind clicked into momentarily sharp focus—here at the start of the footpath Lisa had taken that last night of her life. He saw her with unearthly clarity, gliding along like a girl in a dream, Lisa on her way to death.

Peck had clambered out and was issuing orders to the four members of his force who had also piled out of their car and were gathered in a huddle around him. Two of them were to stand guard here at the roadside; two were to come with him in search of the missing parties. As for Janet and Bax, they were to stay where they were, safely out of the way of any action that might develop.

Left to himself, Bax might just possibly have obeyed these instructions; it turned out that Janet had other ideas. She waited until Peck and his fellow searchers were on their way and the two guards had moved off on an inspection tour of the three abandoned cars. Then she whispered, "I want to see what's going on. How about you?"

They slipped quietly out under the wheel, unnoticed by the guards who by this time were absorbed in the Volkswagen. Bax heard one of them say, "Hey, look, a gun. Here on the floor. He left his gun."

Janet had been listening too. "So it was Carlos in the Volkswagen. And it's perfectly safe now. He's not going to shoot anybody."

"No, but I think he had a knife. Yes. He used it to cut the clothesline." Again something stirred in Bax's memory. Almost surfaced. Sank before he could get hold of it.

"Sh." He could feel her trembling. Poor Jannie, the place had its connotations for her, the shock of finding Lisa wasn't something she would forget in a hurry. All the same—maybe for that very reason—she refused to stay safely out of the way tonight. Well, and so did he. They had seen the start of it; they must see the end. And this had to be the end, all of them converging here, as if drawn by Lisa herself. All of them: Carlos and Quentin who had loved her, Grace Leonard and Rhoda Verdell who had hated her, Margaret Robinson who might or might not be quite as much of a bystander as she seemed.

From the path ahead came the sounds of stealthy movement—Peck and his men trying to be quiet, and doing surprisingly well at it. They were the ones to watch out for; though the guards back on the road were sure to discover that Bax and Janet were gone they wouldn't risk leaving their posts to follow. Wouldn't risk raising an outcry, either.

So the trick was to keep a healthy distance between themselves and the searching party and to be even quieter. At least that was how Bax figured. Again Janet had another idea. "We could cut through the brush. They'd be less apt to spot us."

Bax was preparing to argue the point when he became aware of a change in the character of the noises up ahead. The rustling-movement sounds had given way to what seemed suspiciously like a whispered conference. Then Peck's voice came through, muted but distinct: "You better take a look, Ed. See if anybody's back there."

They cut through the brush.

Actually, it wasn't much rougher going than the path. And Bax had to admit it afforded more cover. They worked their way along at a cautious half-crawl, pausing now and then to listen. To nothing, for the most part; they had apparently diverged far enough from the path so that the search party was no longer audible. After a while they could hear the sea. And the clumps of scrub were sparser now. They must be getting close to the rocks.

During one of their breathers Janet gave a little start. "My word, Bax, you're still in your sock feet!"

So he was. Now that she mentioned it, so he was. And she was still in her cocktail party dress. It would never be the same. For a moment longer they huddled together. Waiting. Listening. But there was only the measured swell of surf against the rocks. Bax shivered slightly. The chilly night air. Fatigue. Nerves. Unless he was way off on his bearings—always a possibility—they must be quite near the ledge where Lisa had fallen. It was too dark to be sure about anything.

Then, as they began inching forward again, the moon sailed clear of the clouds, outlining in ghostly light the stones underfoot, the leaves on the bushes, Janet's profile beside him. And the ledge. It was closer even than he had thought, just beyond the last steep downward slope of thirty-odd feet.

A man and a woman were standing there, motionless, facing each other in tense absorption. Like figures in a theatrical scene, thought Bax, an aura of unreality about them. Then the woman spoke, very low, a kind of hurried croon. She put out her hand in a curiously violent gesture. Threatening? Imploring?

There was no ambiguity about the man's reaction. He recoiled, as if from a snake.

But the woman could not or would not believe. Her hand remained outstretched, and after a pause she resumed her crooning. Until he broke in savagely; then she cried out: "Carlos! My boy!"

Again he shrank away from her. "No! Don't touch me! Don't you understand? I was here that night, waiting for her down by the rocks, I saw you, what you did, you ... Why do you think I've been hiding? Because even though I knew, I couldn't—even though I know, yes, and hate you for it, I still can't—ahhh, what's the use?" He covered his face with his hands.

His mother made no further move to touch him. Her angular figure, etched in moonlight, seemed to Bax to sway back and forth, desolate as a blasted tree. He had a premonition, he knew she was going to ...

Everything happened at once. From the path, somewhere off to the right, Peck's voice boomed out, lights flashed, footsteps thudded. Janet gave a squeaky little sob. Down on the ledge, Carlos whirled to face Peck and his men. And Rhoda Verdell flung herself off the ledge to the rocks below.

After a while Bax croaked, "Let's get out of here."

Halfway along the path Margaret overtook them. "Quentin went on down. I thought you were up there on the road. In the police car." She spoke calmly, but very slowly as if she had to fumble for the words. "Peck said I was to wait there with you."

"We didn't stay there." Janet didn't sound as crisp as usual, either. "We saw it too."

"Oh. You saw it. He said to wait. A few questions, he said."

Naturally. A few questions. A few loose ends to be tied up. They plodded on a moment in silence; then Janet clutched at Bax and stammered, "Grace Leonard. She—what happened to Grace Leonard? Margaret? Do you know? Did you see—"

But Margaret shook her head.

They found out what had happened to Grace Leonard when they reached the road. She was more or less stretched out on the front seat of her car, with one of Peck's men hovering close by. "Waiting for the ambulance," he reported. He adjusted the cushion under her head. "Don't worry, ma'am, they'll be here in a minute."

"I'm all right," said Grace dimly. Her eyes were open, bewildered looking, the eyes of a scared child.

"Sure you are, ma'am. Coming around fine." He turned aside to Bax. "Mrs. Verdell conked her over the head with a flashlight. Didn't want her along when she caught up with that boy of hers, Carlos. We found her slumped down here back of the wheel. Out cold for a couple of minutes. And by the way"—he fixed Bax with a steely eye—"I'd like to know what the hell you thought you were doing, taking off like that.

Behind our backs."

"No other way to do it," Janet pointed out. "If you'd been watching you'd have stopped us. In case you haven't heard what happened—"

"Sh. She don't know yet." He cleared his throat uneasily. "Yeah. I know. Ed came back and told us. Carlos didn't give them any trouble at all, he said. No fight left in him. Kind of like he was glad it was all over, Ed said."

Grace's voice wavered out again. "It was me. Hadn't been for me, Rhoda would never have come up here. And I didn't believe that tale of Emerson's...."

The earth tilted beneath Bax's feet. "Sweet Jesus," he breathed. Emerson. The kid. He had been down in the cellar too, must still be there, Carlos had tied him up too, oh, sweet Jesus.

"Bax," said Janet sharply. "What's the matter with you?"

From the footpath came the approaching rumble of Peck's voice.

Bax squared his shoulders—well, tried to—and tottered off to meet him.

THE END

Jean Potts Bibliography (1910-1999)

Mystery Novels:
Go, Lovely Rose (1954; winner Best First Novel Edgar Award)
Death of a Stray Cat (1955; reprinted in omnibus as *Dark Destination*, 1955)
The Diehard (1956)
The Man With the Cane (1957)
Lightning Strikes Twice (1958; reprinted in the UK as *Blood Will Tell*, 1959)
Home Is the Prisoner (1960)
The Evil Wish (1962; finalist Best Novel Edgar Award)
The Only Good Secretary (1965)
The Footsteps on the Stairs (1966)
The Trash Stealer (1968)
The Little Lie (1968)
An Affair of the Heart (1970)
The Troublemaker (1972)
My Brother's Killer (1975)

Mainstream Novel:
Someone to Remember (1943)

Short Stories:
The Lady Afraid (*Woman's Home Companion*, Feb 1942)
You're All I've Got (*Woman's Day*, March 1942)
The Other Woman (*Collier's*, Aug 24, 1946)
Restless Redhead (*Liberty*, Feb 1948)
The Box of Apples (*McCall's*, March 1949)
A Family Affair (*McCall's*, Nov 1949)
The Bracelet (*McCall's*, Dec 1951)
The Heart Must See (*McCall's*, Apr 1952)
The Engagement Ring (*Thrilling Love*, Oct 1952)
Let's Start All Over Again (*American Magazine*, Apr 1953)
The Girl He Didn't Marry (*Woman's Day*, Jan 1954)
A Long Day's Journey (*Cosmopolitan*, July 1954)
The Ideal Gift (*Family Circle*, Oct 1956)
The Withered Heart (*Ellery Queen's Mystery Magazine*, Feb 1957)
Murderer # 2 (*Alfred Hitchcock's Mystery Magazine*, Jan 1961)
Just Like Jessica (*Redbook*, Feb 1963)
The Only Good Secretary (*Cosmopolitan*, July 1965; condensed version of novel)
The Inner Voices (*Ellery Queen's Mystery Magazine*, Apr 1966)
In the Absence of Proof (*Ellery Queen's Mystery Magazine*, July 1985)

Two on the Isle (*Ellery Queen's Mystery Magazine*, Jan 1987)
The Lady Macbeth Case (*Ellery Queen's Mystery Magazine*, Nov 1990)

Family Circle "Family in Trouble" series (commentary by John L. Schimel, M.D.):
Families in Trouble (April 1969)
Families in Trouble - Alone Again! The Agonizing Problem of A Lonely Wife (June 1969)
Families in Trouble - "My Youngster Is Taking Drugs" (Oct 1969)
Families in Trouble - "My Job Made A New Woman Out Of Me!" (Feb 1970)
Families in Trouble - The Credit Card Nightmare (March 1970)

Unpublished Short Story:
Lady Bountiful

www.ingramcontent.com/pod-product-compliance
Lightning Source LLC
Chambersburg PA
CBHW070930190726
48292CB00004B/1191
* 9 7 8 1 9 5 1 4 7 3 5 5 6 *

THE MAKE-BELIEVE MAN

Norma Hovic is recently widowed and living with her 11-year-old son in her mother's house. When her mother leaves to stay with Norma's sister, who is expecting, Norma is at first pleased to have the house to herself. But then Cliff appears. Cliff had been her mother's roomer until Norma came to live with her. She had heard all about Cliff. But the Cliff who shows up at her doorstep is another matter altogether. There is something not quite right here. This Cliff makes her nervous. His face is wounded and he keeps babbling about a man he had worked for who had humiliated him. He almost seems to resent Norma's presence here. And that's when he tells her that he wants to stay…

A FRIEND OF MARY ROSE

Mr. Nicholas is 83 and blind, living with his son and daughter-in-law in a neighborhood which has seen better days. In fact, today the family is moving. But Mr. Nicholas is afraid that his personal trunks will be left behind. So, after spending the day at Mrs. Thompson's house next door while the movers are at work, he sneaks back into his house at night to make sure the movers took them. But he discovers instead a young girl being hunted in the attic by a drunken letch of a man. Mr. Nicholas has never paid much attention to his neighbors before. He has no idea who the young girl could be. All she tells him is that her name is Mary Rose. Now they are locked in a dark room together, being hunted by someone who is an even greater mystery…

Elizabeth Fenwick Bibliography (1916-1996)

Mysteries:

The Inconvenient Corpse (1943; as E. P. Fenwick)
Murder in Haste (1944; as E. P. Fenwick)
Two Names For Death (1945; as E. P. Fenwick)
Poor Harriet (1957)
A Long Way Down (1959)
A Night Run (1961)
A Friend of Mary Rose (1961)
The Silent Cousin (1962)
The Make-Believe Man (1963)
The Passenger (1967)
Disturbance on Berry Hill (1968)
Goodbye, Aunt Elva (1968)
Impeccable People (1971)
The Last of Lysandra (1973)

Mainstream Novels:

The Long Wing (1947)
Afterwards (1950)
Days of Plenty (1956)

Children's:

Cockleberry Castle (1963)